The WITCH'S DREAM
A Love Letter to Paranormal Romance

The Order of the Black Swan
BOOK TWO

by Victoria Danann

VICTORIA DANANN

Published by 7th House.com,
a Division of Andromeda LLC
395 Sawdust Rd, 2029,
The Woodlands, TX 77380
817-548-7737
www.7th-House.com

isbn 978-1933320632

Printed and bound in the U.S.

Cover image: Collage including images purchased from Getty Images.

Reading the serial saga in order is highly recommended. The first book is *My Familiar Stranger*, available at Amazon.

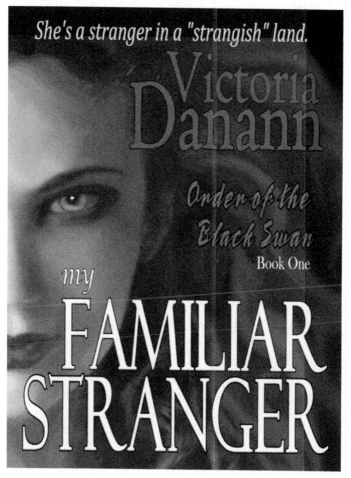

She's a stranger in a "strangish" land.

Victoria Danann

Order of the Black Swan

Book One

my FAMILIAR STRANGER

Praise for *My Familiar Stranger*

"This book was a ride! I simply cannot say enough great things about Victoria Danann and the genius that is *My Familiar Stranger*. Danann's writing style is uniquely honest and captivates her audience with both plot and characters in a well-developed and thoughtful world (or 'worlds' as it seems)."

- Between the Bind.

"Firstly, while this may be the author's first foray into fiction, PLEASE don't let it be her last. Wow, is she good! This book is amazing. Love the story, love the concept, can't wait for number 2. If I could write like this I would never do anything else... "

- Books, Books, and More Books

"I do see shades of Lara Adrian's *Breed* books and shades of J R Ward's *Black Dagger* books but this story is unique enough that it stands out all on its own and can stand up alongside those other books and I think given time will elbow them out of the way with the rich storytelling and deep emotional core."

- Musings of a Bookworm

"This book is not the usual paranormal story that I am used to reading. It is way better. ... There are many surprises and in this reviewer's opinion this book had it all."

- The Paranormal Romance Guild

"*My Familiar Stranger* was a wonderfully engrossing paranormal romance with just a dash of science fiction that grabbed me from page one and didn't let go! Ms. Danann absolutely knows how to get a series going."

- Bitten by Paranormal Romance

"Let me just say I am (im)patiently awaiting the next installment. I loved this story. I loved how Ms. Danann didn't make this story into an instant love, it progressed over time. It was a wonderfully intriguing romance with its own twist on the paranormal world and I loved every page."

- Bitten by Love Reviews

"*My Familiar Stranger* is a very complex book that is beautiful and heartwarming. There are numerous laugh-out-loud moments, as well as several nail biting, edge-of-your-seat moments. The adventure quotient is high, but not too much so. The romance in the novel is built in seamlessly, exquisitely enhancing the story. I absolutely loved this novel, and cannot wait for the next one!"

- Night Owl Reviews

I absolutely loved this book! Paranormal romance isn't a genre I usually read but after reading the plot, I was intrigued by this book and decided to broaden my reading horizons and give it a try. I'm so glad I did because I devoured the book in less than two days!"

- Book Nympho

"... emotional, sweet, moving, funny, heart-wrenching, action-packed and totally enthralled me from the get go! On the edge of my seat I was hitting the turn key on my Kindle trying to figure out what was going to happen next. Nothing is predictable."

- Emily Guido, author of the Lightbearer Series

"Go sneak off to your reading nook, get comfy and get ready to dive into a new dimension with horrors, villains and true love that will keep the pages turning till the very end leaving you wanting more, but satisfied!"

- Addicted to Reading

CRITICAL PRAISE FOR *The Witch's Dream*

"...dramatically fun, sexy, and addictive."
                                              - *Between the Bind*

"...an awesome follow-up to *My Familiar Stranger*." - Book Maven

"...the writing is tight, descriptive and flows neatly along a path that often is twisty, but always seems to resolve with a satisfying feeling of "what will they get into next.

This world is so unique and the writing so constant and detailed with little pieces of information drop like breadcrumbs until the loaf is completed. You will be turning pages as you need to get to the end - and then re-reading as you await book 3 in this series."
                                              - *Booked and Loaded*

"Wow, Danann does it again. The lady knows how to weave quite the story. Filled with magick, love, and jealousy *The Witch's Dream* is a sweet and sexy good time."
                                 - *Bitten by Paranormal Romance*

"Sometimes sequels can be a bit of a disappointment, but Victoria Danann has written an intriguing sequel that surpasses *My Familiar*

Stranger."
> *- Ramblings of Coffee Addicted Writer Blog*

"The story itself begins fast and never once slows down. The characters from the first book are back and smarter and sassier than ever. There is plenty of blazing hot romance, as well as plenty of adventure and dimension jumping. For fans of the series, this novel certainly will not disappoint."
> *- TOP PICK, Night Owl Reviews*

"Victoria definitely has a way of pulling you in and making you feel like you're part of the family."
> *- Bitten by Love Reviews*

"There is a witch, a demon, a psychic, a berserker - yes, I know, I was unsure what that was before, too - an ex-vampire, modern day knights, heroes, werewolves, elves, fae... you pretty much name it in the Paranormal realm and you will find it in *The Witch's Dream*. Oh, and that's a good thing.

Well, they work, and how! I began reading it and could not put it down! If you love Paranormal, Fantasy, and or Romance, run, don't walk and pick up a copy today!"
> *- Alyson LaBarge for Sniffer Walk Books*

"This is a wonderful series of handsome, macho men and beautiful, intelligent women. I highly recommend this series and look forward to book number three."

-The Paranormal Romance Guild

"Victoria pens her characters well developed and realistic in this magickal, romantic paranormal book. All the characters you followed in the first book are back and not forgot along with new ones being introduced. Victoria does not disappoint and I find myself waiting for the next in the series. A must read for all fans of the romance, paranormal and magickal genre."

- Cozie Corner Book Reviews

"I was a little worried because of how much I liked Book One, but needn't have - Book Two is as good. We meet new characters and they are as well done as expected - carefully created with all those things you look and fall for, making you feel like you know them and are right there with them. The storyline is wonderful, intriguing and entertaining with just enough romance and action. I love Victoria Danann's writing style and her use of language, a bonafide wordsmith! I can't wait to get started on Book 3."

- Beverly, The Wormyhole

The Order of the Black Swan, A Team.

Amanda Zafris
Ashley Logan
Christine Merritt
Elizabeth Qunicy Nix
Frances Royer
Janice McNamara
Jen Albright
JoBeth Sexton-Harris
Karen Berglund
Karen Bradbury
Leah Barbush
Liz Cabrejos
Margaret Nolan
Martha Smith
Mary K. Koval
Maxine Murphy
Maya Bowen
Nelta Baldwin Mathias
Tabitha Schneider
Heather Poindexter

Thank you to my BETA readers. You're the best.

FOREWORD

Thousands of dimensional variants are anchored to Earth each one believing it is "the world", *the* third planet from the Sun. As might be expected, many of those have developed simultaneously with cultures expressing almost identical parallels to ours. Mystics and magicians have always been aware that our dimension is not alone.

Religions allude to these with names like heaven, hell, purgatory, summerland, and nirvana. Myths call them by names such as Shangri La and Merlin's crystal cave. They are real places on Earth. They just aren't real places on *our* Earth. Interactions with other dimensions are often explained as ghosts, poltergeists or myriad other paranormal phenomena. Sometimes people and things simply vanish.

Just one small deviance from our own history, here or there, could have drastically changed our reality. Imagine, for instance, what the U.S. would be like if we had reached the twenty-first century without a Civil Rights Movement. What if there had been no Henry Ford? Were you to visit one of these other worlds you might be struck by the juxtaposition of the alien and the familiar, the familiar sometimes manifesting in more than curious ways.

PROLOGUE

Book Two picks up where Book One, *My Familiar Stranger*, ended. Following is a brief synopsis of what has happened previously.

There is a very old and secret society of paranormal investigators and protectors known as The Order of the Black Swan. In modern times, in a dimension similar to our own, they continue to operate, as they always have, to keep the human population safe. For centuries they have relied on a formula that outlines recruitment of certain second sons, in their early, post pubescent youth, who match a narrow and highly specialized psychological profile. Those who agree to forego the ordinary pleasures and freedoms of adolescence receive the best education available anywhere, along with the training and discipline necessary for a possible future as active operatives in the Hunters Division. In recognition of the personal sacrifice and inherent danger, The Order bestows knighthoods on those who accept.

Ten months ago, the elite B Team of Jefferson Unit in New York, also known as Bad Company, lost one of its four members in a battle with vampire. A few days later Elora Laiken, an accidental pilgrim from another dimension, literally landed at their feet so physically damaged by the journey they weren't even sure of her species. After a lengthy recovery, they discovered that she had gained amazing speed and strength through the cross-dimension translation. She earned the trust and respect of the knights of B Team and eventually replaced the fourth member who had been killed in the line of duty.

She was also forced to choose between three suitors: Istvan Baka, a devastatingly seductive six-hundred-year-old vampire, who worked as a consultant to neutralize an epidemic of vampire abductions, Engel Storm, the noble and stalwart leader of B Team who saved her life twice, and Rammel Hawking, the elf who persuaded her that she was destined to be his alone.

This story begins at Rammel's home in Derry, Ireland. B Team has been temporarily assigned to Edinburgh, but they have been given leave for a week to celebrate a handfasting for Ram and Elora, who have learned they are expecting.

.

CHAPTER 1

It's true that love expresses itself in myriad forms. Occasionally it manifests as the perfect alignment of two beings that almost creates the balance the universe seeks and can never quite achieve. That alignment is sometimes achieved by bringing opposites together and sometimes by matching pairs.

Natives of the fire dimension of Ovelgoth Alla take their sustenance from various forms of emotion-generated energy. All Ovelgoth Alla demons are born with the ability to slip dimensions through any deliberately constructed portal or naturally occurring vortex. by a simple mental process. They are not immortal, but, like their brethren called angels, have much longer life spans than most of the humanoid races.

Abraxas demons are one of the races who call Ovelgoth Alla home. Abraxas are the spiritual expression of sex - which has two faces - the power of love and joys of mutual sharing or its opposite: domination, humiliation, sadism, cruelty, selfishness.

Abraxas demons procreate in matched pairs of light and dark. In a cosmic reenactment of an endless play of futility, light offers love to darkness knowing that darkness is incapable of receiving the gift; like offering a beautifully wrapped package to someone without hands to take it from you. Light's gift is predestined to be misunderstood, predisposed to be desecrated, doomed to be wounded.

Incubus demons are the get of a tragic match. They are not evil in themselves, just as pleasure is not evil in itself, but can be made so by its interpretation or application. Like all of us, incubus demons bear traits of both parents and are capable of expressing a range of behaviors from chillingly depraved to spiritually transcendent.

To the woman looking for true love, commitment and emotional security, the incubus is a devil. To the woman in need of a boost to her belief that she is sexually appealing and a simple body buffing, he is an angel. Incubus demons are highly adaptive and flexible. They can be almost anything to anyone. The one thing they cannot be is monogamous.

The incubus demon, Deliverance, was the progeny of such a mating between a dark male named Obizoth and a light female named Ariel. He was conceived in the deep green waters of a fossilized lava pool and, three days later, walked full grown onto the shore in all his glory as the masculine personification of lust. If Deliverance had to be described by one word, it would be irresistible - not in the ordinary usage of the term, but in the true meaning of raw compulsion that *cannot* be resisted.

Earth Plane X, Loti Dimension, year 7213 D.H.

Deliverance never cared much for his father. Why should he? During the near millennium of his life, he had probably not spent the total of a day in his company. Still, Terrans could not be allowed to go around offing demons with impunity, even when they deserved it.

Terran was the name given the dominant species occupying Loti Dimension by the other beings who share the plane. Terrans, of course, were unaware of what they're called by others just as they were woefully provincial, unaware of most things in the Multiverse. They referred to themselves as human.

Even though demonic family structure was loose at best, survivors of a departed who met a deliberately perpetrated end were expected to seek retribution in kind. So, in the interest of custom, as the only surviving offspring, and for no other reason, Deliverance half-heartedly undertook a vendetta for Obizoth's killing.

It didn't take long to track down the responsible party. Once in possession of the target's name, Deliverance wasn't in any particular hurry. He reasoned that, if the killer died by some other means while Deliverance was working up the motivation to tackle the chore, it would simply save him the trouble. Win. Win.

After a year had passed it came to his attention that there was some public grumbling among his more blood thirsty relatives, which meant he had run out of "reasonable" stall time and needed to start taking retaliation more seriously.

The only relative he cared about was his mother, who was too good to want anyone executed - not even Obizoth, who sort of had it coming. He hadn't seen his mother since Rosie disappeared, but he "felt" her often enough. No, she wasn't part of his reason. It was a simple equation. It would be easier to carry out a vendetta than to put up with gornishit public insults and denouncements for the next thousand years.

Sir Chaos Caelian, usually known as Kay, was everything you expect from clichés about Texans. He was six inches over six feet tall, well built and easy-going to a fault. At least that is the persona he had carefully cultivated.

The back-story is that he was part of the youngest generation of a legendary line of berserkers who had immigrated to South Texas almost two centuries ago and stayed. Kay was unique in the sense that he was the only berserker to ever work for The Order in any capacity, much less in the Hunter Division. Kay had done an outstanding job of mastering the berserker side of his psyche - so much so that he often seemed to be the only voice of reason when other members of B Team were overly emotional.

Kay loved his family, which, in some ways, would have to include his B Teammates because they were that close and had been through too much together. Yes. He loved his family and his friends. But he adored his fiancée, Katrina, whom he had identified as the love of his life when they were children. Kay had never looked at another girl in a romantic way. He'd never asked someone to dance without knowing in advance what the answer would be. Never flirted his way toward enough courage to inquire about a possible dinner and movie. Never studied a stranger surreptitiously while wondering what it might be like to be her lover.

Fortunately, Katrina felt exactly the same way about him. The phrase "made for each other" had been coined to describe the two of them, and in a few months, a lifetime of love was about to culminate in a late summer wedding that would include the entirety of the Houston Social Registry along with corporate clients of Katrina's event planning business.

A year ago, more or less, B Team had been dispatched to New Persia because The Order's Psychic Division had reason to believe a sex trafficking operation was receiving assistance from a paranormal source. The operation had turned ugly overall, but had become super dicey when Kay's berserker made a rare appearance.

The misery of the captives, girls who had been kidnapped or sold, who were forced into acts of the vilest depravity, which often included torture, had provided the Abraxas demon, Obizoth, with a rich source of emotion for a long time. To a dark Abraxas, misery is a delicacy - tastier than joy, longer sustaining.

When Kay witnessed firsthand the suffering visited upon these females, his berserker would not be contained. He took one look at those women and saw in their place the sorrowful faces of his own mother, sisters, and wife-to-be. A berserker's rage, once loosed, was a force beyond the natural. Once the berserker part of the personality took charge, it stayed in control and did not recede until it believed there was no guilty party left to kill. Even when the killing was over, the berserker often continued to mete out rage in terms of property damage and destruction until the well of emotion was spent or satisfied. It was a mindless condition over which the saner side had no control and dangerous in one as strong as Kay because it could persist for an indeterminate amount of time.

The Abraxas demon, Obizoth, was present when B Team raided the New Persia facility. When he encountered Kay, he literally lost his head as the Black Swan knight in berserker form wrenched it from his body with both hands. It was a sight that Rammel, Lan and Storm would never forget.

Once Deliverance had gained access to the manifest of females who had been recovered from the raid, it was a simple task to track them down one by one and manipulate them into recounting the events of their rescue. The sixth girl on the list had been an eyewitness to Obizoth's murder, although she did not know him by that name. She was able to describe the angel of vengeance who had liberated her so that there was no doubt whatever.

Obizoth's revenge was to be visited upon a Black Swan knight named Chaos Caelian.

Deliverance traveled to the Jefferson Unit of Black Swan at Fort Dixon, New Jersey where Kay was stationed. The Unit, protected on all sides, even overhead, by a functioning military base, was impossible to access. Impossible for Terrans. For an incubus demon? Minor speed bump.

The demon first identified the popular, local, recreational destinations for personnel who were off duty, then made a point of frequenting those establishments until he made a connection with someone who could get him on base. He preferred to visit Fort Dixon at night because his long black hair was less a red flag among the buzz heads. Once on base he made his way to the nondescript, apparently windowless, fifties-style building that housed Jefferson Unit and waited for female employees to emerge at the end of their shifts.

Most of the people working at Jefferson Unit resided there, but a few lived off site. With little effort, Deliverance was able to learn that Kay was not in residence at the time. The informants were not able to divulge his present location with certainty because that information was well-protected, but did pass on that his permanent address was Houston.

Deliverance located a pass a short distance away; a pass is a naturally occurring vortex that, as the name suggests, allows passage between dimensions. These are the "doors" used by angels and demons, among others, to come and go between dimensions.

Del, which was what he called himself these days, entered the murkiness of the pass with an address on his tongue. He took two steps and came out the other side next to an ATM in a River Oaks upscale strip mall. A woman shrieked when he materialized in front of her.

"Oh! You scared me. I didn't see you there."

He needed a ride to Kay's townhouse, but such things were rarely so much as an inconvenience to a creature with his gifts. The woman he had surprised was a mid forties brunette returning to a Bentley carrying a small black shopping bag tied with gold satin ribbon.

"I need a ride." He walked along beside her.

She took one look at Del's laughing black eyes and couldn't think of anything to say except, "Get in."

He was wearing his hair tied at the nape over an ivory linen sports coat and jeans. It wasn't the sort of outfit that you'd see on a runway showing for Dolce and Gabbana. It was better because it said, "I'm so beautiful I can wear anything and look good in it. And I'm so rich I can do what I want without caring what you think."

Like most incubus demons, Del liked women. He didn't think of himself as using them, but chose to believe he offered a valuable and needed service in exchange for fuel. He left them feeling marvelous, at least at that moment. Of course he knew that he had doomed them to live out their lives being disappointed by sexual experiences that must inevitably be substandard, but he chose not to focus on the less agreeable aspects of his job description unless it suited him to do so.

He left women with their bodies humming. They left him gassed up. So far as he was concerned, it was a perfect symbiotic relationship. Win. Win.

Del said goodbye to the lady in the Bentley in front of Kay's townhouse. He didn't have to ring to know that no one was there. He could sense that the unit was not currently occupied by any animated life form. One of the perks of being a demon.

A neighbor three doors down had come out to pinch the dead heads off red geraniums, when she looked up and saw Del. Her first impulse was to go back inside, but his gaze held her in place as he closed the distance between them. Another perk of being a demon.

Liz Tinsley, from three doors down, said she didn't see much of Mr. Caelian because his work kept him away a lot. However, she did happen to be outside a few days before and hear one of his sisters say, "See you in Ireland," before jogging from his door to her car, giving the neighbor a bright smile and wave on the way by. Del thanked her and turned away to find a pass to the land of magic. He had nothing against being lover to older women. He was simply full at the moment.

No further research was needed to find Kay. He'd already learned about the exploits and obviously exaggerated heroics of the elite B Team. He knew their names, their habits and their strengths and weaknesses. Most importantly, he knew that, if Kay had gone to Ireland, there was a very good chance he was visiting Prince Rammel Hawking's ancestral home, the palace at Derry.

The prospect of Ireland brightened his interest. The island state was teeming with ripe sources of nourishment who welcomed beautiful demons with long, shiny blue-black hair, laughing black eyes and flawless skin kissed with a touch of bronze fire. Well, he laughed to himself, the same could really be said for any place.

Most importantly, he had learned that the target had a gaping weak spot just begging to be exploited; something he valued much more than his life. Kay was devoted to a girl he'd loved since childhood. When Deliverance learned about Katrina, the plan for his vendetta began to morph into an appropriately painful alternative. Deliverance wasn't big on killing and got no enjoyment from it for its own sake, but he was big on his own self-interest and what he needed more than anything was a semi-constant supply of fuel provided by sex. He would take Kay's girl and let him know that she was going to be thoroughly used in every conceivable way; that her incubus lover would enjoy it immensely, but, more importantly, she would, too. The knight would be driven insane by his own imaginings. A brilliant retribution, if he did say so himself. Win. Win. Win.

He would wait for the perfect opportunity to grab the Terran female then keep her on tap for a while, like a staple in a larder. When the retribution fervor passed and even the most distant cousin had forgotten all about it, which wouldn't be long, he would send her back. If Kay still wanted her, he could spend the rest of his life in frustration trying to find a way to satisfy her. The idea of that made Deliverance laugh out loud. As if.

CHAPTER 2

Edinburgh, Scotia

Litha turned out the lights and drew the drapes back so that the historic district of Edinburgh could cast a night-light over her small room. She took a minute to appreciate the view. It was captivating by day looking across the gardens to the castle sitting high on the crag, but was even more magical at night when the grand monuments were lit by spots. Having a room on the view side of the building was one of the things she liked most about being temporarily stationed at the headquarters of The Order.

She crawled between cold sheets and let her teeth clatter like one of those battery-operated skulls at Halloween. Somehow listening to the sound of that made waiting for the covers to warm go faster. It might be the first of April, but chill lingered late so far north and her blood wasn't thick like the Scotia fae. She drifted to sleep, the last thing on her mind a Pacific breeze blowing from the west to warm the Northern California bay where she grew up. She liked her work with Black Swan and felt privileged to have it, but sometimes she missed home so much she understood the sentiment of pining for something.

As soon as she was warm, she fell into a deep sleep and dreamed. She was standing on a green, grassy plateau rising from an ocean of black water that churned and raged against the rocks below. She felt like she could turn in a circle and see the whole world. The sky was overcast with charcoal colored clouds moving unnaturally fast, defying what was thought to be true about how physics operated in the world; swirling, blending gray with silver, white, and black like paints on a palette, gathering storms in every direction. Tornadoes twirled down from dark clouds like ribbons of tempests spinning, lingering for a few seconds, back lit by lightning strikes. As she stood there, she knew the appropriate response should be concern for survival, the appropriate action the seeking of shelter, but she was so entranced by the terrible beauty of such a display of unimaginable power that she couldn't find motivation to move.

She faced toward the breeze blowing from the west, strong and warm, her hair loose and free behind her. She wore a simple silk gown the rich saffron color of the togas worn by Hari Krishna monks. As the gale pressed against the front of her body, the garment conformed to her curves like a second skin. The back of the skirt was a train formed by yards and yards of the marvelous fabric that was, at one time, as precious as gold. Against the backdrop of the storm, it looked like liquid sunrise when the breeze caught the silk, making it dance in the wind like a watercolor come to life, billowing like a sampan at full sail.

To her right stood a tall, beautiful, dark-haired man, shirtless, with enormous black wings - at rest, the tips of the wings skimmed the ground. As he was talking to her, he swept one hand across the horizon as if to illustrate a point he was making about the panoramic event unfolding before them. In her dream, she absorbed a whisper of the words 'storm angel'.

Suddenly and without explanation, as often happens in dreams, there appeared in her hands a bow and arrow. As the angel stood by watching, she aimed toward the clouds, seventy degrees above the horizon. She tried to pull the bowstring taut, but did not have the strength to do it. She turned to tell the angel that she was not up to the task, but when she looked into the piercing intensity of his black eyes, watching her quietly and calmly, she decided to try again. This time she added fast resolve and the metaphysical force of spiritual commitment to her physical strength and the string drew back easily, responding to her command like a virtuoso playing a violin.

When released, the arrow, aimed at the darkest gathering of clouds above the horizon, flew along its foreordained trajectory cutting a path of visible electricity in its wake across the sky. When it reached its mark, there was a deafening clash of thunder followed by a series of rolling rumbles that could be felt vibrating the earth beneath her feet. Clouds parted at the point of arrow strike revealing a patch of blue sky and impossibly fluffy white clouds whirled into peaks like meringue. The dark and angry ocean below the precipice was overtaken and forced out to deeper sea by waves coursing a friendlier hue of Pacific blue, calming the churning to quiet tidewater lapping at a coastline garden thick with floral blooms.

The bow disappeared from her hand as her attention was redirected to a miraculous display of grape vines sprouting upward from the earth all around them. They were rapidly maturing into healthy, thriving plants as flowering, low growing, yellow mustard blooms blanketed the earth beneath them. She laughed and looked at her companion whose wings were gone. The figure standing next to her was a man whose intense, black-eyed gaze was focused on her so completely she felt as if nothing else existed apart from the two of them. His presence gave her a sense of peace, contentment, and belonging. Even in her dream, her heart cried out for that. Longed for that. She reached out to touch his face with her fingertips and woke to a crash of thunder, her arm outstretched in the air.

With drapes left open, there was enough light in her third story room to see the myriad images covering her walls; art renderings of a pink Italianate villa with a slate roof and red bougainvilleas blooming profusely, trailing from big iron pots set on the steps of terraces as the vineyard stretched down toward the sea. She knew the place well and had been recreating it from memory for years in every medium imaginable: oil, watercolor, paint marker, charcoal, pencil, even crayon. She supposed the casual observer would think her obsessed and, objectively speaking, she would probably have to agree.

Her thoughts wandered back to the dream she'd been having just before she woke. There was something about it that she wanted to remember. She had tried to hold onto the images and the feelings, but they swirled and pitched and, within seconds, both had evaporated like smoke.

VICTORIA DANANN

CHAPTER 3
The Palace at Derry, Ireland

Happy mating had quieted Ram's emotions. It had been so long since he'd felt the rise of his notorious hot temper that it seemed foreign, like it was no longer a good fit with his body. Especially when aimed at Elora. Being angry with her felt wrong and feeling guilty made him glower at her even more.

"You said you could *never* be mad at me!" Elora didn't have to play the lady anymore. She could yell and scream and pound on walls if she wanted to, though that would be extremely ill advised since her strength might weaken, if not bring down, even palace walls.

"When I said that, how could I know that we would be makin' babies together and that one day you would propose somethin' so fuck-it-all stupid as puttin' yourself and our little one in harm's way?"

"It's supremely simple, Ram. If the baby's father is going, the baby's mother is going. Baby's father stays home, baby's mother stays home. Your choice."

Ram's color reddened as he turned to face the wall to shout frustrated Gaelic at the top of his lungs.

She examined her nails nonchalantly, completely unfazed. "It will do you no good to curse in Irish. I can't understand it."

"You are the most fractious woman to ever walk the earth!"

"Nonetheless." She rolled a shoulder in a pretty shrug indicating she would not be moved in this. "You know I'm good with dogs."

Ram's mouth fell open and he gaped at her with wide eyes. "Elora! Werewolves are not dogs."

"If it looks like a canine…"

"It does no' look like a canine, Elora. It looks lupine."

"Oh, what-the-hell-ever."

Ram laughed. "Pub speak, my girl? Where's Ms. Perfect Princess Propriety now?" He stopped and grinned. "Say that three times fast."

She gave him a pointed glare. "Off topic, Rammel."

Ram faced the closed suite door raising his arms and his voice in a mock plea of distress. "Help! She's callin' me Rammel. I'm in trouble now!"

"You know you are asking for it."

Very slowly he turned his head and gave her a lupine smile if ever she saw one. In the spirit of giving credit when due, she had to hand it to the love of her life. He didn't need to say what he was thinking out loud to be clearly understood.

There was no one near the east wing of the palace who didn't know an argument was underway between the prince and his soon-to-be bride. Not being used to the way the newly mated couple interacted, the staff gave each other poignant looks and donned personal listening devices to keep from eavesdropping.

Of course, the staff was aware of Ram's temperament or, rather, temper inherited from his mother. When he was a child, he had fought constantly, sometimes with his father, sometimes with his older brother, Aelsblood. When the environment of conflict became too much, even for him, he would run away to an uninhabited hunting cottage in the New Forest Preserve and stay for long periods of time.

When he wasn't fighting, however, he was more fun than a pint of Guinness. Emotional outbursts are hardly foreign to the Irish character. It's something of a cultural pastime. And everyone knows that fits are easier to overlook when the owner of the temper is also a renowned joy-giver as was the case with both Ram and his mum, the queen.

However, adding Elora Laiken to the mix seemed to have raised the intensity of Ram's tirades. Or at least the volume.

Having heard the disturbance on the way to breakfast, like everyone else in that wing of the palace, their teammate, Kay, decided to seek out Ram's little sister for help. Since coming to Derry for the wedding and meeting Ram's family, he had learned that the beautiful and lively Aelsong was an extraordinarily talented clairvoyant - just the thing needed to restore peace in a super-sized household.

After asking around Kay located her having coffee and croissant in the solarium while she pored over details of the pending handfasting. She and Ram's mother had taken it upon themselves to make this wedding the event of the century and that sort of staging required mega organization and dedication. Kay asked if - just between the two of them - she could please look to the future and see the baby.

Ram couldn't remember ever wanting to throttle *anyone* more. Since that wasn't a possibility, he did the next best thing, which, according to his somewhat unique logic, was to grab Elora and kiss her like he hadn't seen her for months.

Kay knocked on the door twice, but the occupants of the room were too preoccupied to take note. He opened the door, expecting to find his teammates locked in combat or throwing things at each other. Instead, he and Aelsong were greeted with the sight of Ram and Elora rolling on the floor and groping each other desperately, like teenagers in the back seat of a car.

Aelsong barked out a laugh. Kay blushed and looked at Song thinking that Ram and his sister really were like twins because laughing in such an awkward situation was *precisely* what Ram would have done.

"Song!" Elora laughed with embarrassment as she untangled herself from her mate and pulled at her zip-up sweater to make it come back together in front.

Ram sat up and glared, looking from one intruder to the other with lines drawn between his brows. "By all means. Please do no' be put off by the *closed* door."

Kay was clearly more embarrassed than Elora.

"Sorry," he finally managed. "I thought you were fighting."

"We are." Ram didn't look at all less angry. "I'm tryin' a different form of persuasion. What has that to do with you?" His attention swiveled to Song. "And you."

"Well, Aelsong is psychic."

Ram gave Kay a look that was priceless. "I know that, Kay. She's my sister."

Kay gestured toward Aelsong. "Well, go on then. Tell them."

Aelsong looked down at the couple still on the floor and flashed them one of Ram's signature high beam smiles. Of course, Elora had fallen in love with her sister-in-law within seconds of meeting her. How could she not adore someone who was so very like Ram?

"'Tis a boy! He looks exactly like you, Ram, except for Elora's turquoise eyes and somewhat strange hair." She looked like she was going to tear up. "He's *so* beautiful. I can no' wait for you to see him."

The lines on Ram's forehead smoothed away. "You're talkin' about the baby."

Aelsong nodded enthusiastically.

Ram looked adoringly at Elora. "*Our* baby."

Elora sucked in a breath and jerked her gaze away from Ram. "Song. I'm begging you. *Please* tell me he has Ram's ears. I mean, ears like Ram's and yours."

"And why would he no'? Cosmetic surgery has no' affect on genetics."

Elora froze and stopped breathing. She'd just

bungled the cover story. This business of hiding everything about themselves and their real lives was harder than it sounded. Then she noticed the gleam in Aelsong's eye. *She knows and is teasing me.*

Aelsong's laugh was like the sound windchimes would make if they were vocal chords proving that she was well-named indeed. "Aye. Indeed his wee ears are comely elfin. And his name is…."

"No!" Ram held out his hand like a traffic cop, as if he could stop words in mid air. "Do no' tell us!"

Kay, with his ever-steady wisdom and calm demeanor, so necessary for keeping his berserker side in check, was good with solutions. "Look, my friends, the point is this. If Aelsong sees the baby in your future, then the argument is moot. Right?"

Ram seemed to be considering. "Song, did you also see Elora?"

"Aye, and..." She stopped.

"...and what, Song?"

"I do no' want to say too much. Much of the fun of livin' is in the mystery, findin' out what's to be."

"Mouths of babes and all that, Song."

Elora cocked her head to the side and looked at Ram. "What does that mean?"

"'Tis from very old writings, the beginnin' of a sayin' about young speakin' wisdom beyond their years."

"Oh. Well. Why is that part of this discussion?"

"My meanin' is that she must finish what she started because I'll no' abide her hidin' behind adages and the like."

Elora looked at Song. "I agree. Spit it out." Before Aelsong could say anything, Elora sucked in a gasp. "You did see Ram in this vision as well?"

"Aye. You two be at ease. I see the both of you, the sweet babe who is so pretty he could near break your heart with just one of his twinklin' smiles... And somethin' else."

Ram and Elora both spoke at once. "What?"

"He is sittin' in the green grass while black puppies crawl all over him waggin' their little tails and nippin' at his tiny fingers and toes. I can see him laughin' so hard in his adorable baby way that he is gettin' hiccups and his skin is turnin' adorably pinkish."

Ram and Elora exchanged a smile that said they needed the room cleared in a hurry as it was needed for overdue make-up sex.

Kay turned toward the door. "Well, seems my work here is done..."

On the way out, he said to Aelsong: "You know those croissants you were having? Where did you get those? Did they have some deer sausage and gravy to go with that?" As he pulled the door closed, they could hear him tell Aelsong. "*My* sisters are coming in later with my fiancée, Katrina. You'll like her. Everybody does."

An hour later Ram and Elora had showered, dressed, and were about to go down for breakfast.

"...and they've got us dressing up in these ridiculous sixteenth century costumes. I mean, what is it with royal families and period costumes?"

Ram laughed. "Do no' know. Maybe 'tis a

heyday thing." Instead of opening the door he gently pushed her back into it with the front of his body and said in a voice that implied intimacy. "Do you mind? We could just run away to the New Forest and spend a week fuckin' like minks." He nuzzled her ear and then talked into the most sensitive part of her neck. "'T'would be fine by me."

Elora's laugh got caught low in her throat as she felt her body respond to the feel of her mate pressing against her, which was amazing considering that she had been so recently and so thoroughly loved and satisfied. On the floor. In the bed. In the shower. All before breakfast which meant that she was hungry. Really hungry. Eating for two and all that.

"There's a part of me that would very much like to take you up on that offer, my darling. All this is way too close to my own upbringing for comfort. But I can't take this away from your mother and your sister. You should see their excitement and dedication. It's become their raison d'être - a modest little affair for fifteen hundred people. How do you think they're going to come up with that many costumes? It's impossible, isn't it?"

Ram chuffed lightly at that one spot in her ear that always made her knees threaten to buckle. "If we're to be doin' this then let's have some fun with it. I very much plan to enjoy showin' you off to fifteen hundred of my mother's closest friends."

She laughed. "If only jokes would sustain me, I would never leave this room. But, alas, I need food as well."

"Did you actually say 'alas'?"

"See? The period costumes screw with your head. Now, feed me or get out of the way so I can find a man who will."

He pulled back and looked at her through half hooded, half smiling eyes. He lowered his voice to the tone he used for raspy pillow talk. "That's no' gonna happen."

Fond memories of the last time he'd said that to her triggered a rush of images that made her tummy flutter. He gently pulled her away from the door so that it could be opened. In unapologetic contradiction, after just saying no, she brushed past him suggestively and had to claim one more sweet, lingering kiss before heading downstairs.

Elora had only met Ram's family a few days before. They had come up with a cover story as to why her ears were different. Supposedly a childhood accident with a bicycle had left one ear irreparably nipped so her parents had decided the best cosmetic result would be to round both ears to match. It was a good story that she had almost blown by babbling about her acute desire that the baby have ears like his da.

Ram had said it was impossible to hide much from someone as psychic as Song, but that she was better at keeping secrets than anyone he knew. "She does no' tell other people's news or thoughts or secrets." There was no mistaking the pride with which he bragged about her.

His parents had turned the kingship over to Aelsblood for reasons that were unclear to her. Ram's older brother was nothing like him, but was very much like his father in looks and temperament. Both had light brown hair, grim, serious personalities and were buttoned up, tightened down, zip locked for better or worse. Judging by her first impressions, Elora was not the least surprised that the king was unmarried. Fate couldn't be so cruel as to mate some poor girl with a man who seemed so cold and distant. Except that, apparently it *had* happened to Ram's mother, Tepring.

Ram's mother and younger sister both looked and acted like Ram: emotionally effusive, bright as sunshine on snow, lively as a kickin' dance of the reel. Fortune had blessed the three of them with beauty, charm, magnetism, optimism, and golden auras that were just barely out of the range of human visual acuity, but sensed nonetheless.

When they'd arrived, Ram's mother had burst into tears on seeing the scar on his face for the first time and was inconsolable for two hours. His father, Ethelred, took one look at him and said, "An' how'd the other fella fare?"

Ram cocked his head for a second and then laughed, never taking his eyes away from his father. "Come to think of it, the other fella got away with no' so much as a scratch."

Elora watched her father-in-law-to-be draw his mouth into a judgmental purse of the lips. She started to rise up in Ram's defense, but he grabbed her around the waist and drew her into an embrace so snug that she almost lost her breath, while his smile never wavered. She got the message. *Families do no' know what we do.* But - oh, how she wanted to say - "I'll have you know that a few days from now my elf will be the first knight in the whole of this century to be inducted into The Order's Hall of Heroes."

Aelsong's response to this exchange was to laugh and ask Ram if she could have the "other fella's" phone number. Elora stared at Song. *Great Paddy! She's Rammel in female form.*

Ignoring his daughter altogether, Ethelred continued to pin Ram with an unflinching stare, accusation all over his face. "An' how is it this happened again?"

"Knife fight in a bar," Ram answered without hesitation and with the same unflinching stare. The thought fluttered across Elora's awareness that Ram might actually be enjoying this exchange on some level. He seemed to like pissing his dad off. At least he wasn't shying away from it.

Not a muscle moved in Ethelred's face and yet a palpable wave of condemnation penetrated the space between Ram and his father. Ethelred was firm in his position of censure. Ram was just as firm in his position, which had all the signs of a third finger salute.

Elora was aware that Aelsblood was watching the warring emotions cross her face. Her peripheral vision was very good and there was no question he'd been assessing, and perhaps evaluating, too.

Of course, in his position he must be practiced at interpreting communication in all its complex and nuanced forms, not just words, and, in a flash of intuition, she somehow knew that he knew. Her eyes swiveled to meet his and found a smile there. It did not touch any other part of his face, which was a trick in itself. But for a fraction of a second, she thought she might have seen admiration in Aelsblood's expression. For what? Wanting to defend Ram? To have the truth be told about who and what he was?

Looking at Aelsblood she tried to project a telepathic question. She asked if this was typical behavior between the two of them. He responded with a nod so slight she could barely discern it, then turned, and left the room without another word.

It was surprising to learn that Irish surnames were passed by matrilineal descent and that Hawking was Ram's mother's name. As soon as they were alone in the suite of rooms that had been Ram's as a boy, Elora had to ask: "So, will you be changing your name to Rammel Laiken?"

"If you wish," he said, walking toward the bath without missing a beat.

When she didn't respond, he stopped and looked over to find her staring at the floor and frowning.

"What just happened?" he asked.

She looked up. "I love your name. And I'm not just saying that. I really do. It's kind of fai..., uh, elf-tale-like. It brings up images of falconry or shape shifting."

Ram laughed as he walked over and put his arms around her. "You do have a very fine imagination, my girl."

"The thing is... I love my name, too. I mean... it's *mine*. Maybe we can keep our own names?"

"Elora, this does no' even show up on my list of

priorities. You can call me dickhead so long as I get to be the one who sleeps with my leg thrown over your beautiful body at night."

She smiled and kissed little circles around his throat. "I like the way you think."

"Ha! Since when?"

Elora's time at Derry had felt like a whirlwind of activity. Aelsong and Tepring tried to involve Elora in the event planning, but with the exception of preference of flowers, she had finally just turned it over to them. Even so, she still had to be available for fittings, for learning how to say the vows in Gaelic and learning how to dance a reel. Rammel had given her a tour of the palace, which took most of the day. Every turn seemed to inspire another story about him being in trouble for this or that as a child.

Finally overwhelmed by tales of a parent's nightmare, she sat down on a step of a little-used, side staircase and began absently stroking her flat stomach with her fingertips. "Okay. You're scaring me now. Just what am I in for here?"

Ram frowned. "Are you tired?"

"Of course not."

Ram gracefully lowered himself to the step next to her and snuggled close, smiling as he put his arm around her. "The babe has two parents who are Black Swan knights. If he was no' a little firecracker, somethin' might be off."

Elora laid her head on his shoulder, turned her face into his shirt, and groaned. He chuckled softly.

"Even if he turned out to be exactly like me, I

believe I would handle it better than did my own da. We will sure no' have him livin' on his own like a half feral. You and I, we're goin' to keep him close and smother him with hugs and kisses every day whether he wants 'em or no'. He's goin' to know we want him.

"As for us, my feelin' is, that if we can survive vampire, we can survive strong-willed offsprin' and find a way to have fun doin' it." He had a way of rearranging perspective so that things never sounded half bad.

"I love you, Ram."

"You know, if you did no' weigh near three hundred pounds, I'd be scoopin' you up and takin' you to bed for naps."

She laughed and raised her head to look at him. "Wonder how much the baby's going to weigh. You think you're going to be able to pick *him* up?"

"Very funny."

He stood. She raised her hand. "Help me up?"

Ram cupped his hands and yelled down the hallway: "We need a winch and pulley in the mud galley stairwell!"

She slapped at his leg, holding her stomach and laughing so hard no sound could come out.

The day promised to be busy for guest arrivals. Kay had come in the night before. He'd caught a commercial flight from Houston and said he was amazed that even first class on commercial airlines was crowded, uncomfortable, and generally barbaric.

Baka was expected from Edinburgh mid

morning, Storm in mid afternoon, and Kay's entourage - composed of sisters and fiancé - would be arriving late in the afternoon.

The breakfast room at the palace in Derry, the seat of the Irish monarchy, was a long rectangle with twenty-five-foot ceilings, original wood floors and a wall of tapestries that were almost as old as elfdom. The other side of the room was a wall of windows ten feet high that looked out on gardens built in terraces above idyllic sheep pastures beyond. Spring flowers had begun to show themselves and Elora could see that the display would be dazzling in another month.

Residents and guests had come and gone from breakfast, but Ram and Elora were lingering with Tepring until late morning. The three occupied one end of a dining table that would accommodate fifty, yet somehow Ram's mother made it seem like an intimate family conversation. One of the staff brought Elora a small silver pot of hot chocolate and set it in front of her with a smile, which Elora returned with thanks and an expression of delight.

"Is the cord ready?" Tepring asked Ram, including Elora in the question with a glance her way.

Ram blinked.

"The cord?" Tepring was beginning to look concerned. "Rammel?"

"Um. I did no' think about it. I've no' done this before, you know."

Tepring made a regal huff and turned to Elora. "We must have a cord for the handfastin'. Traditionally the bride and groom choose the materials and braid it themselves. 'Tis customary to keep it somewhere prominent in the couple's bedchamber, as a symbol of the way you felt on your weddin' day. 'Tis a gift to yourselves really because there may be days when the physical, visible reminder may help you get through times that are no' so fun. There's still plenty of time, but you should attend to it sooner rather than later."

Elora nodded. It wasn't one of her traditions, but she liked the sound of it and it certainly couldn't hurt. "How long should it be?"

"Split the difference between your heights."

She looked at Ram absently while she mentally pictured how much that would be. "Okay. Any suggestions about materials?"

Tepring looked out at the gardens for a few seconds. A wistful smile took over her expression. Elora thought her mother-in-law could not possibly be remembering her own wedding to that walking coat rack with any fondness. Tepring suddenly jerked her focus back to the meeting in progress as if she had heard Elora's thoughts.

"I've noticed you like to wear clothes made from pure natural fibers like silk, linen, wool, and cotton." She leaned toward Elora and lowered her voice. "No' a thing wrong with a few wrinkles here and there."

Elora assumed she was still talking about clothing and smiled. "You're very observant."

Tepring returned her smile. "No' really. I may be overly fond of clothing."

Her eyes slid to Ram. She gave the Black Sabbath tee shirt and faded, threadbare 501's with a tear in the knee a pointed once over. Elora snickered at the implied put down. Ram just smiled, shook his head, crossed his arms over his chest and leaned back in his chair as if to say, "No' a thing new."

His mother sighed. "No danger that anyone will accuse you of that, Rammel. Anyway, you could start with thick embroidery threads. Or it would go quicker if you used yarn. As you're braidin' you can weave mementos from your courtship or symbols of what you love into the braid. You both like to ride so you could add some horsehair. Elora, the flowers you chose will begin arrivin' later today. If you weave a few into the cord, they will dry prettily."

Ram looked at Elora. "You chose the flowers? Stargazer lilies, red roses, and no baby's breath."

Ram's mother laughed and clapped her hands. "That's right! Rammel, you turned out to be romantic!"

Ram gaped at his mum. "And since when have elves been concernin' ourselves with romance? I thought 'twas a human thing."

Tepring looked at Elora and rolled her eyes and that was all that needed to be said.

After asking Tepring where to find yarn, Ram and Elora went on quest for cord materials and some quiet time to combine braiding with enjoying each other's company, but as they were starting up the wide staircase leading to their wing they ran into Baka, just arriving and being shown upstairs.

Elora rushed to give him a hug which he returned far too enthusiastically to suit Ram.

Istvan Baka had lived his life as a human for thirty years before living as a vampire for six hundred years. As a result of the brand new cure for the vampire virus, developed from the antibodies in Elora's blood that had been hard won at her expense, Baka had very recently resumed life as a human. Because of his long-time ties to The Order and his unique circumstances, he had been hired to create and head up a special task force to bring about the great vampire inversion. As part of that assignment, he had been transferred to headquarters in Edinburgh where he was to reside semi-permanently.

Implementing the inversion was a monumental task and would be daunting if the prospect of ending a millennia-old plague on humanity wasn't so exciting. Sometimes, when change happened, it revolutionized with lightning speed. Overnight the knights of The Order of the Black Swan, Hunters Division, who had spent most of their lives training to become vampire slayers, were about to be retrained and retrofitted as vampire healers instead. The new mission would be to tag vamps with antidote capsules or, as the new slogan said, Shoot to Cure.

As head of the new highly specialized task force, Baka anticipated that finding and curing the vamps would be the easiest phase of the operation. The tricky part would be figuring out what to do with them afterward. There would be hundreds, perhaps even thousands of displaced souls globally, who would "wake up" to find themselves alone in the world - family and friends having aged beyond recognition or passed away. They would need help acclimating to a new life and help with motivation. Meaning that Baka expected widespread depression among the cured vampire, who would confront loss of life as they had known it, coupled with knowledge of the crimes that their bodies had perpetrated without consent. As someone who had lived through this himself, he would even go so far as to say that widespread suicide was a possibility if they didn't come up with a methodical series of steps back toward the light.

Baka foresaw that this posed endless problems of logistics relating to halfway housing, personnel, education, funding, and probably a closet full of problems he hadn't even thought of yet. As musician extraordinaire and successful author of a popular vampire romance series, making the transition to administrator would present some personal challenges. He rather liked not being accountable to anyone else for his time. But he'd do it because he loved what it represented. Not only did he get a chance at life again, he got to spend his days helping others claw their way back to lives worth living. If there was a touch of grace to be found in good works, he was willing to spend some time looking for it there.

Engel Storm wasn't especially happy about the appointment. He thought turning Baka into a bureaucrat was a waste of rare, natural talent; that Baka would have made an excellent addition to The Order's Hunters Division. Truthfully, he would probably have liked to see Baka take Elora's place on B Team, at least while she took pregnancy leave.

VICTORIA DANANN

Assuming Rammel would be able to convince her to take pregnancy leave. She had a super-annoying habit of keeping no counsel other than her own.

Baka was easy to get along with and surprisingly, he and Storm saw eye to eye on most things. Including their mutual attraction to Elora Laiken. Perhaps there was a seed of commiseration over the loss of a shared fantasy.

Ram and Elora decided to put off the cord quest so that they could have a nice lunch with Baka, play hosts, and make him feel welcome. Ram stopped by an in-house phone to call the kitchen and request light fare for three in the solarium while Elora strolled that way with Baka. On the way, she gave him as much of the tour as she could, given that she, herself, was basically a guest as well.

She had loved the solarium on first sight. It was basically a glass room held together with white iron grids forming frames around individual panes of glass narrowing as they reached toward the sky to form the complex and beautiful shape of a convex roof. The room housed a lush indoor garden, peacocks and a large fountain featuring the statue of a young elf with bow and arrow.

"Here we are," she said as they stepped through the open doors. She gestured to the room. "Wonderful, isn't it?"

"Indeed it is, my la...Elora." Baka's smile was part conspiracy and part sheepishness. "It's hard to remember."

Elora smiled and nodded. "Come sit. How have you been? I still can't get used to the color of your eyes. I guess I always knew they'd be blue, but I

50

couldn't have guessed the shade."

He pulled out one of the wrought iron chairs for Elora, then held up a finger to his lips to indicate that her slip was even worse than his had been. She laughed. "It *is* hard to remember, isn't it?" She leaned in closer. "What can we talk about safely?"

His eyes danced with laughter.

Elora leaned closer and spoke quietly. "Not the fact that this will be the first time I've seen you eat actual food."

His eyes sparkled with amusement. "No. Not that."

"And who is this?" The exchange was interrupted when Aelsong breezed into the room wearing a red silk dress, the slightest suggestion of expensive perfume, and as much self-confidence as can be contained in one personality.

Baka stood up as she approached saying to Elora under his breath, "Yes. This will do."

Elora smiled at Song. "This is Istvan Baka. He's a business associate of Ram's. Baka, meet Aelsong, Ram's sister, if there was any chance you couldn't tell."

Aelsong was captivated. She held out her hand. Baka took it and smiled, "Pretty name. And I *love* red." He glanced at Elora just long enough to insure she knew it was a joke intended for her.

Aelsong giggled a most attractive version of her tinkling, wind chimes laugh while Elora snorted as inelegantly as a person raised behind the bar at a roadhouse.

Song looked at her as if to say, "What's your problem?" Then, turning big, blue-eyed attention back to Baka she proceeded seamlessly, "An *unmated* associate?"

Baka stepped closer without breaking the connection with her upturned gaze, lowered his voice, and said pointedly, "*Completely* unattached."

Song's mouth spread into an appreciative, well-what-have-we-here smile.

Elora was thinking that this flirtation was fascinating to watch, as smooth as a professional tango.

Ram came in and without breaking his stride or acting as if anything was noteworthy, walked around Baka, who was still holding Aelsong's hand. "Song. You havin' lunch with us?"

She withdrew her hand and looked at her brother. "Absolutely," she grinned.

"Okay. I said three, not four, so go pick up the phone and get blessed out by Bridget for changin' the request. And while you're doin' that, tell her I forgot to ask for an extra chocolate for the baby." He sat down next to Elora taking her hand and looking at her like she was the first female in the history of the world to conceive life.

"She is probably goin' to say, 'What baby?'" Song said dryly. Turning back to Baka she cheered immediately. "Keep me company? 'Tis no' far. Just over there."

Baka gave Ram and Elora a quick glance. "Be right back."

When Ram and Elora were left alone he reached over and ran his fingers through her hair, like he couldn't stand to go for another minute without touching her. She noticed that he seemed completely relaxed about the fact that Song was aggressively flirting up a recently cured ex-vampire, one who may also be a notorious womanizer.

"The fact that Baka's trifling with your sister doesn't seem to bother you."

Ram looked confused. "Why should it? She's grown, healthy and unmated. And he's the poor devil who's spent the last hundred years whackin' off in a tower keep."

Apparently elves in this dimension were progressive about sex even when it came to younger sisters. She recalled the section on pre-mated sex from the book he had given her: *Everything You Ever Wanted To Know About Elves But Were Afraid To Ask*. It did seem to indicate that rampant promiscuity was to be expected from both sexes before mating.

Somehow the four of them managed to make conversation without discussing the subject of vampire, the business of The Order, or anything else about their lives that would be considered strange by civilians or treasonous by Black Swan. When it was time to leave to pick Storm up from the airport, Elora asked Baka if he would mind doing it as a favor because she and Ram had a handfasting task to complete.

She hadn't asked Ram about it in advance, but it seemed like a good solution, partly because Storm genuinely liked Baka and partly because the awkwardness had not yet been ironed out of their relationship. That sad fact was compounded by the fact that Storm was Ram's Best Man. What a cluster!

Ram had felt like asking him was rubbing salt in the wound, but how could he not ask? If Lan was alive that job would have been his, but there was no question that Storm was next in line, and passing him over would be like punishing him for being in love with the woman Ram was marrying. So he had asked Storm to stand up with him and Storm had simply said, "Of course."

"I would be happy to retrieve the dark and broodin' one."

Aelsong laughed her musical laugh that made everyone want to freeze in place while the pleasure of the sound washed over them.

Baka was delighted that she acknowledged his dry wit with magical sounds that, apparently, only elves could make. "I take it you've met the pilgrim of whom we speak?"

"Oh, aye. He has visited a few times. As you say, beautiful, but broody."

"I'm certain I didn't say beautiful."

Maybe her own feelings of guilt were too close to the surface, but Elora felt defensive about Storm. It sounded to her like they were making fun of him when he was not able to speak for himself. "Well," she began, "say what you will, but, as Kay once put it, someone has to be the grown up. Since I would not be sitting here if that dark and brooding one hadn't saved my life. Twice. I can't help but object that you seem to be having fun at his expense and, more to the point, in his absence."

Aelsong looked stunned. "'Tis misunderstandin' pure and simple. I'm quite fond of Ram's friend."

"Likewise," Baka said, looking unusually sincere, "I meant no disrespect. As you know, I also owe Storm a great debt for... several things including recommending me for the position I now hold. The reprimand is unjust, but stings nonetheless."

Elora smiled brightly. "Okay then. So long as we understand each other. I don't mind retrieving him myself. "

Ram laughed. "Oh! Retrievin' him yourself, is it? Great Paddy in the flesh would no' agree to ride in a vehicle with you at the wheel. You've no' even mastered drivin' on the right hand side of a parkin' lot yet." Elora glared. "O' course I would *love* to drive you."

"No need," said Song, taking charge in a remarkable imitation of her mother. "Baka, I will go with you to fetch our esteemed guest..." She turned her high beam smile Elora's way. "...whom it is our very great honor to host."

"So. You got your brother's silver tongue as well as his looks and his smile."

"No' at all." Song's mouth curled seductively as she stepped closer to Baka. "My tongue is sweet and pink."

Elora looked at Ram as if to say, "No. Way."

He took her hand in his and laughed softly in response.

Baka looked down at Aelsong with the amused confidence of someone who had been playing the seducer longer and better. "Nothing would please me more than to have your delightful company, but I'm afraid I rented one of those two-seater sports cars."

Song chuckled. "Autos are hardly a problem, em... Do you want to be called Baka?"

He glanced at Elora again. "I've grown accustomed to it. Baka is fine."

"Well, Baka, what do you say? Unless you need to be alone with my brother's friend?"

Baka laughed. "No. I neither need nor wish to be alone with your brother's friend." He leaned closer and lowered his voice. "I would much rather be alone with you."

Song responded with the obligatory giggle of a flirtation ritual as she rose from her chair and said goodbye to Ram and Elora. "We've gone to the garage to choose transport."

As she led the way, Baka looked at Elora over his shoulder and grinned. She smiled and gave him a little chest high wave.

What a pleasure it was to see him enjoying life. He deserved it, but unfortunately, didn't believe that.

When Kay's bunch arrived, it suddenly seemed as if the one hundred seventy-five room palace on twelve thousand acres would not be nearly big enough. The Caelian family had migrated to South Texas in the nineteenth century and found it agreeably inhospitable. Berserkers enjoy a good challenge. So they founded an organization to clean up the mess, taking on rowdy itinerants who heartily embraced a get-it-done, no-rules philosophy, and called it the Texas Rangers. Were it not for the early wave of berserkers it seems unlikely that the frontier mix of Comanche, desperados, and javelina could have been subdued so relatively quickly and by so few.

Chaos Caelian was named by his maternal grandmother as was her privilege in berserker society, but had come to be affectionately known as Kay, a nickname bestowed by his teammate Rammel Hawking soon after they'd met. Ram had thought a knight named Kay - like the foster brother of King Arthur from Arthurian legend - was amusing. So Chaos became Sir Kay and it stuck. Even his own parents eventually began calling him Kay.

Yes. Everybody knew the near-giant knight as Kay except for his three older sisters who flatly refused to give up calling him Bubba, never letting him forget for a minute that he was the "baby" of the family. The four youngest Caelian children were close in every way including age, only a year apart. There was a much older brother, but he and their parents almost seemed to comprise a separate family. The three preschool girls started out calling him "brother", but something in the Southeast Texas atmosphere caused that to quickly degenerate into Bubba. And it was clearly not going away.

Their grandmother, sometimes called Evil Gran by those she had named, gave the girls similar hardships to bear. Having inherited the "sight" from her own grandmother, Evil Gran claimed she knew three girls were coming and set out to name them after the Norns, the three keepers of time according to Norse myth. Hence, they were named in order of linear time - past, present, and future: Urda,

Verdandia, and Skulda. In a triumph of sibling camaraderie and conspiracy over custom, their names had morphed into something more suitable before they entered kindergarten. Urda became known as "Urz", Verdandia as "Dandie" and Skulda did a triple twist into "Squoozie" which, odd as it was, seemed like a custom fit.

Kay was fond of saying that opening the door to his boyhood home was like going through the wardrobe to the land of "Nornia".

The entire family resembled the popular perception of Vikings: tall, fair haired, fair skinned, with blue eyes, an abundance of athletic ability, and an indomitable desire to know where to plunder the best jewelry. Fortunately the family had accumulated multigenerational wealth in land, cattle, and oil in the late nineteenth and early twentieth century so the quest for jewelry did not require going a-viking as it was known in the old days. Kay's sisters were content with the occasional plunder of Gump's, Tiffany, and Cartier.

Ram and Elora had dutifully set themselves to the task of gathering materials for their handfasting cord. Some of the flowers had indeed arrived after lunch. Elora had suggested they each pick one red rose to go into the braid. They had also borrowed a few long, coarse strands from the manes of two horses. Elora had been drawn to a dapple-gray mare with a pretty face, an intelligent expression, and a wavy mane that just begged to be laced with flowers. She also happened to be pregnant.

Ram argued with a magnificent black stallion

over giving up two strands of mane, but after some alarming hoof strikes echoed against the stall's wooden walls, he jumped over the stall to land in the breezeway looking deliriously victorious. Grinning at Elora wickedly, he came straight for her and proceeded to crowd her against the wall where she waited. While still breathing deep to get his breath back, he whispered something in her ear about stud horses and fertility. It got the *exact* reaction he was hoping for and he laughed with the delight of a mischievous boy.

"'Tis a first. I made a knight of the Black Swan blush *and* giggle at the same time."

Back in their suite they were laying out the components they'd gathered and were discussing who would hold the knotted end and who would braid the strands when they heard the commotion of Kay's troupe being shown to their accommodations down the hall. They took one look at each other and dropped what they were doing, scrambling to the door to go and see the show.

The far end of the hall was beyond excitement. It could only be compared to a three-ring circus. The three sisters were assigned to a suite of two bedrooms with shared bath while Katrina was planning to room with Kay. Ram and Elora stood in the hallway at a suitably safe distance to enjoy the theater of commotion. There was arguing over beds, giving directions as to where luggage should be set down and which way it should face, questions about additional hangers, opening and closing of windows and doors, and, of course, running back and forth between rooms to make sure that nobody else got a better deal.

Kay noticed his teammates looking on like wide-eyed spectators. He sauntered over to stand next to them, out of the way of the feminine siege, but looking strangely at home in the middle of a situation that would bemuse a lesser man. The staff had finished delivering luggage and was clearing out, happily, when Katrina noticed they had attracted an audience. She came straight toward Elora with a grin that showed off dimples Shirley Temple would envy.

Elora had guessed she must be Katrina because the three sisters were taller, blonder and bore a family resemblance to each other as well as Kay. Katrina had hazel eyes, a heart-shaped face and a head full of shiny brown curls with a touch of red in them. She was pretty, but more importantly, her manner gave the impression - even before she spoke - of someone who was kind and gracious; both highly valued traits in Southern society. She had the singularly self-possessed bearing of a woman who had never experienced loneliness, rejection, or a broken heart. And she never would.

When Katrina approached, she leaned toward Ram for a kiss on the cheek. Elora extended her hand with the intention of introducing herself.

"Oh, put that away and come here." Katrina laughed as she ignored Elora's hand and pulled her into a hug. "You could only be Elora. Kay's warned us not to invite you to one of our late night poker games unless we want to lose everything."

Elora smiled. "He couldn't be more wrong.

Ram's the shark. Blackball him."

Katrina laughed and glanced up at Kay with a look that was proprietary and adoring at the same time. When her attention came back to Elora she said: "This is *too* much fun! An elf wedding. Wow. Maybe I'll pick up some ideas."

"Well," Elora said, "if you do, I can't take credit. Ram's mother and sister are the architects of the event of the millennium. I'm along for the ride and glad to have somebody else taming the details."

Kay's sisters suddenly took the hallway. In a dizzying flurry of femininity, they said hello to Ram then grabbed Elora, pulled her into their suite, and closed the door, leaving their brother and the groom standing in the hall alone.

Kay looked down at Ram with a tiny shake of his head and a crooked little smile that implied this was nothing unusual.

Ram said: "I happen to know where the tenants of this monstrosity keep some very fine Irish whiskey."

"Lead the way." Kay immediately looked more optimistic about the prospects for a pleasant afternoon.

They had only gone a few steps when the girls' door opened. Dandie stuck her head out. "Hey. Any chance we can get some..." Her head disappeared momentarily while there was apparently some appended discussion, then popped out again. "...Arnold Palmers sent up here?"

"Sure." Ram shrugged offhandedly.

Without thanks or further adieu, the door closed, leaving the two men staring at an empty hallway. After a few seconds, they turned and resumed their quest for whiskey, but were stopped by Squoozie this time. "We need snacks, too. That airline food was just... well, you know. Y'all got stuff down there to make chicken cheese nachos?" Someone was saying something. She looked away for just a second. "With jalapenos." Another voice was heard coming from inside the room. "Not the sissy kind."

Ram took a deep breath and put his hands in his jeans pockets. "No nachos, Squooze. Why do you no' come downstairs to the solarium or the library or the game room? We can drum up some cheese and fruit. Maybe tarts or popovers."

She opened her mouth to say something, but Ram held up his hand shaking his head. "No' a single jalapeno in the house."

She contemplated that for a minute, ducked her head back into the room, then reemerged smiling brightly. "That'd be great, Ram. Thanks, hon." The door slammed, but reopened three seconds later. "We'll be down in twenty minutes."

Behind closed doors four single ladies piled up on the beds next to Elora and insisted that she give up details on how she "bagged" the world's most eligible and allegedly "active" bachelor. While Elora found the company of other young women novel and exhilarating, she had to get very creative with her story to ease around the fact that she was an alien from another dimension with extra physical abilities, who was employed by an ancient secret society of knights and paranormal investigators who guarded innocents from harm by occult or supernatural forces sometimes using occult or supernatural forces in the process. She found that she was able to stay close to the core facts while tiptoeing around specifics that would require security clearance.

When she recalled her time with Ram at the hunting cottage in the New Forest Preserve, she repeatedly heard sighs and noticed that eyes had glazed over with longing. Well, it *was* a good story.

She was less prepared for a question about where she got her hair color done. After a couple of beats of indecision, she said, "It's natural."

The four blinked at her for a few seconds, uncertain how to respond, then simultaneously exploded into a fit of shared laughter. Squoozie said, "Good one, Elora."

Sometimes honesty really *is* the best policy.

The other women were so open and easy to be with, that by the time the little group emerged an hour later to make their way toward fruit, cheese, tarts, popovers, and Arnold Palmers, Elora felt like she had known them for a long time. She noticed that Kay's sisters alternately called his fiancée "Trina" or an even more affectionate "Trinnie".

On the way downstairs Elora pointed out what she had learned so far about the palace and how to get around without getting lost. She headed straight for the solarium while they talked about costumes for the handfasting and who would be wearing what. They were just traversing the grand foyer when the giant doors opened and in walked Baka, Aelsong, and Storm.

Elora's eyes went straight to Storm's and locked there. She hated feeling uncomfortable around him and wished that she could run up to him and give him the same sort of unself-conscious hug she had received from Katrina an hour before. Instead, she froze where she was and simply nodded. He did the same, but was quickly distracted by Kay's women swarming him to say hello. Elora made herself useful introducing Aelsong and Baka, who seemed to be enjoying the female attention immensely.

Aelsong gave instructions to staff as to where to put Storm's bag.

"We were going to the solarium for a Texas style tea. It's an iced thing called Arnold Palmer. Ram and Kay are together somewhere, but I don't know where."

Aelsong turned to a maid passing by. "Where are my brother and his gigantic friend?"

"The library bar," she replied.

Aelsong thanked her and turned to the women. "I will show these two to the library bar and then join you for Texas style tea if 'tis no' presumin'?"

After assuring Aelsong she was more than welcome to join them, the little group dispersed, going in opposite directions. Elora looked back over her shoulder at the same time Storm was doing the same. She would have to talk to Ram about a way to get past this touchy situation. There must be a way to back a relationship up, call a romantic truce, pledge friendship, and move on.

When the men decided to drift toward the warmth and excitement of feminine company, Storm excused himself to his room saying he would unpack and settle in before dinner.

In the solarium, the conversation quickly turned to questions about the handfasting. Shortly after they'd been joined by the men minus Storm, Elora's mother-in-law-to-be arrived to talk about the various activities scheduled. They were all to enjoy dance lessons in the ballroom after dinner. The women responded with enthusiasm. Kay and Baka groaned. Like most elves, Ram loved to dance so it was okay with him.

Dinner was served in one of the small, intimate dining halls since there would be only twenty-one guests including a few of Ram's relatives. The average person would have been so impressed they might have been tempted to call it theater, but the six-course production was nothing extraordinary for the royal family.

Tepring sat Aelsbood at one end flanked by two of the Norns and put Storm between one of the sisters and Katrina, with Kay across from her. Aelsong and Baka were next to each other across the table from Ram and Elora which gave the betrothed couple a ringside seat to the seduction underway.

Ram found the interaction between Song and Baka more or less comical. He reached for Elora's hand under the table and gave her a smile promising a midnight encounter hotter than anything the ex-vampire could dream up, but toward the end of dinner, he began to seem preoccupied. When everyone rose to make their way to the ballroom, he steered Elora off to the side.

"I thought of somethin' I must do. I'll be away for a few hours."

"Ram," Elora looked concerned, "what...?"

"I'll tell you everythin' when I return. Promise."

"Wait. What's going on?"

He pressed his lips to hers and lingered so sweetly it reminded her of their first kiss. "'Tis a surprise. Go and dance with the others. Leave our door unlocked. And keep the bed warm for me." He left Elora standing in the doorway wondering.

The ballroom was lit so brightly it was dazzling. It was amazing that the centuries-old building had been wired for modernity; a sort of miracle in itself. Tepring had hired the same musicians who would play at the handfasting to be on hand for dance lessons that evening. She was thoughtful enough to have young, virile-looking gentlemen partners on hand for whichever two of the three Norns would not be dancing with Storm. It was becoming clear that Tepring was a genius at planning and organization, never missing the slightest detail.

Aelsong and Baka were happily paired off and lost in their own world. When Elora showed up with no partner, Tepring promptly sent for her other son, the king.

Aelsblood arrived, wearing a certain stiff politeness if not genuine pleasure at being summoned from whatever he was about. Though lacking the personal traits usually paired with dance instructors, Aelsblood proved to be an adequate teacher and Elora could see that he possessed the basic athleticism of his younger brother.

Were it not for the entertainment factor in watching people make fools of themselves, the elves, excluding Elora, would have been bored to the core going through steps they had learned as babies. But there was an inherent fun factor in an Irish reel and, by the time everyone was up to speed, the laughter threatened to interfere with keeping the dance steps in time. Even the king flashed a split-second smile, revealing a spark that reminded her of the magnetism Tepring had passed to Ram and Aelsong.

When the dance stopped, Aelsblood bowed from the waist. As he did so Elora projected the thought, "So. You hide a second nature."

He cocked his head almost imperceptibly and allowed the corners of his mouth to turn up as his lips flirted with a smile. Even that tiny change transformed his appearance from mask to semi-handsome face.

"Good night." He nodded slightly as he started away, a modern day version of a bow she supposed, and a rousing demonstration of warmth by Aelsblood standards.

"Stop right there!" Tepring commanded, proving that even kings relinquish command to the firmly stated wishes of mums. "We are no' done here. Your sister-in-law needs a partner for the waltz."

For a heartbeat Aelsblood looked like he might tell his mother to fuck off. No matter how much Elora liked Tepring, for the king's sake, there was a part of her that hoped he would.

To Elora she said: "After the handfastin' you

and Rammel will greet our guests in the receivin' line. Immediately afterward you will lead a waltz."

"Alright. You can free the king from dance duty because, I assure you, I *do* know how to waltz."

Tepring smiled brightly. "Well, then, Aelsblood will very much enjoy bein' first to dance with the bride." She stepped back. "The rest of you can join them after a few bars." She waved a sweeping hand at the musicians. "The Shannon Waltz."

This was the first time Elora had seen Tepring's imperious side and had to admit it was impressive. Her future mother-in-law would have made a passing good field general.

The king was an excellent dancer. With her right hand in his left, her left hand on his shoulder, and Aelsblood's right hand pressed firmly between her shoulder blades where he could exert the most control, he guided Elora around the floor effortlessly, the two of them demonstrating that they had both been born to pretension. Of course, Ram's family could not know that. Ever.

"You're a wonderful dancer. Can you waltz The Shannon and talk at the same time, your brotherness?"

"No' awed by the elfdom then?" he deadpanned without looking directly at her.

"Is that what you're accustomed to? Awe?"

Aelsblood had danced them toward a far corner, where he stopped and dropped his hands. "Unlike your mate, Ms. Laiken, no' all of us can go about selfishly actin' out our fantasies like carefree children. Some of us have interminable responsibilities."

And there it is.

"Were you ever a carefree child?" She saw something flicker behind Aelsblood's eyes, something that said she had pinched a sore place. "Please don't misunderstand me. I'm not making light of your job. Only a loon would want your burden. But maybe you could gain some mastery over that burden before it swallows you whole?"

He smirked, which was okay with Elora. She was thinking any emotion at all was an improvement. "And what would you be knowin' about it?"

With complete solemnity she looked into his face. It was time to find out if he could read her or if she was imagining things. "More than you might expect."

He pulled back, stared at her for a couple of heartbeats, then turned and strode away like a man late for an appointment. Fortunately Tepring was busy elsewhere and didn't notice.

Left alone, Elora's attention riveted to Storm, who was across the vast ballroom space, clearly out of place with waltzing, and having no fun. At all. His discomfort was a sharp contrast to Kay and his sisters who had taken ballroom dancing classes as juveniles so that they would be prepared for the demands of social registry functions.

When the music stopped, Tepring drifted toward the entrance thanking the extra young men for coming. Saying goodnight to their employer, the musicians left everything in place because they would be back in two days and because they did not fear theft. Elora caught Storm's eye and motioned for him to stay behind. He looked like he'd rather take a beating.

When Kay reached the door with his brace of female flurry, he turned back. Elora said to go ahead, that she and Storm would be just a minute.

Storm stood with his hands in his back pockets and sighed deeply.

"How are you?"

"Okay. I heard you're expecting."

"Yes. Expecting." She smiled. "It was quite unexpected."

Storm looked at something behind her off to the side and blinked, but made no reply, didn't even change his expression.

Okay. So no jokes. "I hate this, Storm. This... being uneasy around each other. Everything about it is *so* wrong. It feels... so wrong." She thought she saw a shadow of emotion flicker over his features, but again, he didn't respond. It seemed he didn't have any intention of making this easier. Finally, she shook her head and continued. "You owe me an invoice."

He squinted and shook his head like he had no idea what she meant. "What?"

"You told me you would keep a running tab of my expenditures so I could pay you back when I started earning money."

Storm looked around the ballroom. "Yeah. I guess money's not going to be a challenge from here on out."

"You're trying to goad me. I don't mean Ram's

family money and you know it. Farnsworth assures me that I have enough to cover my debt to you. Just let me know what it is."

"Okay." He looked around as if to say, "We done here?"

"I noticed you could use some help with the waltz. Everyone's gone. It's just us here. Let me show you."

He looked her full in the face for the first time. "What are you doing, Elora?"

"Letting you know in no uncertain terms that you're still part of my life. You're my best friend and I'm not letting you get away without a fight."

She moved toward him and insisted he assume classic dance pose. He was reluctant, but complied. She started at the beginning, going over the steps. By the time they had practiced to the point where he could do it without thinking, he had relaxed and was looking a little more like himself.

She stepped back. "You're a quick study, as good at this as at everything else you try."

He smiled a little at the compliment.

"Every woman is going to want to dance with you tomorrow night, Storm."

"Why wouldn't they?" he asked with mock arrogance. "I know how to waltz."

She laughed and they walked out together.

A couple of hours before dawn Elora felt the bed move. Half asleep, she reached for Ram. "Where've you been?"

He opened his arms so that she could snuggle into his side and warm him. He nuzzled her ear and kissed her temple. "'Tis a surprise. Show you tomorrow."

She wiggled in closer. He was wearing drawstring sweat pants and nothing else. "Missed you."

"And I you. What else did I miss?"

"I danced with the king."

Ram caused Elora and the entire bed to shake as he laughed silently.

"And 'twas a roarin' good time I suppose?"

"Well, he is a little stiff."

"You had better be meanin' that in the sense of bein' dead and no' in the sense of bein' excited. Make that aroused. He probably does no' get excited even when he comes."

"You're very funny for an elf who's been up all night". She snuggled closer, wiggling until she was satisfied that she was as close to Ram as possible without intercourse being involved. "And with Storm."

"I have no' been with Storm."

"No. I also danced with Storm, practiced the waltz. Everybody else knew how." Ram was silent. "He seems a little broken and it's hard to watch. He doesn't have his usual..."

"Swagger?"

"Um, I was thinking confidence. You think he's going to be okay?"

"Give it time. He'll find the one who's meant for him. 'Tis no' you though. You know that."

She raised herself up so that she leaned on one elbow. There was enough moonlight coming through the tall window to see her hunky elf's outline on the white sheet next to her. It would be a full moon in two days and Elora secretly thought a handfasting on the occasion of a full moon was most auspicious.

"Of course I know that," she said with just the right measure of indignation. "It would serve you right if I said I wasn't sure and was rethinking things." She then set upon his ticklish spot with a vengeance and without pity for the fact that he'd been up all night and was running on empty.

When Ram woke the next morning, Elora had already taken a long bubble bath, washed, and dried her hair, and put on a sleeveless, pink, linen dress that made him think about licking strawberry ice cream.

"How late have I slept?"

She turned toward the bed. "Late. I'm going to grab a muffin, but I'll come right back. I'll get a couple extra and bring you a coffee."

She opened the door to leave the suite, but the knob jerked out of her hand as the door shut quickly in her face. She turned around to welcome an elf fresh from the bed, pressing his still warm and relaxed body into hers. She opened her mouth to ask how he had moved that fast, but the question was drowned by a kiss that stole her breath and made her forget all about breakfast.

When he pulled back, she moaned deep in her throat.

"Hmmm. The second sweetest sound in the universe." He was staring at her mouth.

"What's first?" she asked with a lazy smile.

He raised his gaze to her eyes and laughed.

"The way you scream when you come, o' course."

"I scream?" She looked guileless as a summer's day. "I don't remember."

"You do no'?" His eyes traveled slowly to her mouth as he began pulling the zipper down the back of her dress. "I can help you with that."

"Stop! Ram!" She laughed softly as she pushed him back carefully, remembering to be gentle. Since becoming dedicated lovers, they had suffered a couple of mishaps when she'd been excited and forgotten how strong she was. "Quick muffins and coffee. Then zippers and slow fornication. Okay?"

Ram tilted his head back. Half shuttered eyelids couldn't hide his amusement. "'Tis no' fornicatin' if we're mates."

"It is if we're not married. Or handfasted. We still have a day and a half to fornicate."

He pressed his face into her neck and talked into her skin. "Then hurry up with breakin' your fast so we can fuckin' fornicate our asses off."

She left gigglin, with him thinking that was another sound he loved hearing.

When Elora returned, it was not with a large coffee in a to-go cup fixed the way Ram liked it. His mother had sent two servants carrying trays: one with a complete silver coffee *and* tea service, the other with covered plates of soft Irish bacon, scrambled eggs, and halved tomatoes fried with black breakfast pudding and mushrooms in sausage fat.

Elora poked her head in to see if he was decent. He heard the door and stepped out of the bathroom with wet hair, wearing a thick white terry, bath sheet tied around his waist and using a smaller towel to dry his upper body.

With raised eyebrows and a look that spoke volumes Elora said: "*We* have arrived with full Irish breakfast."

Ram was mildly amused. Elora felt a familiar stir of interest, watching his pecs move as he towel-dried his hair. "Let me guess. My mother," was all he said.

Elora nodded in confirmation and held the door open for the troops. They put the trays down on the large desk. "Sorry. I don't have any Irish money for a tip." The young men just stared at her. "It was a joke?" she offered.

"Aye, mistress." They gave her the same nod she'd received from Aelsblood after their dance, and left.

Ram chuckled and went back into the bathroom to comb his hair.

Elora followed and stood behind him. "So what about the disappearing act?"

He looked at her through the mirror then turned around. "I was thinkin' about our handfastin' cord."

"Uh huh?"

"Come see."

He walked over to the dressing table and retrieved a bunch of greenery tied with a red ribbon. He held it out to her like a bouquet.

"'Tis holly. It grows by the door of the, uh, our huntin' cottage."

Elora looked at the greenery, accepted it into her hands, and was instantly overcome with emotion. Her eyes filled with tears, her nipples beaded, and fine goose bumps formed all over her body.

"Ram," she said so softly. "You went all that way in the middle of the night? Through the woods in the darkness? Just to bring something from our time there?"

The tears were running down her cheeks and onto her pretty pink linen dress. Ram took a step forward and, in a gesture that had become all too familiar, cupped her face, and pushed the tears away with the pads of his thumbs. He kissed her lips with all the tenderness of an elf who was doubly blessed to be both mated *and* in love.

"I've never heard of anything more romantic." She looked into his eyes. "I'm the luckiest person alive."

"Oh, 'tis no' so, my girl. That would be myself."

After breakfast, the guests spent the morning in comic pandemonium sorting out who would wear what costume and having them fitted. The women were thrilled. The men were disgruntled about tights and codpieces. Except for Baka who was already two hundred years old when the style came in vogue.

At the end of a lunch break, they dispersed for personal pursuits. In mid afternoon Kay was making his way toward the library bar to see if somebody might be up for a game of cards when he heard Dandie, his sister the firebrand, shouting. He rounded the corner just in time to hear her finishing up a tirade. "Get the hell away from me or my brother is gonna kick your ass."

"Whose ass am I kicking now?" Kay asked calmly as he entered the room to find her staring at Baka with hands on hips.

She motioned toward Baka. "This *player* thinks he's got a shot at sleeping his way through the Norns. Just last night he was in somebody *else's* bed and now he's putting moves on me." Smirking at Baka, she said, "Credits for stamina - maybe. Debits for sleaze."

Kay looked at Baka who shrugged and smiled innocently as he walked behind the bar. "I'm making up for lost time." Turning toward Dandie, he said, "Yesterday's lady and I had an understanding."

"No doubt." Kay leveled a meaningful look at Baka. "You need to find something else to occupy your time."

"That's it?" Dandie was incensed. "You're letting him off with a warning?" She shook her head at Kay reprovingly. "Wow. That government job has made you soft, Bubba."

In the middle of pouring a whiskey, Baka stopped at that to bark out a laugh. He turned to Dandie and appeared to agree with her. "That's exactly what *I've* been saying! Kay, you and those other people you work with are simply too soft." He shook his head as he poured Scotch over ice. "God in heaven, you people are fun." He held the bottle up toward Kay in a gesture that asked, "How about you?"

Kay ignored him and looked at his sister. "Dan, that vampire and I have been through a lot together."

She looked blank. After a few blinks she drew her brows together. "Vampire?"

Kay paled a little when he realized he'd slipped. He looked at Baka, who grinned brightly and raised his glass as if to say, "Cheers," before bringing it to his perfectly chiseled lips.

Kay stared at Baka for a moment before finally deciding what to say. "It's an inside joke."

Dandie turned to Baka as if to get confirmation. He waved the glass in his hand toward Kay. "Indeed. Nothing quite says *funny* like vampire."

Dandie considered that for a moment, stepped closer to Baka and said: "Come near me again and I'll kick your ass myself."

In response Baka gave her his best sardonic smile and rubbed a forefinger in his ear. "I'm sorry. Did you say kick or lick?"

Dandie's eyes grew impossibly wide and her face reddened, making it look like she might spontaneously combust.

Baka seemed intrigued by the demonstration and watched with interest. "Kay, my friend, do your sisters berserk as well?" Kay stepped in front of the ex-vampire. "Never mind. That was a silly question. Given the right circumstances all women berserk."

Kay advanced with a more threatening tone. "Baka..."

"Alright. Alright. I'm going." Baka looked around like he'd lost something. "Has anybody seen Aelsong?"

Kay, who had turned toward his sister, gritted his teeth and wheeled around like a parent who'd been pushed too far. "Baka! Give. It. A. Rest. *Everybody's* sisters are off limits. Am I making myself clear?"

"Kay," Baka chuckled, "most women are somebody's sister."

Kay took a step forward in an aggressive mannerism that was universally understood as provocation-gone-too-far. The fact that it was out of character for Kay was a little alarming. So, in an unprecedented display of good judgment, Baka set his glass down, held up his hands, and began backing toward the door.

Having witnessed the entire scene without saying a word, Squoozie now hurried out the door after Baka. When she caught up to him, they were still close enough for Kay and Dandie to hear their sister say: "My *baby* brother doesn't speak for me, Baka. I'm sure Aelsong is busy right now. But *I'm* not."

VICTORIA DANANN

CHAPTER 4

On the day of the handfasting, the palace became a blur of activity between deliveries and the hustle and bustle of staff, both permanent and temporary. Katrina and the Norns kidnapped Elora from the breakfast table and insisted that Ram could not see her again until time for the ceremony. Elora was touched that they wanted to fuss over her and help her get ready.

When Song heard about it, she showed up and the suite was alive with feminine laughter and excitement. In mid afternoon she said, "I'm goin' to go check on the groom."

A chorus of voices sounded all at once, the gist of it being, "Don't tell him a thing you've seen or heard!"

Song found her brother in his suite and offered to braid his hair behind his ears. He sat quietly in front of the mirror and enjoyed reminiscences with his favorite sibling, who was quick to assure him that she found Elora Laiken a treasure beyond compare. He tried to pump her for information about what Elora was doing, but Aelsong resolutely kept her pledge of silence. When she was sure that Ram knew exactly how to put on his own costume along with where and when he should report for the ceremony, she gave him a quick kiss on the cheek and returned to the bride's ready room.

VICTORIA DANANN

Tepring and Aelsong had spared no expense on
the bride's gown. She had chosen white for no
reason other than that Ram loved to see her wear
white. The dress was raw silk with decolletage that
showed the right amount of bosom - not too
scandalous, not too prude - and a tight fitting bodice
beaded all over with real pearls. There was so much
fabric in the skirt that a weaker woman might grow
tired carrying it around.

Tepring arrived in late afternoon holding a box
wrapped in forest green satin sheen paper with
white and gold ribbons woven together then formed
into a bow. Elora sat down on the settee to open it
saying how much she hated to disturb the perfection
of the wrapping. The gift inside was the perfect
complement to her dress - a four strand pearl choker
necklace - all the more precious because it was a
family heirloom, having belonged to Ram's great-
grandmother. When Elora started to tear up, there
was a sudden rush of group admonition insisting
that no tears were allowed once make-up had been
applied.

Aelsong then handed Elora a smaller gift in
identical wrapping.

"For you from the king. 'Tis somethin' new,"
Song said quietly.

It was a pair of stud earrings with pearls
identical to those in the choker. Each pearl sat on a
foundation of emeralds. Song then handed her a
bracelet of four strands of pearls. "This one is mine,
but it matches the necklace so I insist you wear
them together today."

"It's beautiful, Song. Are you sure?"

"Oh, aye." Aelsong's tinkling laugh made the space joyful. Elora gave her a hug. The pearls for the dress, though smaller, had been chosen to match the exact same tone and luster. The result was stunning.

As oldest, Urz took the leadership role. "Trinnie's got one more thing from us." She gestured to indicate the other four women.

Katrina handed her yet another forest green box with gold and white ribbon. Elora looked from one to another with delight and anticipation. She tore off the wrapping with more abandon each time she opened a gift. This box contained a wide blue, raw silk garter with a luxurious excess of ruching, accented with a single pearl centered on a white satin bow.

"Something blue," said Katrina.

Elora had no idea why Katrina thought it important to point out that the garter was blue, but over the past half year, she had gotten pretty good at covering when she didn't understand a cultural reference. Elora thanked each one of them individually, then pulled the garter on and up to the top of her white, thigh high hose while being modestly careful not to reveal that she was getting married without underwear.

Last they placed the traditional partial wreath of holly, tree fern, and fine, diaphanous white silk feathers on her head.

When she was fully dressed and ready to go down, she was such a vision that the other women just stood and stared until she became self-conscious, wondering if the plan had not come together. With her unusual hair and the natural high coloring in her cheeks, they could certainly understand why the groom liked seeing her in white.

"What's wrong?"

Song took her by the hand and smiled. "'Tis so no' wrong. If my brother did no' already believe himself to be a very lucky elf, he will be thinkin' he's died and gone to heaven."

Elora grinned at her. "Song, you are *so* like your brother."

"Well, since 'tis rumored on good authority that you love him, I shall take it high praise."

Elora squeezed her hand. "As you should."

Urz answered a knock at the door. Right on time, the king's mother had sent a herald to fetch the bride.

Song handed her *the* rose. Katrina had stayed with her, sipping white wine while Song and the Norns raided the "floral room". It was usually a large dining room, but was temporarily converted into a hub for arranging and distributing thousands of blooms. They had spent an hour there, first searching and then arguing over which was the single most perfect flower.

Elora had kept back a sprig of holly, which she tied together with the perfect rose using the red ribbon Ram had brought her.

She took a deep breath and looked at the others. "Here we go."

Descending the stairs, they could hear the noise of music and many voices talking at once. The hall, more aptly called a thoroughfare, was deserted except for the royal guard in dress uniform, posted every few feet for security watch although it was a formality. The elfdom was populated by millions of citizens willing to die for the king.

When they reached the ballroom entrance, the music stopped and the crowd grew quiet. With one last encouraging look, the other women went ahead of Elora, leaving her standing alone outside the entrance. She turned and looked at the soldier standing nearest her. His response was the barest hint of a smile and a wink which, oddly enough, calmed her nerves.

The guests had parted to clear the wide strip of forest green carpet that marked a path to the circle in the center of the room where Ram, his family and the people closest to the couple waited with the Old Ways priest who would guide the ceremony. Elora had been instructed by the planners to listen for her musical cue then follow the carpet to the circle where the groom would be waiting.

The processional was the traditional "Star of the County Down" played on wooden flute, tin whistle, fiddle, tiompan, and bodhran. When she heard the prelude, she took a deep breath, winked back at the guard, and walked to the entrance, where she could see the ballroom for the first time. The number of people looking at her expectantly was expected, but still overwhelming. She had never liked lots of attention.

Her gaze flew straight to the end of the carpet where stood an elf who challenged the bride for beauty and, in her opinion, won the contest without a fuss. Nonetheless, there was a collective sound of approval from the throng when she appeared in the doorway at the head of the carpet, a mixture of little gasps and murmured oohs and aahs. The groom had to swallow a lump, as he was thinking: "Exactly right buggers. And ne'er will you again see a creature so beguilin'."

Rammel was wearing the male version of her costume: white raw silk and a vest of tufted velvet with matching pearls in the furrows. His sister had done a masterful job of braiding his hair behind his ears and had pulled the rest into a catch at the nape of his neck. His smile and golden aura were in full bloom.

Ram and Elora held each others' hands with crossed wrists and repeated vows as the priest sealed their joining with the cord they had braided while laughing and talking about the future. Out of the corner of her eye Elora saw both Song and Katrina brush away stray tears. She was aware of where Storm was standing, but resolutely refused to look his way because she wouldn't chance having her wedding day compromised by sadness no matter how much guilt she might secretly hold in her heart.

When the cord was unwound, Rammel surprised her by producing a gold band etched in Celtic knot weaving with a large, oval emerald of the deepest green. And it fit perfectly. She was expecting a chaste kiss, but should have known that her elf would not be shy about public displays of affection. By the time he released her, she was blushing like a Victorian virgin.

It seemed to Elora that they had been standing,

greeting guests for hours. When finally she saw the end of the line, she leaned over to whisper in Ram's ear. "Let's sneak away for a few minutes. You know some place nearby with a good lock on the door?"

Ram's body immediately responded to the suggestion underlying her request and he suddenly had a new appreciation for the practical side of codpieces. The light in his eyes signaled his agreement. He rushed the last few people along, grabbed her hand and they dashed for a side door before someone could block their escape. He led her straight to a small and little-used morning room. It was a parlor outfitted in Victorian furnishings both uncomfortable and too formal for modern tastes. It was no wonder it wasn't visited often.

He closed and locked the door while she laughed with the excitement of a schoolgirl cutting class. When he reached for her, she ducked out of the way.

"For the last five hundred people in line I've been thinking about how to do this."

He grinned. "Aye. Well, I would give witness that you do, in fact, know how to do this."

"No. I mean with all these clothes." He watched with interest as she grabbed a chair with no arms from in front of a small writing desk and brought it to the center of the room. "Sit," she commanded. And he did. Gladly.

"Now let's see about freeing you from this thing." She began to fumble with the codpiece.

He laughed and offered assistance, releasing a proud erection, its intense coloring a sharp contrast and graphic invitation as it jutted from the pristine white, silk costume. Looking down, she saw glistening drops of moisture on the head. He hissed in air when she took him in hand lightly and spread the precum with her thumb watching his eyes darken to the navy blue that meant he was ready. She stood his cock at an angle she judged right and directed him to hold it right there while she gathered yards of skirt and straddled her new husband.

Having imagined this moment for the past two hours, brushing up next to Ram while greeting well-wishers, she had no further need of foreplay. She eased down on him, her eyes closing from the sensation, glorying in being filled to the hilt, then she bent forward and covered his mouth with a kiss of pure possession. There in the gloaming light of a seldom used parlor, his hands under the skirt of her vast and costly wedding gown fit for a queen, fondling the bare skin of her hips and upper thighs, he was thinking that, however unlikely, this might be the single most erotic thing that had ever happened to him. He stared up at his singularly beautiful - and commando - bride, transfixed on her face as she moved torturously slowly, massaging the arousal that was now throbbing a tattoo of demand, while she purred, "Ah, Ram, you feel *so* good."

He moved his hand so that his thumb grazed the sensitive pearl of her sex every time she came to rest while, at the same time, he was captivated by the feel of her sex meeting his with his hand. She cried out her release, moving faster and harder until he joined her. They stayed where they were, catching breath, exulting in the pleasure of each other and their new status as officially mated. After a moment he looked down, spied the blue garter, and smiled broadly.

"And what is this?" Ram asked as he hooked two fingers under the elastic.

"Katrina made a point of pointing out that it is blue."

Ram laughed. "'Tis a weddin' tradition for good luck. 'Tis a rhyme as well. The bride wears somethin' old, somethin' new, somethin' borrowed, and somethin' blue."

"Oh. I wish I'd known the significance. Your mother gave me the necklace," she touched it as she spoke, "saying it belonged to your great-grandmother. I guess that qualifies as old. The earrings are a gift from Aelsblood. Song even said, 'Tis something new' when she handed me the box. She insisted I borrow this bracelet that matches the necklace." She covered his face with tiny kisses then sat up. "So this means we'll be blessed with good luck?"

"'Twas already proclaimed. Happily ever after and nothin' less." He pulled her down into a kiss then removed the garter. "I believe this is intended to become the property of the groom."

"Who says?"

Ram shrugged, pulled it on over his sleeve until it circled his bicep then popped it suggestively with a broad smile. That's when they heard banging at the door. Elora rose and tried to rearrange the skirt of the dress hoping she had saved herself from becoming noticeably disheveled. She knew the color in her face would be higher than usual. It always was after making love to the stunning, garter-wearing elf whose pleasure-giving cock had just disappeared behind a codpiece.

They opened the door to find Tepring standing there with hands on hips.

"Mum! Come to offer us congratulations?" He grinned mischievously.

She was not to be put off her mission. "You two are supposed to be leadin' a waltz. Remember?"

Elora looked embarrassed by the situation and Ram suddenly felt defensive. "You are embarrassin' my bride, the mother of your grandson. The whole lot of wankers in there is no' worth that."

Tepring pursed her lips while she contemplated being corrected by her second son. Then she turned to Elora. "Rammel is correct. 'Tis your weddin' day and you should have some say o'er what transpires. Shall we proceed without you?"

"Not at all," Elora said. "We're on the way. One waltz coming up."

Tepring nodded and started away, but stopped suddenly and turned around. "Grandson. The baby is a boy? How do you know?"

"How do you think? Aelsong." Ram was not as respectful as he could have been, but he was feeling perturbed toward his mother.

"What's his name?" Tepring's entire posture had changed. She looked as enraptured as if she had just learned about the baby on the way.

"Do no' know. My bride is goin' to name him." He looked at Elora like he idolized her. "'Tis my gift to her."

"Oh, well, if you need suggestions..."

"She does no' need suggestions, Mum."

Tepring looked at Elora. "With all the planning I may have been remiss in no' tellin' you sooner how happy we are." She didn't wait for a response, but rushed away with a spryness that was admirable for someone her age.

"Do no' be embarrassed, Elora," Ram said in her ear. "She's right. 'Tis *our* weddin' day and we can spend it in each other's arms if we choose."

She smiled at Ram. "Let's dance."

Engel Storm was the sort of person who believed there are very few gray areas in life and even fewer when it comes to questions of ethics and morality. He believed that the right thing to do was always evident to someone who was looking honestly for it and that, once that "right thing" had been identified, it was an acquired target; something to be done without further debate or question.

If sometimes that happened to be hard, well, that was just too damn bad. Not up for debate. That was the personal code that had kept him in good stead for as long as he cared to remember, certainly ever since he had been recruited by Black Swan. Even with the horrors he had witnessed as a field active knight, he usually slept well.

The day of the Laiken-Hawking handfasting was the first time Storm had ever confronted a "right thing" that felt impossible to execute. He hadn't struggled too much with accepting the invitation to come. It was the right thing to do. So he did it.

He hadn't struggled too much with being

included in the wedding party, with learning reels or watching the happy couple at meals or even letting Elora teach him to waltz. But he couldn't figure out how he was going to make himself get in that receiving line and give his congratulations to Ram and Elora. A lump formed in his throat when he pictured it in his mind.

It was the right thing to do. No question about it. Still, he stood alone in a small alcove with a large ale, away from the festivity, and argued with himself for some time. He tried to tell himself that there were so many people, Ram and Elora wouldn't notice his absence. He tried to tell himself that he could always congratulate them later. Last, indulging in a completely foreign and ill-fitting moment of self pity, he told himself that he had already done enough.

That was right before Engel Storm's nobility marshaled his innate character and triumphed over every argument, or excuse, that might have been made by a lesser man. He set down the ale, pulled his shoulders back and emerged from the alcove with determination, only to find that the receiving line had dispersed. The newlyweds were nowhere in sight. He felt a momentary jab of panic, thinking he may have lost a once in a lifetime opportunity to do the right thing by adding his well wishes to those from others.

He searched the ballroom asking first one person, then another, if they had seen the bride and groom. When he was sure they were not within, he rushed out into the wide hallway. He looked to his right and saw only a long expanse of white and black checkerboard marble tiles with formal military security posted every ten feet. He looked to his left and, to his very great and visible relief, saw the pair hurrying toward him hand in hand, the two of them looking so perfect together.

As he started toward them, Elora closed the distance between them, flew into his arms and squeezed him like she was holding on for dear life. He held her tight with his strong left arm while he looked at Ram over the top of her head and held out his right hand in an age-old male gesture of goodwill. Ram clasped Storm's hand with affection and sincerity and, in a wordless conversation, the two men reaffirmed that their dedication to each other was not subject to any mitigating factor. Their shared history as B Team knights, having long ago committed, each within his own heart, to die for the other without question made them far more than friends. More even than brothers.

Storm opened his mouth to try and say the word. He got as far as, "Con..." But, Ram didn't ask for more. He let go of Storm's hand and stepped in close to share the hug. After a few moments, the three of them released each other.

Elora used the backs of her hands to wipe at tears. "You men are always making me cry."

Ram and Storm gave each other a look that said somehow it would work out and be okay. They would get through even this.

CHAPTER 5

Normally the trip from Derry to Edinburgh would be by small craft charter, but The Order had sent one of the small jets to pick up B Team and Baka. The small caravan had driven right up to the plane and the drivers were transferring luggage from the road vehicles to the cargo area below. Katrina and Kay's sisters were hitching a ride to Edinburgh. They were planning to stay for a couple of days, see the sights, then do some shopping in London before heading back home.

Ram and Elora stood on the tarmac in the morning chill talking to Baka when one more car pulled up. Aelsong emerged carrying a bleached, canvas duffel and offered a cheerful, "Good mornin'."

Ram stood blinking and looking as discombobulated as Elora had ever seen him. "What do you mean, 'good mornin'? What are you doin' here?"

"I did no' think the time was right to share my news durin' the handfastin'. I've been recruited by The Order and I'm goin' to Edinburgh." She glanced up. "On this very fine plane as a matter of fact."

"The fuck you are! 'Tis no' safe for us in Fairyland, Song. I forbid it."

Aelsong gave him a laugh with more meat than wind chimes. "Right. 'Tis why you're stayin' here, is it? Get out of the way, brother."

Aelsong jerked her duffel onto her shoulder giving Ram the sort of snarky smirk that siblings reserve for each other. As she started for the plane, he took a step after her, but Elora pulled him back. "Ram, you know you can't stop her. Like you said, she's grown. It's her choice."

"Great Paddy's Balls Afire. You women will be the death of me!"

Cars and drivers were waiting for the troupe at the Edinburgh private hangar. One of the cars took Katrina and the Norns to the Balmoral Hotel while the other transported their luggage. B Team, Baka, and new recruit, Aelsong Hawking, were taken straight to the General Headquarters building where they would work and reside while on assignment there.

B Team was on loan to help Baka set up his task force at his request. The office at The Order's headquarters in Edinburgh also planned to take advantage of their specialty. Since their own staff of hunters was spread thin, B Team was to assist with a werewolf sanction. They had been receiving disturbing reports of werewolf activity in one of the most populous districts of London.

The timing of Ram's induction into the Hall of Heroes made the entire gig a perfect marriage of efficiency and necessity.

For the time being, thanks mainly to Baka, things were relatively quiet at Jefferson Unit in New Jersey. The vampire infestation had been neutralized along with their chief habitat. It would take them some indeterminate time to regroup. Before that happened Baka and his new task force should be making headway with permanent eradication through cure.

It was misting when they arrived in Edinburgh. Elora had visited the city before; at least she had been to the Edinburgh in her dimension as a child. She remembered thinking there were things about it that were magical in a fairytale sort of way. Now, from the perspective of an adult, she could understand why she remembered it that way. It *was* magical. The mist made it seem all the more so.

Driving along Princes Street, the castle, rising out of the crag at the head of the Royal Mile, looked like something out of a dream. The High Street buildings were blackened by centuries of coal burning, but the color seemed to add to the charm rather than detract. The historic skyline overlooked the city gardens and the Royal Museum from the hill leading downward from the castle to Holyrood Palace, where the fae monarchy was in residence most of the year.

High above the palace a smaller version of a Parthenon-like temple sat on Calton Hill which was the city's own Acropolis. Eight times a year processions climbed the hill to celebrate pagan festivals. Some were riotous and some were solemn, but all of them were sacred to the national character of the fae. The rest of the time, Calton Hill served the community as a park with an excellent view of the city.

The division of the Edinburgh unit of The Order of the Black Swan, where they would be stationed, was housed in a nineteenth century building occupying an entire block of outrageously expensive real estate on Charlotte Square. The basement level housed operations that were never viewed by people not employed by The Order. The ground floor was offices, conference rooms, and dining. Floors above were a mix of office and living quarters.

Locals believed it to be the seat of a network of charitable organizations and, from a certain point of view it was, in the sense that The Order performed services benefitting the entirety of the human race. And they did it without pay.

When the transferees came to a stop in front of the building, Elora could hardly contain the excitement of being reunited with her dog, Blackie. They had decided before they left the States that it would be easier on him to go straight to Edinburgh and settle in rather than be transported here and there, always adapting to new circumstances. So, Glendennon Catch, an eighteen-year-old from Jefferson Unit, had already been in Edinburgh with the dog for four days.

Glen, himself, was one-quarter werewolf. He didn't shift or have any of the notoriously inconvenient traits, but he did have a way of seeing things from a different perspective. The Order employed educators who served as part teacher and part talent scout. The most important part of their task was observing, evaluating, and helping to develop special abilities and interests. Glen's teachers at Jefferson Unit had agreed that he would make a fine hunter, but that he would be better utilized in the division of General Investigation as he had an extraordinary gift for identifying details that went unnoticed by others.

When the current assignment came up, it offered a perfect opportunity for Glen to do a part time internship with G.I. in Edinburgh while helping to take care of Elora's dog, the former Jefferson Unit mascot. Werewolves didn't automatically get along with dogs. In fact, the opposite was often true, but Glen and Blackie liked each other enormously.

Glen was ecstatic about the appointment, saying something like, "Mysteries, dog walking, and fae girls? I'm in!" He was a cute kid with a slightly unkempt sort of devil-may-care appeal: rich brown hair skirting his collar and eyes that defied description because they appeared green or brown depending on what he wore and where he was. His frame still held the angularity of teens, no fat, all bone and muscle, but he was going to be as big as most of the knights when he filled out. Last, but not least, he was good natured and easy to be with.

Elora wasn't worried about his adjustment. She figured he wasn't going to be alone in Edinburgh unless he wanted to be. Fae girls would be all over him.

The main foyer of Headquarters general offices building was originally designed to make a grand first impression. And it did. Though it had been modernized with elevators, air-conditioning, and state-of-the-art plumbing, the improvements had been made without compromising the essence of the era. The building entry featured a pair of wide, wrought iron and turned oak staircases that rose from the polished marble of the ground level floor and gracefully curved toward each other ending in a mezzanine gallery that joined the two halves of the building.

Litha was crossing the mezzanine on her way to the Office of Letters when the little band of travelers arrived. She slowed just a bit, curious as to why people had come out of their offices and were now standing by the railing looking down at the front entrance. She heard a whispered conversation off to her left and slowed even more. One person said to another, "Do you know who that is?"

"No. Who?"

"That's Bad Company."

"No shite? B Team from New York?"

Litha looked down at the group just as Storm looked up at the mezzanine. Their eyes met for an instant, but, unlike hers, his eyes kept moving and didn't stop until he had thoroughly surveyed the environment. She wished she could look away as easily, but she was frozen in place, staring.

She thought that she could have seen this man in a mall, at a fair, in a bank lobby, it wouldn't matter. She would know him anywhere. He was the furthest thing from metrosexual, the furthest thing from soft or malleable. What she was admiring was a man born to be a knight. She had no idea or warning that there was a place in her heart that harbored a secret desire. But, just like that, in the blink of an eye, Litha suspected that the feeling that washed over her, leaving an indelible impression, was love.

She thought of herself as a person who had a reasonably healthy interest in men and sex, but, for some reason, had just never thought of herself as being *in* love; had never expected it or envisioned it, or hoped for it, or planned for it. Love was something that happened to regular people.

The Order's personnel files were full of extraordinary biographies and resumes; people who were gifted or accomplished. Litha was one of a kind: a transplant from Northern California who was both witch and tracker. She knew she was scheduled to be temporarily diverted from more important work to help B Team with a werewolf fiasco that anyone with rudimentary dousing ability could handle. She had been thinking of it as a nuisance assignment, right up until she saw Engel Storm walk into the foyer of her building.

When Litha was finally able to make herself put one foot in front of the other and move forward, she was talking to herself under her breath. "Of all the secret societies, in all the towns, in all the world, he had to walk into mine."

One of the two coworkers who had been standing close by said, "What was that?"

She stopped long enough to scrunch up her face then looked at them. "Love! Shit!"

Resuming her errand she walked away a different person from the one who had started across the mezzanine bridge a few minutes earlier.

The two coworkers thought nothing of the outburst. The Order was a veritable hot spot of interesting personalities. Some might say quirky.

There were those with unique talents and those with miraculous skills. It was simply a fact of life that special gifts were often paired with unusual disposition and/or social adjustment that was a little off center. Of course, there were exceptions, but there were days when even the exceptions gave themselves permission to act out.

That was why ramrods like Sol and Simon were so vital to the organization. Somebody had to keep the menagerie herded into a working group.

Litha closed the door to her office and leaned against it, doing a personal checklist. The Great Palpitating Revelation came with a distinct lack of the accompanying symptoms it was supposed to trigger. There were no bells ringing. There was no sense of walking on air. She did not feel high. Loss of appetite? No.

What she really felt was a damn foreboding sense of looming inconvenience. This was definitely not part of the plan. Her plan.

She pushed away from the door restating the initial accurate assessment of her true feelings, once more for good measure. "Shit! Love!"

The fact is that nobody believes in love at first sight. Until it happens to them.

Since Ram and Elora were the rare married couple working for The Order, and the only one with a pet, they were given a spacious corner apartment on the top floor with bedroom, living room, and bath. Glen had been assigned a small room next door for quarters, but had been sleeping on their sofa so that Blackie could feel more settled.

Elora heard the dog barking when the elevator door opened. He already knew they were there. Glen opened the apartment door and let him run down the floral carpeted hall to greet Ram and Elora. She got down on the floor with him and gave him a good long, hello tummy rub while quietly assuring him that she missed him and was very glad to be reunited with him.

The temporary apartment home was decorated in muted, restful colors of sage and brown. Someone had provided water bottles, fresh fruit, and fresh flowers with a card that read "Honeymoon Headquarters". Making an educated guess, Elora thanked Glen for his thoughtfulness. Since he didn't deny it, she assumed she had guessed right. She had read his file and knew that he had spent a semester assisting in the Operations Office at Jefferson Unit. And Elora knew firsthand that a kid didn't train under Farnsworth without learning a thing or two.

Their work schedule was free until the next morning. Their social schedule was free until dinner. So they decided to unpack quickly and try out the new bed. After all, what could top a cool and drizzly afternoon with nothing to do but make love and nap in each others' arms?

Kay went out for dinner with Katrina and the Norns. Aelsong had already met some people close to her age in the Psychic Division and was off doing something with them. Ram, Elora, Baka, and Storm were invited to dine at the Director's table.

Simon Tvelgar, Head of Agent Affairs, was to be their direct supervisor for the duration of their assignment in Edinburgh. Ram's first order of business was to interrogate Director Tvelgar about Aelsong's recruitment.

Director Tvelgar, was about the same age as Sol, but, unlike Sol, he wore a permanently pleasant expression. Like all the administrators who had begun their careers as knights, Simon retained the hardened physique of a warrior and the presence of an underlying tension that implied that the civilized manner was pure veneer. In close proximity to such a personality, the subconscious mind of the innocent registered a feeling of comfort and security that they would be protected if necessary. On the other hand, that same presence created an urge in blaggards to flee.

Tvelgar seemed somewhat amused by Ram's questioning and was more than patient with the concerns of an older brother, especially since those concerns centered around the fact that there were Elves now living in the fae capital.

The Director said that he had planned a private lunch for the next day in which he would introduce personnel who would assist them until Baka had established what his permanent personnel requirements would be. They had cleared away space on the second floor designating a "War Room" with three adjacent offices.

It was nine o'clock by the time they finished a nice dinner of charred salmon with mustard, boiled potatoes in butter, and unleavened bread. Even in April the sun set late that far north. Ram's mouth twitched as he reached for Elora's hand under the tablecloth. He knew that, after the dinner plates were removed, she was looking around wondering when chocolate would be available and in what form.

He leaned over and whispered: "Do no' worry. We shall adjourn shortly and go on cocoa quest."

She squeezed his hand and, thinking no one was looking, brushed her lips across his cheek suggestively. Storm saw the exchange out of the corner of his eye and felt his heart seize ever so slightly. He wondered if it would always be that way.

CHAPTER 6

Across the dining hall, Litha Brandywine half listened to her companions while she watched Storm dine with Director Tvelgar, a man with model cheek bones and piercing blue eyes, and two people who were obviously a couple - a beautiful couple. He was either elf or fae. If there was any difference, she'd never been able to detect what it was.

After dinner, she decided to make her way to the Office of Records and find out more about the tall, dark, and striking knight.

Twenty-seven years earlier, Litha had started life as a Dickens cliché, having been left on the church steps in the tiny village of Clitheroe on the edge of Pendle Hill, Lancashire; a region of

Britannia most noted for legends of witchcraft and strange goings-on. The Anglican priest who discovered her was entertaining an old friend at the time; a Cairdeas Deo monk visiting from California. When discovered, the pretty baby was not crying and fussing, but kicking happily at her blankets while patiently waiting to be found.

Brother Cufaylin, who had one of the seven gifts, recognized her as something special. He appealed to his friend, Father Daugherty, to let him take the child home to the monastery four thousand seven hundred miles away. He vowed the other monks, his brothers, and he would love her like a daughter and dedicate themselves to seeing her thrive, helping her reach toward her potential and find her destiny - whatever that might be. While Father Daugherty had his doubts, he'd heard too many stories about the bleak futures of hapless children who were orphaned or abandoned to a system that worshipped nothing but bureaucracy. Brother Cufaylin's offer to give the little girl the best of everything was very tempting. In fact, he didn't see how he could refuse.

Although he never would have offended his friend, Father Daugherty also had misgivings about the nature of Brother Cufaylin's beliefs. The Cairdeas Deo sect was far too mysterious for his comfort. There were even indications that perhaps they were not *strictly* Christian. Still, he supposed the baby's fate would be better off with atheists or alchemists than the alternative.

So, they managed to acquire the credentials that would allow Brother Cufaylin to pass through immigration and attain legal guardianship. After a quick course on the care of an infant from a village woman who had served as nanny to the high-born when she was younger, he carried the pretty babe home to the vineyard monastery at Bodega Bay.

The Cairdeas Deo monks had been "hiding in plain sight" for centuries, disguised as a Christian sect since the term automatically created a societal mystique that functioned as a protective barrier against close examination or typical standards of rational thought. The Cairdeans actually served the twin masters of the Merkaba: truth and life force, privately calling themselves the Friends of Life.

Brother Cufaylin brought the child home to the Sonoma Coast winery on the very day of the Summer Solstice and dubbed her Litha in celebration of the Feast Day of that name. The monks were, at the same time, celebrating a very fine review of their handcrafted, bottled-in-bond, one hundred proof, seven-year-old brandy. So she became Litha Brandywine, precious daughter to seven monks who could not have been more surprised that an odd twist of fate brought them the opportunity to be proud parents.

They were in a unique position to help Litha develop and channel her very special talents. Her mind was polished and refined on the turning wheel of free thought. She was exposed to every myth, doctrine, superstition, and philosophy according to the principle that minds with little education form a narrow palette of capability which is far too easily manipulated. Their view, that mental strength requires a perpetual diet of new material to digest, found perfect expression in Litha's step-by-step development.

She never felt that she missed out by not experiencing a more typical family environment. Nor did she ever spend a minute of her life wanting for love or attention.

What Brother Cufaylin saw in the infant that day at Father Daugherty's Anglican church was his secret, but he judged truly when he concluded that she was special.

In point of fact, Litha was the daughter of a practicing Pendle Hill witch and the demon she conjured.

Litha's mother had been told that her great-great-grandmother was reported to have summoned a demon. The seed of that tale grabbed hold and took root in such a way that her future was then deprived of real choice. No one knows what sets the heart on an intractable course, but Litha's mother yearned to repeat her great-great-grandmother's adventure into the occult and worked tirelessly to discover the key that would enable her to do so.

One of the central issues in the practice of witchcraft has always been unpredictability and the inability of the witch or sorcerer or magician to replicate results. In the case of demon summoning, the craft took a wrong turn sometime early in the Dark Ages that could be traced back to a practitioner who successfully conjured a demon and documented the episode. The problem was a faulty conclusion based on incomplete data. The magician's assumption was that a recipe of steps involving tools and words of power had wrought the event whereas that was only true in part.

The practitioner had accurately performed the steps necessary to cast an ether net which was the *true* cause. The effect though, was not that a demon had been summoned, but that a demon slipping dimensions had been *caught* within the net that was cast. Future witches and sorcerers would ponder the unpredictability of summoning for centuries without ever realizing that the process is exactly like fishing. Cast an ample net in which you may or may not catch a demon.

Tomes on craft were full of legendary accounts of the downsides to conjuring. Naturally demons were rarely happy about being caught in a witch's web. For one thing it was a little painful, like getting a righteous zap from static-filled carpet.

Further, it was quite unsettling, even for demons, to set out for one destination and suddenly end up in another. And a pissed off demon wasn't likely to be in a mood for granting favors.

Of course there are exceptions to every rule and one was the case of Litha's mother, Rosie Pottinger, the apothecary's daughter, who caught the incubus demon, Deliverance, in her web. He appeared within her Circle with a loud pop that startled her into releasing an embarrassingly tiny squeak and jumping back. She was taken by surprise partly because of the noise and partly because of the shock of being successful. After all, who ever *really* ever expected to conjure a demon?

She gaped as he hissed and roared. "Cromm the bloody Crúaich!" Through a red haze of indignation he spied a culprit, vaguely registering that it was a female witch. "Tarnation woman! Do you know that bloody well hurts?"

Into the palm of his hand he spontaneously pulled a sphere of fire a little smaller than a bowling ball and drew back his arm to launch it, thinking he would teach this witch a lesson to reverberate through the annals of magical notation for generations. As he was about to release the fireball he focused on the woman for the first time. The flames spit a couple of sparks, turned blue and then evaporated in his hand as he stared.

Rosie Pottinger still stood wide-eyed and gaping at the demon while he stared back. He sensed a trace of something more than human in the young witch who could have taken her name from the brilliant color in her cheeks. Apparently Rosie's great-great-grandmother had done more with the demon than just summon him.

Deliverance dropped his arm as his mouth spread into the sort of spellbinding smile that could only be managed by an incubus.

He lowered his volume to dulcet tones and, when he said hello, Rosie Pottinger felt her knees go weak. His accent was tinged with a gypsy dialect that was far from aristocratic. That was because he had learned Anglish in the shadows of The Tower of London.

The shirtless figure stood before the witch inviting her to look her fill as he drew her nearer to a trap of his own device. The candle flames danced in his black eyes like they were mirrors as they tracked her tiniest movements. His thick, silky hair fell to his waist, the color so intensely black that it reflected light like the glossy surface of polished slate. His coppery skin gleamed with a promise of heat and molded lovingly over musculature that demonstrated the artistic principle of shadow being equally important as light.

Indeed. Deliverance was fashioned as the personification of female sexual fantasy and desire, a perfectly designed instrument of seduction.

There are many degrees of desire. Temptation means that denial is possible. Deliverance inspired the sort of desire that burned two steps beyond that. Just the sight of him was enough to push the strongest-willed woman past need, past longing, all the way to compulsion.

Deliverance wasn't an actual sex god as demons are not deities in the sense of mythos. They are simply a distantly related race of beings, but why quibble over details? Deliverance had never known the disappointment of rejection because he was - quite literally - irresistible.

Within the hour the apothecary's daughter, with her comely curves and light brown hair, lay on the stone floor inside the Circle that contained the demon - or so she thought - being pleasured beyond the limits of mortality.

Certainly you might expect to know what is on the next page; that the incubus demon, Deliverance, took his pleasure from slightly misguided Rosie Pottinger and continued upon whatever demonly errand had occupied him before the interruption of his journey. But that is not the way the story goes. The demon may have intended his encounter with Rosie Pottinger to be a brief and pleasant diversion, but her demon blood called to his and, as he slowly stroked her luscious body with his own, the sweet fucking turned into lovemaking.

He stared into the witch's eyes, green as the water standing in the lava pools of Ovelgoth Alla, absorbed her scent into his essence as he nuzzled her neck, and fell in love.

Every night when Rosie's father, the widower apothecary, had drunk himself into a stupor, Deliverance came to the witch's Circle with gifts and stayed to hold her through the night. While she slept he would whisper, "My sweet, sweet, delicious Rosie. You please me well."

It is a well-known fact that demons produce sperm when coupling with other creatures who have demon blood, no matter how small the proportion. Of course, he knew that pregnancy was a possibility. What he did not know was that it was possible his love could leave him, in one way or another.

When Rosie Pottinger realized she was pregnant with the child of a sex demon who could not be faithful to her, she first became despondent and then depressed. The more melancholy she suffered, the more she became convinced that the cause of her suffering was sin in the Christian sense; specifically the sin of cavorting with a demon. Though she had never been religious and had not been educated in anti-demon doctrine, she sought out the Church as a possible source of comfort if not resolution.

She went to a priest and confessed everything from the means by which she had deliberately conjured the demon to the pleasures that she had found with him nightly on the pallet inside her Circle.

The priest never doubted for an instant that she was mentally troubled; that, at the least, she suffered delusions of sexual fantasy. The fact that she was fantasizing about intimacy with a demon was deeply disturbing.

The village priest was ill prepared to counsel those in need of psychiatric analysis or those who encountered paranormal phenomena. So he did the only thing he knew how to do. He blessed her and sent her home with a verbal instruction to be thereafter chaste in mind, body, and spirit. Unfortunately, Rosie did not find in that simple instruction the means to cope with her sorrow.

When the baby was born, Rosie wept over the child's beauty, seeing some of the father's traits stamped plainly upon her face. After leaving the newborn on the steps of a church in another village where no one would suspect her birth was "tainted", Rosie took her own tragic life with drugs easily obtained by an apothecary's daughter.

Deliverance, who had always been as happy as a demon can be, was devastated by the loss of the witch he loved and was left alone with what was theretofore considered impossible: an incubus with a broken heart. Since he had not seen or touched the infant, he gave no more thought to his offspring. He never, in fact, so much as troubled himself to learn whether Rosie Pottinger had given birth to a baby that survived. Simply put, deprived of his lover, Deliverance cared about nothing, which is why, thereafter, he embraced his dark half and began to behave more like his father than his mother.

Of course Litha knew nothing about her unusual heritage or the source of her extraordinary gifts. She could not know that she had her father's black hair and a light kiss of his bronze tinted skin that gave her color even through a long Scotia winter. She could not know that she had her mother's deep green eyes, rosy cheeks, and luscious lips so naturally red they never needed artificial color.

What she did know was that she was different. The monks had gone to great lengths to teach her from infancy that those differences must be carefully hidden from most of the people most of the time. There were some things that not even The Order knew. For instance, she had a miraculous resistance to the dangers of fire. In other words, she couldn't be burned.

CHAPTER 7

After dinner Ram asked Elora to please wait for him in the lobby. In less than five minutes he showed up with jackets and an I've-got-a-secret smile. When she looked at him questioningly, he helped her into her jacket, put his arm around her shoulders and gently nudged her toward the door. "How about goin' out for a bit."

He was clearly enjoying himself so she didn't grill him about what he was up to.

They walked straight south in the direction of the castle. Before they started down the steps to the gardens they stopped at a newsstand where Ram bought one Toblerone chocolate bar and handed it to his bride. Ten minutes later they were standing in front of the National Museum. It would normally be a five-minute walk, but they strolled leisurely in the late Northern gloaming while Elora enjoyed her after dinner chocolate fix.

"Here we are," Ram said.

"Ram, it's almost ten o'clock at night. The museum is long closed."

"No' for us," he grinned and steered her toward a side door.

He knocked and the door opened as if someone on the other side was waiting there. They ducked inside and removed jackets while Ram shook hands with the security guard and thanked him for letting them in.

Their footsteps echoed loudly in the vacuous marble expanses as they hurried past irreplaceable treasures of art and history. They passed dozens of armed guards who nodded as they walked past the central stairway and descended a small staircase at the rear. The lower level was illuminated by low level lighting. They walked for some distance in the immense building. Elora noticed there was a higher concentration of armed guards. After passing through several Employees Only checkpoints, they arrived at what seemed to be a dead end. It was a plain, nondescript door that, once again, said "Employees Only". If pressed, she would have guessed that a utility closet would be found on the other side of that door, but instead, it opened to a vault entrance much like the one in Baka's former prison. She looked at Ram, who smiled like he could hardly wait for her to see what would happen next.

The guard punched in a code then stepped aside while Ram did the same. With a hiss, the hydraulic locks spun open. The guard pulled back on the wheel centered on the twelve-inch thick door to reveal the space beyond. He smiled at Elora. "There's nothin' more secure than the king's museum. Unless, of course, it would be the wing that belongs to The Order."

Elora was surprised to hear this museum guard speak about The Order.

When the door was pulled open Elora could see that the lights came on inside. Ram motioned for her to enter. Inside was a gallery perhaps a hundred and twenty feet long and thirty feet across. There was no furniture other than a few ornately carved wooden benches on the periphery. Nothing but large, framed paintings on both walls, facing each other. Each was a portrait about eight feet high and four feet wide.

The space vibrated with an energy that was difficult to describe, but Elora got a mental impression that she was in the presence of something held sacred.

"Is this...?"

He nodded and looked around with pride, imagining he was seeing it for the first time through her eyes.

Slowly she began to walk the room, taking in each visage, trying to imagine the knight portrayed as he was when he had lived. Beside each was a brass plaque engraved with their name and the year they had been memorialized.

Some of the oldest wore actual armor and held shields with family crests. What they had in common was a posture and determined expression that she knew oh so very well.

After half an hour, she came to the last space currently occupied. A portrait hung there, obscured from view by white silk draping. When she realized what it was, Elora's hand flew to her mouth. She took in a deep breath having vowed to stop being such a weeper. Her eyes watered, but did not overflow. She stepped close enough to the plaque to read: Sir Rammel Aelshelm Hawking, Knight of The Order of the Black Swan, Prince of Elves. She looked at her new husband who was waiting for her reaction.

She smiled. "I guess it would be bad luck to look underneath?"

He chuckled and kissed her mouth. He broke the kiss, put his lips next to her ear where she could feel his warm breath and said: "Let's go home. Our new bed is no' yet broken in." He pulled back just far enough for her to see his puckish smile. "If you like, I can put on a kilt and you can look underneath all you like. Maybe have a feel as well."

She turned her face and breathed into his beautifully pointed ear. "I only sleep with heroes."

He laughed and pulled her away.

Litha sat alone in front of a computer that held biographical data. It had the facts of Storm's career with The Order, but much had to be "read between the lines". Apparently he was a textbook example of the ideal profile of a Black Swan knight. Since he was now rumored to be at the top of his vocation, the process must have gotten it right.

One of the surprises was learning that he was from Oakville, California, only thirty-five miles from the monastery where she was raised. It was strange to think that they had been growing up so close together and were so unaware of each other, but, contrary to the popular adage, it is not a small world.

She could see from records that Storm had been in trouble at school from the first day of first grade. Like a lot of the knights, he was too smart to be suited for the public school curriculum and the system wasn't set up to cater to individuals. Also, most adults had a really hard time liking children who were smarter than they are.

He seemed to have been born knowing things, like math for instance. His mind would grab on to a concept on first presentation and then, while his classmates struggled, he would be looking around for something to do. That something usually ended up being disruption.

Storm was loved by his parents, but school faculty was another story. He had a reputation with the teachers for instigating pandemonium in the classroom. He was the triple threat: smart, bored, and a natural leader. It wasn't that he was a class clown, nothing so obvious or exaggerated. He just quietly went about doing whatever the hell he pleased and ignoring objections. In short, no one in his life to that point had given him adequate reason to believe that anarchy was not the best policy.

Peers wanted to be like him. If that wasn't possible, they would settle for doing whatever he was doing. So Storm's experience of the public school system was time spent in the hallway, the principal's office, or in trouble at home with his parents agonizing over what to do.

At one point they thought sports might be the answer. He had an extra helping of athletic talent and one of those bodies that would have said yes to any physical demand. He just never saw the point. To him, sports represented an endless, mindless repetition with some arbitrarily established goal that made no sense when he broke it down and it turned out to be… well, boring. Put it all together and he was a public school educator's nightmare. He was also a textbook ideal candidate for Black Swan.

VICTORIA DANANN

One day he was sent to the Vice Principal's office under protest claiming that, for once, he wasn't doing anything wrong. He sat down in his usual chair to wait for the usual carpet ride, but instead, the door opened to reveal too many people crowded into a smallish room. That included the V.P., Storm's parents and a tall, serious-looking guy with a piercing gaze and an unmistakable air of authority.

Storm sat up a little straighter and had only one thought. *Uh oh.*

The stranger wore slacks, highly polished loafers, and a sports coat. He guessed the man was old, thirty-five maybe, but he looked hard all over like one of those athletes who can't repeat enough Iron Man triathlons to please themselves.

Engel Storm's father worked for the Randolph Moldavni vineyards as head winemaker. The work was personally fulfilling and he wasn't chained to a desk in a cubicle, but it didn't cut a path to either greatness or riches. His mother worked part time as library receptionist at the local branch of the University of California. Between the two they made enough to take care of three kids in solid middle class fashion. They could eat steak, but not every day. They had good health insurance with the vineyard. They could take a summer vacation if they drove and stayed in motels. It was an upbringing no child should complain about, but most did anyhow.

Storm's background hadn't afforded an education on the finer points of better men's' clothing, but even to an untrained eye there was a

120

vague sense that the stranger's style was expensive.

"Have a seat, son." Vice Principal Rodgers motioned to an ugly metal chair with a green leatherette seat and back. Storm noticed that there was a small tear in the seat that showed a little white stuffing. His mind was racing, partially occupied with the fact that Rodgers had called him "son". He decided that meant he was in even bigger trouble than he thought, but on the other hand, his parents looked serious, but not mad. The tall guy leaned against an old book-case and looked really, really out of place against the backdrop of venetian blinds that were partly bent and a room that needed repainting.

Mr. Rodgers, better known to the student body as "Tums" as it was said his tummy entered a room five minutes before the rest of him, sat down with a plop that forced air out of the vinyl cushion seat. Another boy his age might have had to suppress a snicker, but Storm sometimes seemed more like an adult than a kid.

When the wheezing subsided, Tums said, "Engel, this is Mr. Nemamiah." Storm looked up into flinty blue eyes that didn't blink or apologize for staring. After a couple of seconds he wanted to look away, but pride wouldn't let him. So he raised his chin just a hair and determined he wouldn't give in first. Mr. Nemamiah's expression didn't change at all, but Storm thought he saw a little light flicker in those steely eyes. Nemamiah let him off the hook and looked away first.

Tums continued. "It seems he's taken an interest in you and your education."

Storm was starting to panic. *Not military school. Please. Please. Please don't let it be military school.* It was then he started calculating how long it would take him to be up, out the door, and hitchhiking on I80.

"It's been noticed that your test scores are extraordinary. To say the least."

Wow. That wasn't what Storm had expected to hear next.

"Mr. Nemamiah is in a position to arrange a scholarship to a private school that develops talent such as yours for possible future work with a quasigovernmental agency. He asked that I make this introduction so that you would know that he and his organization are legitimate."

"Develops talent? What does that mean?" Storm demanded. He directed the question to Tums, but Nememiah interjected answering in a gravelly voice.

"It means specialized training. Highly specialized."

Storm stared at Nememiah for a couple of breaths and then barked out a laugh intended to imply rebellion, irreverence, and a healthy dose of cynicism. "Spy school? You want *me* for spy school?" He laughed with his whole body as only boys can - for a few seconds. Then, in the time it took to draw another breath, Storm raked a gaze up and down the older man sizing him up, reasoned through the bizarre nature of the offer and decided that first, it would not be boring and, second, it might be cool. "Okay. Sign me up."

Mr. Nemamiah almost gave in to the

temptation to smile. While such behavior might be seen as rash, impulsive, or even schizophrenic in the mundane world, the ability to quickly sort through an equation and make hard decisions on the fly was one of the traits his organization prized. Neither parent was particularly surprised. With Storm they knew the one thing they could count on was unpredictability.

Nemamiah talked directly to Storm as if to say from now on this is between you and me. "Clean out your locker and say your goodbyes to your friends. Let them think you are going to military school. I'll be by your house tomorrow morning at ten o'clock. You and your parents will have an opportunity to ask questions. You may consider it an interview if you wish. If, at that time, you are satisfied with my answers, we will leave together. You may pack some personal things into two duffel bags, but that is optional. Everything you need will be provided for you from now on. You're going to receive a first-class education, the kind money cannot buy, from people who will be honored to teach you."

Storm blinked and his brows came together to form perfectionist lines that would be permanently etched into his face by the time he was twenty-five. *People who would be honored to teach him?*

Mr. Rodgers cleared his throat. "Well," he stood and held out his hand to Storm's father to shake. "Thank you for coming." He nodded to Mrs. Storm. "Give us a call tomorrow and let us know what you decide."

Everyone in the room knew Tums would feel

like he'd won the lottery if the troublemaker kid was on the way to being somebody else's problem.

Storm's parents waited in the car while he cleaned out his locker. In the few minutes that took, he had already made a list of questions. He couldn't keep himself from peeking into the classroom where he would normally be looking for something to occupy his restless mind and body. When the other kids looked up and saw him at the door, he gave them a goofy smile and a wave, just so they'd know he hadn't been led away crying or something disgraceful like that. He wanted to leave with his reputation intact.

Prune Face Blackmon followed the eyes of her students to the classroom door which stood open to the hallway. "Mr. Storm. Do you have someplace you need to be?"

He didn't want to give her the finger. He really, really, really didn't want to give her the finger. But he gave her the finger, and trotted away grinning at the uproar of laughter from the poor douches who were going to be stuck in that hellhole the rest of the hour.

"Not a bad exit," he thought to himself. "Points shaved for lack of planning, but..."

He didn't know where he was going or what he was going to do. But he would have felt really good about the whole thing if he had known that Sol Nemamiah would have laughed, on the inside, had he witnessed the teacher receiving a prime example of bird as a parting shot. What you want at your back if you're heading into a nest of unknown fuck all is not a man who was afraid of a little authority as a kid. That guy would just as likely freeze and shit his pants or vice versa.

Sol's philosophy, had he ever been asked, would have been something like: "Give me a kid with a proud third finger and I'll give you back a vampire slayer."

The Storm family stopped at McDonalds drive-through on the way home, then settled down at the Formica top kitchen table with a yellow legal pad and the goal of making a comprehensive list of ask-now-or-hold-your-peace questions.

What was the scope of this "first class education that money cannot buy"?

Did it include geometry, foreign language, literature, biology?

Would he be receiving a diploma?

Would it be accepted by desirable institutions of higher learning?

Where would he be going?

Could he leave if he didn't like it?

Would he be able to call home whenever he wanted?

Could he visit them?

Could they visit him?

Would he have a room of his own?

Would he get spending money?

Would he have an opportunity to spend spending money?

Would he be signing up to get an education or pledging himself to pay off the investment in service to a job that wasn't his choice?

Would he have an opportunity to interact socially with others his own age?

And, did they know it wasn't all mind-blowing test scores and high I.Q.; that he had been in trouble at school pretty much nonstop since first grade?

By the time his two siblings got home from school, Storm and his parents were agreed on which questions were deal breakers.

He and his dad pulled down two duffels they kept in the attic for camping. After packing everything he wanted to take, he hadn't even completely filled one. That realization gave him pause, but not as much as the fact that he didn't have any friends worth lying to about where he was going.

He didn't sleep that night. At all. He didn't know whether he should be excited or apprehensive. So far the information he had was cryptic at best. What he did know was that it was an adventure come knocking at his door and that this kind of thing didn't happen every day. In fact, he'd never heard of it happening to anybody. Ever. The idea of a school that *wanted* him was so outrageous it made him smile to himself in the dark.

The next morning Storm said goodbye to his older brother and younger sister when they left for school, then sat down at the kitchen table with his parents to wait. His duffel was by the front door just in case. At precisely ten o'clock the doorbell rang.

Nemamiah was invited in. He graciously accepted coffee and the four of them sat down in the modest living room for a question and answer discussion about the future of a very special boy. After all their questions had been answered, to everyone's satisfaction, Mr. Nemamiah clicked open an old-fashioned, battered, brown leather briefcase and withdrew a contract.

Storm's dad put on his reading glasses. Every one of the questions they had asked was covered in the contract already. It spelled out what they would do for Engel Storm. It spelled out that the initial choice of facility would be theirs, but that he might be transferred at any time at the discretion of Saint Black's which was the parents' code name for the organization. Storm and his parents agreed not to say anything other than that he had been awarded a scholarship to a private school. When Mr. Storm was finished reading, he handed the contract to his wife and asked Mr. Nemamiah to excuse him and his son. He took Storm into the back room, closed the door, and gestured for him to sit on the bed.

"Your mother and I want to do the right thing, the best thing, for you. If you decide to accept this offer, we want to be sure that you're doing it for you and not for... any other reason. We love you enough to let you go if you're inclined to think this is the best thing, but we want you to stay if it's not. Do you understand?" Storm nodded and tried to swallow back the lump in his throat. That was the longest speech his father had ever made, that he knew of, and he heard the love in it loud and clear. "Alright. You know what you want to do?" Storm nodded again.

So Storm and his parents signed the contract. He gave his mother a big hug and tried not to notice how hard she was working to keep the moisture in her eyes from spilling over. He was already two inches taller and could look down on her when she wasn't wearing heels. He was more trouble than the other two put together... more trouble to the third power. Even so, although she would never admit it even to herself, he was her favorite.

He stowed the half-filled duffel in the trunk of Nemamiah's understated black sedan and waved to his parents who were standing in the front yard watching him drive away. He had just turned fourteen.

They drove south toward San Francisco. Nemamiah wasn't big on small talk, but he told Storm he was welcome to listen to whatever radio station he liked. He then rolled the driver's side window part way down and lit a little, thin, black cigar.

They kept driving until they reached the naval base at Treasure Island. They were headed for the compound in the middle surrounded by a twenty-foot wall. They passed three checkpoints where guards recognized Nemamiah and waved him through. As they passed a gorgeous old graceful mansion with lawns and tennis courts, Nemamiah said it had once been an Admiral's home, but that it was being used for the school now, that Storm would eat and enjoy leisure time there.

They parked next to a brick building, opened the door with a key card, and entered a long dormitory-style hallway. Each door had a nameplate. When they stopped mid way to the end, Storm looked at the door. The nameplate said Engel Storm.

He reached up to run his fingers over the lettering. "Wow. You must have been pretty sure

I'd come."

Nemamiah didn't smile, but his eyes did soften just a touch. "We've been doing this for a long time, Mr. Storm. We know what we're looking for." He turned the knob and swung the door open. "And you're it."

Elora got up early enough to take Blackie out for a run. She put him on leash, thanked the doorman for his cheerful, "Good morn'" and started jogging down Princes Street to the east. The north entrance to Calton Hill was rarely used because the ascent by small, paved trail was a straight up heart attack waiting to happen even for young legs. But it was exactly the sort of workout Elora and Blackie needed. So they ran up.

When they reached the top, Elora unsnapped the leash and pulled a tennis ball out of her fanny pack. When Blackie saw it, he was so excited that he spun round in circles so fast he looked like a Tasmanian devil. She threw it toward the other side of the park and laughed out loud to see how joyfully he tore after it. They played in the park for the better part of an hour, then jogged back.

Elora's hair was still damp from showering when she joined the others at breakfast which, for her, was a fruit cup, cranberry scone and hot chocolate.

They were to get a complete tour of the building before lunch and a little orientation on the old part of Edinburgh just outside the front door. Elora had seen a little of that the night before.

B Team was assembled for their private lunch

in the room that had been set aside for their exclusive use. Director Tvelgar, who had asked to be called Simon, was in attendance. The War Room was a lovely large space. It held an oblong table for eight, suitable for work, conference, or eating. The wall behind featured a large screen monitor flanked by electronic pen screen boards on either side. The rest was furnished with comfortably plush lounge seating. There was a small bar with complete coffee service, a small, but well stocked refrigerator, and a quarter bath for the sake of convenience.

An inviting buffet lunch had been set out on the bar. When Litha arrived, Storm had just gotten up to serve himself. As she breezed up to him, he turned to look down into deep green eyes enhanced by the matching green of her lightweight and clingy cashmere sweater. She was wearing a shin length, A-line skirt that fell into a drape swishing around her legs with a captivating femininity, and flat heeled shoes that gave her movement the grace of dance in progress.

"Hi," she said in an American accent. "I'm Litha Brandywine."

He got a flash impression of dark clouds rushing by on the wind. Before he could stop himself he said, "You smell like a rainstorm."

As Litha looked up into Storm's handsome face, her red, bow-shaped lips formed a bewitching smile. "What a nice compliment!" she said in a voice that was naturally sultry without affectation. "There's nothing more wonderful. Something about the rumble of thunder that's so primal, so carnal. It's the ultimate turn on. Add the smell of a rain storm coming and you have a witch's dream."

Storm wanted to look away, but seemed to be hypnotized by the illusion of tiny little flames dancing in her eyes. He shook himself internally, wondering if he had heard right. Did she just say carnal at the exact same moment his dick twitched in his pants in response to that smile?

"I'm not looking for a relationship," he blurted. He was thinking it must be a day for wondering because now he was also wondering what had happened to the simple security of having a mouth that cooperated with his brain. He was the kind of guy who liked control. Everything about the idea of his tongue going rogue was disturbing on a cellular level.

Having heard his part of the exchange, since he had added volume to the force of the proclamation, everybody in the room had stopped what they were doing and turned to look at him with a giant unspoken, "What the hell?" on their faces.

Litha's expression never changed. Nor did she miss a beat. She acted like his out-of-left-field comment was the most natural thing in the world. The beauty of her poise and composure bore through the stunned haze of Storm's humiliating behavior long enough for him to register that Litha Brandywine was extraordinary. Even the tease of her smile had never wavered.

"Oh," she said lightly, "I hadn't realized I was planning our wedding out loud."

That broke the tension and drew a few muffled chuckles, but Storm's friends were still regarding him with a question mark. The fact that she was so unflappable while he was acting like a dunderhead was annoying.

Simon came to the rescue and interjected: "Litha is here in the capacity of tracker. She's on loan from Magicks for the purpose of helping you isolate targets."

"Witch?" Elora asked.

"Best we've got," answered Simon. "You know, Storm, Litha's also from wine country."

Litha tore her gaze away from Storm, who was still staring at her and wondering what had happened. She glanced around the room at everyone present and nodded as she set her things down next to Elora. "Yes indeed. Cock Bay."

Elora's eyes widened at the remark.

"Sorry." Litha chuckled. "It's just a little bit of local color. Back in the fifties Alfred Hitchcock filmed a movie called 'The Birds' at Bodega Bay. Since it's our only claim to fame, the locals started calling it Hitchcock Bay. Eventually it got shortened."

Elora smiled. "Oh. I just assumed there must be a unit of Black Swan knights there."

Ram snickered and grinned at her like he couldn't be more proud.

Turning to hang her sweater on the chair, Litha knocked her satchel off the table strewing papers on the floor. In the messy stack were some sketches and a little watercolor of a pink, Italianate villa with red bougainvillea trailing from pots on steps.

Squatting down to help gather the spill, Storm picked up the small square of colorful art and examined it. "What is this?"

"Oh nothing," she took it from his hand. "It's a pretty little vineyard close to where I was raised. It sits high up on a cliff, the ocean on one side, the Russian River Valley on the other." She smiled at the little square. "To me it's heaven on earth."

Storm stared at her for a split second then straightened and walked to his chair. He had a photograph of the same villa in his luggage. It was dog-eared from being with him wherever he went. It had been in his pocket that Yuletide day when he walked away from Elora Laiken. He had been planning to show it to her on the plane, hoping with all his might to see her face light up with a description of his dreams for the future. He'd been in love with that place ever since he was sixteen, but had kept that fact hidden from even his teammates, because there was a part of him that was afraid his desire for it was dangerously close to obsession.

For over half his life, he had been saving so that one day, when the time was right, he could walk up to the front door, ring the bell, and say to the owner, "How much?"

It was hard for Storm to concentrate on the details of the briefing. His mind kept drifting to the unlikelihood of such a coincidence. Plus his eyes kept wandering back to the witch's red, red lips. Or her dark, green eyes. Or her skin with the bronze patina that made it look heated from the inside. Or her mess of black hair that fell to her shoulder blades and curled like she had just been well loved.

Completely aware that he was taking her measure, Litha finally looked him straight in the face, not bothering to hide that she hadn't been kidding about wedding plans.

When they had finished lunch and were ready to begin structuring the new department, the door opened and a young woman hurried in carrying a large stack of papers. The latest arrival hesitated, eyes darting around the room, registering that the only vacant seat was next to Baka. He took in her chestnut curls, amber eyes, and generous curves in one practiced sweep - along with her hesitation about taking the chair next to him.

Simon glanced over his shoulder. "Ah. Help has arrived."

Baka gestured to the empty chair next to him. "Please."

She appeared to be gathering resolve. Once decided, she walked to the end of the table purposefully and sat next to Baka. With conspicuous formality and unmistakably Anglish dialect she said, "How do you do. I'm Heaven."

"I can see that," he said in his usual flirtatious manner.

"Right. And I've never heard that one before, have I?" Turning her attention to Simon she said, "The newly arrived employees *are* familiarized with sexual harassment policies are they not?"

Before Simon could decide how to answer, Baka had bristled at the suggestion that he would sexually harass Heaven or anyone else and had taken personal offense. "I beg your pardon. What I meant to say was that Heaven is an excellent stage name for stripping, but most 'dancers'..." He formed air quotes when he said the word 'dancers'. "... take on more understated names when they enter respectable occupations such as this."

Her amber eyes took on an angry glow and narrowed on him while the flush on her face began to spread downward.

"I don't know much about stripper names, Master Vampire." She drew out the word vampire and said it like it was something the plumber would throw away after clearing a drain. "But I did a two-year internship in Chronicles when I was taking certification in demonology and read some of your history. Until, what? Three weeks ago *you* were classified a demon yourself. Was that the sort of respectability you had in mind?"

They stared at each other with enmity having instantly taken root and growing by the second. Baka was speechless. His jaw tightened visibly revealing that he was clenching his teeth.

Tvelgar thought it might be a good time to mention why Heaven McBride had joined them. Looking at Baka, he said, "Meet your personal assistant." The Director's tone managed to be dry and wry at the same time.

While Baka stared at Simon like he must be deranged, Heaven was saying, "Not by choice I assure you," under her breath.

Baka wasn't pleased to let her have the last word. The conflict he was experiencing was almost painfully unnerving. He was attracted to her and repelled by her at the same time. The first was understandable. The second was not. Something about her put him on edge and made him want to flee the room.

The rest of the afternoon was spent sorting out a starting point for one of the biggest and most involved projects of the century: a mass migration of refugees from hell to the everyday problems of humanity, including shortcomings like weakness and mortality. Every time Baka gave his assistant a task, she glared at him, eyes flashing, nostrils flaring. It was most unfortunate that her new boss enjoyed the fallout of her distress. When he had realized that the nature of the job gave him the upper hand, his mood was restored to stable, if not outright euphoria.

Elora had decided that, since Katrina and Kay's sisters were leaving the following morning, she would organize a night out: pub food, live music, and maybe a pint or two. She included Baka, Aelsong, and Litha in the invitation then had a nice long chat with the doorman about the best place in walking distance for good stew and an unplugged jig. He suggested a pub in the shadow of the Balmoral Hotel, six minutes walking distance. So Elora told everybody to meet in the lobby at eight. Ram was not all that excited about a night out in Fairyland, but Elora wanted it so, naturally, he agreed. Kay said he would go by the hotel for his women and meet up at the pub.

When the meeting broke up, Litha stopped Storm in the hallway and held out the little watercolor to him. He started to reach for it, but then pulled his hand back.

"What's this?"

"You seemed interested in it so I want you to have it."

He stared at the colorful square in her hand for a few seconds. Finally, he raised his eyes to meet hers, but didn't raise his hand to accept the gift.

"I can see myself sharing it with you," she said.

He gaped, completely incredulous at the bold and ridiculous assertion. He was also starting to wonder if she could be a little psycho. He'd heard about such things. "Anybody ever told you that you move kind of fast?"

She was undaunted. "I was home schooled. I guess I never learned the point of not saying what you mean. Seems like a senseless waste of time."

Storm's stubborn streak was compromised by his curiosity about the witch's odd behavior. "Okay. I'm as much a fan of honesty as the next guy. Why me?"

"Why am I not being bashful about letting you know I… like you?" He said nothing. "A lot?"

"Yeah."

She studied him for a minute while she was deciding what to say. "I guess it's like an antique puzzle box where all the cylinders have to be arranged in a particular pattern before the box will open. When I saw you, all my cylinders lined up and clicked into place. I guess nobody believes in love at first sight until a stranger walks into the room one day and..." She trailed off. "What is it *you're* looking for?"

Wanting to simply put an end to the inane and pointless dialogue, Storm quipped, "Someone entertaining."

Litha considered that for a moment. "I can be

entertaining."

He blinked, trying hard not to find that response just a little bit adorable. He wanted to ask how in the worst way, but forced himself to look uninterested, turn and walk away. Without the watercolor. Even though his fingers had itched to reach out and accept it.

CHAPTER 8

It wasn't easy to commandeer space for eleven people in a bar on a night when they were featuring live music. But with a combination of large corner snug and two tables pulled close, they managed to form a loosely structured group. The Norns were going to be trolling the bar all night anyway so there was no point in saving seats for them.

Though Aelsong had her back to the room, she kept getting the feeling that someone was staring. She finally turned to see who it was and her eyes locked on the navy blue gaze of a dark haired angel sitting across the room. He didn't look away or try to hide the fact that he'd been staring. She let her eyes wander down his body and back up again before turning back to her group.

The pub had better food than Elora had expected. Everybody had eaten well and seemed to be having a good time. Well, everybody except Litha. Storm had decided to nip the pursuit in the bud by making a big show of flirting with an array of unattached women in the bar while ignoring her. Observing this, Elora concluded that he must be very afraid of Litha's potential power over him, to engage in such un-Storm-like behavior.

Song also seemed more distracted than anything. Several times more she turned around to see what her admirer was up to. He was out with friends, raucous friends, but whenever she turned his way, he stopped what he was doing and looked back like she was the only one in the room of any importance.

Out of nowhere someone yelled, "Elves!"

The music stopped. The talking stopped.

Aelsong said, "Great Paddy. The crap has hit the wind."

Ram looked at Song and Elora and said: "Stay here," forcefully enough to let both know he meant it. As she slid out of the booth right behind him to follow and cover his back, Elora wondered who in the world he thought he was talking to.

When Ram reached the middle of the room he was facing several perturbed-looking fae, but he was also flanked by a recently cured vampire and three Black Swan knights, one of whom was a berserker and another of whom was his wife, who could destroy the building if she had cause.

He said to the crowd in general. "We do no' want trouble. We are here on official business. If our presence makes you uncomfortable, we'll be leavin'."

One of the fae staring down Ram smirked, raised his voice and said: "Hey, Duffy. The Fen is sayin' he's here on official business."

Aelsong's angel came through the crowd and stood in front of Ram. As she approached, she noticed he was as tall as her brother, which meant he was tall for a fae. She stopped beside Ram in a show of solidarity.

The angel looked down at her. "You're with him, then?"

"For all eternity. He's my brother."

The prince's mouth turned up at the edges. Then he looked at Ram. "And what is the nature of your *official* business?"

"Again, we do no' want trouble and are willin' to leave, but why should we be tellin' you our business?"

One of the challengers pointed a thumb at Song's angel. "Are you daft? You're talkin' to Prince Duff Torquil. You could be sayin' he's the last word on official."

Prince Torquil noticed that Ram showed no outward sign of being either intimidated or impressed.

Aelsong raised her chin and let her eyes wander over him again. *A dark fae*.

"'Tis no' for public consumption," Ram said.

"I see. An' is your sister privy to this intrigue?"

"Aye."

"Very well. Have her come o'er here and whisper it in my ear."

"My sister is no' chattel. I do no' tell her what to do."

At that so very public statement of confidence, Aelsong's heart swelled with pride and affection. She looked at her brother with unconditional adoration for all of two seconds before she walked to the Scotia prince purposefully and stood on tiptoe to whisper, "Black Swan," in his ear.

Duff experienced a moment of sensory overload, a little light-headedness, when Song came near enough to kiss. He couldn't decide whether to focus on her very arousing scent which would have to be called Carnal Knowledge if it could be bottled, or the warmth of her breath on his ear, or the sound of her tinkling windchimes voice, or the actual words she said. When he managed to restart his mental processes, it registered that she had mentioned The Order.

He looked down into those hypnotic Hawking blue eyes and said loud enough that everybody in the bar could hear, "The elves are in Scotia under my protection." Under his breath, quietly enough that only she could hear, he said, "Fae's gods, it can no' be."

Aelsong swallowed and looked up with wide eyes, her heart shaped mouth forming a silent "o". She started to take a step backward, but he grabbed her wrist. "What's your name?"

"Aelsong Hawking."

He looked like his future had just turned inside out and his brows drew together as he looked down at her. "Hawking?" His heart was sinking.

She backed up a couple of steps unable to look away then Duff's boisterous friends grabbed him and dragged him away.

Storm went straight back to the bar and grabbed a girl for a dance, making sure they were within Litha's vision so she could see them rubbing against each other suggestively. Litha had never felt jealousy before. She'd never cared enough about what someone else did to be emotional about their behavior. But sitting in that booth, watching Storm's hands drift further down the girl's body while she rubbed up against him made Litha grow warm with anger. The longer it went on, the hotter she got. In fact, she was so mad she was fuming and could have sworn she smelled smoke. That was when someone yelled, "Fire!"

She looked down and saw that her skirt and the booth were on fire. She quickly got herself under control and extinguished the flames on her clothing by patting them out. Not knowing that Litha wasn't in danger, Elora, who was closest to her, pulled her away from the fire thereby setting her own shirt ablaze. In a fit of quick thinking, the people in the next snug doused her with pitchers of beer which, thankfully, had so little alcohol it didn't act as fuel and turn her into a human torch. As an added bonus, it also cooled her skin so that she wouldn't burn. On the downside, she was covered in sticky, smelly beer.

The bartender, meanwhile, had grabbed a fire extinguisher from the kitchen. When the danger had passed they were standing in the middle of a mess composed of smoke, sloshed beer, white foam, and burned leather that smelled so bad patrons couldn't wait to get to the nearest exit. Elora, sensing that somehow this was Storm's fault, insisted that he get out his Platinum American Express and pay for both the damage and the owner's loss of business for the night. Storm and Elora yelled at each other for a couple of minutes before he produced the plastic and handed it over. He was seething, angry enough that he could have set the bar on fire himself. Mostly because on some level he also suspected it was his fault, although he couldn't see how.

He looked around to see if Litha was okay and

if she was still watching him. She wasn't. She was leaving, but she did pause at the exit and turned around just long enough for him to see hurt in her eyes. *Son of a bitch.* He'd wanted that. Now that he had it, he hated himself for it. How fucked up was that?

Ram took off his shirt and gave it to Elora. In the Ladies' she removed the ruined blouse she'd worn, threw it in the rubbish bin and used damp paper towels to dab away some of the disgusting beer smell. She put Ram's shirt on, thanking the gods that they were only a few minutes away from her bath. Ram wore his jacket over his bare chest and they left making sure they had Song where they could see her.

When they got out of the elevator, Elora stopped Storm in the hall before he unlocked the door to his room. She didn't care that she was standing there in an oversized shirt, smelling like smoke and beer with her hair hanging down around her face.

"Storm, for gods' sakes, don't let what happened between us ruin your chances to have what I have."

Storm's shoulders tensed. After a few beats he turned and gave her a hard, this-is-none-of-your-business expression. "You're overstepping, Princess."

"I can't overstep with you, Storm. I may not be your family, but, in this world, you're mine. I'm going to see to it that you're happy if it's the last thing I do. If I have to tie you to a chair and set her on your lap."

He stared at Elora until he couldn't keep that image from softening the corners of his mouth.

"Yeah." She nodded. "That's what I thought." She started toward her own apartment, then said over her shoulder: "I'm not blind, you know. And don't call me Princess!"

Ram went straight to the bath and started filling the deep tub that just happened to be big enough for both of them with steamy hot water.

"Hey," she protested. "*I* was going to take a bath. I'm the one who smells like a burned brewery."

He dropped his jacket and leered while removing his boots and unbuttoning jeans.

"Hold your ire and kick your knickers off. I do no' mind sharin'." He smiled at her like the cat who stole the cream. How could she protest that?

When Elora had rinsed the beer smell out of her hair she lay back against Ram, relaxing into the pleasure of his bare skin and the security of his arms.

"Elora, you're no' responsible for Storm's heart. You have no' done anythin' to feel guilty about."

"You're making too much out of it."

"If it makes you happy to play matchmaker, then 'tis fine with me so long as I'm the one crawlin' in bed with you at the end of the day."

CHAPTER 9

Storm threw the keys on the table, closed his door and leaned back against it. The image of being tied to a chair while Litha sat on his lap made him hard. He figured he must finally be losing it. And who would blame him? He'd had a year of fucked up. Hell. It hadn't even been a whole year.

First, Lan was killed by a vamp and there wasn't a thing that he or Kay or Ram could do to stop it. Next Elora had literally materialized out of thin air as an unrecognizable pile of goo. When she'd recovered they learned she was an alien who had been forced into this dimension. He fell in love with her. She chose Ram and broke his heart. End of story. Boo hoo.

Did he want to be interested in a woman? No.

Was he interested in a woman? He wanted to say, "Not only no. But hell no." Problem was that might not be the truth. In his mind, he replayed the look on Litha's face when she was leaving the pub and it made him feel like he had to be the biggest bastard who ever lived. How fucked up was that? *Deep and wide.*

Storm pulled on the light drawstring sweats he liked to sleep in, threw the covers back, turned off the lights, and lay down on top of the sheet. He thought about jacking off, but went to sleep before he could follow through.

In his dream he undid the drawstring on his sweats and pushed them down far enough to expose the erection that pulsed against his abdomen, begging for attention. When his hand traveled down and cupped his balls, he hissed in a breath while he tried to remember how long it had been since he'd needed release so badly. He slid his hand up to the thick width of his cock and wished it was her hand encircling him, applying just the right pressure, in just the right way.

As his hand started to massage the pressure of aching arousal he saw the wall beyond the foot of the bed begin to shimmer. Litha stepped out of a diaphanous light and walked forward to stand at the foot of the bed. She was a vision, wearing an old-fashioned white cotton nightgown, sleeveless and loose, with a low cut neckline revealing the swell and the sway of her unbound breasts. Even in the darkened room he could see how red her mouth was and he knew even without touching that her hair would feel like silk when he fisted it in his hands.

This dream was sexy. Sexy and romantic and there was something about having her stand there watching him caress himself that aroused him even more. On some level he knew that he moaned out loud in his sleep.

"Here," she said softly, "let me do that."

She raised the skirt of her nightgown above her knees so that it wouldn't catch and, never taking her eyes off him, started to climb onto the bed.

"I'm not interested in a relationship." His protest seemed somewhat compromised by the fact that he held an engorged penis in his hand. If he'd been awake, he would have been painfully self-conscious about that, but his dream self was not the least inhibited.

Kneeling on the bed next to him, she cocked her head to one side. "This isn't a relationship. It's a dream."

"It feels real."

"But it's not." Her gaze skimmed over Storm's exposed body appreciatively. When her eyes came back to his, she smiled. "You can be yourself. You can do what you truly want."

Without asking for permission she straddled him and then released the nightgown so that it drifted down and settled feather light on his legs. When she leaned toward him, he stared at the pendant that fell between her breasts and caught her rainstorm scent.

"Is this a dream spell? Are you using magicks on me, witch?"

She looked surprised and cocked her head to the side, studying him. "This is *your* magick, Storm. You called me from *my* sleep."

He considered that, assessing the odds and, oddly, coming to the conclusion that she could be telling the truth. "And you had to come?"

"No, of course not. It's my choice to be here." She looked down his body. "Were you thinking about me?" Gently, but insistently she moved his hand, replacing it with her own, wrapping around him. "Is this what you were thinking? Did you imagine my hand here instead of yours?"

His gaze darkened and his breath started to come faster. Seeing that he liked what she was doing, Litha leaned over him so that the loose neckline of her bodice drooped exposing her breasts to his view. His eyes locked on them like heat-seeking missiles.

She leaned even closer so that she could speak close to his ear, increasing the intimacy, and she felt his erection swell even bigger in her hand. "Beautiful knight. I love that you compelled me. You could have summoned anyone, but it was I you called to in your sleep. Would you rather I watched you?"

Storm was so switched on he thought he might come out of his own skin. He'd never been so hot. When the pad of her thumb skimmed up his engorged staff and began to massage vee just under the base of the head, he grabbed fistfuls of bedding with both hands, and gave a tight shake of his head in answer to her question. She smiled. Eyes never leaving his, she leaned down and lazily drew her tongue across the drops of precum that glistened in the darkness. His organ jerked in her hand and he let out a sound that was something between a moan and a shout.

He was too excited to continue to lie there passive. He had to touch her, had to feel in charge. He let go of the bedding, grabbed her face with both hands and pulled her red mouth into a possessive kiss, a kiss of claiming, one that said: "Mountains may crumble. Seas may go dry, but I will *never* let you go'."

His tongue invaded her mouth and then she was the one who was moaning. She let go of his cock so that she could lower herself and press her body where her hand had been. Her moans implied that her arousal was keeping pace with his own. Feeling the soft swells of her breasts and the vibration of her murmurs against his chest ratcheted his passion even higher. He was thinking he hadn't known that it was possible to want something so badly and, now that he did, he would never be the same.

When Litha pulled back from the kiss she was breathing hard. "Take what you want."

Suddenly he knew exactly what that was. He flipped her over so that she was under him, pulling her nightgown up as she curled her pretty legs around his waist. "Take what you want." Every repetition of that was said more urgently until his tachometer was on overload.

He sat up long enough to take the pretty white nightgown in both hands and jerk it open unceremoniously so that little pearl buttons went flying. For a split second he stared at the miracle of the woman who was laid before him, then he remembered it was just a dream. *Just a dream.*

He lowered his body to hers and felt the dizzying rapture of skin on skin for the first time. *Perfect.* He wanted to slow things down, to savor touching her, feeling her. He wanted to learn her body slowly with hands and then slowly with his mouth, but his need was too far gone for that. The smoldering desire burst into hot flames and he was suddenly pushed to a frenzy by the demanding way the witch pressed her naked entrance against him.

When he pulled his hips back and drove into her she cried out in triumph and surprise. In response, he made a sound that was more animalistic than human. He didn't care. The only thing in the universe worth thinking about was the luscious witch who was writhing under him, chanting his Anglicized name in fevered whispers.

"Angel. Angel. Angel."

As their bodies moved together, she made him feel like his thrusts were heroic. She made him feel like he was the only man ever born who could make her ripple like a river. He wanted her to know that she was the *only* woman who could bring him out of a half-life haze and make him crazy for her.

In his dream Storm was so close to orgasm that he had taken a breath to yell out. Then he woke.

Both erection and dream dissipated almost instantly leaving him waking face down with his draw string pants around his knees and a draft of chilled morning air cooling his bare backside. He groaned, pulled a pillow under his face and muttered curses into the down. He stayed like that until he had to choose between moving his face away from the pillow or not breathing again.

After another moment's hesitation, he turned over on his back feeling empty, unsatisfied, disturbed, and inexplicably angry at Litha for reasons that were unclear even to him.

He couldn't deny that there was a part of him being held hostage by the green-eyed witch with her red, red lips and her, oh so feminine and romantic nightgown; just the kind of thing a fantasy was supposed to wear in a dream. But the other part of him was repulsed by the idea of being teased and manipulated by magicks. And what other explanation could there be for such an occurrence?

CHAPTER 10

After breakfast the next morning, Storm waited on the mezzanine catwalk so that he could catch Litha and talk to her before going into the War Room. When she came into sight, she saw that his gaze was fixed on her so she headed straight for him. His expression bore down on her like a thing with physical weight.

He didn't waste any time on salutations or other pleasantries, but spoke to her in a demanding tone like a man who was used to having his way. "I'd like to know your philosophy on witchcraft."

A telltale look of injury flickered across her face before she gathered her protections around her and laughed. "Well! Not exactly the way I had imagined this conversation might begin. Would you like that in ten words or less?"

"This is not a joke. Do you use witchcraft to manipulate?"

Litha was instantly serious, narrowing her eyes as her expression became guarded. "Are you accusing me of something, Mr. Storm?"

"That's Sir Storm. And answer the question," he demanded as his eyes moved downward of their own volition and locked on the pendant that fell between her breasts.

"That doesn't sound like a respectful request..."

With effort he jerked his eyes back up to her face. "I will answer you for reasons that escape me at the moment, but I want you to know that I resent the implication. No. I do not use Craft to manipulate humans in any way, for any reason. Never have. Never will. Witches' honor."

Storm barked out a sarcastic laugh that was both rude and startling. "That's very funny. Witches have no honor."

"Really?" she asked. "I hope that's not true, but in my opinion, a man who would say such an ugly thing for no reason other than to hurt someone else isn't qualified to judge who does and does not have honor. In my opinion, such a person shouldn't be knighted, Mr. Storm." And with that she turned and walked away, leaving him standing there alone and wanting to argue some more.

Certainly that was a first. No one had ever accused Storm of being short on honor before. And questioning the worthiness of his knighthood was beyond outrageous. He was furious for a few seconds until he heard his own voice saying that maybe no one had ever questioned his knighthood because he'd never behaved like a lunatic before. What he had said was uncalled for. That led him to the next logical question which was, why did he do it?

And the inescapable answer was because he *had* wanted to hurt her. Again. *Deep and wide.*

Sure as he was that he was losing it, he couldn't stop himself from pursuing her. He took three long strides and caught her arm.

"Tell me the truth, witch. Did you use a dream

spell on me?"

Litha slowly turned, pulled her arm out of his grasp, and studied him a minute before answering. "Like I already told you..." Her gaze bore right through him saying, 'listen up because this part is important'. "...the magick was *yours*. Maybe you have some latent aptitude that's surfacing in reaction to being around me. That's all the truth I have for you.

"I will say this though." She stepped back far enough to let her eyes drift all the way down his body and back again. Slowly. "If *I* was casting a dream spell, it wouldn't be over nearly so fast and it certainly wouldn't leave us both so... unsatisfied." She drew the last word out until there was absolutely no mistaking her meaning.

He wanted to tell himself he was shocked, but he wasn't that good a liar. It *had* been real. At least in the sense that their psyches had shared an extra-body experience. Of course it wasn't as real as intimacy with actual bodies, but it was a whole hell of a lot more than fantasizing. And he was the one who had originated the encounter? Was that even possible or was she just fucking with him? Well, yes, she was fucking with him. *Wait. Had she just accused him of being a rookie witch and a ham handed lover who pulled the trigger prematurely?*

"By the way," she continued, wrenching his attention back from his own reverie, "if you try it again you may not find me so cooperative. If I respond at all, it won't be so quickly. Or so sweetly." She punctuated that with a smile that was sweeter than sugar. He wanted to grab her with both hands and kiss that provocative, taunting smile off her face and replace it with an expression of desire - for him - like the one he had seen just before he woke up.

And wanting that so much made him even angrier. And more confused.

Storm didn't know if that was a threat, but at the least, proclaiming that she would not be quick, cooperative, or sweet sounded like a promise of retaliation. He stared dumbly while she turned and walked away...again... taking with her his gaze firmly riveted on the graceful roll her hips gave that pretty, dark print skirt. The fact that she was so calm, so unruffled and so in command somehow cranked his agitation higher which was a feat because, at the moment, he was pretty damn agitated.

He stood in the hallway not knowing what to do next. That had to be another first. He was wondering if that was what people mean by indecision. Uncertainty didn't sit well with him. He was very decided about the fact that he didn't like how indecision felt. At all.

When he arrived at the War Room a few minutes later, Litha was stirring coffee and chatting with Elora about what colors were best for nurseries. She studiously avoided acknowledging his presence for the rest of the day. Not so much as a glance. He knew because he rarely took his eyes away from her.

Litha was undeniably distracted, her attention divided between the meeting and the exchange she'd just had with Storm. She alternately scolded and berated herself for having gone and fallen for a tall, outrageously handsome knight without knowing anything about him. Other than that he was tall, outrageously handsome, and surrounded by a magnetic field that almost pulled her off her feet when in his presence. What she hadn't known about him were the little things like, for instance, that he was rude with a nasty mean streak, and, worse, clearly prejudiced toward witches.

Not to mention that he was way out of touch with his own feelings. *Fine, then. Let him just sit and stew in his own poisoned pile of denial. Alone!* Let him stay there until he figured out that he was on the wrong side of his own argument. She had never seen a man more in need of being put in time out.

It would be hard to imagine how she could have picked a guy who was more aggravating or less self-aware. Not to mention the fact that he had been the catalyst that had caused her emotions to spike so far out of control with jealousy that she'd morphed into a firestarter for craps' sake.

She knew she couldn't be burned like other people, but had no idea that sufficient emotional turmoil would generate actual flame in her hands. Now, in addition to everything else, she was afraid that, if The Order found out, she'd be reclassified as dangerous. Oddly enough, no one ever questioned how the fire in the pub had started. Perhaps they were too caught up in the elf versus fae drama.

Late that night, when it would be early morning on the Pacific coast, she had called home and asked

Cufay if he had any previous indication of her fire-starting. He was surprised, but didn't seem the least worried, saying he knew she would work it out.

So adding to the list of Storm's undesirable qualities of being mean, rude, and hostile to witches, he was a trigger for a heretofore unknown ability that threatened the safety of persons, property, and perhaps even Litha's own future and freedom.

Maybe he was right. Truncating the highly unconventional beginnings of a relationship that wouldn't work for either of them was the best thing to do. Better now than later.

B Team came to dinner in their dress uniforms. Like her teammates, Elora wore the black sileather pants, black long sleeve knit shirt, Black Watch tartan sash and Black Swan pin. She was surprised by how many people were in attendance.

They had allowed Aelsong to come since she was officially employed by The Order and was the inductee's sister. Only one other honoree was still living and, at eighty-seven, said he wouldn't have missed it. The royal family had sent the prince as their representative.

When they removed the silk draping from Ram's portrait, Elora didn't even try to stop big tears from rushing down her cheeks and falling on the wool sash of her dress uniform. He looked exactly as he had that Yuletide day she arrived at the cottage in New Forest, with his hair pulled back behind his ears, in hunting costume, and his Black Watch Tartan gathered around his shoulders. The artist was as masterful as Rembrandt. The portrait, beautiful beyond description with mere words, but not nearly so beautiful as the elf himself. He beamed as she pressed her lips to his ear and told him there never had lived a male more glorious.

It hadn't escaped Elora's notice that Prince Duff Torquil and Princess Aelsong Hawking continually stole furtive glances at one another throughout the ceremony. She was hoping it had escaped the attention of everyone else.

As inductee, Ram was toasted with champagne and asked to personally speak to everyone in attendance. While he was busy, Elora saw an opportunity to have a word with the fae prince, who was, in his own right, handsome as any fairytale ever imagined in his kilt which was probably his uniform for official state occasions.

She knew she might have only a couple of moments to talk without being overheard.

"Your highness," she began, "I'm Elora Laiken, proud spouse of the honoree."

Up close she could see that the dark blue in his eyes was coupled with shades of violet. They were so unusual she may have stared just a second too long.

With a smile he said: "I well remember seein' you in the pub last night."

"Was that just last night?" She looked genuinely surprised and he laughed. "Is it difficult for you being here to honor an elf?"

The prince's smile didn't falter, but he seemed to be trying to judge what she might be after. "No' at all, madam. Like many of my contemporaries, I believe 'tis time to put our differences aside. So far as I can tell, it serves no constructive purpose. In short, 'tis silly to continue for the sake of continuin'. But, if I see that in a headline on the morrow claimin' to quote me, I will deny it 'til the Highlands look level."

"I'm pleased to hear your progressive views on the subject. I vow your secret is safe with me though I must add that, if everyone keeps their more abrasive views secret, nothing ever changes."

The prince pursed his lips and nodded. "A good point and well said."

"These contemporaries who share your views were not with you at the pub."

"'Tis true. You caught me sneakin' out on my miscreant night." Elora had to laugh. "Boys from school who can be a little rough after a few pints."

The young prince had an engaging way about him. "It's been very nice to have this talk. I will try to get my husband to reexamine his position on the feud." The prince's lips twitched when she said the word feud. He was thinking that only an outsider could so minimize the past thousand years of elf and fae at war with each other. "And I will also work on my esteemed brother-in-law from the inside."

"Esteemed. A cautious compliment I would say." Torquil's eyes twinkled.

Elora laughed. "You've met him?"

The prince shook his head slightly. "Certainly no'. Let us say I have heard he is no'... a lot of laughs." They both shared a chuckle at the expense of the King of Ireland.

"Perhaps you could begin to ease your own reservations about the status quo into the discussion in your household as well?'

"'Tis a good plan and certainly I enjoy a conspiracy as much as the next prince, but my elders are no' showin' signs of bein' moved either in their political views or away from the throne. 'Twill likely be a long time fore I am king.

"If I may ask, though, what is your mate's position on this question?"

"He's never spelled it out as such, but the night I first met him, he turned red in the face and turned over a chair at dinner because he thought I was calling him a fairy."

The prince looked serious. "Were you?"

She smiled. "It was an error of innocence. I come from a culture where everyone knows a collection of stories by the name fairytales. Something about that was mentioned."

"I see. And he was much offended."

Elora nodded. "Well, one step at a time then?"

"Always a sound policy."

"Meanwhile, do you think I can trust that my young sister-in-law will be safe in your country? She's the one over there who could *almost* challenge my husband for good looks."

The prince regarded her with amusement as if to say: "I know that you know and you know that I know. The question is does she know that you know what I know?"

"Fae's gods I pray 'tis so and 'tis no' said casually." He looked past Elora to where Aelsong was talking to guests and stealing glances at him.

Sensing that Elora might prove to be a valuable and trusted ally, he leaned a little closer to her. "'Tis most unfortunate that I can no' see to it personally. Tragically so, as a matter of fact. One of the problems with your traditional approach to diplomatic relations is that diplomacy takes a very long time."

"Forgive me for saying that is a youthfully impatient remark, your highness."

"Oh, aye," he laughed. "And how old be you, Madam?"

She patted her tummy and smiled. "Old enough to be someone's mother. Soon."

"Congratulations to you and the hero of the hour."

"Of the millennium," she corrected.

"So. 'Tis a love match then." He grinned and cast a glance in Aelsong's direction without realizing he had paired the phrase 'love match' with a need to look her way.

At the same time, Elora saw that her conversation with the prince had drawn Ram's attention and that he was regarding her with distinct curiosity. Not wanting to press her luck, she said good night to Duff Torquil who stopped her long enough to shake her hand as he palmed off a card with his personal number on it. "Let us no' lose touch as the Americans say."

Elora walked away wondering where she could put that card. She thought about her bra and then laughed to herself. Had she seriously entertained the idea, even for a millisecond, that her bra might be a safe place to hide something from Ram? She walked straight to Kay and told him she needed him to keep something for her, no questions asked. As she knew he would, he pocketed the card looking straight ahead, no questions asked.

Gods. She loved Bad Company.

"Later," she said and hurried to her mate's side smiling brightly. When she reached him, she pressed herself tightly into his side and whispered behind his ear. "I'm *so* proud to be your partner."

Storm lay in bed looking at the patterns the lights from the crag made on the walls and ceilings, examining his feelings. He wanted to end the strange series of interactions with Litha Brandywine that had begun with him turning to her and blurting out, "You smell like a rainstorm." As if he had Tourettes for gods' sakes.

She hadn't made eye contact with him since he'd gone out of his way to insult her which was a good thing. Exactly the result he wanted. With every intention of bud nipping, he could not have made it any more clear that he was *not* interested in a relationship.

What had happened with Elora still felt like an open wound and it was one that he didn't expect would ever heal. The last - *the very last* - thing he wanted or needed was complications of the feminine variety. The best case was that it led to confusion and irritation, as two days of green-eyed witch had just born out. The worst case was that it led to feelings of bleak emptiness coupled with fistfuls of hopelessness.

He wanted nothing more to do with that damn,

blasted witch. He was absolutely sure of it.

So why was he lying there with edgy, tingly feelings of anticipation about a possible repeat dream encounter? *You can do what you truly wish.*

At some point during the night Storm was lucid dreaming, the surreal experience of knowing he was dreaming while at the same time feeling the distinctly different quality of waking reality. In his dream he sat up in bed and stared at the spot where Litha had materialized before. He waited, but there was no shimmer in the air and no romantic white nightgown.

He knew he'd called out to her. Not with words. It was involuntary like a muscle reflex, but of a spiritual nature. The part of him that his dream self represented felt sad that there was no response. He wanted to take the witch in his hands, kiss her again, and hold on longer this time. He wanted her warmth and softness pressed against him. He wanted the silky friction of his skin moving across hers. He wanted to see those red lips part in welcome.

Storm woke with a start and, before the dream faded like smoke, he knew he had called her, knew also that she had heard, and that she stayed away. He sat on the side of the bed and asked himself, for the umpteenth time, what the fuck he was doing.

One thing was for sure. This was different. Elora had never made him feel out of sync and off kilter, like he didn't know whether he was going or coming. Yeah. *Deep and wide.*

CHAPTER 11

Ram and Elora woke to pounding on the door of their suite. Blackie stood at the door alternately barking warnings and snarling about the disturbance while Ram pulled on a robe. He left Elora sitting up in bed and hurried to answer. She heard Storm's voice, understood the sense of urgency, but couldn't make out what was being said. Whatever was the matter, she knew she'd better get up and get moving. She was pulling on her robe when Ram came in.

"Storm's here. Best come and hear the news together."

Elora said she'd be right there. She hurried to the bathroom, used the facilities, and splashed a little water in her face. When she emerged from the bedroom, she was looking into two very familiar, but unusually grave faces.

"What's happened?"

"Katrina is missing." Storm looked between the two of them.

"What? How do you know?" Elora asked. When receiving shocking news, people often respond with questions that are not well thought out.

"She went downstairs at the hotel in London to cash a traveler's check and didn't come back. There's no record of a transaction at the cashier's desk and nobody at the hotel saw or heard anything unusual."

"Where's Kay?"

"Getting ready to go to London. A company plane is landing in an hour. They have to refuel then they'll be ready to fly south. I'm going with him. Right now Tvelgar is waiting for us in his outer office ready with whatever resources we need."

"Song." Ram was moving toward the bedroom to jerk on some clothes. "We need Aelsong."

Storm looked at Elora.

"He's right. She's marvelously gifted. If she can get a fix on this situation, she can tell us everything we need to know right now. We'll get her and meet you downstairs in Simon's office."

Storm opened the door to leave.

"Storm?" He stopped with his back to her and didn't turn around. "I'm sure it goes without saying. Ram and I are on that plane, too." He nodded and let the door close behind him.

Elora called Glen on the phone. Even though he was next door, she thought that was a better way to wake him. She let him know that there was an emergency and that he needed to care for Blackie until further notice.

Ram was pulling on a shirt. He just gave her a look that said, "Hope this works."

Elora took a two-minute shower then pulled on working clothes which, for her, meant stretch pants, riding heel boots, and a long sleeve, silk weave shirt that would be comfortable to wear for days without changing if necessary. She combed out wet hair, dabbed on lip balm in lieu of makeup, and threw a leather bag with jacket and toothbrush over her shoulder while Ram was letting Glen inside.

Simon Tvelgar's outer office was sized like a medium hotel lobby with three seating areas and a large conference table by the windows. It was decorated impeccably and featured some items that were clearly priceless, such as the museum quality tapestries decorating two walls.

Ram, Elora, and Song arrived before Storm and Kay and were surprised to see Litha waiting. Tvelgar had asked for her assistance, anticipating how useful her tracking abilities could be in a situation like this.

Ram asked Aelsong if she wanted anything, before going to the bar to draw a coffee for himself and a hot cocoa for his mate. Elora thanked Litha for getting there so quickly and assured her that they would be grateful for any help they could get. Baka straggled in without saying a word and took a seat out of the way in a far corner. Elora wondered who had called him, but, whoever it was, she was glad for it because she was oddly grounded by his presence.

Kay walked in looking gray as death and anxious as hell. Storm showed a momentary flicker of surprise to see Litha, but said nothing.

Without further exchange, Ram told Aelsong to say what she needed from them.

She looked around, chose a large, overstuffed chair with arms and sat in it. She told the little assembly to choose their places and get comfortable because she was going to need them to be still and quiet.

While everyone was finding a seat, Song said that she had a pretty good chance of picking up something since she had met Katrina and spent time with her recently. She said she was ready to begin and everyone went statue still.

Song closed her eyes, relaxed her shoulders, and started to take three long, deep breaths in preparation. On the second breath her eyelids began to move. When she got mid way through the third inhalation, her breath suddenly caught in a way that looked painful. Her eyelids moved faster and she didn't seem to be breathing at all. Suddenly her head swiveled on her shoulders, coming to rest facing Litha. When her eyes flew open there was accusation plainly written there.

Kay stood. "What is it, Song? Tell me now!"

Song dragged her gaze away from Litha and looked at Kay. "Nothin' can be gained from goin' to London, Kay. She is no' here."

When Song glanced at Litha again, Elora gave Ram a pointed look to say, "What is that about?"

"What do you mean 'not here'? Where the hell is she?" Kay was getting agitated.

Ram caught his sister's eye. "This is no' the time to be cryptic, Song. Please. Spell it out plain."

She shook her head and looked at Kay like she was offering condolences. "She's been taken by someone no'..." She seemed to be struggling for the right words. "...no' like us. And he has taken her to a... reality outside this."

"You mean another dimension?" asked Elora.

"Aye." Song nodded at Elora, grateful to be understood.

The room went dead silent while each individual contemplated the implications of that in his or her own way. A few months ago there was no evidence that multiple dimensions, or alternate realities, shared common physical space or were anything more than fantasy or science fiction. But that, of course, was before Elora materialized out of thin air. If her arrival alone was not sufficient evidence, she had brought with her scientific documentation in the form of encoded data that proved the premise beyond refutation. With an alien from another dimension standing in the room, it would be hard to use impossibility as an argument.

Kay was first to speak. His normally quiet and assured, easy-going, Texas drawl was tinged with anxiety and his volume was several notches above his norm. "What does he want with her?" Song looked like she was searching for the right thing to say. "Out with it, girl. Just spit it out!"

Kay had risen, walked toward Aelsong's chair, and was now looming over her. Normally he would be cognizant of the intimidation factor, but he was too preoccupied to think about it. Seated, with Kay's giant figure towering over her, she had to lean her head way back to look him in the face. With a tone full of apology and sorrow at being the message bearer she said, "He wants to punish you."

Kay looked like he'd been slapped. Gaping at Aelsong, he backed up two steps until the back of his legs caught the sofa facing her. Looking stunned, he more fell into sitting position than sat.

Elora wanted to rush in and put her arms around him, but somehow thought that might make things worse. So she kept her full weight glued to the chair.

"Punish him for what?" Storm demanded.

"The abductor believes Kay is responsible for the death of someone... Father maybe?"

"What else can you tell us?" Ram asked. "We need to know everythin' you saw. Do no' think that any detail is insignifi...."

"Alright," Storm interrupted, "If nobody else is going to say it, I don't mind being the one to ask. Why were you looking at the witch like that?"

"Like what?" Song looked completely confused.

"Like you thought she did it. Or had something to do with it."

"What?" Song frowned, looked Litha square in the face and then shook her head. "No. I did no'."

"That's bullshit! What are you hiding?"

Elora read her new sister-in-law's body language. The effect of having so many larger-than-life men standing over her making demands was showing. Her arms were crossed in front of her and she had pulled her legs up into a defensive posture that made her look so much smaller. It was disconcerting to watch someone with Song's normal self-confidence and lustful personality reduced to looking victimized.

Storm was coming dangerously close to browbeating and Elora was on the verge of intervening when two things happened. Peripherally she saw Baka rise out of his chair in the corner, clearly with the same idea in mind, but before either of them acted on their protective impulses, Ram passed in front of Elora like a flash and was standing between Storm and Song.

"'Tis my sister you're speakin' to, lunker."

Storm held out a finger pointing at Kay. "That's my partner sitting on the couch looking like he's been stabbed in the gut!"

Ram gaped at Storm like he had lost his mind. "And now you're thinkin' you're the only one in the room who cares about Kay, are you? My sister is no' the enemy. She's here, voluntarily, to help *our* teammate find and recover his female."

Storm and Ram, with faces only a foot apart, stared at each other for a few beats at impasse. Finally, Storm blinked twice and looked at Song.

"I'm sorry, Song. I shouldn't be taking this out on you."

He shot a brief, but dangerous glare at Litha then turned away.

"I have impressions I can share. I do no' know if they'll be helpful," Song told Ram.

Ram knelt beside her chair and said softly: "Tell us what you saw. How do you know they're no' in our reality?"

Song shook her head. "I can no' say exactly. 'Tis hard to describe. 'Tis a sensin' that comes to me. She is no' terrified nor hurt, seems more hypnotized. The creature who has her is beautiful enough to be a god. He's no' a god, but he's no' a man either. Long black hair, black eyes, bronze skin. I hear the word..." She paused and frowned while looking down at the carpet in front of her.

"Can no' be right."

"What can no' be right, Song?" Ram urged her to continue.

She looked him in the face. "Demon?"

Litha stood up. "What kind, psy?"

Everyone turned to look at the witch.

Aelsong closed her eyes to see if she got an impression. "I do no' know if this makes sense."

Litha could see that Aelsong was showing signs of nerves, growing more reticent and unsure of herself by the second. She approached the young seer, speaking in a tone of calm assurance with a hint of big sister patience.

"I know you've just arrived and barely unpacked. You haven't had time to prepare for the pressure of reading in a situation like this with emotions so high and so much at stake. I'm sorry you had to jump straight into the fire, but since you know the subject personally, there's no doubt you're the best bet.

"You know The Order doesn't recruit just anybody with a little sixth sense. You're special. Trust that. Just say whatever came to mind and let us judge the validity."

Aelsong looked at her. "Incubus." There was an audible, collective gasp right before they felt a low rumbling, vibration. "But they are no' real are they?" Her entreaty made her sound so young and inexperienced, but Litha couldn't afford to be distracted by sympathetic impulses.

At first Elora thought the rumbling was a minor earth tremor. Then she heard the growl paired with it and saw that her husband had turned toward Kay and paled.

Storm lunged for Kay, grabbed him by his impossibly wide shoulders, and began shaking him.

"Caelian! No! This will not help us get Katrina back. Stay with us. We'll hear from the kidnapper and find out what he wants."

Seeing the potential crisis, Song seemed to regain some of her self-possessed demeanor she normally wore like skin. She scrambled off her chair toward Kay, knelt in front of him, and took his hand. "Kay, Trina is alive. Alive and unharmed."

Seeing that she could add nothing to the way her partners were handling the situation Elora took Litha by the arm and pulled her to the far side of the room.

"What do you know about this?"

Litha faced Elora, letting her see an open expression showing that she had nothing to hide. "No more than you."

Elora reached out with her intuition to try to ascertain whether Litha was telling the truth or not. Certainly she saw no wariness or defensiveness. "Why do you think Song looked at you the way she did?"

"I don't know. Maybe because I'm going to be involved?"

The rumbling quieted, which meant her partners had helped Kay stay in control. For now.

"How?"

Elora saw the other woman take on a resolute expression as her mouth set in determination. "I'm going to track the berserker's bride."

"Bride-to-be," she corrected. "If Song is right,

if it is a demon and he has taken her to another dimension, how are you going to track them? It seems..." She glanced over her shoulder at the others and lowered her voice, "...impossible."

Litha cocked her head to the side. "How long have you worked for The Order?"

"A few months. Why?"

"Because we don't like to think the word 'impossible' until we're positive there's nowhere else to go. We have the best resources in the known universe."

"I know that."

Litha smiled slightly. "Well. There's knowing and there's knowing."

"What the hell does that mean, Litha? I'm not in the mood for riddles."

With a little shake of her head that was charming whether Elora liked it or not, Litha answered. "Sometimes preparation meets opportunity. Sometimes we get lucky. Sometimes we make magick. And sometimes the result is that we manage the impossible."

Elora nodded in understanding. Her estimation of the witch was growing and she was starting to feel good about Litha batting for their team. "That berserker over there is family to Ram and Storm and me. Any of us would do *anything* for him. Just tell us what we can do to help. Anything," she repeated.

"Just keep the big bastard in his skin until we get this sorted out."

Litha walked over to Simon Tvelgar and told him they could use a demonologist on the scene. He said she was already on the way.

When Heaven arrived, Litha asked Aelsong to join them. The three withdrew to a corner where they could talk quietly without upsetting Kay. Litha had Song repeat what she had seen for Heaven's benefit and then asked her to clarify details while the visions were still fresh in her memory. Any information, no matter how meaningless it might seem on the surface, could be the very thing that helped her track.

Litha asked Song to describe the environment, or backdrop, of the scenes she had witnessed. Aelsong had seen Katrina leave the hotel with the black haired man willingly. The next thing she saw was Katrina sitting in a windowless room staring straight ahead.

Kay's phone rang. He was working so hard at controlling his rage that it took him a few seconds to register that it was a call for him. He pulled the phone from his pocket, looked at it, and felt a chill run through his veins when he saw the Caller ID. It said simply, "Got Your Girl."

His hand was shaking badly as he raised the phone. "This is Caelian."

"And this is Deliverance, son of Abraxas, Obizoth, whom you murdered. In lieu of the blood debt you owe me, I have decided to take your female. She is much sweeter retribution than killing you. Every day you will imagine how I enjoy having her in my bed and at my mercy as she pays for your transgression."

Kay stared straight ahead not seeing anything or anyone around him. His gray eyes had glazed over and looked silvered. Only he could see the red streaking across the gray haze in his vision, gradually overtaking it. His voice croaked low, barely more than a whisper. "Please, demon."

Deliverance laughed and ended the connection.

Kay dropped the phone as he began vibrating visibly. The rumbling they had heard earlier turned into deafening roars of rage and grief and helplessness. When Storm approached, Kay threw him aside then began dismantling furniture.

Simon called security and told them to bring tranquilizer guns on the double. By the time they arrived, Kay had torn the priceless tapestries from the walls and was ripping them to shreds. Storm was trying to get through to him, but Kay was beyond   words.

Keeping her body between the berserker and the others, Elora steered everyone, including Simon and Baka, out of the room, leaving only the four members of B Team.

Two security guards burst into the room leveling tranq guns on Kay. They fired with amazing speed and precision. When Storm saw that they were shooting Kay with darts, he lunged for them screaming, "No!"

Ram tackled Storm before he could reach the guards and got him in a chokehold from behind where he could say in his teammate's ear: "They're no' hurtin' him, Stormy. They're helpin' him. Savin' him from the pain. Look at him. Look close. That's no' Kay."

Storm stopped struggling and, after a few minutes, he nodded. Ram instantly released him.

Two large orderlies rolled Kay onto a gurney, strapped him in, raised it, and wheeled away. The medical staff had been ordered by the Director to keep him lightly sedated so that he would not harm himself or others while they sorted out this muddle.

When Elora caught Ram's eye, she motioned for him to step aside with her and talk quietly out of earshot of the others. "We've got to think of a cover story for the Norns."

Ram exhaled a heavy sigh and ran his hand through his hair. His eyes were so full of sadness she could barely look at him. They worked out the details of what to do about Kay's sisters with Simon.

The Order had someone situated high enough in the Greater London Metropolitan Police Department, unofficially known as Scotland Yard, to call off the search. Ram took it on himself to call the three sisters. He told them that Kay was beside himself with worry, but that he would be able to deal with the situation better knowing that they were safe at home. Amazing even himself, Ram was able to talk the girls into flying back to Houston and said that a police escort would pick them up and see them onto the plane.

Elora watched her husband from across the room as he closed his phone. She could see that Ram felt a hundred years old. And it wasn't even time for breakfast yet. She remembered Kay once saying that, within the team, group dynamics were always in motion. When she first met the other three members of B Team, Ram had generally been thought of as an immature hothead and prankster.

Today, seven months later, he looked like the foundation that B Team was standing on. Her heart swelled with pride to have witnessed the journey of the man he'd become, but also grieved a little because, each time he shouldered a new burden of responsibility, the gregarious elfin boy she'd fallen in love with retreated a little further and she feared one day he could be lost forever. She wanted so badly to comfort him, but knew there would be no such thing as comfort for any of them so long as one of Bad Company was in crisis. One for all. All for one. It had never been said because it didn't need to be.

After Kay had been subdued and removed, the little group drifted back into the ruined room and stood silently surveying the damage. The mood couldn't have been more solemn.

Ram took charge and said to the group in general. "Why do we no' move upstairs to the War Room?" Looking at Simon he said: "Perhaps you could ask someone to bring us breakfast while we hear the tracker's thoughts on where to begin?" To Litha he said: "Is there anythin' in particular you will be needin'?"

"For now, more time with Aelsong and Heaven. I have more questions for both."

As Litha passed by Storm he reached out and grabbed her wrist. "What do you have to do with this?"

"I'll tell you what I have to do with this, Sir Storm. So far as I know, I'm the only hope your friend has for ever seeing his fiancée again." She jerked her wrist free and continued on her way once more leaving him standing there watching her go and feeling like a Grade A prick.

While they waited for some news from the tracker, Storm sought out the infirmary so that he could see for himself that his partner was in good hands. When he opened the door to Kay's hospital room, he found Elora sitting by Kay's bedside with her back to the door. She turned her head to see who was there, but didn't speak. Remembering he wasn't alone in caring for Kay took the edge off some of the pressure Storm had been applying to clenching his teeth together.

His eyes came to rest on Kay's relaxed features and substantial form covered in white starched sheets with a white cotton weave blanket on top. He looked around the room. The high ceilings made it seem expansive. That was good. He didn't want Kay in small, confined quarters. The feeling was airy and bright – the exact opposite of what was in his heart. Walls were painted pale, pale yellow and there was a nice view of treetops through a tall window with wrought iron panes. Sunlight filtered through the new spring leaves on those trees, causing light and shadows to dance on the walls and ceiling with an optimism that was welcome even if it was so out of place. He was grateful that the room wasn't gloomy.

As he stared out the window, a bird landed on a branch and fluttered his wings excitedly.

Elora had been watching him, following his gaze. She saw that his eyes had glazed over and that he was in a semi state of trance. After some time, she said, simply, "Window."

His lids flickered, awareness returned and he looked her way, their eyes meeting in acknowledgement of a poignant moment of shared personal history. Both of them were remembering that, when she was new to this world and injured beyond anyone's expectation to recover, she had asked for only one thing: a window. Storm had spent a season of his life coaxing her to rise from helpless and vulnerable lost girl to, perhaps, the most formidable creature in his world. He thought... well, it no longer mattered what he thought.

No one ever knows where their personal breaking point is until they reach it. Most are never pressed to such a limit that they find out. Storm wasn't that lucky.

Suddenly, without warning, Storm reached his. Emotions finally overflowed and culminated in an eruption that looked and sounded a lot like a sob. It surprised him as much as it did her. In an instant, before he could suck in a breath to replace the air that had just gushed from his lungs, she was there with her arms around him.

In the past ten months Storm had been through several levels of hell and without once succumbing. No tears. No self-pity. Which also meant no blessed release.

There, at the foot of Kay's bed, with his best friend drugged into oblivion and the only woman he had ever loved trying to give him comfort, the dam finally broke open and he let go of some of that tight control; that tight control that kept muscles painfully rigid, temper on edge, laughter and joie de vive always just out of reach.

He let himself grieve for his late teammate, Lan, the brother-in-arms who had taught him how to hunt vampire and stay alive while doing it. He let himself feel the deep psychic wound of Elora's rejection. He let himself feel fear for a forcefully sedated berserker who was closer to him than any other living person besides Ram. He let himself be comforted by his fourth teammate, the first and only female knight in the history of The Order of the Black Swan; the one who had chosen somebody else.

Elora tried to stem her own tears of empathy and just be there with Storm while he rode it out. Whatever it took. For as long as it took. She might not want to marry him. She didn't love him in that way, but she *did* love him, more even than her own two brothers – if they were still alive. She loved him unconditionally and without reservation and there was nothing he could ever do that would change that. Certainly he had done this and much more for her.

She recalled an early October morning when he had stood in place with his arms around her while she clutched onto him for dear life and wept into his chest, her heart brimming with desolation. Gods. Had that really been less than a year ago?

Their roles had reversed. Life never fails to be strange.

When he finally began to quiet and pull away, he said, "You won't tell."

It was such a young, unguarded, and unexpected thing to say she almost laughed, not in ridicule, but in the hope it gave to see his human side peek out.

"It was one of my first lessons. Remember? As a matter of fact it was Kay who taught it to me. What happens with Bad Company stays with Bad Company."

He tried a little smile and it almost happened.

"How about a coffee?" she asked.

He nodded. Turning away she brushed the residue tears away from her own face and went out to get a big, black, and bold with one sugar - just the way he liked it.

When the door closed, Storm turned toward Kay feeling drained, tired, embarrassed, not necessarily better, but different somehow. A step back toward life instead of away from it. His perspective had rearranged itself in the tumbler of emotional upheaval and he thought that maybe, just maybe, there was the tiniest bit of hope that they would find their way to the other side of this.

He remembered that Ram had read fairytales to Elora when she was unconscious and that she'd heard him. So he decided to talk to Kay and tell him they were figuring this out, that they had the world's best tracker, who was also a powerful witch, and that she was working on it at that very moment.

Having said that out loud to his comatose partner, he realized for the first time that he might have a tiny grudging admiration for Litha. He even felt a small, and quite inexplicable, twinge of pride when he had said 'world's best tracker' out loud. Of course Storm wasn't naive. He knew that no power on earth could bring Kay's fiancée back from another dimension. Litha couldn't get Katrina back. No one could. She was gone. Forever. And the devil would be collecting a truckload of pain from Kay when the day came that he had to wake and confront that.

Still, even for a battle hardened, battle weary knight like Engel Storm, there was a miniscule part of inner child that protected a belief in magic. Whether he recognized it or not, whether he would admit it or not, that part of him hoped the beautiful and indomitable, green-eyed witch had a miracle in her pocket.

He told Kay to sleep and dream of honeymooning on a beach in the South Pacific with rum drinks and a bride wearing little or nothing.

When Elora returned with coffee, the two of them walked back to the War Room to join the others for the vigil.

Elora and Storm didn't need to ask if there had been any word. It was easy enough to read the faces that turned their direction when they entered. Ram walked over to Elora, put his arms around her, and then let one hand slide down to cover her stomach as if he couldn't go any longer without making a connection. In hushed tones he asked about Kay's circumstances and she assured him that it was the best situation possible.

CHAPTER 12

When Litha was satisfied that she had learned all she could from Aelsong, she turned to Heaven for a briefing on incubus demons; insight into their known characteristics and typical behavior.

Breakfast was a dismal event and most of the food went untouched. Litha told Kay's friends and colleagues that she would retire to her sanctuary, where she would try to track Katrina and would let them know the results, one way or the other, by mid afternoon.

Litha went to her room first where she filled a large, old fashioned, porcelain tub with hot water and sea salt. She soaked for twenty minutes, clearing her mind and her aura of emotional turbulence - her own and what she'd picked up from the others as a result of this experience. Some of it was quite resistant to expulsion. Afterward she assembled a collection of clean clothes, not worn since they'd been laundered. She pulled on black tights with no feet, a black leotard, a wrap around skirt, ballet slipper flats, and the pendant necklace she always wore.

Litha's "offices" were far from what would typically be pictured when thinking about someone's workspace. She occupied two rooms adjacent to the Ancient Books section of the library that had been designed according to her direction, specifically to her needs. The Ancient Books section was seldom accessed which made her corner of the east wing a very quiet place to work with few distractions - just the way she liked it.

The room that could be entered from the hallway looked very much like a traditional office except that all the wall space featured floor to ceiling shelves. Considering that the ceilings were twelve feet high, that was very impressive. Her shelves were filled with books and all manner of curious goods. Some belonged to The Order. Some were part of her personal collection. The only furniture in the room was a chair, a large carved chest, and a large French rococo desk, black with gilded accents, and priceless if it came up for auction at Christie's.

On entering she went straight to the pretty window seat. She pulled the cushion and decorative pillows away, then lifted the solid wood top that formed the seat and set it aside. Inside the hollow space was a heavy carved chest secured by a modern combination lock that had been warded, making it highly unlikely that anyone other than she would ever open it. The ward was designed to confuse the mind of anyone trying to focus on the numbers, because they appeared to blur, transpose, and shift.

After removing the lock, she opened the chest and withdrew a hooded cape made of red velvet. Then she unlocked the wrought iron French door behind her desk and stepped over the threshold of her small, private terrace into the motorized hum of an Edinburgh morning. She shook the cape out in the sunshine, being glad, for once, that she was on the east side of the building and that there was sunshine that particular day. After twirling it about in the air a few times, she was satisfied with its essential "cleanliness" so she reentered locking the terrace door behind her.

The room she thought of as her inner sanctum was protected by a keypad lock with wards similar to the one used on the chest lock. She punched in her code, donned the cape, removed her shoes, opened the door and stepped inside, feeling the muscles in her body relax even more.

The room was round. The architect had initially grumbled about wasted space, but she had persuaded Simon by pointing out that maximum results require maximum equipment. The east wall featured a small window, placed high up, with wind chimes hung from the ceiling so as to hang in front of the window's perfect center. Another wall featured a fine stone fireplace that looked considerably older than the building in which it was housed, as if it had been transported from elsewhere and reassembled. Another wall featured a fountain flowing from the mouth of a dragon-faced gargoyle into a wide pedestal bowl. The last wall featured an indoor garden of herbs and flowering plants that were thriving with a combination of magick and semi-fluorescent lights.

The walls and ceiling were painted the same pale gray as the polished, flagstone floor. Litha went immediately to the fireplace where she lit seven candles of various colors. The small window provided some light, but not so much that the reflection of the candle flames couldn't be seen on the smooth stones.

Other than the features representing the four ancient elements, there was nothing else in the room except for the large globe in the center of the room nestled in the cradle of a priceless dragon's wings. The centuries-old dragon statue, beautiful, powerful, and magnificent in its own right, had been taken from a pagan temple in Teutonia two millennia past for safekeeping else it be destroyed by misguided Christians like so many other thousands of priceless artifacts.

Objects of power were not created deliberately nor did they spontaneously spring into being. They came from humble beginnings, being no more extraordinary than a typical river rock or knife or fork. Objects became infused with power when energetic residue was repeatedly transferred from beings with accumulated magickal power. The exact number of contacts that equaled critical mass was non-calculable.

Sometimes objects of power are identified by those who are either talented or proficient in the occult. When not discovered as such, their energy sometimes went awry, their very presence wreaking havoc without intent, direction, or cause. The Order had been collecting these artifacts for centuries, rescuing them from destruction by zealots and protecting the human population from the effects of wayward magicks. The location of the treasury had moved around from time to time, often dependent on wars and the dangers they posed.

At present the artifacts not in use were stored in what many agreed was the best location to date: the western boundary of Idaho Springs, Colorado. The vaults were located deep under the Rocky Mountains – which would withstand any destructive device available to date. It was cool, dry, near the Interstate, and only an hour away from a major airport. In short, a perfect storage facility. The excavation currently underway in Brazil was rendering frequent additions to the cache. Only an institution with The Order's connections could remove articles of antiquity from the locations of their discovery with impunity.

It was Litha's great honor to have the dragon temporarily in her keeping, as he had been recognized as a potent object of power and in service to magick for millennia. The proud Teuton dragon currently served as The Order's own version of Prometheus, silently holding the world on its shoulders while also protecting its treasure: a precious crystal ball held lovingly in its curved claws. The multifaceted crystal ball picked up every color in the room and reflected it back onto walls and ceiling as rainbow prisms. The effect was a space that was magical as well as magickal. Litha's dragon, and she thought of him that way as she was his temporary caretaker, was charged with several tasks and he performed each admirably.

The globe, rendered in shades of green and brown, was perhaps a foot and a half in diameter and hinged, very much like one of those liquor cabinet parlor tricks. It would separate at the equator and become two parts of a sphere, one half stationary, one half lid. When opened, it revealed one of Litha's two most prized treasures, a concave, black glass scrying plate the same diameter as the globe's equator. The dragon stand had been built so that, when standing barefoot, the scrying plate was at exactly the same height as Litha's navel.

She reached out and lovingly ran her hand over the dragon's head as if he was a living pet. Sometime during the past two thousand years, his eyes, had been replaced with black glass. The candle flames and rainbow prism danced together in his eyes, making them seem so intelligent and lifelike that it was easy to imagine him as a familiar.

Litha pulled her red robe closer as she paid homage to the Spirits of the Four Winds, whom she would be summoning to assist with Locating Magicks. Real witches were risk takers, came with the territory. Even so, few witches would have dared wear red when practicing the magickal arts because the color red possessed powerful attraction properties. That meant red can be a shortcut in summoning, but that it also attracted the bad as well the good. Litha came from a rich history of witch ancestors who tended to act according to a philosophy of "great gambles bring great rewards" and at some point, it had become part of the family's genetic legacy. It was partly natural to her and partly logical since Litha knew she was powerful, or practiced, enough to hold a sufficient protection barrier while admitting friendlier Powers of Assistance and accepting their help.

The witch took up a large purple candle and

THE WITCH'S DREAM

began circling the globe in the center of the room in a clockwise direction. She carefully counted nine revolutions as she sang an old medieval melody with lyrics written and substituted by the witch herself. Her singing voice was quite pleasant although the quality of performance would have no bearing on outcome. The melody was not more magickal because it was medieval. It was simply a useful hook on which to hang the quatrains she had quickly, but specifically composed for chanting, which would be crucial to outcome. She wrote the four-line rhymes in her head while she was bathing and now repeated them in magickal form while she raised energy by stirring the atmosphere into the equivalent of a small whirlwind.

After completing nine circles and chants, Litha used the flame of the purple candle to light a large white candle with three wicks. She then sprinkled a mixture of Dragon's Blood resin, Solomon's Seal, white sage, and crystalline salt directly onto the candle's flames. When the herbs caught fire, she invited into the circle those who could be of service whether spirits, guides, or elementals, with the caveat that they were welcome so long as they wished her well and would not prove to be a lot of trouble later on.

When she was satisfied that conditions were optimum, she opened the globe. She always felt a rush of satisfaction upon viewing the gleaming surface with alphabetical, numerical, alchemical, and Theban script symbols etched on its surface in circular patterns. Taking hold of the pendant necklace that she always wore, she pulled downward to remove the outer cover, which was a crystal with planed edges forming a heptagon. No one would guess that the crystal was a cover disguising a pendulum of black opal, perfectly weighted for scrying, encased in a Celtic knot filigree of white gold matching the necklace chain.

The pointed stone was the rarest black opal, alive with deep red flecks called "fire" by jewelers. Litha's pendulum had been hand crafted for her by the monks of Cairdeas Deo and given to her on her sixteenth birthday. Or, rather, the day that had been arbitrarily established as the day they would celebrate her birth.

That birthday was a milestone because it was the day she had been given the freedom to legally drive by herself. In the process of celebrating by doing exactly that she came across a scene that would forever be etched in her heart: a pink Italianate villa sitting high above the Sonoma Coast with vineyards terracing toward the sea, neighboring hills covered with flowering yellow mustard so that it looked like something from a fantasy. She had pulled the car over, taken a mental snapshot, and knew that someday she would drive through the gate and it would be hers.

She ran her finger over the pointed end just to reestablish the connection - which was never really broken.

When she held the pendulum over the glass, it immediately dropped into place and stilled, awaiting instructions from its mistress. She began to trace Katrina's name, one letter at a time, while picturing Katrina - replaying the snapshot moments of their brief time together - and "hearing" the sound of her voice. Then she began to add details about Katrina's current situation and state of mind that had been gained from Aelsong's visions.

By the time she reached the "i", the pendulum was moving on its own to complete the specification ritual. Out of the corner of her eye, she could see candle flames dance and flicker as if a draft had blown through the room. For Litha spontaneous movement of air was a more or less commonplace occurrence, at least when she was scrying. If others preferred to think of the phenomenon as invisible, or discarnate entities, it made no difference to her.

She closed the globe and moved so that she was facing Scotia, then held the pendulum above it simply saying, "Where?"

The pendulum did not move. Which was a first. Frowning, Litha repeated her command a little more firmly, "Where?"

No response.

She lowered the pendulum, took it in her hand, and rolled it around in her palm a few times while deliberately focusing on an image of Katrina.

Again, she held the pendulum above the globe. "Where?"

No response.

Remembering that Aelsong had said Katrina was no longer in the same reality, she decided to alter the question. She held the pendulum above the globe and asked, "Near where?"

Almost instantly it began to pull toward the east like it was magnetized. Allowing enough slack so that it could go where it wanted, Litha allowed the point to slide over the map of Europe. Across France. Past Genoa. It came to rest just south of Florence. Siena.

"Got it."

She quickly returned the pendulum to its pretty crystal housing, thanked the Powers That Assisted while politely and respectfully dismissing them, unwound the charged energy of the room by retracing her steps in the opposite direction, doused the candles, and reset the keytouch lock on the room as she left. Litha knew that people were anxiously waiting for some word from her, but nonetheless some tasks could not be hurried. She removed her red robe and carefully rolled it up to fit in the top of the carved chest that held her most precious, personal tools. She renewed the wards on the lock, replaced the window seat so that no one would be the wiser, secured her wrap-around skirt, and hurried upstairs.

The atmosphere in the War Room vibrated with tension. Every now and then Storm would venture out into the hallway, look up and down then walk back slowly. Just so he could feel like he was doing something. He had just exchanged a look with Baka and sat down on the end of a sofa when Litha came rushing in. Storm was up again like there was a spring in the cushion seat.

He knew the instant he looked at her that she'd been successful. She wasn't smiling, but her eyes were burning brightly. He knew.

"We've got a starting point," she said, looking

around the room. "Siena."

Everybody started talking at once. There was no shortage of questions. The emotion in the room went from gloom to excitement in ten seconds.

After some considerable debate about how to use this information, Elora said the only logical thing to do was to call Monq. It would be around dinnertime at Jefferson Unit and he wouldn't be hard to reach. So they called and put him on speakerphone. Elora told him who was present in the room. After giving the short version of events, with a couple of corrections and interjections, Monq was up to speed.

When asked if he had thoughts about how to proceed, he said that, in this case, magick was the only tool available. Everyone in the room, to a person, turned simultaneously and stared at Litha. She didn't shrink away or begin offering protests or excuses. Instead, she blinked, sighed, and seemed to begin contemplating how she might go about creating a magickal rescue. Watching her face as she accepted the burden of being the only hope, Storm's admiration grew past grudging to full flowering respect. He thought to himself that, in her own strange and feminine way, she was also a knight of The Order. Of sorts.

Of course he knew The Order was a big tent, broad reaching operation, but somehow, in his arrogance, he had always assumed that it was the field active knights who were the *real* agents of the spirit on which The Order was founded, and that everyone else were variations on a theme of clerical help or administrators. Watching this scene play out he realized how wrong he had been. Courage wears a lot of different faces. Importance wears a lot of different roles.

"Litha, is there something you can do?" Simon asked quietly.

Storm thought he could see wheels turning as he watched her liquid green eyes come up to meet Simon's. He watched even closer when her tongue peeked out to wet her naturally red, bottom lip.

"I honestly don't know." She shook her head. "But I've heard that you can't win if you don't play. And that sounds right to me."

"Well said, my dear. You'll have the entire journey to come up with a plan." Simon turned to Storm. "Sir Storm, I'd like you to accompany our tracker as her escort."

Ram took a step toward the Director. "We usually do things as a team. I know we're one down, but at least allow me to..."

"One of you is going, Sir Hawking: Storm, you, or your wife. The other two are needed to deal with the reason you were brought here in the first place - the werewolf sanction."

Ram gave Storm a look that was half apology and half worry.

Storm knew Simon didn't tender the escort assignment as a request. It was a direct order from his temporary commander so he didn't bother to verbalize a protest. What would he say anyway? *"Please don't make me go with her because she's a maddening, indescribably beautiful and intriguing woman who makes me squirm. And I'm a pathetically fucked up asshole."*

"Storm!"

He shook himself internally and, pulling it together, realized the Director was addressing him. "Yes. Sorry."

Simon turned to say something into his cell phone and waited for an answer. Litha was studiously avoiding looking at Storm, which made him want to rankle her by staring until she felt prickly all over.

Simon snapped the phone closed and looked at the two of them. "Your plane will be full of petrol with a fresh pilot and ready to go at 0600."

Litha nodded, turned, and walked out of the room without another word or glance backward.

Storm slept fitfully. He dreamed that he rose from his bed having decided that if the witch would not come to him, he would go to her. He walked straight through the walls of several apartments between his and hers, passing sleeping occupants as if the walls were visible, but not solid. Even in his dream he recognized that it was odd he knew he could do that. Finally, he stepped into her room where she was sleeping soundly in her white nightgown.

He left her undisturbed while he slowly perused the artwork, marveling at the fact that the room was virtually papered with representations of the Sonoma Coast vineyard, the same one that he had picked out for himself when he was home visiting family and not yet out of his teens. How could she possibly be obsessed by the *same* place? Unless she was using magicks to trick him.

The room was lit by moonlight, but somehow, in the most surreal way, he was able to see each piece of art clearly. There were pencil sketches, charcoals, oils, acrylics, and watercolors. He spotted the little watercolor Litha had tried to give him and was sorry he'd said no. All he had to do was reach out, take it, and say, "Thank you." Like a halfway decent person. He wished he'd done exactly that. He wanted that little watercolor square more than any priceless art treasure to be found across the Princes Street Gardens in the National Museum of Scotia.

After he had studied every rendering, he was drawn to stand over her bed. He could hear her deep breathing and found that he was breathing in and out with the same rhythm. He should have felt like a voyeur, but didn't. Clothed in white nightgown, lying on white sheets, he thought she could have been an angel in peaceful repose on the fluff of a cloud. The pale background made the contrast of black hair and red lips all the more inviting. As if she could feel the weight of his stare, she stirred and turned onto her back and was, to his mind, the essence of beauty sleeping. *You can do what you truly   wish.*

Impulsively he bent down and kissed her slightly parted lips softly, then brushed his own lips back and forth so that he would imprint the sensation and not forget the exquisite feel of her.

"Storm?" As Litha's sleepy voice poured over his phantom body it seemed to give him more substance. He pulled back as she sat up in bed. "What are you doing?"

"After hours visiting."

"Hmmm." She studied him as she contemplated that and then suddenly said, "Well, go away."

He was deflated from being summarily dismissed, but decided to man up and give her another chance to reconsider. "You sure?"

"What do you want, Storm?"

What did he want? He looked around. To look at the art? To see where she lived? To watch her sleeping? Yes to all of those things. But that wasn't all.

He opened his mouth to say: "I want you to move over so I can crawl into bed with you," but, instead, found himself waking in his own bed to a shout of frustration. He brought his fist down on the mattress beside him and growled hard enough and long enough to leave his throat scratchy.

Litha's dream self lay back and chuckled. The finer points of nightwalking require a little training, a little talent, and a *lot* of practice. Still, she had to hand it to him. He did try.

CHAPTER 13

Storm knocked on Litha's door at 0515. There had been no plans made for him to call for her, but he wanted a chance to see the inside of her room. He had to know if it would look like what he remembered from the dream.

She opened the door looking as bright and awake as if it was noon, wearing a dark print skirt and a white silk, v neck tee shirt under a deep forest hoodie that made the green in her eyes pop even more than usual. Abruptly she opened the door wider and turned away saying: "Come in. I just have to zip up my bag."

Litha's personal living quarters were tiny compared to her spacious work space, but everything was in its place. The floor was carpeted with a large rose floral pattern on a background of forest green like the hallway outside. Her small, black leather shoulder strap bag was sitting on top of a bed made with an old-fashioned, white, popcorn crochet spread.

Girly. And romantic. But what he had come to see was the walls. He couldn't see the walls though. They were covered with art renderings of his vineyard, exactly the way they looked in his dream, except that these were in color.

Litha saw that he had stopped in front of the little square watercolor she had tried to give him and was staring at it.

"If you change your mind," she said with a kindness he didn't think he deserved, "I'd still like you to have it." He shook his head no. "Suit yourself," she said, pulling the bag onto her shoulder.

Without saying a word, he eased the strap of the bag off her shoulder and onto his own then picked up his own bag waiting in the hallway outside her door.

"This is heavier than it looks. What's in here?"

"I brought some tools." She smiled slyly and shook her head in that way that he was coming to realize was a signature mannerism of hers. "Just in case."

Litha thought chivalry looked more at home on Storm than rudeness, meanness, and the other unattractive variations on orneriness she'd witnessed the past few days.

They walked in silence to the front lobby. When they reached the entrance, the doorman blew his whistle and a car pulled in front ready to take them to the private jet hangar that served as The Order's hub for air travel. While the driver stowed their two bags in the boot, Storm opened a rear car door for Litha.

The plane was empty except for the two of them. Normally air travel would be planned with more efficiency, but Simon Tvelgar had given this project as much priority as possible and authorized the expense.

Storm went straight to the back of the plane, sat

down in one of the big overstuffed recliners, and pulled out a carryall computer. Litha supposed that meant he didn't want to chat, which was just as well because she should be trying to keep her mind clear; an open channel for any bright ideas that might like to make themselves known. Anytime now.

This was not her first seat-of-the-pants mission, but nothing had ever held stakes like this. There were so many people counting on her to come up with something, and that something was looking as elusive as a unicorn. She was grateful that at least no one had actually said the words, "You're our only hope," or worse, "You're our last hope."

So far Litha's best idea was the method called: *"Go as far as you can see to go and then hope to Hades that, when you get there, you'll be able to see further".* Meanwhile, she didn't want to shake the optimism of Kay's loved ones by not appearing confident, even if she didn't know what the bleeding hell she was going to do. Certainly "loved ones" included the big, silent, semi-sulky guy sitting in the back of the plane by himself. Much as she didn't want to amend that, she simply had to correct to say big, silent, semi-sulky, *gorgeous* guy.

It had been cute observing him looking around her room to verify that he had successfully generated and executed a nightwalk all on his own. *After hours visiting indeed.* She had hid a smile. Though he might be a long way away from proficient, she was a little impressed that he had managed to get that far with no training of any kind.

Storm emailed Monq to say that he was

escorting Litha on her mission and to ask if there was anything he could do to prepare or help. As the person who had meticulously studied the scientific journals of his counterpart, who had pioneered inter-dimensional travel in Elora's home world, Monq would know if anyone would. Since it was lunchtime at Jefferson Unit, Eastern Daylight Time, he shouldn't have any trouble getting an answer from Monq before they arrived at Siena.

A few minutes later Storm got a text from Elora wishing them gods' speed with Fortuna's blessing and asking that he please stay in touch and keep them posted. He texted back that he would and asked her to keep an eye on Kay.

Her reply: "Goes without saying."

They had originally planned to land in Florence and have a self-drive car waiting, but, an hour into the flight, they encountered driving rain and enough turbulence to have Litha looking a little alarmed. Storm took a look toward the forward part of the cabin. He could see that she was uncomfortable, but trying to hide it. He respected that. He wouldn't give two cents for a person with no sense of pride.

"It's just air pockets," he smiled as he eased into the seat next to her and fastened his seatbelt.

"But it feels real," she said, giving him a shiver of déjà vu.

The flight attendant approached. "Bad news. The front is hovering and we can't get clearance to land at Florence."

"How close can you get us?" Storm asked.

She went back to the cockpit and returned a minute later. "Zurich?"

He nodded. "It'll have to do." To Litha he said, "We'll catch a train from there."

The Zurich train station was one of the busiest in the world because of its central location. It provided rail access to Spain, France, Italy, Austria, Germany and beyond. The underground was a crowded, bustling, merchantplex with hundreds of shops and eateries all one hundred percent dependent upon modern fluorescent lighting.

Storm put Litha's bag over his left shoulder, carried his own bag in his left hand, and used his right hand to guide her through the terminal. Normally they would have been served breakfast on board the company plane, but it had been too bumpy for that. They agreed they were too hungry to wait for dining car service, so they stopped and got two coffees and croissants. Litha carried them in a little take out tray since she was the one with free hands.

Storm had bought four first class tickets so that the two of them wouldn't have to share the space with strangers, because you never know who those two other people might be. And anyone who has travelled very much knows that sometimes fellow travelers can make you want to jump out the window.

They would be changing trains at Milan in about six hours and then it would be another hour from there.

Storm stowed the bags on the compartment overhead rack. They sat on upholstered bench seats next to the window, facing each other. Once settled in, Litha handed Storm his black-with-one-sugar coffee and reached into the paper sack for a croissant. Miraculously, they were still warm and smelling fresh from the oven. Opening the sack released the aroma to tease and entice. She pulled the paper tissue part way down for him, then handed Storm a croissant before taking one for herself. He thanked her, shoved it into his mouth, and bit off half.

Recovering from the surprise of seeing a person eat half a croissant at once, Litha bit off a pointed end, closed her eyes, and moaned, partly from the pleasure of eating, as she was way past famished, and partly from the sensory experience of fresh, warm croissant baked to French Swiss perfection.

Watching Litha's eyes slide closed while hearing her moan would have been an unwelcome turn on under any circumstances, but the close proximity coupled with the implied intimacy of an enclosed cabin made the demonstration way personal. Storm froze, stopped chewing and grew instantly hard, not necessarily in that order. When he realized he was salivating, he resumed chewing while taking up a mental chant. *I am not interested in a relationship. I am not interested in a relationship.*

"These are *so* good."

He longed to hear her talk about him in that same tone of voice, with the same inflection, and the same look on her face. "What?" He realized she was waiting for a response. "Oh, yeah, good."

Litha laughed softly. "How would you know?

You wolfed yours down like there was no tomorrow."

He responded with a sort of perverse masculine pride in being accused of eating too fast. He didn't want to smile. He really didn't want to smile. So, of course, he gave her a tentative smile because lately his body always did the opposite of whatever he directed it to do.

When the train began to move, both of them looked out the window. As they pulled away from the terminal and out into the open, they could see that it was still densely overcast and raining. In ten minutes' time they had left the unattractive, industrial underside of Zurich and were looking at what was unquestionably some of the world's most beautiful scenery, at any time of year, in any weather. The snows had melted, the trees were showing buds, and grass was starting to green.

Litha crushed the paper bag, set it aside, and took a sip of coffee, looking at Storm over the top of the cup. "Have you been to Zurich before?" she asked.

Still looking out the window he nodded, then faced her. He folded his big hands loosely in his lap.

"We... my teammates and I... were here two years ago on our way to Prague. Just like now, we didn't stop."

"Have you done a lot of traveling?"

Storm barked out a laugh. The feeling it conveyed was more sarcasm than humor and the force of it had been a little startling. It caused Litha to wonder just how much anger Storm was sitting there percolating.

"Yes. I've done a lot of traveling."

She looked down at the coffee cup she was holding between two hands in her lap and back up at Storm. "How much was for fun?"

His lips pressed a little tighter together. "Working for The Order isn't a commitment to good times and you know it."

"I do know that," Litha agreed. "But it's not supposed to take everything from you either."

Storm narrowed his eyes and settled back against his seat. "You gonna try to psychoanalyze me?"

Litha shook her head slowly. "Not qualified."

"It's good to know our limitations."

Not knowing how to proceed with this dialogue, Litha looked out the window. Storm continued to stare at her for a few minutes. "So. You have a plan?"

There it was - the question she'd been dreading. She didn't want to have to tell him that she didn't have a clue, past finding the spot she'd scryed. The last thing she wanted to see written across those handsome features was disappointment, especially when the disappointment was with her.

"Truth?"

"Always," he nodded.

"I got nada."

She waited for judgment or recrimination. What she saw, instead, was enough twinkle in his eyes to indicate amusement.

"I suspected as much. Thanks for being honest." She opened up the paper bag and set her empty coffee cup inside. "So, how about a little more truth?"

"Alright," she answered warily.

"Is this a fool's errand?"

Storm watched her carefully. He was trained to read body language, facial expression, tension in voice, any sign that sent non-verbal messages. And of course, she knew that. She dragged in a big sigh.

"I'll tell you the same thing I told Elora." She noticed the almost imperceptible wince, the way he blinked and shifted in his seat when she said Elora's name. After all, she had the same training he did. "That I'd rather not think impossible until there's nowhere else to go. Sometimes we get lucky."

"You've done this kind of thing before?"

It was Litha's turn to bark out a sarcastic laugh. "Nobody's done *this* kind of thing before. And that's the crux of our problem."

"So we're going to go to the spot you tracked and then..."

"Yes."

"Okay."

"Look, if you have a better idea, by all means don't be bashful. Jump on in. I'm receptive."

"I'm just the escort, ma'am," he drawled.

She rubbed her right hand over her mouth in frustration. That would be frustration with him and he knew it. And enjoyed it. Why in gods' names should that please him on any level? He was such a dick. Why couldn't he stop needling her?

He was thinking that if the red color on her lips was lipstick she would have just made a comical mess. Instead, what remained was a tantalizingly fetching, rouge colored pout that was just begging to be smothered in a demanding kiss.

"It's going to be a long trip, isn't it?" Her eyes slid slowly to his as she waited to see if he'd answer.

He moved his head in an I-don't-know-about-that gesture. "What do you want to talk about?"

"Okay." She crossed her legs taking up more of the space between them, seeming to close the distance. "Is there something going on between you and *Mrs*. Hawking?"

Storm looked like he'd been baited and was rising to a challenge, but rather than sounding angry or irritated, he went stone cold in both expression and tone of voice. He leveled a stare and spoke evenly enough to get the point across that all pretense of companionship was kaput. "First of all, she's not Mrs. Hawking. She's married to Sir Rammel Hawking, but her name is Laiken. Lady Laiken. Second, my relationship with my teammates is none of your business."

With that he stood, unzipped his bag, and pulled the carryall computer down from the overhead. For the next three and a half hours he ignored Litha. Never so much as looked up once. Suddenly he shut the computer with a click, set it aside, stood up and said, "I need protein. Let's go to lunch."

Litha was thrown off balance by the sudden change of mood and wondered if that was what he had intended. If he was playing games, she decided then and there she was in over her head. She reached for her purse and stepped into the aisle where he indicated that he would follow her to the dining car.

They were seated right away. Litha's humor lightened just by the change of atmosphere. Though it was still cloudy and raining, there was much more light in the larger space. She hadn't realized that being so close to Storm, and so alone with him, felt more oppressive than intimate since he made it abundantly clear he didn't like being with her.

He unfolded a menu. "This looks good. What'll you have?"

His change of mood was abrupt, but she wouldn't question any favors from the Fates whether large, medium, or small. "I hadn't decided. Maybe fish?"

"Fish?" He looked over at her and shook his head. "I'm thinking steaks."

She looked confused. "You mean you're ordering for me?"

He looked confused. "Of course not. Why would you think that?"

"Because you said steaks. As in plural. More than one."

"Yeah." He smiled sheepishly in spite of himself. "We get teased about how much we eat when we're away from Jefferson Unit." He chuckled. "And we have a habit of taking it poorly."

"I see."

"No. I didn't mean I'm taking it poorly with you."

Litha looked down at the menu written in German with French and English translations underneath each item. Suddenly she closed the menu and said: "You know, I've decided to go with optimism. If I need heavy-duty magicks, I need to be grounded to the earth. So I'll have a steak, too. Just this side of well done. Green salad with arugula if they have it, extra spinach if they don't. Vinaigrette on the side."

Storm looked up from his menu and blinked a couple of times before his mouth spread into a slow, sexy smile that went all the way to his eyes. When the waiter arrived at the table Storm ordered in German without ever referencing the menu or taking his eyes away from Litha. By the time he was finished and the waiter was gone, her smile matched his.

"Your German is good."

He shrugged. "My mother."

"Are you close?"

"We're not close in the sense that I call her every day, but I don't have any parent issues. The folks are alright. I didn't end up at Black Swan because they did anything wrong."

"Do you think you ended up at Black Swan because you did something wrong?"

He flashed a grin just long enough for her to see for the first time that his teeth were straight and white. "Well, let's just say my behavior, my mostly *bad*, behavior attracted the kind of attention that eventually got me noticed by Black Swan's network of people who watch for such things." He chuckled. "I was recruited by the guy who's my boss today."

"How old were you?"

"Fourteen. And absolutely positive that I already knew everything worth knowing." He shook his head in self-deprecation, but he was enjoying talking about himself and Litha was enjoying a glimpse of what he was like when he wasn't wound tight as a top or seeing her as the enemy.

She got him to talk about Sol, about his training as a teenager, and about his family. He talked about being partnered with Kay and teamed with Ram, who was B Team's most senior member, and his late partner, Sir Landsdowne. When the dishes were cleared away, he asked if she wanted dessert.

When she said no, Storm laughed and said Elora would be more likely to pass up the entre and go straight to dessert, but only if it was chocolate.

"I'm not Elora." When Litha saw the transformation come over the man across the table, she wished to seven shades of Hecate that she had kept that to herself.

"Of course you're not," he said seriously. "I wasn't comparing you." He pulled his napkin out of his lap, put it on the table and said, "You ready?"

She started back the way they had come. Just as they were starting into the noisy breezeway that connected to the car their cabin was in, a clutch of rowdy boys came dashing through - some sort of young sports team on the road, oblivious and narcissistic as kids that age are.

Litha plastered herself against the outside door and Storm turned into her to protect her from being jostled. Their bodies were swaying back and forth with the movement of the train, a hair's breadth away from touching. He was looking down into her upturned face, hands on her waist to steady her. He was thinking that her features seemed even more perfect when he was close; flawless skin, large liquid eyes, and red, red lips that drew and held his stare. It was disconcerting, which led him right back to the same conclusion he kept coming to again and again. She was indiscriminately and unethically using magicks. Had to be.

Once again, he caught the scent of rainstorm, a distant childhood memory that prompted a potent visceral reaction. Visceral *and* genital. He liked it. Liked it too much. And that meant he needed to be careful around the witch. Careful with enough distrust to be smart.

"Um," Litha said, "they've gone."

Storm took a step back and used his right hand to open the breezeway door to their car. He held it open for her to pass by ducking under his arm.

When they reached their seats and settled back in, Storm said: "Tell me about the pictures in your room."

To his surprise, she lit up like a floodlight when asked about the vineyard. She told him the story, holding nothing back. How she had just gotten her driver's license and was driving two lane roads on the coast feeling as free as if she was flying. She came over a hill and almost slammed on the brakes. It was quite surreal for Storm to listen to this other person, who wasn't him, describe his experience and his dream as if he was the one speaking.

No. That wasn't strictly true. She recalled minute details and talked about the villa in romantic ways that he felt, but wouldn't have been able to articulate. He was enthralled. So much so that when she stopped talking he wanted to ask her to start again and repeat everything she'd just said.

Instead he said, "What do you know about being a vintner?"

"A lot actually!"

That answer was clearly unexpected. Storm let the surprise register on his face.

The subject matter proved to be a source of instant animation for Litha whose excitement permeated the compartment. "I was raised in a monastery that supports itself by making wine. Great wine, I might add. You should see their reviews. Some of them are framed. That's even how I got my last name, Brandywine. I came to them when the brandy had just gotten a lot of great press exposure because of the reviews of some celebrity sommeliers."

"You were raised in a monastery?"

Litha grinned and nodded. "The Cairdeas Deians. Not everybody gets that mom, dad, 2.2 kids, 1 dog thing. In my case it was a little black haired girl and seven monks wearing long sleeved, floppy tunics. Quite a picture, I know. And I wouldn't trade it for anybody else's situation."

Storm looked fascinated and wanted to hear more, but wasn't sure about how the questions running through his mind would be received. So she decided to cut him a break.

"How did it happen?" she asked.

He just nodded.

"The story goes that I was left on church steps in a little village in England." She leaned in conspiratorially and made his heart speed up with her wicked smile. "A little village that's very near a place famous for witches, by the way." She stood up and started to pull off her hoodie. Staying seated where he was he grabbed the wrist of one sleeve and held it in place while she pulled her arm free. He didn't plan to make a study of the way her white silk tee shirt pressed against the curve of her breasts when she stretched, but he was at eye level.

Litha noticed where his attention was, but pretended not to. She got a rush of pleasure from imagining that Storm was thinking about her in a sexual way and it made her smile on the inside.

She didn't think she was pin up material and never intended to find out, but she wasn't embarrassed about her body either. Somewhere she had read that girls who were home schooled had a shot at escaping the "system" as free thinkers and with a healthy dose of self-esteem intact since it was never eroded away by either the systemic sexism or the sadism of other kids - girls or boys. In short, she felt good in her skin and, from what she could see, Storm was more than okay about her body. Even if he wasn't ready to admit it.

Once off, she tossed the hoodie onto the seat, sat back down and crossed her legs while leaning back. Storm couldn't hear the friction of skin sliding against skin or the rustle of skirt fabric over the noise of the train, but he imagined it.

"Anyway, one of the monks - I call him Cufay - was visiting a priest friend in England when I was found. Cufay has the sight and knew I was different. So he talked the friend into handing me over and brought me to California. He rescued me from being an orphan. And from being Anglish, too." She laughed silently.

"How did he get you out of the country?"

She arched a brow comically. "I think perhaps you underestimate clerics. They can be *very* resourceful."

Storm was staring with his lips parted.

"What's wrong?"

"I don't know whether to be horrified or happy for you." She smiled and opened her palms as if to say 'all's well'. "And how did The Order hear about you?"

"Oh. Well, in some ways that's the best part of the story. The Cairdeas Deo monks are not actually part of The Order, but they are - shall we say - loosely associated with it. When Cufay brought me home, he expected that I might be a resource someday. The monks set up my education so that, in a way, I was custom designed for The Order."

Storm wasn't sure that was a good thing, but decided to take the conversation in another direction. "My father is a winemaker. He works for one of the big outfits."

"Really?"

"Yes. When I was little he used to take me to work with him on days when I wasn't in school. It was really the only time I didn't get in trouble. I think I loved it." He chuckled. "My mom tried to take me to her work once. She was a part time librarian. That didn't go nearly as well."

He looked up into Litha's face and his breath caught because she was looking at him like... No.

Not a chance. There was no fucking way she could be in love. With him.

Had he not told her in the most concrete, definitive, and loud ways that he was *not* interested in a relationship? He glanced at her again to see if that beatific expression was still directed at him. It was. Holy hell.

The transfer in Milan went smoothly. They already had tickets to Siena, but it was a much smaller train with no first class or pre-assigned seating. After walking through two cars Storm found a bench seat with enough room for the two of them if they didn't mind a tight fit. He motioned to Litha to go ahead and sit down next to a woman with white hair pulled up on top of her head in a do that would have seemed chic on a young person. Apparently she was traveling with grandchildren and a daughter who looked like a younger version of herself sitting on a facing seat. With Litha's help Storm stowed the bags beneath the bench and then eased down beside her.

Both of them were independently marveling at how warm the other's body was. Storm had taken off his windbreaker and stuffed it in his bag. He was wearing a short sleeve knit shirt that was expensive and looked it. Litha shifted around trying to find a position that would be fairly comfortable for both of them for a one-hour ride, but Storm had an imposing upper body. She finally decided that it worked best for him to bring his right shoulder in front of her. At least it kept her from crushing the woman on her right.

Litha was happy enough with that arrangement.

The only downside was from Storm's point of view. Litha's left breast was now pressed tightly into his bicep, moving rhythmically every time she breathed in and out, and jiggling with the movement of the train. He was not going to be able to think about anything else until they got off the train, which had been designed for Italians and not Germans, much less German-descended warriors.

By the time the train pulled into Siena, Storm was pretty sure he needed a shower. The two of them climbed the steps to street level and stepped out onto the sidewalk in front of the station. Storm stopped and looked around like something was wrong. He asked a couple of passersby something in Italian. They smiled and answered. He thanked them and then muttered curses under his breath.

"What's wrong?" Litha asked.

"Not the best timing. It's the first Palio race of the year."

"What is that?"

He motioned to a taxi pulling up. "Come on. We're lucky to get one this fast."

Storm gave the driver the address of the Siena residence. The Order owned and maintained such places in every city of consequence all over the world.

"For centuries the old family groups have been holding these horse races three times a year. Each family has an entry. The piazza is covered in dirt so that the race can take place in the center of the old town. It gets crowded like Times Square on New Year's Eve. If we didn't already have a place to stay, we wouldn't have found a bed between here and

Florence."

"That won't affect us unless we can't get close to my location."

He turned to look at her. "We'll get you there."

She envied the utter confidence he held in his ability to complete his part of this mission.

In seven minutes the taxi pulled up in front of an old stone building facing a narrow cobblestone street. A man waited by the front entrance. "Mr. Storm, I presume," he said in decent English. It wasn't a question.

Storm didn't commit until the man offered a key, which he took and then asked which Contrade the man would be supporting in the race. He said he was Drago, grinned with pride and pointed to the dragon banner hanging from a building at the next corner.

Inside, he and Litha climbed three flights of stairs and were rewarded with an apartment that looked out onto the tower of the thirteenth century square and down onto one of the prettiest piazzas in Italy. It was covered with dirt for the race the next day.

There were two bedrooms, one a loft open to the living area below. Litha wouldn't want to admit it to Storm, but she was tired. He pointed her toward the enclosed bedroom, saying he would take the loft and that she might want to take a little rest, that they would venture out for dinner later, and start fresh in the morning to find the spot she'd scryed.

Grateful for the respite, she fell down on the bed and was thrilled to be greeted with the smell of fresh laundered linen - no perfumes, just good, clean soap. The windows were open to a lot of excitement below, but not enough to keep her awake. She was sound asleep in minutes.

When she had fallen down on the bed there had been a couple of hours of sunset left, but she woke in the dark, disoriented. She located a light and tromped to the bathroom. The mirror said she looked like she'd been run over. She took a shower, pulled her hair up in a ponytail, put on a red silk shirt and covered her shoulders with a huge silk and linen scarf.

Storm was sitting on the sofa reading. He looked up when she came out. He'd changed his shirt and the damp hair over his collar indicated that he'd taken a shower, too.

"Hey," he said. "Hungry?"

"Are you?"

"If it's dinner time, I'm hungry." He stood up and started moving toward the door. He had an impulse to tell her she looked good in red, but thought it wouldn't be fair to lead her on since there was definitely no future with him.

"I'm with you."

"Nope. Other way around."

"What do you mean?"

"We're going to stroll around until you say, 'Stop here'."

Everything about that offer sounded delightful. And suspicious. She narrowed her eyes and put her hands on her hips in a gesture he found curiously appealing. It made him want to circle both wrists with his hands and pull her arms around him. It would be nice to transform that challenge into a begrudging smile and admission of affection.

"Are you thinking this is a last meal kind of thing?"

He laughed and stood up. "Come on." He held the door open for her.

The streets around the main square of Siena at night were as charming and romantic as you might imagine. There was a lot of pedestrian traffic, but not so much that they couldn't walk freely and at their own pace. The evening air had cooled off enough so that she wished she had on something more than a silk/linen blend scarf. A woman stopped sweeping a pretty entryway with potted geraniums long enough to look at them and smile. Litha knew she was thinking they were a couple; lovers, maybe more.

What Storm had been observing was how many men were taking overt notice of Litha. It was a little unnerving. Of course he knew she was attractive, in a witchy sort of way, but she was collecting way too many double takes from guys who ought to be paying attention to the women they were with instead.

The ambling felt comfortable. Storm seemed relaxed which was practically an occasion for notifying the press.

"I read the bio in your file, you know."

He angled his head in her direction and looked down at her with what could have been curiosity or amusement. "Oh?'

"Hmmm."

"And was it gripping reading?"

She chuckled. "There were some interesting bits. Like the fact that you were an athletic boy who shunned sports."

"Shunned?" He laughed, then rolled a massive shoulder in a half shrug. "Just didn't get it. Seemed like a complete waste of time to me."

"What did you think was a good use of time?"

He hesitated for a minute like he was trying to decide how much to share. "Well, wine making for one thing." He looked her direction and saw that she was waiting for him to say more. "It's an accomplishment. Something you can be proud of. I loved going to work with my dad. He told me that it feels good to coax and nurse these delicate plants to give you back a harvest of special fruit, then turn that into something that's food, but so much more. If you put a bottle of wine on a dinner table it elevates the meal into something entirely different. It suggests pleasure and contentment and well-being..."

"Romance."

Storm smiled at Litha in a way that made her feel like she'd just won a prize. "Yeah. That, too. Definitely that, too."

"You were actually listening to your father wax poetic about wine while the other boys were playing baseball?"

"Like they say, it takes all kinds to fill up the freeways."

They had probably passed a dozen restaurants before she spied "the one". It was tucked into an alleyway behind the cathedral and could easily have been missed. Still, enough people had found it that the place was packed. Storm fully expected to be told that there would be a lengthy wait, but they were ushered straight to a table for two by the fireplace.

When they were seated, he leaned over and quietly asked, "Did you do that, witch?"

"Do what?" she looked around with wide eyes as if to decipher what he might mean.

"Did you get us the best table without a wait and without a hundred dollar bill?"

She broke into a husky, throaty laugh that massaged his erogenous zones like expert fingers. He'd never heard her laugh before. If he was a guy interested in a relationship, he might want to hear that laugh again, often and without reservation.

"You know, Storm, sometimes people have plain, old-fashioned good luck."

A waiter came by to ask about wine. Litha told Storm she could afford one glass and still be good to go the next morning - a nice red to keep the chill away. Storm told the waiter they were hungry and asked for menus. He ordered a flatbread appetizer with sausage, pepperoni and ricotta. She ordered a salad and a penne with mushrooms, spinach, sundried tomatoes, caramelized onions, Feta and pine nuts. Storm had the same, plus a double order of the grilled chicken with bacon and fresh Parmesan.

Litha smiled at Storm. "You wanted beef didn't you?"

He smiled in return. "We can't always get what we want."

It sounded like he was trying to get a larger

point across. A glass of red wine was set down in front of her. She took a sip and closed her eyes to enjoy the little burn as the warmth seeped into her system.

Through dinner they chatted amiably about operations in their respective units and some of their more unusual assignments. When the dishes were cleared away, Litha looked around and saw that only a few people remained. Reluctant to let the evening end, she asked for another half glass of red wine.

"Dinner was wonderful. I'll never forget it." She put her hand on top of Storm's in a gesture of affection that made him feel warm and fuzzy and uncomfortable all at the same time. He looked down at their two hands and she withdrew hers. "What happened between you and Elora?"

Storm had let himself relax and was caught completely unprepared for that question.

"I told you it's..."

She interrupted and finished the sentence. "...none of my business. I know what you said. Consider it my last request if you need to."

"You know that putting it like that is cheating."

She rolled her shoulder in a way that accentuated her femininity. "Didn't you say witches have no honor?"

Okay. So she was charming. He had to give her that.

He sighed as he surrendered. "Short version only."

"Fine."

He opened his mouth and then stopped, looked

around, raked a hand through his hair and finally said: "Wow. I guess this is even harder than I thought." He glanced at Litha who waited patiently, still as a statue looking elegant and at home seated at the best table in the joint.

"Kay, Ram, and I had just lost our teammate. We were in debriefing when Elora materialized in the air and landed at our feet. She was so injured we didn't even know what she was; looked more like ground meat than anything. Sol didn't want us to touch it. Ram said we should kill it. But I saw this thing reach out to me and I..."

Storm's voice broke a little. She felt a pinch of empathy and was starting to be sorry she'd pushed this, but he composed himself quickly and went on.

"I decided to try to save whatever it was regardless of consequences." He looked up at Litha." I had to disobey a direct order to do it. Kay had to help lift. Later on we found out she weighs as much as I do." Litha's eyes widened. "Yeah. She was designed for another dimension. The trip to this one tore her up so badly... well, nobody really thought she could survive it, and she was in recovery for months.

"Kay and Ram went home on three months' grief leave. I stayed because I guess I felt responsible for the thing that turned out to be Elora. I spent every day with her, visiting, letting her know somebody was on her side, watching her turn into a person, a..." His gaze darted to Litha. "... person.

"As you know, she turned out to be a miracle: strong, fast, brave. She fought her way into B Team and took the place Lan left vacant as Ram's partner. Even though I tried to stop it and kicked up a fuss, I agreed she deserved to be there.

"To wind it up, I asked her to marry me. She chose Ram. We just came from their handfasting a few days ago. And..." He blew out a breath and gave her a rueful smile, "...they're expecting."

Litha didn't have to be a genius to figure out that there were a lot more painful details to be read between the lines. She searched her heart for something to say, but nothing felt right so she said nothing.

Finally, he said, "Now I have a question for you."

She looked into his eyes. "Alright. I guess anything you want to ask is fair."

He smirked. "So now we're talking fair?"

"Ladies' choice."

That earned her a genuine laugh and lines smoothed away from his forehead. "Funny, Litha."

She thought it might be the first time she'd heard him say her name and she loved the way it rumbled over his baritone.

He reached into his shirt pocket and withdrew a photo that was faded and ragged around the edges and set it down on the table face up. It was a picture of the villa she had recreated a hundred times from memory. He watched her carefully.

She frowned trying to figure out what this meant. "That's my vineyard. Well, I mean... you know what I mean."

"I do. Because that's the same thing I would have said."

Litha jerked her gaze up to Storm trying to grasp his meaning. She shook her head, still frowning. "I don't..."

"I took this picture the year *I* was sixteen. *I* found this place when *I* was out driving all by myself. I borrowed my older brother's Polaroid and went back to take this photo the next chance I got. I've been putting back money to buy this place ever since then - planning to walk up to the front door someday and ask the owner what they'll take for it."

Litha stared at him for a few beats. "That's a pretty big coincidence."

"I don't believe in coincidence."

"Synchronicity?"

He shook his head.

"Serendipity?"

He stared quietly.

All of a sudden she smiled as brightly as if someone had switched on a high beam spot. "How about destiny?"

Storm looked incredulous. "You aren't serious."

Litha nodded looking very self-satisfied. "Well, it looks like you've got a decision to make. You can either get into a bidding war with me or we can pool our resources and live there together. You and me. There." She looked down and pointed to the photo on the table. "In our villa."

"*Our* villa?" Storm was still gaping. "What part of 'not interested in a relationship' don't you understand?"

She looked at him completely seriously and said, "The part with the 'not' in it." Then she smiled like she'd just won the lottery and he felt the rest of the ice that had formed around his heart fracture.

Was that what he wanted? A woman who was relentless? He didn't know the answer to that, but maybe, just maybe, he should stop putting all his energy into being an asshole and find out. She wasn't undecided about what she wanted. She had no doubt that it was... him. And who wouldn't be flattered to be somebody's end game? Especially when that somebody was the enchantress sitting on the other side of the dinner table.

"When was the last time you took 'no' for an answer, Litha?" he asked quietly.

"I do. Often. It's just that nothing else has ever been this... big."

As Storm sat drowning in the hope he saw in the depths of those deep green eyes, he realized he hadn't fought for Elora. It never even crossed his mind.

The return trip to the apartment was faster because it was too cold to stroll. Litha closed the bedroom window and searched for more blankets. She went to sleep happy, thinking about the bizarre turn of events. How unexpected it was to discover that she and Storm had settled on the exact same dream, in the exact same way, at the exact same time in their lives - that they had grown up so close to each other without their paths ever crossing. Until now.

Then there was also the fact that she seemed to be wearing him down. Elora Laiken had broken his heart, but maybe not so badly that she couldn't put it back together.

What she needed to do now though was put

VICTORIA DANANN

aside girlish day dreams and concentrate on getting Kay's future back. Nothing would make Storm happier.

The next morning she found him in the kitchen with food. While she'd been sleeping he'd rounded up juice, fruit, and bread that he had toasted. It was still early, but the noise was starting to pick up outside as crowds were overrunning the city.

Storm could see that Litha had her game face on. She was ready and it showed in her tension and her serious expression. She had her bag with her.

"You're taking the bag?"

"It has things I might need. I won't know until I get there." She looked down at it and back up. "Also, once I find the place, I want you to get away from me. Magick can be... unpredictable. I'll feel better if I know you're not too close." He just looked at her without committing one way or the other. "Say yes."

"Yes."

"Are you telling the truth?" His eyes flared with that twinkle she was starting to understand translated to amusement. "You *are* lying."

"I'm not lying. Exactly. But you do know that when I was assigned to escort you, they didn't mean come along and be your travel guide unless it gets a little dicey and then save myself. They meant be your protector. You've got your job. I've got mine."

"That's all well and good except there's a mitigating factor."

"Okay," he said cautiously. "Speak."

"Your take on doing your job may compromise

my job if part of my focus is distracted because of my feelings for you."

He seemed to consider that while he blinked at her. "Let's just see how it goes. I don't want to compromise your concentration."

Truthfully, he was torn between telling her to do all possible to get Trina back for Kay, and pulling her back from the mission. Even having that thought was so not Storm.

She nibbled at a corner of the toast he insisted she eat then Storm picked up her bag and followed her downstairs.

"Do we need a taxi?"

"Don't know yet." She took her necklace off over her head, pulled the housing free, and held the pendulum out from her body far enough to read the direction it pulled. She began to follow. It was harder than usual with so many people in the streets and so many bodies passing close by. Storm was trying to run interference and keep people away from her.

The good news was that the further they got away from the square, the less crowded it was. They found themselves back at the cathedral near where they'd had dinner. The pendulum pulled down a narrow side street that was completely shaded from the morning sun. A cheer rose from the square, but it didn't faze Litha. Years of practice had perfected her concentration so that not even Palio races would keep her from a goal.

She stopped half way down the block. The pendulum thunked against the solid wall of a thirteenth century palazzo. Litha looked up and around. Overhead a gargoyle stretched out from the cathedral roof as if it was guarding the spot. Or pointing to it.

She put the housing back on her pendulum.

"Well," she said, shrugging, "this is it."

Storm raked his gaze up and down the stone wall, up and down the alley, and looked dubious. "Litha, there's nothing here."

She pulled on her earlobe and shook her head. "I know that's what it looks like. But that's why they pay me the big bucks, right?"

"You get big bucks?"

"No, gorgeous. I was totally joking."

He glanced around again, feeling inexplicably nervous. "Let's go. There's nothing here."

"Seriously, Storm. Here's what I need you to do. Go wait at the corner." He looked toward the end of the alley like he was considering it. "Wait! Kiss me first."

He turned back to Litha, his eyes going to her mouth and resting there for a beat before looking into her eyes. "Did you just call me gorgeous?"

Her lips parted. He hated to encourage her, but he'd seen a lot of strange shit in the years since he'd been an active Black Swan knight. There was always a chance something might happen, and if he refused, he knew he would regret it. After all, it was just a meaningless kiss.

Putting his hands on either side of her waist, he gathered the material of her dress into his fists. He pressed her back into the wall with his body, intending to give her the kiss he'd been subconsciously obsessing about ever since the night she walked into his dream in her pretty, white nightgown and palmed his cock like it was the most natural thing in the world. *Here. Let me do that.*

As he pressed her back, he felt a momentary heat when their bodies came together. Then she was gone. Instead of holding handfuls of luscious, tempting witch, his knuckles were shoved against solid stone.

It took a few seconds for his mind to catch up with events. Then he yelled her name. "Litha!"

He pressed his hands over every square inch of the wall. Then he did it again. Over and over again. There was nothing there but cold stone.

He couldn't afford to be disheartened. Maybe she needed him. Maybe there was some hidden key. He told himself he had to keep trying because it was his job as her escort. She was his responsibility and he would feel just as panic-stricken no matter who he'd been charged to protect. He started over and did it again and again. And again. Finally, he rested his back against the wall and sank down to the ground. He sat there without moving for the rest of the day until after dark.

He saw the crowds disburse and grow thin. And still he sat there not really knowing what to do, not wanting to leave, but having nothing to act upon. *Nothing to be done. That's a new one.*

He was sure that if Litha came back she could find her way to the apartment. It wasn't far. He got to his feet slowly, picked up her bag, and trudged away feeling very tired and very alone. He stopped at the end of the alley and stood there for some time, giving her one last chance to get her curvy ass out of that wall and explain herself.

When he closed the apartment door, he dropped the bag, sat on the couch, and called Simon with a report saying he would not be leaving until Litha returned. Simon agreed to leave it like that for the time being and hung up.

Storm sat there for a while staring straight ahead, still stunned even after all the hours that had passed. He'd been over it in his mind a hundred times. Then his eyes fell on the leather bag where he'd dropped it on the floor. He pulled it toward him and unzipped it.

There were a few clothes on top that he moved aside. Then he came to a thin, delicate and very feminine, white, cotton nightgown with lace edging and little pearl buttons. He pulled it out and, without thinking or assessing motive, gathered it in both hands and buried his face in it so he could drag in her scent. Rain.

After a while he lowered the gown, but didn't set it aside. He left it curled in his lap while he went through the tools in the bottom of the bag: a tone chime, an athame, some herbs, various crystals, and a notebook that looked like a journal. He pulled out the notebook and opened it. It seemed to be a diary of sorts; a record that was a combination of personal thoughts or experiences and documentation of magickal undertakings.

He carried the book to the kitchen, sat at the table, and started to read. When his stomach growled because he hadn't eaten since early that morning, he had some of the bread and fruit he'd gotten for Litha, while he continued reading.

Eventually he lay down on the sofa close to the door, but didn't stop reading. On some level he felt like he was maintaining a connection, a lifeline.

Just before midnight he came to the entry she'd written the day he arrived in Edinburgh and saw it retold through her eyes.

I was walking across the mezzanine bridge when I heard someone whisper that the famous B Team of Jefferson Unit, a.k.a. Bad Company, had arrived. I looked down into the foyer and thought perhaps my heart had stopped. No matter how foolish it sounds, how foolish I feel for feeling it, I cannot help but admit that I have fallen in love with a beautiful, dark knight who never even noticed me.

This is a lesson in the pitfalls of skepticism. Cufay always said I ridicule other people's experience of the world at my own peril. I have taken pride in condemning such fanciful notions as myth or even psychosis. A very fine joke on me.

The second entry recorded the encounter in his dream.

I became aware that I was nightwalking when I found myself standing at the foot of his bed witnessing the most erotic sight any woman could ever have fantasized. He called me into his dream, but did not know how to keep me there and it ended, I believe, before he intended. That was a shame because the pleasure was exquisite, far exceeding any sexual encounter I have ever experienced in waking reality.

The third entry said:

Tonight there was an incident. I cannot commit all the details to writing partly because it was disturbing and partly because it could be dangerous to do so.

I was included in a social outing with some of his friends. The knight in question was intent upon making a point that he was neither interested nor available to me while actively pursuing the attentions of every other unattached female in the establishment. Even though I suspected he was staging a show for my benefit, it was painful to watch him touching other women. I think what I felt was an acute case of jealousy. It was awful. I should hate him for it. And I wish I did.

The fourth entry contained a reference to him.

I felt him call to me in my dream, but I refused to go. It seems I have chosen poorly indeed. I love a man who does not know his own mind. Worse, he harbors prejudice toward witches of all things and has three times demonstrated a proclivity toward meanness. A happy outcome seems unlikely.

Storm's chest felt like it was held in a vice grip. Reading what he had meant to Litha, the good and the bad, made the vice tighten painfully. Absently he rubbed the fabric of the white nightgown between his fingers while he read as if he thought that could soothe the emotional battery he had delivered. For no good reason.

There was only one more notation after that.

I am tracking a missing person who is missing from this dimension. It feels like the most important task I have ever undertaken because my knight's happiness is dependent on the outcome. I am in over my head and have more questions than answers, but there is no one else. I must try to find a way.

Among the many things that could be gleaned from reading Litha's diary, it was clear she was innocent of using magicks on him or against him. Coincidences were just coincidences whether the almighty Storm believed in them or not. Feelings were simply feelings and he needed to start owning up to his instead of looking for somebody to blame. Her only crime had been picking somebody seriously fucked up to love.

The journal was still in his hand when he woke. He stopped and got breakfast on the way to his post at the wall where he would spend another day waiting for some sign of a green eyed witch who had literally slipped through his fingers. He took the journal and reread it with his back against the wall. Literally.

CHAPTER 14

One minute Litha was feeling Storm's body press against hers while she was preparing for a kiss that would last her a lifetime, if that's all she ever got. The next she was in the "no place" that separates realities, a state of being without geography, a grayness where nothing is solid, where direction isn't concrete and therefore doesn't exist. It took her mind a few seconds to adjust to the shock, but she had been trained to keep her wits about her even when circumstances defied conventional reference points.

She decided the most logical course of action would be to begin by asking for what she wanted. She took the housing off her pendulum and without removing it from her neck, said simply, "Katrina."

A whirring, rushing sensation filled her ears even though she felt no movement of air. Suddenly she landed unceremoniously on her rear end on the sand floor of a limestone room with torches on the walls and randomly placed dark puddles of some viscous substance that was on fire. Fortunately the sand had absorbed the sound of her entry. She quickly took in the scene.

Katrina sat in a cane and rope chair staring straight ahead. She was not looking worse for wear physically, but she did look scared and disoriented. And her wrists were bound. When she saw Litha, she opened her mouth to say something, but the witch put a finger to her lips and then turned to assess the figure, whom she assumed must be the incubus in question, who now had his back to her. As Aelsong had correctly related, his hair was black as night and hanging to his waist. He was shirtless, wearing loose, dark colored pants that draped his form like fine, soft suede.

Litha got to her feet as quietly as she could and had risen to her full height before the demon turned and saw her standing there. It would be a gross understatement to say that he was shocked. In nearly a thousand years no one had ever found their way into his private lair. Without entertaining whether there might be merit in asking questions first, he gathered an impressive fireball into his perfectly formed hand, drew back and launched it at the intruder.

The fireball was aimed right at Litha's torso. Out of pure reflex, she raised both hands and caught it in front of her midsection using exactly the same movements one would use to catch a basketball. For a moment she held still, staring, then, as if she knew what to do instinctively, she clapped her hands together. First the fire was extinguished then it vanished as if it had never been.

Lowering her hands to her sides, she calmly raised her eyes to the demon, and waited passively to see what he would do next. There was a part of her mind that was questioning her bravado, saying it would be more appropriate for her to be, at least, judiciously afraid. And yet she was not.

In fact it was the demon who was afraid. Just

as he had released the missile, he was struck by the fact that the creature standing before him was the very image of Rosie Pottinger. He was mortified that he might have acted rashly and hurt her. Oh, how he cursed himself and wished, a millisecond too late, that he could recall the flame to his hand. But whether he deserved it or not, the gods had been merciful. He was granted a reprieve from punishment for acting without thinking. Miraculously, the fire had caused no harm. And so it happened that Deliverance found himself staring into the eyes of the witch he loved, dark green as the lava pools of Ovelgoth Alla.

"Rosie?" he whispered.

"No. My name is Litha. And you are?" she said in a matter-of-fact tone.

The demon cocked his head to the side as if he could study her better from that angle. Her manner was decidedly more assertive than Rosie's, but she spoke with Rosie's voice. Just as he was about to ask, "What are you?", he saw that her hair was not brown like Rosie's. It was black. Like his. Her lips were red like Rosie's. So much so that the reminder made his heart hurt to look at her, but the creature's skin was also not so fair as Rosie's. It was tinted with fire. Like his. He did not then suspect, but *knew* that this woman who had arrived in his lair, this woman who was not susceptible to fire, was the baby he had forgotten about once he knew that Rosie was beyond his reach. She may not have been invited to the demon's private lair, but she was oh so welcome.

As she was being studied, Litha was likewise

assessing a male who was every bit as remarkably formed as incubus demons are purported to be. When the stunning creature before her began to smile, his appeal increased exponentially and just seconds before, she would have thought that impossible. Her previous conceptions about ideals of beauty were being revised minute to minute.

"Deliverance." He gave the impression of enjoying his own name and said it with a little bow. "In these days of fashionable informality people usually call me Del, but I think you should call me..." He smiled even broader. "...Dad."

Litha didn't react to that visibly. She was calculating whether to proceed as if he was insane or allow him to make the case for his claim of paternity. She decided there was enough of a chance to allow a little exploration into the possibility.

As surprising as it might be, even to her, she took this information in stride. After all, she knew she had been fathered by someone. She also knew she had abilities that were unusual and, in light of the disturbing firestarting incident, growing more unusual lately. Truthfully, being fathered by a demon could explain a lot.

"You believe you're my father."

"No doubt," he said.

"Do you have any proof?"

"Well, first, there's the fact that you're standing here." He swiveled from the waist and gestured around him. "In my lair. How many witches do you imagine have ever managed that?"

"Three?"

He shook his gorgeous mane of hair and smiled indulgently. "That would be one."

"Okay. What else?"

"Daughter, except for the fact that you grow *my* hair and wear *my* skin, you are the image of your very comely mum." He turned away and then back again. "Whom I loved, by the way."

Litha frowned. "An incubus demon in love?"

He shrugged. "Happens."

"Not that I've heard about."

He waved his hand and the fires burned lower. "Not often, I grant you. But she was very special. Sweet, delicious Rosie." The last three words were said in a lowered voice, almost to himself. "Your family has been passing demon blood for generations. None of them had as much as you of course, but enough to make babies."

"The Pendle Hill witches."

"Indeed. You're powerful - *and* quick - for a halfwitch."

"Please don't call me that. It sounds way too much like halfwit."

He tilted his chin up and scrutinized her until she began to feel uncomfortable. "I can see I made a mistake missing out on your childhood, but I just turned the fire down because you look a little warm."

"Well. That should make up for it." He said nothing. "How did I get here?"

"You don't know?"

"No."

"Were you looking for me?"

"Of course not."

"Were you looking for her?" He glanced in Katrina's direction.

"Yes."

"Well, there you go. And, now that you're here. What can I do for you?"

"Let the woman go."

"What is it to you?"

"My job."

"What is it to you?" As if someone pressed replay, he asked it again in the exact same way without missing a beat. Litha didn't respond. "If you will not tell the truth, we have nothing else to discuss."

"She   is   someone's   love."

"I'm aware. How does that involve you?"

"It's important to the one I love."

"Ah. And how badly do you want this?" She didn't answer. "You're not going to cry, are you?"

Litha was insulted. "No. I'm not going to cry. I don't cry. I stopped crying when I stopped getting skinned knees."

"Hmmm. It's just as well I missed the young times then. I don't like crying."

"What's   your   proposition?"

He smiled. "That's my girl. What I have in mind is a win, win. If you agree to stay with me, I will return the woman. Then I will tell you what you need to know about your demon side, about manipulating fire, about your heritage, about riding the passes."

"Riding the passes?"

"It's how you came here from the Loti Dimension." She looked puzzled so he clarified.

"The dimension the Terr... humans think of as the *only* reality." He rolled his eyes as if to say, 'How stupid can they be?'

"For how long?"

"How long have humans been clueless? Since they were single cell organisms that crawled from the muck. Although that's secondhand information. I'm not *quite* that old."

"No. How. Long. Me. Stay. With. You?" She made hand signals like she was trying to communicate with someone who spoke a different language.

"That is *so* precious! You're acting out because I abandoned you, aren't you?" He smirked. "Well, you need to stay long enough for us to get past the juvenile snits." He crossed his muscular arms in front of his muscular chest and considered that. "A year."

"A day."

"A season."

"Till Beltane."

"Done."

"Doesn't really matter. I could stretch time and pack a year into a week."

"That's cheating."

He laughed. "What did you expect? Dad's a demon."

"I heard that was just bad press."

"Clever girl. And rightly said because public sentiment could have gone either way. It's a P.R. matter that we've never cared to correct because it's more trouble than it's worth. 'Cause really. Why should we care what Terr... humans think of us?"

Then, as if he was enjoying a private joke, he laughed. "But wait until you find out how far the Nephilim will go to get *their* way."

"Angels?"

"They prefer we use their own language to describe them. But why should we care what they prefer? By and large, what have they ever done for us? I say fuck 'em. Angels it is!"

"Do you think you would know if you were mentally disturbed?"

"Have some respect. I'm your father."

She ignored that. "Have you hurt the woman?"

"Certainly not." He sounded offended. "My beef is not with her. She's a tool."

"I assume you mean that in the conventional way? Not in the slang sense?" He looked blank. "Never mind. If I stay with you, your, um, *beef* will be considered satisfied." After thinking better of it, she appended the demand. "That means the debt will be voided by you."

"No new conditions. The deal is already struck."

"I'm half demon. I don't have to keep my word, do I?"

Deliverance threw his head back and laughed with his whole essence. It was mesmerizing. "You learn fast."

"Well?"

"Very well. My revenge against the lover will be satisfied if you voluntarily stay until midnight, Beltane Eve."

"And how can I be sure I can trust you to honor your agreement? *Dad.*"

"If we make a pact of fire, it can't be undone without dire consequences to the breaching party."

"Dire consequences, huh?"

"Yes." He looked sincere, but she suspected that sex demons were especially good at looking sincere.

"Leaving that alone for now, what's a pact of fire?"

"Generate fire in your hand. I'll do the same and we'll clasp hands."

"I don't know how to do that."

"It's just like shaking hands. I put mine out..."

"No! I don't know how to make fire!" He grinned at her. "You're being deliberately obtuse, aren't you?" She didn't know herself if that was rhetorical.

"Maybe. You really don't know how to gather fire?"

"I did it once - recently - and it was an accident."

"Hmmm. I guess you're wanting me to release her soon?"

"Yes. Naturally."

"Well, you need to make fire so we can conclude this transaction. Let me see you try."

Litha held up her right hand, stared at it, and imagined fire. Nothing.

Deliverance walked over to Katrina and pinched her on the upper arm until she wailed. "How about now?"

"What the hell?"

"Exactly. Do it." He pinched Katrina again harder. She screamed and Litha could tell it really hurt. It made her so mad both hands burst into flame. Deliverance grabbed one of her hands with his and said, "Congratulations. You just sealed the deal." He made an air whistle sound and the fire went out. "You're now the proud owner of one damsel in distress."

"You know I was just starting to think I might learn to like you. But you really *are* evil, aren't you?"

He scrunched his face up like he was thinking about it then sort of wiggled his head back and forth. The aggravating thing was that she recognized that stupid head wiggle. She did that! And not even scrunching his face made him unattractive. That was super annoying.

"Not really," he said while he was pulling on a shirt and tying his hair back at the nape of his neck. "I'll just drop her off where I found her and be right back."

"Hold on a minute. I need to send a message with her." Litha knelt down in front of Katrina, who was rubbing her arm and looking more frightened than she had when Litha first arrived. "Katrina, he's not going to hurt you anymore." She turned and gave the demon a look that promised retaliation if he made a liar out of her. Then turning back to Katrina she used a tone she hoped would calm her. "You're going back and I'm going to stay here in your place. I need you to give Storm a message. Can you remember for me? It's important."

Katrina nodded, glancing at Deliverance and looking wary about going anywhere with him.

"Tell Storm that he's not interested in a

relationship with anybody but me and that not even demons can keep me away forever." She smiled. "I don't know if that will please him or scare him, but tell him anyway."

Katrina nodded again. "Thank you."

Litha stood up and turned to Deliverance. "I'm starved. Get me a hamburger on the way back, okay? Well done with everything including onions. No ketchup."

"A hamburger from London? I don't eat food and even *I* know that's a terrible idea."

CHAPTER 15

"And take Heaven with you."

"What? Why?" Baka scowled at Director Tvelgar.

"Simon says," Elora quipped.

Baka turned toward his former crush with a dry tone. "Unforgivably amusing, Mrs. Hawking."

"Why thank you, Fang."

"Great Heavenly Days! Does Nemamiah have to put up with this all the time? This isn't a playground for aliens and ex-vampires to squabble like siblings."

B Team and friends had been in Edinburgh for just a short time, but apparently, it didn't take long for them to convert an unflappably calm and composed administrator into an irritable man with semi-paranoid feelings of losing control.

Ram joined the conversation without looking up from something he was doing with his intelliphone. "Pay no mind. They talk to each other like that, but in the wash, 'tis harmless."

"You think so?" Raising her eyebrows, Elora turned on Ram with a challenging tone.

"As I was saying, Ms. McBride needs field experience and I think this would be a great opportunity. Take her with you. It's just one werewolf. So far as we know now. Should be a walk in the park for half of B Team and Istvan Baka."

"If *she* goes, the experience will be neither

great nor heavenly, I assure you." Baka wasn't giving up the protest until he was sure beyond any reasonable doubt that he wouldn't have his way.

With a thoughtful expression Ram looked up from his phone. "As you've said correctly, Simon, 'tis just one meager werewolf - so far as we know. So 'tis really no' a good reason to involve the women at all. Why no' just have the vampire...?"

"...EX vampire," Baka corrected.

"...aye, the ex-vampire and I go on along and take care of the beast ourselves?"

Elora gaped at Ram. "You really don't give up, do you!" Ram shrugged without the slightest repentance or willingness to give ground. "Look here, elf." Elora grabbed Ram's face in both hands. "If you're going, I'm going." And she laid a kiss on his very inviting, death-by-sex mouth that drifted across generally acceptable boundaries for public displays of affection in Scotia and most other places in the world.

Simon flopped into an overstuffed chair in a very un-Director-like way and looked toward the window like he was searching for a source to garner patience. "Anyone like a graphic demonstration as to why there's a no-office-romance policy?"

Reluctantly, Elora pulled away from her mate and turned to Simon. "I'm sorry. That was so uncalled for. Can we chalk it up to pregnancy hormones? And I *will* try to behave better, I promise."

Ram, for one, was hoping the resolution for better behavior never gelled. Elora had spent her first twenty-three years living an extremely repressed, highly public role as a Briton royal in her own world. Once she'd had a taste of personal freedom, she wholeheartedly embraced the concept and Ram had done all possible to encourage her adventurous, lusty side.

"But," she said more seriously, "do not conspire with my husband to keep me from him."

Simon wondered if that was a threat and decided not to ask. He simply sighed and looked at Ram. "I sympathize with your conflict and your predicament, but B Team is already limping. The Lady Laiken goes."

Ram swung away from Elora and muttered some mild curses.

Simon turned to Baka. "If you feel that strongly about taking Heaven, you can go as three."

Baka gave Simon one of his half nod, half bow gestures. "Thank you."

"You're welcome," Simon said with a hint of wry. "Plane leaves in three hours. As you know, Litha was working on this, but her talent as tracker was wasted because all the reports of sightings were close to London Bridge within three blocks of Magnus the Martyr's Church of England."

Ram turned to Baka. "Either relent regardin' your assistant or get us a map." Baka reached for his intelliphone. "No. We need a real, old-fashioned map, big enough for the three of us to look at together." To Simon, Ram said: "I want to see those reports. And have you made arrangements for us to stay over?" Simon nodded and began speaking instructions into his own phone.

Ram turned all the way around to find Elora

standing behind him. "And might you be available to throw a couple things in a duffel? In case we're delayed past midnight?" He started out fully intending to dole out her assignment objectively, but as he spoke, he moved closer and closer like he was being pulled by an invisible force until the last few words were nuzzled next to her ear, giving her both shivers and giggles.

Ram heard a noise of exasperation behind him and turned his head. "Sorry, Director. But we *are* on our honeymoon you know." Elora got a smile full of promise.

"On my way." She eased around him, brushing past his body with just enough contact to let him know she would be collecting on that promise later.

Ram, Elora, and Baka arrived at the private planes terminal at London City Airport which was not nearly so far out as Heathrow or Gatwick. They readily agreed that Ram should drive since he was at home on the left-hand side of the road and didn't have to conscientiously think about how to use a right-handed gear shift.

Not wanting to call attention to themselves, they had dressed in the sort of urban casual, pedestrian clothes you would expect to see in that neighborhood and picked a Vauxhall four-door sedan out of The Order's fleet. Elora took one look at it and said, "Baka can ride in back," which an understated way of calling 'shotgun'.

When they were close to target area, they left the car in a pay-to-park lot and started off on foot. The plan was to find a pub and have dinner while waiting for darkness to settle in. They knew the werewolf wouldn't show itself until full-on night.

"I love pub food. It's my favorite."

Ram snorted. "'Tis what you say about *all* food these days."

"That is *so* not true and *so* snarky of you to say. Ugh! I wish *you* were the one who was pregnant."

"Sorry." His eyes twinkled as he reached out and put one arm around her while rubbing her yet-to-be-round tummy gently with his other hand.

"I like it, too," said Baka.

Ram looked at him. "I beg your pardon?"

"Pub food. Shepherd's Pie, ploughman sandwiches, goat cheese quesadillas."

Elora laughed at him. "Goat cheese quesadillas are not pub food."

"Then why do they have it on the menus so often?"

"Because they're not pub purists?"

"Pub purists. Okaaaaay."

"You know," Ram said, "Simon is right. The pair of you do no' bring out the best in each other."

They spent the rest of sunset in relaxed conversation - more or less. Elora did make the point that it was surprising to have a werewolf problem in the middle of a big city. Everyone knew that werewolves preferred areas with lots of open space. They usually gave big cities a wide berth for the same reason feral wolves do.

When it looked dark as could be expected on a quarter moon night in one of the world's largest artificially lit cities, they took one more look over their map, reviewed the plan, and headed out on a mission of the 'simple' sanction, to use Simon's word, of one 'meager' werewolf, to use Ram's word.

Ram was wearing button down jeans, a heavy metal tee shirt and a nondescript, tan trench coat outfitted as an arsenal. Elora wore a skirt with flat-heeled ankle boots and a leather jacket. She didn't carry much in the way of weaponry, but she didn't need to.

"Hey," Baka sounded more cheerful than usual. "Have you ever heard the song 'Werewolves of London'? Maybe if we sing it, it might make him mad enough to show himself."

Neither of his companions broke their stride as Ram said, "How does it go? Sing a little for us."

Elora slid a sideways smile toward Ram. Usually people withdrew suggestions about singing when put on the spot and they both expected Baka would do the same. Instead, he launched an uninhibited, full-throated, baritone rendition. He had gotten as far as the line about 'beef chow mein' when they overcame their surprise enough to stop him.

"We are no' tryin' to giddle the beast. We're tryin' to curtail the terrorizin' of citizenry."

Baka looked disappointed. "Right."

After a couple of hours of patrolling, Elora had outdistanced the men a little and walked a ways uphill from them. As Ram ambled alongside Baka, he found himself feeling especially content and waxing philosophical.

"You know, Baka, a few months ago, I watched through a glass wall as my wife sat down in front of you and became so fearful I actually hyperventilated and had to breathe into a paper bag. It was fuckin' humiliatin'."

Baka smiled. "I suppose there are some advantages to being feared?"

"I hope you find there's more on the plus side in bein' human. I am walkin' along with you this very night because my teammate, Storm, and that marvelous creature just ahead of us both think so highly of you."

"That pleases me very much, Sir Hawking."

"The thing is, I know there is some sort of weird connection between you and my mate. Though I can no' account for it, I am nonetheless grateful that you were instrumental in savin' my wife from death by vampire."

"Was my finest hour. No doubt."

"I also know you seem intent on pollinatin' all the flowers now that you're free. And certainly 'tis no' a thing wrong with that. I've been unmated myself." Ram stopped on the sidewalk and faced Baka to emphasize a point he wanted to make. "Just be very sure your stinger is limp and securely in your pocket when you're 'round my wife. Or I will be forced to feed your balls to the lady's great, black beast who has such a profound and inexplicable dislikin' of you."

Baka opened his mouth to tell Ram not to worry, that he had, in fact, lost interest in 'pollinatin' all the flowers', but that was forgotten when every hair follicle on his body surged to life and stood on end. There are few noises as frightening as a werewolf's threatening snarl. It is the stuff of nightmares. Once heard, it is never forgotten and that ominous sound was coming from just ahead in Elora's general direction.

The werewolf was crouched on a stone fence a few feet above her head. He was not fully turned, but was far enough into the shift to be hirsute, fangy, and all round bona fide terrifying. Plus he was a big son-of-a-bitch. Ram was instantly smacked by a huge release of adrenaline that surged all the way to the marrow in his bones. That combined with the acute fright had him trembling, shaking so hard he could barely reach for a weapon.

He might have been at risk for a heart attack if he hadn't been so young and physically fit. The sight of an aggressive, angry, half-turned werewolf sitting just above Elora's head, growling at her, well, Ram had only thought he'd known fear before that.

Oddly, his mind flashed on the image of Kay's face saying, "Please demon." That's exactly what Ram wanted to do - fall to his knees and say, "Please werewolf."

Very slowly, trying not to alarm the creature, he reached inside his coat and pulled out a draw'n hook. It was a weapon modeled after a crossbow, in miniature version, except more powerful and instead of an arrow, it shot a three-pronged hook attached to a line. The hook was curved and barbed like a fishhook, so that, once embedded it would hold. If he could get a shot off, he could grab the line and pull the werewolf away from her – dead or alive, but he would have to shoot before the creature moved.

While Ram raised his weapon, Elora was

standing very still watching the werewolf. It almost looked like he was her prey and not the other way around. When he leapt for her, she simply waited for gravity to pull him close, then, without batting an eye she stepped aside, reached up and in lieu of a scruff, grabbed him by the back collar of his shirt in a manner similar to the way a mother wolf would discipline a cub. Except that a she-wolf would not repeatedly dash a cub against a stone wall while he howled like he was signaling the start of Armageddon.

When Elora released him he whimpered, but made no move to either renew the attack or escape. He slumped against the wall holding one arm and licking it. "Cromm the Bloody Cruiach. That hurt!" he said with a thick Irish accent. "What sort of bloody people do they have workin' for The Order these days?"

By this time Ram and Baka were standing next to Elora. Ram had traded weapons and now had a long barrel gun with silencer trained on the hapless shifter. As the werewolf started to stand, the three hunters backed up a couple of paces giving themselves time to react to sudden movements, but at the same time, making an arc around him so that he was trapped. Unless he wanted to try to jump straight up.

They didn't want to kill him until they learned whether or not there were any more troublemakers.

He was Red Irish with rust colored hair and a beard a few shades darker. His eyes appeared small because his cheeks were puffed and rounded in an unfortunate piggish look and the tint of his skin could only be described as pink. These things combined to a result that meant he was undoubtedly more handsome in wolf form.

Elora was irritable. "Retract your fangs! I can't understand a thing you're saying."

"I did!" He whined in protest. "I have an overbite!"

After a few beats of processing that, Elora simply said, "Oh."

Baka wasn't quite successful at stifling a snicker.

The werewolf leaned toward Elora and sniffed loudly. "You're growin' a pup".

Ram immediately moved in front of Elora. "Step away now or forfeit somethin' you prize."

Elora never objected to his acting out male mate instinct. She secretly thought it was sort of cute and... sexy.

Incredibly, the werewolf looked offended by Ram's repositioning and hostile declaration. "I would ne'er hurt a royal."

Elora regarded him curiously. "What makes you think I'm a royal?"

He threw up his hands. "Excuse me while I say 'duh'." He glanced toward Ram. "The poser does no' need to protect you from me."

"Poser?" Ram was past astonished to be insulted by a werewolf, particularly when said werewolf had been singled out for sanction and was presently facing the receiving end of a terminating weapon.

Elora felt defensive about Ram. "Look here, werewolf, not that it's relevant in any way, but the elf you're addressing is an Irish prince."

The werewolf spat out a disagreeable laugh and looked at Ram. "The poser is lifetimes away from bein' a *real* prince."

Ram continued to gape and his color darkened. "My family has held the monarchy for fifteen hundred years!"

Elora tilted her chin toward Ram and regarded him quizzically. "I thought you don't care about such things, Ram."

He looked a little discombobulated, but lowered his voice. "I do no'."

Puzzled by that whole exchange, Elora decided it was neither here nor there. "Okay, then." Turning back to the beast she said, "So. What's your problem, werewolf?"

"It took you long enough, did it no'? I've been sendin' bloody letters for weeks."

"You've been sending the letters?"

"Aye. Now did you bring the silver or no'?"

Elora looked as mystified by the werewolf's behavior as Ram.

Baka said. "Apparently he wants to die."

Ram immediately raised his weapon. "Here. Let me help you with that."

Elora put her hand on top of the gun and gently - for her - pushed the deadly end down so that it pointed to the ground then turned back to the werewolf. "Why do you want to die?'

He lifted one shoulder and let it drop. "'Cause I'm the last one."

Ram looked stymied and impatient. "The last one what?"

"What do you think, blondie? The last werewolf."

Elora could see that the smart mouth werewolf standing in front of her wanting to expire was about to get his wish because her husband was one remark away from throttling the bugger.

"Werewolf, listen to me carefully. The person standing to my right, whom you seem bent on calling out, happens to be the most famous Black Swan knight alive." Hearing those words pour from that mouth he lived to kiss made Ram stand a little straighter and swell with pride like she'd pulled the cord on an inflatable raft. "I strongly recommend that you cork it until we sort things out. If you persist, I won't intervene on your behalf again. Nor will I feel sorry for you when he shows you why he *should* have your utmost respect. Either take my word for it or get schooled the hard way. Werewolf's choice. Do we understand each other?"

The werewolf hesitated, but nodded. Reluctantly.

"What's your name?"

"Harefoot."

Elora thought Baka could have tried harder to stifle the ensuing laughter. She gave him a dirty look, but he just mimed a zip-it mouth and reached for the little spiral notebook he'd been carrying in his pocket ever since a night in a New York alley when he'd needed to jot down notes.

Even though Baka wasn't currently writing vampire romances, his modus operandi ran along the lines of "you never know what the future might slap you with". So he liked to keep his escape hatches open and handy. Extra long life tends to give one a big picture sort of perspective.

The werewolf watched him start scribbling in his little book and then said to no one in particular, "People usually call me Harry."

At that, Baka and Ram both laughed so hard they were leaning on each other for support.

Elora just looked at them and sighed. To the werewolf she said, "I'll just call you werewolf."

Harry shrugged indicating he didn't care one way or the other. "Suits me."

Baka laughed even harder.

The werewolf was now becoming indignant. To Elora he said: "Either kill me or shut the fuckin' vampire up now."

That sobered Baka quickly. He blinked at Harry like he was a new species.

Elora studied Baka for a minute and then returned her attention to Harry. "Why do you think he's a vampire, uh, Harry?"

The werewolf just looked at her. "Ain't he?"

Elora chewed her bottom lip while trying to decide whether to tell the truth or not.

"No. Not anymore. We cured him of vampirism. Although we can't do a thing about his personality." Elora paused just long enough to give Baka an amused look.

"Okay. Here's the thing. You're not the last. Far from it. There are self-governing werewolf reservations all over North America. In Canada, the Pacific Northwest, Louisiana - although I really don't get that one because... fur is hot. You know?" Harefoot nodded wholeheartedly. "We could find out who is accepting immigrants and arrange for you to connect."

Harry just stared at Elora until Ram finally broke the silence. "You okay?"

"Yes. Thank you," he said meekly, sounding like a changed werewolf. "Can we go now?"

Elora gave Ram a 'what the hell' glance before saying to Harry: "Um, well, you'll need to come back to Edinburgh with us. We'll make arrangements from there. Do you want to pack a bag?"

Harry looked down the block for a minute then said, "Yes. Please."

Ram stepped toward him. "Look here, Irish to Irish, 'tis safe for me to put this weapon down?"

Harry was deceptively contrite. "I said I would no' hurt a *real* royal. 'Tis no' for me to be pointin' out that she married beneath her."

Harry had managed to accomplish what no one else ever had. He'd rendered Ram speechless. He just stared at Harry with his mouth open. Harry looked at Elora. "He's a mouth breather? 'Tis even worse than I thought."

Elora said: "Ram. Maybe there's something seriously wrong with him. It seems like more than a simple social maladjustment. Maybe a true death wish? Or masochism? I don't know. I'm no psychologist."

"Maybe we best be findin' out what's the matter with him before we're responsible for foistin' the fucker off on some poor unsuspectin' tribe. I can just hear it now. Look what Black Swan sent us."

Elora regarded Harry with pity. "You may have

a point."

"At the least he's deranged. As you said, werewolves usually avoid cities."

"Hello! Standin' right here you know." Harry couldn't seem to keep the belligerence out of his tone for longer than two minutes at a time.

"So why *are* you here in the big middle of London, Harry?" Elora asked.

"I'm canine. That means I do no' like bein' alone."

Elora looked at Ram. "See. He *is* canine."

Ram's intelliphone vibrated. He saw that it was Simon and picked up. While Elora continued to talk to the werewolf, explaining why it would be in his best interest to get in touch with his politic side, Ram walked a few paces away and spoke in low tones.

Elora heard the phone click closed and looked up. Ram's eyes were shiny.

"What's happened?"

"She's back."

Elora squinted slightly and started to ask, "Who?" Then her breath caught. "Katrina."

Ram nodded. "She's in the lobby of the Hyde Park Hotel. Borrowed their phone and called Kay. When she did no' get an answer, she called the Norns. Then they called Song. We need to go get her. After what she's been through, we do no' want to leave her waitin' there alone."

Elora nodded. "Let's split up. You and Baka go get Trina. I'll take the werewolf to get his things and we'll meet you at the plane."

"We have one car."

"Werewolf, do you have a car?" Elora turned to Harry. He shook his head. "How far away do you live?"

"Six blocks."

Elora turned to Ram. "We'll get a cab. I don't have a purse. Do either one of you have the fare?"

Baka reached in his pants pocket, pulled out a fistful of bills and placed it in her hand without looking to see how much was there.

All of a sudden, Elora drew up short. She looked at Ram. "What about Litha?"

He just shook his head no.

Elora had planned for the werewolf to gather essentials into a reasonably sized article of baggage, but that would be too easy. When they got to his flat, he went diva on her. By the time he was done insisting on this and that, they had three oversized bags of stuff. The werewolf was turning out to be le giant pain in le derriere.

Baka, Ram, and Katrina were already at the steps to board the plane when Elora arrived with Harry in tow.

The werewolf rushed out of the taxi and headed straight for Ram. "I'm beggin' you. Please make her stop sayin' 'Bad Dog'."

In a new fit of laughter Baka repeated, "Bad dog." Grabbing for his little notebook, he said: "I can't stand anymore. I think I may have broken a rib earlier."

Elora gave Katrina a gentle hug and asked Ram to keep Harefoot at the other end of the plane, saying the last thing Katrina needed after her ordeal was to put up with Harry.

Ram took custody of the werewolf then called Simon to let him know they were bringing him in and that Katrina had an urgent message for Storm. Simon said he'd make arrangements for foster care for the werewolf until they could find a tribe that would take him. Glancing at Harry, Ram said: "You'll have to find people with Paddy's patience and even they are goin' to need to dig deep."

Storm was sitting alone on the uncomfortable cobblestones of a Tuscan side street with his back against a stone wall, when he got the call from Ram that Katrina had been returned to the hotel lobby from which she was taken. He'd been recalled to Edinburgh. Ram had added that Katrina was adamant about wanting to personally deliver a message to Storm from Litha.

He stood up slowly. "Rammel. She did it." It was reverent, almost a whisper.

"Aye. To be sure. I'm lookin' at Kay's girl in the flesh."

Storm stood for a while with the flat of his hand on the wall where Litha had disappeared. Going didn't feel right. It felt like leaving a soldier behind. What if she came back the same way? A big part of him wanted to stay, but there were two problems with that. First, orders were orders and, second, he wanted... no... *needed* to hear that message.

It seemed a Siena taxi driver could be persuaded to go all the way to the Florence airport in exchange for a small fortune. Storm had the driver circle round past that wall in the shadow of the cathedral just one more time and drive slowly, just on the off chance...

All the way back to headquarters, he thought over and over about how he had told her it was impossible. And she had just said impossible is what you think when there's nowhere left to go. The jet landed in Edinburgh before breakfast. Storm knew he wasn't looking his finest, but he was eager to see Katrina, wake Kay up, and last, but certainly not least, collect his message from Litha.

It was so early the streets were practically deserted. The doorman opened the door with a smile and a tip of the hat. Storm stepped into an empty foyer, pulled out his phone and called Ram. If there was anybody alive that he had blanket permission to wake at any hour of the day or night, other than Kay, it would be Rammel.

"Where are you?" Ram answered on the first ring.

"Front door."

"We're in the infirmary and we just got him up."

"Tell him I'm here."

Storm closed his phone, handed his bag to the doorman, and jogged to the infirmary. He opened the door of Kay's hospital room without knocking. Ram and Elora were standing together on the far side of Kay's bed in front of the window. Kay was sitting in a big reclining chair next to the bed where he'd been kept sedated, and he was still wearing a blue cotton print nightgown. Katrina was rolled into his lap in a semi-fetal position with her knees drawn up and her head under his chin. Kay's big arms were folded around her like a shelter.

"Hey, Partner," Kay gave him a little smile with his mouth and a big smile with his eyes.

Ram nodded at Storm. "We have no' even had time to tell him what he slept through."

While holding Ram's eye, Storm pointed to Katrina and raised his eyebrows.

"Simon said under the circumstances we're liftin' the confidentiality rule. Since she already knows about demons, he's takin' a chance on trustin' her with the rest." Ram chuckled. "'Tis an up side to this. Life is goin' to be easier for Kay with her knowin' what he does for a livin'."

Storm closed the door behind him and leaned back against it, suddenly feeling tired.

While Kay stroked Katrina, Ram described how Litha had tracked the location to Siena in secret, then Storm had escorted her there where she disappeared. At that point in the story Katrina's head came up off Kay's chest.

"Storm," she said and looked around. "I have a message for Storm." She sat up on Kay's lap. When she turned and looked in his face, Katrina's bottom lip started to quiver a little. "She made a deal with him." Tears started to run down her cheeks and she swiped at them. "She told him she'd stay with him if he'd let me go. They bargained about how long. She said it was important to remember to tell you that you're not interested in a relationship with anybody but her. And that not even demons can keep her away forever. She said she didn't know if that would please you or scare you, but to tell you anyway." She looked at Storm sorrowfully. "I'm sorry."

Kay asked her quietly, "Did he hurt you?"

"No."

Kay noticed a bruise on her upper arm. "Then what's this?"

Katrina looked at her arm. "He pinched me."

"He pinched you?" Kay's shot a glance Storm's way to see if he could pick up what his partner might be thinking about that.

"Well, he pinched me really hard."

"I see that. And I'm not trying to make light of it. You know every hair on your head is precious to me. It's just that we've never come across a situation where pinching was used as coercion before."

Katrina raised her head to look Kay in the face. "Are you laughing at me?"

He was serious as a judge and shaking his head. "Absolutely not."

"He was trying to get Litha to make fire."

Kay looked confused. "What do you mean? Like build a campfire?"

She shook her head. "No. He could make fire in his hands. He said she could too and that she had to make the fire to seal the deal. She tried, but she couldn't do it until she got mad because he was hurting me."

Storm said, "Litha made fire in her hands?"

"Yes," Katrina went on. "And he wanted her to call him Dad."

He knew that he'd felt empty since she disappeared into that wall, sort of like a hole had opened up in his middle. It would drive him crazy if he thought she was in danger or being hurt. But if the demon thought he was her father, then maybe she would be…

"Katrina, do you think Litha is safe?"

She took her time answering, as if she was replaying everything. "I think so. He was willing to give up his... revenge against the lover..." She looked at Kay. "- I guess that's you - in exchange for Litha staying with him. But I can't say for sure. He seemed... erratic. I'm worried about her." Tears began to fall again. "She sacrificed herself for me."

"She hasn't sacrificed herself, Katrina. She just struck a bargain to get you both home. Can you remember how long she agreed to stay?" Storm pressed.

Katrina closed her eyes. "He said a year. She said a day. They went back and forth. He said something about stretching time. I don't know." She was getting agitated. "I'm really sorry, Storm."

"For your sake and Kay's we're very glad you're back." Storm's eyes met his partner's. "Tell me what you need." Nobody needed to worry about Katrina now that Kay was awake. He was always going to see to her first.

Elora came around the bed like she was cued and joined Storm in his bid for support. "Do you want to try to move to your own apartment? Are you hungry?"

Kay pulled his chin in so he could look down at Katrina and asked her softly, "You hungry?"

"Maybe."

"We can have a quiet breakfast in my room and then you can go to sleep."

VICTORIA DANANN

She nodded.

"You up to walkin' that far?" Ram asked Kay.

"Guess we're about to find out. I'd like to do it in pants though."

Elora looked at Ram. "How about if I get enough breakfast for everybody and bring it to Kay's place. while you find him some pants." Ram nodded and the two of them left leaving Kay, Katrina, and Storm alone in the room.

Katrina got up and said she was going to the bathroom down the hall. She didn't want to use the one attached to Kay's hospital room because of lack of privacy.

When she was gone, Kay's eyes ran up and down Storm. "You know the funny thing about this is that I think I'm the only one unscathed. Hell. If there's any other really bad stuff in my future, maybe y'all can arrange to just put me out of commission till it's over. What do you think?"

Storm couldn't tell if he was kidding or if he was objecting to being sedated.

"You mad about being tranqed?"

"Nah. What else could you do?"

"I don't know, but, if you do, tell me. For future reference. I mean not that... " Storm didn't know where he was going to go with that or what he'd been thinking when he started that sentence.

"It was the best thing for all of us. For me, too. It wouldn't have helped Trina to come back and find me in a Hannibal Lecter suit.

"Right now the only thing I want to think about is how to make this up to her. It was my fault she was taken. He wanted to hurt me through somebody

I love. And he did. If it wasn't for that witch, it could have been a lot worse." Storm's heart felt a little pinch with the reminder that Litha had exchanged herself for the hostage. "The thing is, he wanted revenge because of something I did on the job. Makes you stop and think. You know what I mean?"

Storm was afraid he did know what Kay meant and started to feel uncomfortable about where this line of reasoning was headed. Never once since he'd been paired with Kay had he ever pictured himself working without him. When he tried to picture that, he saw nothing. They had basically spent their twenties as a partnership and he wasn't ready for a change. It was selfish to think that way and he knew it. But there it was.

He didn't want Kay to continue if it would present a serious danger to him or his family, or if it would be too distressing for Katrina. And he *did* want Kay to continue no matter what.

Waking Woden! When did he start having such a problem thinking things through?

He told himself to remember that there was always a right and a wrong. It was easy to figure out which is which. The right thing was always the harder thing. Always.

Elora had not only arranged for a knight-size breakfast, but talked Simon into letting the engaged couple use a suite like the one she and Ram occupied, for the duration of Katrina's stay. She had people putting Kay's things away in the closet while others were setting breakfast out on the dining table. She wasn't present when they arrived, but a few minutes after they sat down to eat, she bustled in with some things to loan the refugee.

She held out an assortment of toiletries, a robe and a nightgown to Katrina. "If you'll make a list of what you need, I'll go out when the stores open." Much as she tried, she couldn't suppress a yawn and ended the sentence that way. "Sorry. We haven't slept. We were bagging a werewolf."

Kay looked at Ram and saw that he was also running on empty. As a matter of fact, everybody in the room, except for him, looked like they would gladly accept an invitation to just fall down and sleep on the floor.

Kay took the robe from Elora's hands. "Much obliged. I'm going to keep her in bed until tonight at least. The shopping can wait. Why don't you help us eat this feast and then go get some sleep yourself?"

"Thanks, Kay. You're still the best mother hen in Black Swan."

Elora told them about Harry while they ate, omitting the sequence of denigrating remarks about her husband. It was evident that Katrina felt like she had fallen into *the* rabbit hole so Elora stopped and turned her attention solely on the other woman. "I know what it's like to feel like the ground was jerked out from underneath you, but let me assure you that you have landed in the most ideal situation possible – surrounded by these three." She nodded toward Kay, Storm, and Ram. "Having these men on your side means you're ready for anything. They don't come better."

Katrina stared at Elora for a few seconds while

she processed that, then looked around the table shyly and allowed herself just a little smile. "I know."

All three men of B Team were a little moved by Elora's sentimental speech. Being men, they were also a little embarrassed and at a loss for what they were supposed to say to that. Thankfully a knock on the door interrupted the silence.

As master of detail, Simon thought to send up a new cell phone for Kay, since his former phone had been destroyed. Ram got the door then handed him the phone.

Kay looked at it for a minute and then ventured hesitantly, "Did I do any other damage?"

Ram barked out a laugh and Elora shoved an elbow in his ribs. "Ow! Great Paddy, woman, that rib has just finished healin' since the last time you broke it."

"Guess that answers my question," Kay said dryly.

Elora rushed in to supply the details before he had a chance to imagine the worst. "There was a little damage to the Director's outer office. It's already been repaired and even he said it was in need of redecorating. No harm. No foul."

Kay smiled at her effort to make him feel alright about losing control. "I'm sorry I called you a dumb ass."

Ram's head jerked toward Kay and his face flushed instantly as his own notorious temper fired. "You called her a dumb ass?"

Elora put her arms around Ram's mid-section laughing. "He's just being funny. It was a long time ago and he didn't mean it at the time. Actually you were there, but distracted."

Kay nodded. "It's true that it was a long time ago. It's also true that you were there and distracted. But I *did* mean it."

Elora just smiled, shook her head, and pulled Ram out the door. Storm said he might as well have a nap and left shortly after, but not before asking Kay to let him know if Katrina had thought of any other details. Kay assured him that his new phone was at the ready if she did.

"Part of me wants to take a hot bath and climb in bed." Katrina was grateful to finally be alone with Kay. "Part of me is too tired to move. And part of me wants to stay awake and talk about all this." She waved her hand in the air. "About what kind of work you really do. We've always thought you had some kind of high clearance government job, but I pictured you working at a desk. This..." She trailed off, looking around the room like something might be hiding in corners, and not knowing exactly how to finish that sentence.

Kay pushed his chair back from the table, reached over for Katrina, urging her to stand up and come back to the warmth, comfort, and safety of his lap. She snuggled in like she knew exactly where she belonged.

"We'll do it any way you want, but the answers to your questions won't change if you have a nice bath and a toes up. The other thing that won't change - ever - is the way I feel about you."

She rested her head against his shoulder. "I was scared."

"I know."

"You know what I really want?"

"What?"

"I don't want to wait until October for the big ass wedding of the season. Now that I understand just how fast things can change, I want to get married right now. I can't even remember what it was we were waiting for." While she talked, Kay rocked her ever so subtly, so glad to have her in his arms and a little desperate to restore her sense of well-being and security in any way he could. "Just our families and your... these people you're so close to. And I want to do it at the place we've both loved so much since we were kids - your family's river house, with all those sweet memories around us like a good hug." Kay let her know he was listening by giving her a little squeeze. "On the grass. In bare feet while it's still too early in the year for chiggers and stickers."

He laughed softly and kissed the top of her head. "Anything."

Kay had food brought in that night so they could stay put. They didn't talk to anybody else except for the Operations Assistant who delivered Katrina's suitcase to their door. Kay's sisters, bless their hearts, had overnighted it, anticipating that she would need her things. She'd been so ever-present all their lives, they loved her almost as much as Kay did.

The betrothed used their time together well. They bathed. They slept. They ate. They made love. They talked at length about Kay's work, about the history and work of Black Swan. Through Kay,

Simon offered Katrina the best on site psychological trauma counseling available anywhere, and, being a reasonable and well educated individual with no false pretenses, she agreed to talk it out with the pros before she left.

Last, the two of them talked about their wedding.

"I'd like to get married on May Day, but it looks like it's on a Thursday. That's not going to work for your sisters because they just took time off work. We'll have to settle for the third. That's the next Saturday after May Day."

Kay ran his huge hand over her hair. "It's perfect, Trina. So why are you sad?"

She didn't cry, but her eyes got red around the rims and he could tell she was working at holding back tears. "I feel so guilty about Litha. I'm here with you. Free of that..."

"Demon," Kay supplied.

"And she's there in my place. I hope she's safe, but I can't know that."

"Just look how resourceful she is, Sugar. There wasn't a soul in this outfit that thought there was a chance in hell you could be retrieved from another dimension. Criminently. I still can't believe it, myself. And here you are." He just had to gather her in his arms again to reassure himself, again, that she was there and okay. Fully present and accounted for. "It was impossible right up until Litha did it. She's a miracle maker. And one of these days she's going to turn up just like you did."

"You really believe that?"

"On my honor as a Black Swan knight." Kay

felt like a shit lying on his honor as a Black Swan knight.

She gave him an I-adore-you look. "You know it's not at all hard to think of you that way."

He smiled. "What's going to be hard is keeping our secret. No one else can know any of this. Not ever. Not even after I leave."

CHAPTER 16

Deliverance returned a few minutes after he'd left. Litha had barely had time to look around. Not that there was much to see.

The demon nodded toward a section of wall. She turned to see why he'd gestured toward it and part of the wall slid open to a large room beyond that was quite contemporary, if not futuristic. Unlike much of contemporary style, there was plush, comfortable furniture set in a minimalist context with a white shag rug on a terrazzo floor and a glass coffee table. What caught Litha's interest was the view of a dark blue lake with pink gravel beach. *Nope. Not in Kansas anymore.*

He handed her a white paper sack wafting a heavenly aroma that smelled like hamburger and made her salivate, then gestured for her to enter the adjacent room, with the hand that was holding the glass longneck of IBC root beer, also meant for her.

Litha took a quick look around at the surroundings and sat down on a divan. One entire wall of the room was glass looking out at the lake which featured large bowls of fire above the water line and near the shore. One entire wall was made up of a grid of dozens of monitors simultaneously playing TV shows, movies and news. Most of them seemed to originate in her reality... the, uh, Loti

Dimension. A third wall could only be described as an altar to fire and the fourth was smooth, rectangular stones, bare except for an enormous oil painting of a woman who looked a lot like Litha except for her fair skin and light brown hair.

Deliverance slouched on the divan facing hers and tracked her every movement. Until that moment he hadn't realized that it was strange for a demon who certainly never planned to entertain guests, to have furnished his living space with a pair of matching divans that faced each other as if inviting dialogue.

She pointed at the monitors. "Bored much?"

He lifted a bare shoulder. "I like to keep up." He had removed his shirt and shoes after handing over the food.

"I thought you said no hamburgers from London."

He snorted. "That didn't come from London. It came from a 6th Street bar in Austin. Casino el Camino." He casually threw an index finger toward the burger. "Well done with everything including onions *and* jalapenos."

"Texas?"

"Not dignifying that with an answer." He chuckled to himself looking mischievous. "Right now I'll bet there's some irate fool standing at the counter yelling, 'Hey. Where's my burger?'"

"Where did you leave the woman?"

"As agreed... " He inclined his head toward her. "...she was deposited where I took her. The lobby of the Hyde Park Hotel, London, Angland, United Queendom of Great Britannia, Loti Dimension,

Gods Save The Queen." Litha opened her mouth to say something else, but he went on. "*And!* She was in absolutely perfect condition, sound of body and mind, at least to the limited extent of her potential."

Litha took a bite and chewed. "Condescending. Don't you have, uh, sex with humans?"

"Sure. Among others. I'm an Abraxas. I'm nourished by emotion. In my particular case, being a subspecies called Incubus, I can only be sustained by sexual excitement. Don't misunderstand me. I like them. But bottom line, they *are* food."

"Excuse me, but, ew. Trying to eat here."

Deliverance looked unrepentant and amused. "Have you ever seen a biogram of a woman's brain when she orgasms? It lights up with an array of kaleidoscope colors like she's powering up the universe." He looked out the window toward the lake and shook his head a little. "It's amazing."

He turned to watch Litha eat. "I'm sure it 'tastes' better to me than that hamburger does to you."

"No way." She chomped down on a bigger bite.

He smiled. "Glad you like it."

"I get why you don't have a kitchen, but, as you can see, I *do* eat actual food. Are you going to fetch all my meals? I'm a grazer. That means I like to eat little meals. Often."

He snorted. "Little meals like the third pound burger you just devoured in six minutes?"

"I was hungry."

"The answer is no. You're going to earn your food."

Litha stopped chewing. "How?"

"You will dine anywhere you wish, eat anything you wish, anytime you wish, but you have to successfully navigate a pass to get us there."

"Is that hard to do?"

"Not for me." He seemed as perky as if it was all a game.

Litha glanced at the wall where the portrait hung. "What about her? Was *she* food?"

The demon's face fell and for the first time, she saw something other than variations on smugness. It might have been a flicker of guilt or remorse or any one of a hundred emotions. Maybe just plain old sadness.

"No," he said quietly. "I loved her. I still do."

CHAPTER 17

When Kay and Katrina emerged from their hideaway the next morning, they looked like they had been rebooted. Katrina seemed polished bright in her own clothes. Kay looked relaxed and happy. They'd called and asked that Ram, Elora and Storm have breakfast with them in the Director's newly redecorated outer office.

When the little group was assembled, they announced their plans to wed in a week's time and shared that Simon had given them all leave to go to Hunt, Texas for the wedding and festivities. Storm took one look at Kay and knew in his heart what Kay had not yet said; that he wouldn't be coming back.

Elora asked Katrina if there was something she could do to help with the event.

"Thank you, but, you know his sisters are not only on the scene, but they're also very, ah, take charge."

Elora chuckled and nodded. "Yeah. Still, if there's anything that requires lots of brute strength, I'm your girl."

Katrina's eyes drifted upward and roamed over Elora's hair. "That really *is* your natural color isn't it?"

Elora sighed. "I'm afraid so. I've thought about changing it to blend in more because I don't like the attention, but I always chicken out."

"That's not chickening out. It's your heart telling you to be yourself. Plus, there's also the it's-amazing factor."

"Katrina, I like the way you think. Now tell me what the bride is wearing."

After breakfast Kay asked Storm to take a walk. They crossed Princes Street to the Gardens side, walked east and turned right onto the bridge. They naturally fell into the easy and relaxed way in which they were accustomed to interacting with each other. They talked about ideas for the wedding, the logistics of getting everybody there and putting it together so fast and, of course, about how badly Katrina's abduction had scared Kay.

Halfway across Kay stopped on the bridge and leaned on the rail looking off toward Calton Hill. "Probably goes without saying, but just to make it official, I'd like you to stand up with me. Can't dive into the deep end without you at my back. You know I was thinking that best man is kind of a funny expression. This may be the first time in history when it happens to be true."

Storm turned and looked at Kay. "You're not coming back."

Kay looked down at his boots for just a second before meeting Storm's gaze head on. "She doesn't want to wait, says now she understands just how fast things can change. And she's not the only one who's learned that lesson.

"I've got enough money so I can spend however long we've got just trying to make her as happy as a person can be - for however long we've got. And that's what I'm going to do. Make her happy. Keep her safe."

Storm took in a deep breath and let it out. "You're right. She's not the only one who's learned that lesson." He was reliving the feeling that he had when he was standing in a Siena side street with handfuls of beautiful, warm, wicked witch one minute and nothing but silent, unforgiving stone wall the next. "Black Swan will be losing its best."

Kay guffawed. "That is *such* a lie. All three of my teammates are better knights than I am."

"Now *that* is a lie." Kay just smiled, while his eyes wrinkled in disagreement. "I don't have to dance disco, do I?"

Kay laughed. "Polish your boogie shoes, brother."

Storm groaned.

Ram answered the door and invited Kay and Katrina inside.

Elora was shocked when Kay asked both of them to stand up with him.

"Well, of course." He barely got that out when Elora plowed into him for an excited hug. "What did you think? This is a progressive Black Swan team. Ladies welcome."

Katrina smiled when Elora looked her way for confirmation. "He's spent the past twenty-four hours explaining things to me and I agree. It's fitting. As it should be."

They sat down and Kay delivered the news that he wouldn't be coming back to The Order after his honeymoon. There was always a sadness accompanying the turning of a page, but there was usually a joyful anticipation of transition as well. Ram surprised Elora by saying that, since his mate insisted on going wherever he went, he'd been thinking that the only way he could keep her safe was to retire from active duty himself.

It was news to Elora that they were retiring, but she wasn't heavily invested in fighting for Black Swan. The reason she had become a knight in the first place was to be sure she could keep those three men alive. What she really wanted was a nice fifty acres of green grass where she could breed wonderful Alsatians, or rather, German Shepherds and at least one, probably rowdy, strange-haired little boy with beautifully pointed ears.

As counterintuitive as it may seem, sex demons are solitary creatures who prefer to live alone. Normally, sharing a residence would have been torture for Deliverance, but there was something almost divine about this creature who was partly him and partly the witch he loved. He dreaded the day, fast approaching, when he would have to let her go and wished he hadn't been foolishly hasty in telling her that a pact of fire binds even him to an agreement.

He had been forced to relent on his proclamation that she should not eat until she could take them through a pass. He fed her for a full two days while she struggled with acquiring the skill, but finally, on the third day she began to show promise. By the fourth day she had the hang of it.

For a demon, or a creature like Litha with sufficient demon blood, slipping dimensions is only slightly out of the ordinary in the same way a yawn is just a different way of drawing breath. Not painful or difficult. Just different.

The first time Litha successfully slipped dimension without assistance she giggled with a child's delight and Deliverance reacted with an embarrassing rush of sentiment. It wasn't like she was a six-year-old learning to ride a two-wheeler for Cromm's sake!

She learned that most of the passes were about the same size as a large doorway, but that some were huge and in flux like the one off the coast of Florida.

Once she caught on to the possibilities she'd gone a little crazy with wanting to exercise the power. He'd watched her crash a beach bake and eat lobster on the coast of Maine. She'd tried twenty-seven different kinds of seared peppers with flank steak in Rio, crawfish on a pier at Fairhope, Alabama, Szechuan beef in Chongqing province, sushi on a deck with a view of Mount Fuji, and Hungarian goulash in a Budapest bistro.

They fell into the habit of enjoying conversation together during her meal, then they would find a place for her to occupy herself shopping while he took care of his own sustenance. As much as she loved sampling the fare and exploring the cultures of her own dimension, he found her to be aggressively adventurous, for a Terran, when it came to some of the more exotic pleasures available in other dimensions.

By that time she had learned to control her ability to gather fire. She could start fire at will without an emotional stimulus and control the size of the flame, making it as big or small as she chose.

He had proudly introduced her to Sylphic Warriors in a wind dimension where they traveled by sailing just above ground on ships with saffron sails like sampans. He told her that some people called them archangels.

"You're friends with angels?"

"Not a lot. Just like fae sometimes have elf friends."

Litha considered that. "What's the difference between fae and elf?"

"There may be a little difference in dialect? Or in their histories, but the origins are the same."

"So you're saying that angels and demons are basically the same as well?"

"We're children of the ancient elements. Like siblings."

"You know what most humans think."

"Well, they're good at naming things and pointing fingers."

"What does that mean?"

"Sometimes it's who gets there first. The Akasus, which is the species you call demons, angels, and some others, are one of the oldest races that evolved on this planet. By the time other worlds began to produce similar species we were advanced, relative to them. The Nephilim made a hobby of watching the worlds to see when a new batch of upright creatures was ready to be impressed with godlike abilities. They have a sort of perverse need to be worshipped. Fire demons weren't into that and didn't care if the Nephilim wanted to fuck around with primitives.

"My mother told me that, in the old days, they were fond of wearing cloaks covered with white feathers when they went among the primitives. That's how they came to be associated with wings."

"And the, uh, primitives saw some of the demons start fire? And that's where the whole demon from hellfire started?"

"Hmmm. There are some advantages to being trusted the way the Nephilim are. But there are also advantages to being feared."

"It all comes down to spin."

"Well said."

"They... you're... just like us, only more powerful."

"Everything in creation that is sentient is light *and* shadow, Litha. The only absolutes are villains in Batman comics."

"You know, you sound a little like the monks who raised me."

"In that case," he said smiling, "I must meet them. I'm sure we would be great friends." He grew suddenly serious. "Certainly I owe them a lot."

Litha looked thoughtful. "You have a mother?"

Deliverance grinned. "Want to meet her?"

"Yes."

"I haven't seen her for a while. Not since Rosie..." He trailed off and seemed to withdraw into himself.

"Have you explored all the worlds?" The question brought her father out of his reverie.

Deliverance laughed good-naturedly. "No, love, a thousand years isn't nearly long enough for that. On this plane alone there are countless dimensions, some hospitable and some not. Some are not fit for travel because of the occupants and some have been ruined by explosive waste or chemical warfare."

"Do you travel between planes?"

He shook his head. "No. Think of it like a multistory building with eleven stories and each story represents a plane. On that story there are hallways with lots of doors and each of those leads to a different dimension, but there's no elevator or stairway to get from one story to another. There's no proof that there are eleven planes, just speculation. It could be more, or less. As to where we are, we could be on the first floor or the eleventh. The main thing is that there are a lot of possibilities on every plane."

"How do you know which ones you've been to and which ones you want to go to?"

The demon beamed at her like she was the brightest student in the class. "Now here is an interesting bit about your heritage. Only a few of the entities tethered to the earth's gravitational field can move between dimensions and, of those, there are only a few who can do it effortlessly." He smiled and held his arms out like a performer inviting ovation.

"And Abraxas demons are among the few who don't break a sweat." She seemed unimpressed. "Of course only birds can fly effortlessly, but that doesn't stop hu... Terrans from doing it anyway."

"First, birds are not the only creatures who fly. Second, what are you talking about?"

"I know somebody who came to my world from another recently. They call it 'slipping dimensions'. She was transported in a machine."

"Uh huh."

"Well, is there a lot of that going on?"

"I wouldn't say 'a lot' per se."

She cocked a hip and shot him a look.

"It's been going on for a while and the traffic is picking up."

"What's a while?"

"I don't know how far back. It's not a subject that has ever interested me, but certainly all my life." Litha seemed to need a minute to digest the implications of that. "But you sidetracked me while I was trying to make a point."

"Okay. What?"

"Do you understand how special you are?"

He waited patiently while she stared at him for a long time trying to sort out her feelings and decide how to answer. "I could learn to appreciate my demon side."

Just what he was hoping to hear. He moved faster than she could track, grabbed her up in his arms and swung her around like she was a featherweight child. She didn't want to enjoy basking in a father's adoration, but it was hard to be indifferent to someone who behaved like she was the best thing since breath moved upon the waters.

A couple of minutes after he set her down, she recovered her footing and her equilibrium. When her brain began working again, she said, "But you didn't answer the question."

"Hmmm?"

"How do you know which ones you've been to and which ones you want to go to?"

"Oh. Well, that's where your 'gift' for tracking comes in. Once you've been to a given world you can find your way back just by thinking about it. After you arrive, you can track the passes by instinct. Every world has them. At least all those I've visited or heard about. Use a pass to step into the aisle, form an image of the world you want, and presto, changeo, abracadabra, calamazam, there you are."

Litha stared at him for a minute while she processed that.

"How about calamari on Santorini?" he asked.

"Mexican fusion and margaritas at Cabo San Lucas."

"Done."

The sun had shifted in the sky since they'd been seated. Litha finished her margarita and put on her sunglasses. "Back to what you were saying about the worlds I haven't been to..."

"It's time to talk about the less hospitable worlds." He looked around. "Right after lunch."

"I just had lunch." Litha found that she enjoyed teasing him.

"Funny. I meant me and you know it. I'll meet you back here in an hour."

Litha set her shopping bag down on a terrace table with a grand view of a Pacific sunset and ordered a second margarita. After a few minutes, a demon almost too beautiful to look at slid up next to her.

"This seat taken?"

"Yes it is. I'm meeting my father."

"If you favor him, he must be very good lookin'." Deliverance sat down across from her looking "full" and satisfied. "Time to talk self-defense.

"You come with some very fine tools at your disposal. Few creatures can withstand fire. Other fire demons, dragons, proto-salamanders, that's about it. Even if you were attacked by a horde of whatever, you could just call more fire.

"Your body can be pierced by anything from an arrow to a nuclear missile. The first you would survive. The second you would not. Sometimes it's best to run.

"The sylphs can protect themselves with their breath. In fact the older ones could blow you off your feet. They also whip up storms when they're aggravated. Or bored. On your world it gives meteorologists fits. 'Where the fuck did that come from? I predicted blue sky all day.'" He laughed like it was a joke she could share. "The undines can call water the same way you call fire and, although a dump of water on your head won't usually hurt you, it isn't pleasant either. The purview of the trolls is mutable. They're pretty much at the mercy of the other elementals which is probably why they're so disagreeable. You could threaten to scorch the earth, but they'd just laugh at you and tell you to go ahead. Never ask one for help. They're likely to do the opposite of what you need.

"You have no natural enemies, but there are those who would destroy anything they don't understand, without asking questions first. I can't teach you how to gather fire and navigate the passes without also giving you skills to defend yourself."

Deliverance insisted that the demon version of martial arts be added to Litha's education, along with familiarization with other creatures and worlds she might accidentally encounter if she traveled the passes without him, and thus were spent their mornings thereafter. They continued to spend afternoons in the same way as before with Deliverance acting as multi-dimensional tour guide while Litha explored wonders other humans would never see or even know about.

On one such occasion they visited a dimension where she could leap hundreds of feet into the air and land without harm, exerting just the slightest pressure necessary for a small jump in the Loti Dimension. He laughed while she squealed like she was on an extreme roller coaster.

Litha loved to swim. Perhaps that was strange for a girl who was half sexy fire demon, but Deliverance took her to enchanted worlds for her laps workout. She swam in flower filled lagoons with Undine Nymphs in a water dimension and put their beauty to shame by comparison. She swam in oceans that were bathtub clear and could be breathed in and out by humans. She swam in lava pools that sprouted flame like fountains on his home world of Ovelgoth Alla.

They had walked on fire together. She had

played hide and go seek with baby dragons while Deliverance petted their mother into a loud, rumbling purr that made the earth beneath vibrate with her pleasure. The dragon was terrifying and beautiful at the same time. She had amber eyes and shiny red scales with hints of green underneath. When they first came upon her den, she brought her great head up and looked down at them with eyes narrowed in warning, while she huffed warm breath, growled low in her throat and spread her great wings. Litha was ready to run, but the demon told her to be still. He said something in a language Litha didn't understand and sent a stream of fire out from his hand like a twirling ribbon in the air. The dragon sniffed at it, then relaxed and shook her head like a horse. Now she stood docile, rubbing her graceful neck against the demon's torso while he talked to her in low, soothing tones, but she kept an eye on what Litha was doing with the babies the whole time.

Of course it wouldn't have been possible for Litha to play with hatchlings if she was susceptible to fire, since they wouldn't develop control for centuries.

"In terms of Loti Dimension, we are very old creatures, Litha. We are mentioned prominently in your most ancient records."

She considered that for a minute then her eyes flew open wide and she whispered her question as if she'd be struck down for blasphemy if she was wrong. "The Lords of the Flame?"

"Yes." He smiled proudly. "You are descended from an ancient and proud race. Not so long ago,

Terrans were fascinated by us and afraid of us. They knew of our existence, but didn't know what to make of the fact that we ignored them while others were so busy manipulating them and vying for their worship."

After a tour of the strange volcanic beauty of Ovelgoth Alla, Litha met her grandmother, who was an angel in the sense most people thought of.

If she had thought it strange to have a father who looked thirty, it was even stranger to have a grandmother who looked twenty-five. Ariel was joy personified to have her son returned to her as his typically happy self. She alternately hugged him and cried, then wept more when she realized he'd brought her a granddaughter.

Ariel lived in what could only be described as a cave. It had some comfortable furnishings, but was blackened from smoke like most things on Ovelgoth Alla, she supposed, from constant exposure to both fire and smoke. It was odd that Ariel wore white that couldn't be brighter, cleaner, or more pristine. Litha spent an afternoon listening to her grandmother recite the oral history of her race and promised to return for a visit.

Deliverance had never in his long life felt so satisfied as he did observing his mother's ecstatic reaction to Litha. Of course Ariel would embrace her. She was the essence of goodness. He, on the other hand, was a hard sell. But, Litha had risen to every challenge and mastered every task with astounding acumen, almost as if she had the natural talents and abilities of a full-blooded demon. In his eyes she was perfection.

They were saying their goodbyes when they saw Ariel's attention diverted to something behind them. They turned to see three of Deliverance's distant cousins on his father's side. The demon's first thought was that such a visit could never be a good thing.

The cousins bore no resemblance to Deliverance other than his coloring. They were much rougher in appearance, with facial hair that Litha would have called unkempt. They wore clothes in shades of black, brown, and blood red that looked like a combination of leather and large animal scales. Maybe they were clean, but somehow those leathers looked like they could stand up by themselves. Thankfully, she wasn't close enough to tell whether they smelled okay and she hoped she never would be. She would bet it was a look that would be all the rage on some world, somewhere, sometime, but her overall impression of her relatives was that she would be declining invitations to family reunions.

"If it isn't the incubus. How about a chorus of 'What The World Needs Now Is Love, Sweet Love'?"

"Sure. Would you care to accompany me, Rysagoth?"

He laughed. "You haven't been seen here, in your own home world, for a time."

"How would you know?"

"Smoke urchins. Been busy?"

"If it's any of your business, yes, I have. Now, if you'll excuse us, we're just leaving."

"Hold! What's this you brought with you?"

Deliverance didn't like the way his fifth cousin was looking at Litha. "*This* is my guest."

Rysagoth turned to Litha. "Is this true, demoness? You're a guest of his?"

Litha wasn't sure whether she should answer, but taking her cue from her father's somewhat hostile response, she gave the interviewer a level look allowing the demon to respond for her.

"She is not your concern. If you have business, state it now. To me and me only. If not, get out of the way."

Rysagoth's eyes slid back to Deliverance and narrowed. "Have you served the blood debt on your father's murderer?"

He hesitated. "Yes. In my way. I chose a suitable alternative, one that serves me at the same time, in keeping with the spirit of Abraxas custom. I kidnapped his mate."

All traces of amusement were erased from Rysagoth's face. It was not a good look for him. "You kidnapped the killer's mate and call that service of a blood debt?"

"Yes."

"Who are you deceiving? You didn't think Obizoth's kin would let that pass."

"It's not up to you or these..." He nodded toward the two sidekicks. "...others. When it's *your* father you can handle it as you see fit, Rysagoth, and I swear to you now I will not interfere with your judgment on the matter."

"If it was *my* father, I would handle it like Abraxas."

"Well, I'm sure you'll get your chance any day

now because, like you, your father likes to push and one of these days, he's going to shove the wrong Akacus the wrong way."

"Are you insulting my father, Deliverance?"

Deliverance laughed. "You take offense that I accuse you of pointless aggression? Why might that seem insincere?"

Litha looked at her father with a burgeoning respect.

Rysagoth's mouth tightened. "This is the killer's mate?" He nodded toward Litha.

Deliverance looked at her like he was checking to see. "No."

Rysagoth took a step toward Litha. "I'll repeat my question and be cordial about it, but only one more time. Who are you?"

"I'm the daughter of this demon, granddaughter of that one." She nodded toward her grandmother. "And presumably also granddaughter of Obizoth whose death seems to be of great concern to you. I wonder if your interest in him was so keen when he was alive."

The three trespassers looked at each other. Incubus demons didn't often have daughters. It was practically unheard of.

Rysagoth turned his attention toward Ariel. "Consort of Obizoth, does she speak the truth?"

Ariel seemed bright and cheerful in a way that was completely out of place with the scenario playing out before her. "Why, yes, Rysagoth. Would you like some tea?"

Rysagoth ignored her. "What we would like is satisfaction. The female will pay the blood debt."

Litha turned her back on the unwanted company and spoke to Deliverance in a low voice. "That doesn't even make sense. Are they playing with the full deck?"

"Full deck?"

"You know. Are they mentally deficient."

"No. At least I don't think so."

"Okay, well, regardless. Are you ready to get out of here?"

"Yes, love. I'm… formulating a plan."

"Hmmm. What about you, grandmother? Do you want to stay here or go with us?"

Ariel looked completely disoriented by the question. "Go? I stay here, of course. I'm serving tea." She brightened suddenly. "Would you like some?"

Litha cocked her head as she tried to suppress an image of the Mad Hatter tea party. The monks had read the colorful, illustrated version of *Alice in Wonderland* to her when she was a child.

Deliverance leaned close to his daughter and spoke in a tone only she could hear. "She doesn't leave here, Litha, but you don't need to worry about her. She won't be hurt. She's the light." Under his breath he added, "I just wish I could say the same for us."

"What do you...?" She stopped, looked at her grandmother, and shook her head. "Okay. Later. Um, good to know though." To Deliverance she said, "Get ready. We're leaving."

"What do you...? Litha, I don't know what you're thinking, but don't be afraid. I won't let them take you even if I have to threaten to seduce every demoness in this world."

"I know you don't want them to, but.... Really? That would work?"

Deliverance crossed his arms over his chest in a gesture that seemed too relaxed for the current predicament. "Well, yeah. Sure. It would be a little time consuming, but it makes a great deterrent. Demons don't like you to fuck their females."

"Oh? And who does?" Deliverance opened his mouth, but she interrupted before he had a chance to answer. "Rhetorical! How far is the closest pass?"

"Over there. Three sectares."

"Um. Could you convert that to metric? Or Anglish measurement?" Deliverance responded with a blank look. "Forget it." Litha turned around to face the problem head on, frustration and all. "Okay boys. It's been real, but we're done here. Say goodbye. We gotta go."

Rysagoth had one of those laughs that held no genuine humor. He elbowed his companions. "When we leave, you'll be leaving with us, young one."

"You're really going to make me say that's not happening?" They just looked at her as if she was a curiosity. "Okay. That's not happening. Now. Get. Out. Of. The. Way."

"Is this a challenge, daughter of Deliverance? I am Rysagoth Ry Feverloch, Rubicon Tier of Abraxas, from the Second House of Eltii. And the blood of Creation runs in me. What have you on your side?"

She didn't know exactly how to answer that and

wondered why she was bothering. "Um. I can count to three in five languages and the Force is with me." They stared at her as if they were waiting for the rest. "Let's make this easy. First choice, you turn around and leave now. No harm. No foul." They looked at each other like this was not going as expected and it was evident they didn't know how to improvise a Plan B on the fly. "Second choice. You get put in the penalty box for a while to think about how bad you've been."

Deliverance looked at her as if he was seeing her demeanor for the first time. She had taken charge of the situation and was stunning. Catching a small movement out of the corner of his eye, he glanced down. She was drawing a little clockwise circle in the air with her forefinger right in front of her navel as she murmured something he couldn't quite hear. The ruffians started toward her.

"Not leaving?" she asked. "I'll take that as Choice Number Two then."

They continued to advance. She suddenly clapped her hands together loudly, saying, "Adstring ensphaerus." Quickly she drew three larger clockwise circles in the air then extended her arm in their direction and pointed. "Specul thither."

The result was three demons standing in her grandmother's "yard", if it could be called that, looking around as if they were locked in a room without seeing a way to get out. They couldn't see anyone but each other and had no idea where they were.

"Come on." Litha motioned to Deliverance to hurry. "Where's the pass?"

As they ran, he said: "That was astounding. What did you do and how did you do it?"

She spoke in little short sentences because she was practically sprinting and didn't have much air for talking. "I bound them inside a bubble lined with a reflective surface like an old-fashioned coffee can so that everywhere they turn they have to face themselves. It's sort of a forced spiritual retreat for purposes of self-reflection."

"Here." Deliverance ran through the pass. She followed him along the ride and in five minutes they were safe inside his semi-secret lair. He caught his breath quicker than she did and stood waiting patiently with a huge smile on his face.

"All this time that I've been trying to give you tools for self-defense and worrying about what would happen if you tried to ride without me... why didn't you tell me you have etherin level magicks?"

"You knew I'm a witch. The only thing that's changed since I've met you is that now I have an explanation for it. It turns out that I'm an hereditary with an extensive and probably powerful legacy. If that wasn't impressive enough for you, it so happens I'm half demon. Why wouldn't you presuppose that I have an advanced command of magicks?"

"Why indeed?" Deliverance grabbed her up in a bear hug, twirled her around and then dropped her to her feet.

"Hey. Still trying to get my breath here."

He grinned. "The Latin was a little cheesy."

"Yeah? Well, everybody's a critic. Worked though. Didn't it?" She grinned back at him.

Deliverance saw this incident as confirmation of what he had already suspected; that the potent combination of hereditary witch and demon had made his daughter more powerful than either one. The whole was very likely greater than the sum of the parts. Only time would tell the full extent of her unique abilities.

Litha had to admit that the days had passed quickly. Occasionally she thought about Storm and wondered what he had thought and done when she vanished right out of his arms. Of course she knew he must have been surprised, but had that been actual desire she'd seen in his eyes before he accidentally pressed her into a pass? It was hard to look at Deliverance without being reminded of Storm because his black-as-midnight eyes were so very much like those of her father... the demon. She tried to avoid examining that too closely.

An errant question about Storm's own lineage danced across her brain, but she batted it away as fanciful. Certainly he could be her own personal incubus in the sense of being irresistible.

Where Dad was concerned, Litha was beset by a little sadness. He said he liked living alone, but that didn't preclude being lonely.

"Stay with me longer," he pleaded. "There is so much more I'd like to show you."

"Not more relatives."

"No. Not more relatives."

Litha sighed. She would never have expected to feel even a little bit torn. "The way you felt about Rosie, that's how I feel about Storm. I don't want to be away from him any longer. It doesn't mean I don't... that I haven't gotten a lot out of our time together. I just need to see him and try to make him love me."

The demon looked alternately shocked and mystified. "He doesn't love you?"

She sighed and looked out at the navy blue water of the lake. "I... think we were moving in that direction when I disappeared, but he's confused and not ready to admit anything. I'll never know what would have happened unless I go back."

An appropriately demonic and very wicked smile spread over Del's face. "Would you like me to persuade him?"

Litha suddenly stood up straighter as panic crossed her features. "No! I don't... you've got to promise me you'll never..."

He laughed as he threw himself into a soft leather chair. "Just kidding. You have your own innate ability to enthrall. Combine my magnetic hotness with your mother's green eyes and red lips? There's not a dangler in any dimension who could resist."

"Dangler?"

He cupped his generous manhood with his right hand.

She gaped. "Ew! And once again let me say ew! Are we coming any closer to observing those ground rules for acceptable behavior we've talked about? Repeatedly?"

"What's the problem? I'm dressed."

Litha just stared at him, thinking she wouldn't live long enough to bridge the cultural gap. She closed her eyes and inhaled deeply. "Well, you might be surprised how many *danglers* manage to ignore me altogether." She sat down across from him using purposefully graceful movements, having stopped just short of throwing herself into a leather chair exactly as her father had just done. Blood will tell. "I'm glad you think I'm attractive. So long as it's in a *purely* paternal way."

His smug look faded as the demon's face became smooth and serious. "I don't think you're attractive, Litha. I'm absolutely positive you're the most beautiful person in Loti Dimension. And I should know."

"Wow. Maybe having you for a dad isn't completely *awe*-full."

"I shall disown you if you ever twist a pun my way again."

"Disown me?" She laughed. "Wouldn't you have to own me first? Come on. Puns are classified as word humor and word humor is intellectual humor. Therefore, the highest form."

"My house. My rules." He shrugged with the practiced nonchalance of someone who had either been an acting parent for a long time or watched a lot of sitcoms. Litha thought his adaptability was really quite something - perhaps a survival trait, the result of a challenging evolution. "Anyway, I do like the name Storm. It's a good demon name."

Litha didn't have the heart to tell Deliverance that Storm's first name was Angel.

"His eyes are a lot like yours."

His interest sharpened. He was clearly enjoying the idea of that. "Well, then. Perhaps he is kindred to Abraxas demons. And perhaps that's why you are drawn to him."

A smattering of information paraded across her consciousness. Storm had demonstrated innate talent for magicks by nightwalking spontaneously, especially during the instance when he was able to direct the projection of himself. According to his file he was scary smart, considered by many to be the quintessential Black Swan hunter with a record that indicated a gift for "hunches". She couldn't help thinking how ironic it would be if The Order's proudest and best turned out to be part demon.

"You're no' responsible for that harebrained mutt. 'Tis Simon's problem," Ram argued when Elora insisted that she couldn't feel good about leaving with Harry's disposition unresolved.

"Technically you're right, but that doesn't change the fact that it *feels* like it would be wrong to just pick up and leave. I'm the one who told him we'd find him a new home. That sounds a lot like responsibility to me."

Ram softened. "You're always creatin' angst-driven, internal conflicts profoundin' the philosophies of honor and normally, I admire you for it greatly. I truly do. But this time is different because Harry is just no' worth it."

Elora looked up. "You made a verb out of profound?"

She was wearing a filmy scoop neck nightie cut to just above the nipples as she sat on the side of the bed mulling over her husband's point of view. Without self-consciousness she appeared to be concentrating on nothing in particular in the direction of the floor in front of her feet. She heaved a big sigh that caused those barely disguised nipples to press against the see-through fabric.

"Oh, 'tis no' fightin' fair."

She looked up just in time to see Ram pull off the tee shirt he'd just put on and lunge at her.

Elora had been on the phone every day as a volunteer in the search for a new home for Harefoot O'Moors. She had finally convinced the leader of the Elk Mountain Tribe in Idaho to consider taking him in exchange for a sizable donation to the Tribe's treasury by The Order. In some ways the idea of buying a home for Harry seemed distasteful, but Elora was willing to compromise idealism for practicality in this instance.

The timing couldn't have been better. The king was coming to Edinburgh to meet Harry and make a decision. Simon had sent a small charter to Coeur de Lane to pick him up and take him to Spokane where there was a large enough runway for one of The Order's company jets. If they could get this adoption wrapped up quickly, she could leave for Kay's wedding with a clear mind.

She was held up in a meeting with people from the Department of Science and the Department of Interspecies Relations, who had been asking for a chance to question her about her experiences surrounding the journey and adjusting to life in a new world. They had started to piece together some information that might prove useful to the future of interdimensional travel.

It was not a "need to know" meeting. The little

round table group was informal and they were happy to share what they knew or suspected. First, they had figured out that Elora's transport device must have been programmed to search out a delivery destination according to two priorities: the dimension had to have a counterpart to her Monq and there had to be an "Elora placeholder". In this case, it was a young version of herself who had died at age twelve from a case of pneumonia that didn't respond to treatment.

They were proceeding on the working assumption that only one life signature can exist in a single dimension at a time; therefore, the need for a "placeholder". But they were quick to add that the idea was theory in the popular sense of the word and not the true scientific sense.

She had stayed to listen to some of the brain storming theories about other versions of ourselves in alternate dimensions, maybe hundreds, maybe thousands that shared a bit of consciousness that was networked through dreaming; the idea was that some dreams were being simultaneously experienced in another reality by another version of ourselves.

The idea was being proposed that, if another very similar dimension - such as Elora's home world - was close to developing the means by which to slip dimensions, others probably already had the technology and still more would be following shortly. That would mean that, at some point in the future, there could be so many comings and goings as to guarantee chaos. It would be a boon to crime and bounty hunters as well. It could also be a worst nightmare scenario for a secret society whose mission was to keep humanity safe.

One of the biggest surprises for Elora was the fact that the person sitting at the head of the table was none other than her youthful dog sitter, Glendennon Catch. She knew he was doing an internship with the Edinburgh office of The Order, but had never asked exactly what they had him doing when he wasn't responsible for Blackie.

It seemed his ability to find patterns that were, in practical terms, invisible to others was being applied to the files of unsolved cases and to issues of preparedness for what multi-dimensional travel might mean to the future of the organization. Elora noticed that, whenever anyone said anything, all the esteemed heads turned to see how Glen would react.

She looked at him like she'd never seen him before and it appeared that, in some ways, she hadn't. She gave him a look that said, "No. Way. Shut the fuck up!"

Joining the wordless dialogue, he gave her a little shrug and a boyish grin that she interpreted as, "I know! Right?"

Just as they started talking about the possible future need for a Department of Multi-Dimensional Anthropology, Biology, Psychology, and Linguistics, she looked at her watch and practically leaped from her chair. Offering quick apologies, she jogged to Simon's office and hoped the werewolf king had been delayed.

To her relief, she wasn't late at all. Simon put his phone away, but as he rose to greet her his eyes moved to fix on something behind her. The werewolf king had arrived.

Elora turned to see a striking male striding toward them purposefully. He might have been younger than he looked. He had a deep tan, and excessive time spent in the sun tends to age skin prematurely and deepen lines. He appeared to be, perhaps, mid thirties in human terms.

Everything about him looked hard and unmoving except for full, youthful lips and long, shiny, silky-looking hair. He wore a silver gray business suit that matched the color of his eyes. It appeared to be an Italian fitted, silk and wool blend with just enough sheen to suggest expense without looking like gangster chic. The fact that it was three pieces made the incongruity even more intriguing.

His medium brown hair fell to his shoulder blades and, though at odds with the look of the suit, he had used a leather thong to catch it at the nape of his neck like a symbol implying, "Do not mistake for domesticated." That hair had the sheen of youth and vigor, naturally highlighted with sun streaks ranging in shades from lighter brown to blond. It was a look that high-end salons in fashion capitals had tried to recreate without success.

Elora was thinking: "Geez. And some people say *my* hair is pretty."

On the streets of Edinburgh he would draw attention for the depth of his suntan alone. Of course, there was plenty more to make him stand out from a crowd than just sun kissed skin.

The werewolf's pulchritude was not the least compromised by the gorgeous fall of hair. If anything, it offset and accentuated his blatant masculinity. He walked with the athletic grace of a wild animal, but also with the self-confidence of a man who had slept in a vat of testosterone. Since he had left his suit coat unbuttoned, the eye was naturally drawn to the fact that every stride pulled the pants fabric tight enough to accentuate that he was well endowed.

Elora gave herself an internal slap for letting her eyes wander toward his crotch. As soon as she realized she had done it, she jerked her gaze upward. Too late. Though his expression was passive, his eyes said, "Caught you looking."

It wasn't that she was interested. She was mated well and true. It was just that he was a commanding figure who was extraordinarily gifted in the department of male packaging.

"Stalkson Grey?' Simon asked.

The werewolf gave no response, but continued to stare at Elora. His expression, which was already hard and unyielding, seemed to be growing stonier with every second that passed.

Ram finally arrived with Harry. As they were approaching from behind, Ram heard a low, almost inaudible, but unmistakable growl coming from Grey.

"Hey! 'Tis my mate you're bloody growlin' at!" When Ram's natural mate instincts roared to life, he forgot all about the fact that Elora was in a better position to take care of herself than any other humanoid on the planet. He started toward the wolf, but Harry grabbed him by the shoulder and spoke to Elora.

"Lady Laiken, the king is becomin' distressed by your refusal to look away." Harry kept a symbolically restraining hand on Ram's shoulder.

Elora did not take her eyes away from Grey, but her expression changed to uncertainty and her brows pulled down into a small frown. "What do you mean look away?"

"Kings do no' like to be looked in the eye for longer than a couple of seconds. They expect others to look away."

At that Elora did jerk her gaze toward Harry. She stared for a couple of beats and then laughed like it was a practical joke. "You're kidding, right?"

Harry shifted his weight from one foot to the other out of nervous habit. Meanwhile, the visiting werewolf held the same unforgiving pose, but seemed just a little less menacing now that Elora's attention was focused elsewhere. "No ma'am. I'm no' kiddin'."

Elora pulled her chin back and gave Grey a look like he was a circus exhibit. "Why would he expect others to look away?"

Harry put his hands in his pockets and studied the carpet by his toes. He mumbled, "To establish dominance."

"Beg your pardon?" Elora tried not to sound exasperated. "Harry, I can barely understand you even when you speak up. Say that again."

Harry looked up at Elora, but seemed embarrassed.

Simon interjected. "Some of the tribes uphold the old werewolf customs." To Grey he said: "Thank you for coming all this way, my lord. We are honored to have you and regret that our personnel have limited experience in the actual presence of lupans."

Grey still did not look away from Elora, who had resumed staring at the king of the Elk Mountain, Idaho reservation lupan tribe. Elora was indignant. Without looking away, she said to Simon: "You're apologizing for *me* because I'm not going to let some pretty boy wolf strut into Order headquarters and behave like a schoolyard bully?"

The corner of Grey's right eye twitched slightly when she said "pretty boy" and she noted, with a little satisfaction, that his eyes sparked right after the taunt. He was probably cursing himself for practically wincing, divulging weakness and his agitation was escalating again. Elora was reacting with hostility of her own keeping pace with the tightening spiral.

"And, furthermore," she said, "I don't really want Harry placed with someone whose self-importance depends on mindless demonstrations of tyranny."

Simon and Ram groaned simultaneously. Simon said, "Crap," pinching the bridge of his nose with thumb and forefinger like he was developing a headache.

"'Tis fine ma'am," Harry found his voice and interjected. "I can adjust to a tribe that's a little old-fashioned. I will just be happy to be with others of my kind."

Elora looked at Harry like he'd grown an extra head. "Harry, you can't mean that you want to go with this..." She scrutinized the werewolf king by unapologetically looking him up and down, "...despot."

That pushed the werewolf to the end of his tether. He took a threatening step toward Elora and snarled so loudly she could hardly believe the sound came from a face that seemed so human. Acting purely out of reflex, before the wolf could even know she had moved, Elora had lifted him and slammed him onto his back. Relative to her capability she used great restraint, but a body slam was still a body slam. And it hurt.

He was initiating snarl phase of the domination ritual. Then, the next thing he knew he was on his back on the floor with no breath in his lungs, with a woman on one knee holding him down. The impertinent female's hand pressed lightly, but with undeniable authority, around his neck, thumb threatening his carotid artery.

She didn't break anything. Thankfully. But the air had been forced from his body. He stared at her face in shock while he turned various shades of blue and purple waiting for lungs to wake up. Finally, he drew in a ragged breath and his color began to return to normal. After a few minutes he had refilled his lungs and was breathing normally again. He turned his head to the side to expose his neck.

When he did so, Harry hissed in a breath and turned away. "He has submitted to you. It's over."

Elora said to the werewolf who was currently on the floor and at her mercy: "Submitted huh. You'd better be bloody glad that I didn't give your snarly snout a firm tap with the heel of my hand or else you'd be returning to Moose River..."

Ram cut in. "...Elk Mountain."

"...yes, Elk Mountain, with a broken pecker."

She released Grey and got to her feet. When she looked around, she realized that all the men were staring at her. "What?"

Ram cleared his throat. "Em, when you say 'pecker', would you by any chance be meanin' the werewolf's nose?"

"Yes. Of course. What else would I mean?"

"Well, in this culture, pecker also refers to... em. Never mind. I'll be explainin' later on then." He gave her a small smile and a pointed look. "In private."

Everyone in the room was prepared for the werewolf king to rise and go storming away in a huff - a version of the-werewolf-has-left-the-building and taken Harry's chances for normalcy with him. Instead, he stayed where he was for a few more minutes and then began making noises indicating amusement. It started with a small chuff that turned into a chuckle and rose to the crescendo of a full out hardy laugh.

When Elora held her hand out to help him up, he took it. Once on his feet he looked back and forth between Simon and Elora.

"Seems I've grown complacent and arrogant in my expectation that everyone in my presence recognize my, apparently exaggerated, importance.

"I suppose I needed a reminder that I'm king of Elk Mountain. Not the world.

"Stalkson Grey." He said his name as he held out his hand to Simon. "I apologize for ignoring you earlier."

Simon shook his hand and nodded toward Elora. "This is Lady Laiken, knight of The Order of the Black Swan." Grey smiled and the redistribution of facial musculature altered his entire persona. He morphed into someone who looked relaxed, approachable, and definitely more handsome. "I believe the two of you have been communicating by telephone about the possible adoption of Harefoot O'Moors?"

Grey's face looked so completely different when he wasn't trying to force others to look away, a concept that would forever strike Elora as, well, stupid. Her feeling was that, if people could walk on two legs and hold a teacup, shifter or not, they should be held to a certain standard of civility.

"Yes. We have." He turned to Elora. "At the moment I'm feeling extremely grateful that you are not wolf or you might be attempting to claim the entire earth. And I cannot say for certain you wouldn't succeed."

Now that it had been established that Elora Laiken was more dominant, Grey seemed friendly, ingratiating, well-mannered, and almost charming. She found the transformation somewhat welcome and bizarre.

Elora introduced Ram and Harry, then Simon invited Grey to sit on one of the sofas. A few minutes after they were seated, a catering assistant wheeled a stainless steel cart into the room laden with a full tea service including mouthwatering pastries, fruit, and, of course, chocolate - the food of the gods.

The werewolf king graciously accepted a cup

of Orange Pekoe tea, but declined sugar saying it slowed him down. Elora quietly snorted into her cup.

They talked about the Elk Mountain reservation, about its pristine wilderness and unrivaled beauty. He shared that in-breeding had become the overriding issue of the day for the heads of tribes and that they were in the process of exchanging wards, young females who would live under the protection of the kings and be raised by the tribes into which they would eventually infuse the blessings of new blood.

"For the past generation we've been whelping far more male than female offspring. Not just my tribe, but, we think, all. We don't have an explanation as to why this is happening, but there aren't enough mates to cool the fevers of young bloods, much less for those like myself who have lost our mates."

"You lost your mate?" Elora's expression toward Grey softened. "I'm sorry." For just a second she glanced at Ram thinking loss of a mate was unimaginable. "How long ago?"

"Seven years."

"And you can't remarry?"

"I could, if there were sufficient females and if I was so inclined. Which I'm not."

"What about humans? Our dog sitter is quarter werewolf. So we know it happens."

The king smiled indulgently. "Certainly we can perform sexually with other closely related species, but only a pure pairing produces shifters."

"Hmmm," Elora started. "Excuse me, I don't

mean to speak out of turn or interpose where I'm not invited..." Ram, who had been taking a drink from his teacup, spluttered at that, choking, and was repeatedly beat on the back by Harry with more than necessary force. Elora shot Ram a dirty look. He, in turn, glared at Harry who just smiled like he had thoroughly enjoyed the experience. "But maybe it would make more sense to have pow wows."

The others in the room looked at each other blankly and then said at once. "What's a pow wow?"

"Well. Where I come from there is a large network of aboriginal human tribes that hold regularly scheduled, intertribal festivals. They take place in various locations and last for days at a time. People come and camp out.

"The gatherings serve multiple purposes. They preserve customs and history. They celebrate the culture with games, music, and dance. They establish contacts that may be useful economically and politically, and..." she looked at Grey pointedly, "the young have a chance to meet each other and interact.

"That way, *all* the burden for healthy proliferation doesn't fall to young females who would, without a doubt, prefer to be with their own tribes and families while they are developing into women. Unless your goal is to traumatize them into abject subjugation so early that they never fully mature."

"Laiken!" Simon was instantly replaced with Director/Diplomat Tvelgar who was on his feet and ready to spit fire.

The werewolf's mouth twitched and he held up a hand toward Simon while he said to Elora: "I appreciate the suggestion, but werewolves are extremely territorial, suspicious of outsiders, and we tend to express that in violent ways. Having so many together in one place could be a very big gamble, the stakes being lots of blood, ruined trade agreements, and the initiation of feuds that could last for generations."

"I see."

"However, we need more than territory and non-interference to survive in the modern world and evolution is all about adaptation. I will consider the prospect, talk to some of the other leaders and see what they think. The potential for reward might be worth the risk."

"Now," he turned to Simon, "is there someplace where the loner and I can talk awhile?"

"Certainly," said Simon, standing and gesturing toward his inner office. "Please use my office. Take as long as you need."

Harry and the king disappeared behind doors and Elora slumped back against the sofa.

"You need a course in diplomacy, young lady." Simon glared at Elora.

"*You* need a course in loyalty, Director," she shot back. "And don't call me young lady. I didn't like that shit when I was one and I *really* don't like it now."

Looking at Simon, Ram sat back shaking his head and crossed his arms over his very photogenic abs. "Oh. You have done it now."

Simon ignored Ram and stared at Elora until

she finally said: "*Please* tell me *you're* not trying to 'establish dominance' by gawking. It can't be contagious."

"Lady Laiken, this situation seems to have turned you out of sorts. I'm sure you do not intend to be challenging a superior."

Ram made some garbled noise that had them both turning to look at him reprovingly.

Elora continued. "Look, Simon, I spent most of my life being *painfully* polite. When I came to your world I was set free to speak the truth and I've been enjoying life a lot more."

Having calmed just a little, Simon nodded. "I believe we understand each other on that account. However, this organization has not endured for centuries, no, not just endured, but flourished, by allowing anarchy within the ranks.

"While you're away on leave for your teammate's wedding, I hope you will carefully consider the merits of a reasonable expectation of discipline. Surely Sovereign Nemamiah had a similar working relationship with you?"

Elora jerked her head at Ram daring him to make a sound. He responded by blinking with the innocent expression of a cherub.

"Okay," she said in a conciliatory tone. "I hear you."

After an hour, Harry and Grey emerged from their closed session. Harry was beaming.

"Director Tvelgar," said the werewolf king, "the Elk Mountain tribe will adopt Harefoot O'Moors according to the terms discussed with your representative."

Simon was clearly delighted. "That's very, very good news. We can arrange transportation for tomorrow evening and hope you will accept our hospitality until then."

"Gladly," he replied. "Lady Laiken, Harefoot tells me you were even more instrumental in this placement than I had known. I would like to personally thank you for being kind and patient with my distant kinsman and with this process."

"No thanks necessary. I'm good with canines."

Grey grinned broadly, showing very showing off beautifully white canines that were just a tad longer and sexier than what is typical for humans. "Lupines," he corrected.

Ram cleared his throat and coughed into his hand. "Told you so."

Turning toward Ram, Grey said: "I apologize for growling at your wife."

"Accepted. Do no' try it again."

The king laughed. "I assure you I will not. Scotia has been conceded to the Lady. And, knowing that she thinks I'm pretty changes everything."

"I would no' be too proud of that. She thinks everyone is pretty."

Ignoring that, Elora said, "One more thing."

Simon, Ram, and Harry all groaned in unison.

"We know someone who is beyond brilliant when it comes to solving problems. Scientifically. He's probably smarter than Einstein."

Grey looked confused. Simon said, "Who's Einstein?"

"Never mind. The thing is, there are never any

guarantees, but he has a remarkable record. We could ask him to look into your gender balancing problem if you like."

For a minute or two Grey seemed to be studying Elora as if he was trying to see into her head.

"Monq?" Simon asked simply glancing at Elora. She nodded.

Looking thoughtful, Grey said, "I'm afraid that any investigation would be handicapped by a lot of restrictions. My people would resist experimentation and would strongly object to researchers wandering around our territory."

"Perhaps there are ways to work around those things. Let's see if we can set up a meeting. One step at a time?"

Grey nodded with his mind racing ahead, already clutching at the hope that they weren't looking at extinction after all. "Thank you."

"You're welcome. Let's get your problem solved and get you mated. I can vouch from personal experience that it will do wonders for your mood," she said.

Simon was gripping the back of a wooden chair so hard he almost snapped it in two, but the werewolf king just laughed a winsome laugh, shaking his head of gorgeous hair, and, once again showing off teeth that almost qualified as fangs.

VICTORIA DANANN

CHAPTER 18

The little band of travelers were packed and ready to leave Edinburgh just in time to avoid the Beltane crowds. Pagan celebrants would descend on the city from all over Britannia and Europa for the spectacular Beltane Fire Festival that took place at the temple at the top of Calton Hill at sundown the last night of April. Some were already arriving to help as volunteers or to set up for costuming or body painting.

On the cusp of May it doesn't get dark until after ten o'clock and is typically quite chilly at that hour for the non-fae, but pagans were a hardy lot and nothing stopped the festivities from going forward.

Elora had found Edinburgh magical in every way except shopping options. The fae were quite woefully lagging behind the rest of the Western world's understanding of contemporary fashion. So she had hitched a one-hour ride on a morning flight to London, spent much of the day shopping and did the reverse in the late afternoon. She hadn't planned on a shadow, but Ram quoted the folkage about the gander and the goose saying, if she was going to insist that he didn't go on assignment without her, he would insist that she didn't travel to London without him. How could she say no to that? Truthfully, he would have gone in any case, but that was superfluous information she didn't need to know.

The night before they left she slipped away to knock on Song's door. New recruits were not assigned luxurious or spacious quarters. They usually got dormitory style rooms for orientation and initial internships. When the door opened, Elora saw that the roommate was in, so she beckoned Song out into the hall.

"Sup?" she said.

"Take a walk?" Elora asked.

Song looked intrigued. "Aye. Let me lay hold of a coat."

"No." Elora shook her head emphatically. "I don't mean outside. Ram would make me pay in ways I can't share with his little sister if I took you out in '*Fairyland*'."

Song chortled. "And what is our Plan B then?" While Elora looked around trying to decide, Song said, "Let us make this easy." She opened the door and leaned back into her quarters. "Gaia. Would you be the best roommate ever and surrender the room for a few minutes? I'll owe you."

"Sure," Gaia agreed cheerfully. "I need a chai anyway. Want something?" She grabbed her purse and smiled at Elora on the way by.

"Gigantic coffee with cinnamon, saffron fluff and a cocoa for the Lady."

"No. Thank you. I won't be staying that long."

Song leaned out into the hall and called after Gaia. "Skip the cocoa."

They heard a distant confirmation that sounded like, "Okay.'"

Song closed the door and motioned toward the bed inviting Elora to sit.

"This won't take long."

"You've got at least fifteen minutes before she returns and, of course, as long as you like afterward."

"So. I guess you know why I'm here."

Song looked mystified. "Em. No?"

"Ram told me you're the..." Elora fanned her hands out in front of her dramatically, "...all seeing eye with steel trap lips."

"What?" Aelsong was starting to wonder if a practical joke was coming.

"I thought you know everybody's future."

Aelsong laughed, shaking her head, and sat on the side of her bed gesturing for Elora to do the same. "A serious misimpression. It does no' work like that. I must be deliberately seekin'. 'Tis all about intention. If I just got images rollin' past willy nilly, I would have gone mad as a mercury press long ago."

"Willy nilly."

"Aye. You know. Willy nilly."

"Okay. Well, here's the thing then. We haven't had a chance to really get to know each other yet, but I grew up oldest of six. I had five sibs in my own world and two of them were girls. So I have experience being a big sis and I'm comfortable in the role."

"Oh. Aye." Song looked like she wondered where this was going.

"While we're gone for Kay's wedding, you'll be here completely on your own." Song nodded. "Away from home for the first time." She nodded again. "So, on that note, I'm volunteering to put my nose where it wasn't invited and offer advice. It will be best if you take every care to avoid Duffy for now."

Aelsong looked a little baffled, a little surprised, and a lot paler. "Duffy?" she asked cautiously.

"The Prince. You do know his name is Duff and his hooligan friends call him Duffy?"

Song nodded ever so slightly while her expression read shell-shocked. "How did you know?"

Elora pointed at her face with two fingers. "Eyes."

"We were so obvious?"

"Apparently not. Astonishing as it is, I seem to be the only one awake enough to see what is plain as day." Song blew out a breath of relief on learning that her brother was unaware. "I'm going to do everything in my power to help you, but it's going to take some time and a miracle or two."

She was looking at Elora with wide, hopeful eyes that could break Elora's heart. "People around here know how to make miracles. Right?"

Elora cocked her head while she appraised Aelsong. "Can you read for yourself?"

Song shook her head. "That would be handy, but my own future just whirls around like... sort of like smoke. If I try to force it, I see bad things - no' the actual future - things scary enough to make me stop askin'."

"And you can't ask anyone else in this department to read for you because of what they might see."

"Aye. Exactly."

"Well," Elora reached over and patted Song's hand, "when we get back I will start working on your mother and your brother. And your other brother. But it must be gradual. It's a big change we're hoping for. And Duff is going to see how far he can get from his side."

Song's lips parted and she hissed in a little air. "I saw you speak to him."

Elora smiled at her sister-in-law's reaction. "Guess what we talked about. Indirectly, of course."

Song's eyes coated with a dreamy expression. "He was *so* gorgeous in his kilt, was he no'? It made my heart hurt."

Elora looked a little wistful, knowing exactly how it felt to love a male so beautiful you never wanted to look away. "Indeed. He is a real life Prince Charming."

Song looked confused. "You mean he's a charmin' prince?"

Elora sighed. She might never get used to living in a dimension without fairytales. "Right. Anyway. He says he has nothing personal against elves and thinks that continuing the feud is silly. That was his word. But he also said that, if I quoted him on that, he would be forced to deny it. He thinks there is a growing movement among some of his peers to resolve the dispute and put an end to the animosity."

Aelsong looked even more enraptured. "He said that?"

"Yes. That does not mean it will happen. He indicated that the mission is daunting from his side."

"Aye. 'Tis from mine to be certain."

"So we're agreed? You'll lay low while I'm gone?"

"Lay low?"

"It means be super discreet and prudent."

Song grinned. "I shall lay low like a rug."

Gaia kicked at the door lightly and they heard a muffled, "Hands full. Get the door."

Aelsong opened the door to let her roommate in.

Elora stood and readied herself to leave. "Don't tell your brother I was here."

"Alright then. Why no'?"

"Because, due to a turn of events that couldn't possibly be more ironic, I believe he thinks I'm a bad influence on you."

Song blinked twice before erupting into a toothy laugh that started in her belly and ended deep in her throat. Enough said. Elora got a quick hug goodbye and was gone.

An hour later there was a knock at Aelsong's door. She opened it to find Ram standing on the other side. As Song turned toward her roommate, Gaia just clicked her laptop closed and said: "On my way for cookies. Want some?"

Aelsong was thinking she could have done a lot worse than getting Gaia for a roommate. "Thanks.

We won't be long." She looked at Ram. "Will we?"

He shook his head.

When they were alone, Ram sat down at the end of Song's bed.

"All packed?" she asked.

"I imagine so. Elora likes to oversee the preparations personally. I believe she's afraid I would take only concert tees and pants with holes if left to my own devices."

Song smiled. "Would you no'?"

He nodded and then smiled just a little sheepishly. "To be certain. I would." Ram cleared his throat and looked uncomfortable. There was no such thing as a bad look on Rammel, but it was an expression rarely seen. "Before I leave you on your own, in this place where we are no' welcome, I want to be sure you understand that the fae are only one cause for wariness. There are others."

He paused to see if she was paying attention.

"Go on," she said.

"The humans are more different from us than... the obvious. Their culture can be very strange sometimes."

"Aye." She prompted him again.

"For instance, in matters of unmated sex, they are full of conflicts and hypocrisies. After all these years among them I have still no' quite got it figured out. The males want sex and find it highly pleasurable, like us, but often, the similarity ends there. Instead of praisin' their gods for the delights of couplin', many of them believe a female is tainted by bein' willin' and that enjoyin' more than an occasional boyfriend compromises her character.

They use ugly names to describe their partners after.

"Truly, 'tis enough to make your head hurt tryin' to sort out." He gave Aelsong a look like he was willing her to understand. "I know it does no' make sense, but this is who they are."

The idea that a woman's reputation could be tied to sexual behavior was foreign to elves, but she knew that what her brother was telling her was true and she was touched that he was trying to protect her from hurt feelings.

She nodded. She could probably count the instances when she'd had a serious conversation with Ram on one hand. "Thank you for tellin' me."

He stood and gave her a perfunctory hug. "Just do no' be tellin' my wife that I was here. She believes, where you are concerned, that I... I think the word she used was 'hover'."

Aelsong grinned. "Swearin' on Paddy's heart I can no' be made to tell."

Travel from Edinburgh to the Texas Hill Country would normally involve at least two changes of planes, but Simon graciously arranged for them to take a company jet all the way to San Antonio at The Order's expense as a wedding present.

Kay's sisters had transport waiting to move passengers and luggage the rest of the way to Hunt. Dandie met them at the private hangar long enough to supervise. She had a van waiting with enough legroom for B Team boys plus Elora and Katrina. She handed the keys to Kay. She had also hired a local kid with a pickup to stash the luggage in his truck bed and follow the van. He was clearly thrilled to get the job. When Dandie was satisfied that all was well, she left for the main terminal to pick up her boyfriend and two cousins.

Soon after the tiny caravan was on the western side of Kerrville, the topography changed dramatically from the dry and brushy goat country they had just passed through.

Kay pulled over for a beer stop. It seemed that setting boots on Texas soil caused Kay to morph into a connoisseur of long necks. Elora noticed that his vowels were more engaged and that his facial muscles seemed more relaxed.

The little log country store at Ingram was open air at that time of year. It had a screen door that swung both ways and a large, black Doberman who sat on a stool by the cash register keeping an eye on things. After looking them over, he jumped down from the stool, picked up his hot-dog-shaped toy, pushed the screen door open, and trotted around the corner out of view.

The cashier, who may have also been proprietor, was an older woman with a ready smile and body language that gave the impression of unhurried, small town warmth and generosity. She had a round face that looked permanently pinked by either heritage, sun, or long necks. Who could say? She remembered Kay and welcomed him back.

When the pit stop was over, the travelers reclaimed their places in the van as if their seats had been assigned and they pulled back onto the two-lane highway. Within minutes they were driving a road that followed right alongside the Guadalupe River, curving when it did, which was constantly, undulating gently up and down with the hills. It was one of those unhurried journeys you hear about that's more important than the destination. Elora thought the water was too beautiful to be natural.

"Kay, do they dye the river water that color like they do at amusement parks?"

Kay and Katrina looked at each other and laughed at the question. "Nope," he said. "It's really that green. All by itself."

Storm said nothing, but silently agreed that he had never seen water look both clear and deep green. It was exactly the color of Litha's eyes. And, for the hundredth time that day, he wondered where she was and wished he knew she was okay.

They came over a rise to a stretch where the river suddenly got much wider and, Storm suspected, much deeper. The road veered away in another direction just as the vehicles turned left onto a white gravel road. Kay's family owned a big, old, white two story house with a huge expanse of lush green grass sloping down to the river where a yellow and green pontoon floated in invitation on water still enough to look like glass. There were several yellow canoes turned upside down and sitting on the grass by the river.

It seemed that Kay's family owned a little piece of heaven. No wonder Katrina had abandoned the idea of a big Houston society affair for a barefoot wedding here.

Kay's sisters had been there for days getting the house ready and making arrangements for a practically impromptu wedding. They came running out to welcome the bride and groom and their guests.

"Come on in and we'll show y'all where you're sleeping." Urz had assigned herself the role of wedding services manager and taken charge of room assignments. She said that the parents and the close relatives would be staying at the resort and some of the nicer river cabins nearby and that it hadn't been that hard to accommodate everyone on short notice since school was still in session.

They had decided to keep the house for the exclusive use of the wedding party.

There were three bedrooms upstairs. She put Kay in one, then asked Ram and Storm which of them would like to volunteer to sleep on the cot on the screen porch in back.

Storm volunteered immediately even though he knew that the word "cot" meant feet hanging off the end. He didn't examine his motives too closely, but truthfully, things had changed so fast his head was swimming. It felt like one day he was firmly and securely entrenched as part of a team of four Black Swan knights, as close as people can be on the outside of the womb. He blinked once and two of them were married. To each other. And expecting.

He blinked again and a third, his own partner, announced he was not just getting married, but leaving The Order. As proof that the world could actually stand on its ear, even the former arch vampire, Istvan Baka, now worked for The Order as the respected, *human* head of the Great Inversion Task Force.

Everyone seemed to have a place in this new world but him. So, taking the cot on the back porch, a place that was neither outside nor in, seemed like the perfect fit - a symbolic representation of the place where life had deposited him. Or spit him out.

The five women were directed to the bunk room which had three built-in bunks, designed to sleep six, so that each of the three girls could bring a friend.

"Stop right there." Kay halted Urz in mid command. "There's enough room for Trina to stay with me and I like her where I can see her."

Urz was resolutely shaking her head. "Out of the question, Bubba. The next time you're sleeping with the bride is *after* you've said, 'I do'."

There was no doubt Kay wasn't completely on board with that plan. Katrina gave him a look of resignation that said: "What can we do? Your big sister has the whistle."

"What about me?" Ram insisted. "I already said, 'I do', and I want this heavenly body..." He put his arm around Elora's waist and pulled her close to him as if to illustrate which heavenly body he meant. "...in the double bed next to me."

Urz looked at Elora with eyebrows raised. "It's your choice, but we thought it would be fun to have a two-night-long slumber party."

Looking at her determined expression and hands on hips, Elora was thinking that not even a Black Swan knight would bite that off without good cause.

"Sorry," Elora told Ram. "But, look, I'll be just down the hall."

"That's no' the same thing."

Elora was trying to remember if she'd ever seen Ram pout before. *Gods*. It was like he couldn't seem to do anything that wasn't thigh numbing sexy. She wanted to throw herself at him and grab that plump bottom lip between her teeth.

Kay had enough experience with his sister to see defeat when it was coming. He rested a big bear paw on Ram's shoulder. "Well, Rammel. I've known these women a long time and I can assure you there's no point in arguing. So, tell me. Did you happen to pack some of that fine Irish whiskey?"

CHAPTER 19

It was the first day of May, known as May Day to some and Beltane to others, the first of four fire festivals in the pagan year. In the Celtic lands of older times, the rituals were initiated with beacon fires lit on hilltops the eve before. It was a day dedicated to procreation and fertility, a joyful celebration of the renewal of life evidenced everywhere the observer cared to look. Sprouts of new crops were breaking through the earth. Young animals were at play in the fields.

While such things might seem to occupy the fringe of our concern in contemporary times, people of European descent had a pagan core programmed deep within the psyche, perhaps on the cellular level, and it unerringly responded to observing the changes of season. Such observances *felt* familiar. Familiar and right. It would have been a mistake to think of Beltane as a simple fuck fest.

Of course, a holiday intended to celebrate fertility and procreation did involve *some* devil-may-care revelry.

"Anybody thought about dinner? I'm getting hungry," Kay asked his sisters.

"Got it covered, Bubba. The Cat House is sending people over and they'll be here any minute. We're eating out in back tonight." She picked up a can of peanuts and tossed it at him. "If you can't wait, crack that open and knock yourself out."

"Cat House?" Ram asked.

Elora gave him a flat handed smack on the six-pack in mock reprimand. "You sounded *way* too interested for my liking and *way* too hopeful."

Ram laughed and reached for her. "You know perfectly well that I'm a well-mated elf who could no' be more settled or more satisfied." He pulled her onto his lap and nuzzled her decolletage. "I would no' trade you for a thousand cat houses."

Kay smirked at Ram. "Better watch what you say or you'll end up with a matched set of broken ribs.

"Cat House is the name of the local catfish restaurant. You aliens, and that's everybody who's not from Texas, are going to get a treat you'll never forget."

The caterers arrived from the Cat House towing a large, outdoor grill. With experience guiding a practiced choreography, they fired up the grill and started frying catfish, French fries, and hush puppies in wide, shallow iron skillets. The air was filled with tantalizing aroma.

Standing outside on the lawn with an ice tea in her hand, Elora leaned into Ram. "I can feel my arteries hardening just from smelling this food."

He grinned at her. "I do no' care. I'm eatin' till I can no' stand up. And, you know, it may damage your credibility as an expert on nutrition when half your daily consumption is chocolate."

Overhearing that exchange, Katrina told Ram to eat slowly and be careful of the bones.

Elora thanked the gods that the Cat House had also brought some mixed green salad along to break up the grease. Sure it all tasted good. Everything tastes great when you fry it in grease. They also brought some pecan pies which held no interest for her whatsoever until someone mentioned the Texas Chocolate Pecan pie with Blue Bell ice cream. She rose to go that direction as if the Morlock gong had been struck. Ram grabbed her arm and pulled her back down to the picnic table bench.

She let him hold her back while he teased. "You should no'. There's plenty of artery cloggin' goin' on in that chocolate pie."

It was her turn to grin and then tickle him until he willingly let go so she could claim her share of pie.

The wedding party sat outside enjoying the soft evening air, talking quietly and joking until after dark. The caterers cleaned up, packed up, and drove away, but they left two huge glass spigot jars, one with sweet tea, one with lemonade, and an enormous chest packed with beer, wine coolers, and soft drinks iced down. After they were gone, it seemed very quiet without the usual city whir of massive numbers of machines or tires humming on freeways.

It was peaceful. And nice. There were several in the group who, no matter what the future held, would be permanently linked by the special bond that sprung into being between warriors who shared mortal risks together. It was a pull that went soul deep. Not the same as passionate love, but every bit as intense. Not the same as familial love, but just as enduring.

At one point Elora said, "Tell me we're not really doing disco."

Katrina feigned haughtiness. "Ugh. Yes! Why does everybody keep asking that? What's wrong with disco?"

Kay leaned forward in his lawn chair like he had something to say. "We gotta keep on truckin' while we get down with the bogue 'cause what-it-is *is* right on bitchin'. I, for real, am sick Bogart for my buff sweetness. So either catch my drift or be a chease weasel. The disconatin' is a far out, flash back, freak out. Don't doubt the deuce dude. If you do, you're untubular self is wacked and jacked and, Zetus-Lapeduz. Catch you on the flip side. Trippy. Yeah."

Everybody stared at the normally introverted Kay for a long time. Finally, Katrina broke the silence. "That was amazing. You're my hero."

Kay stood up and gave Katrina a bow from the waist while everyone cheered. When he sat down again, Ram said, "That was, em, far out. Truly. Could we please speak with Kay now?"

When the Norns said goodnight and went upstairs, the members of B Team, plus Katrina, lingered, reluctant to give up the evening and call it done. The two pairs of lovers weren't eager to pull away from comfortable embraces and separate for the night. When the light was turned on in the upstairs bunkroom it filtered out onto the lawn, casting yellowish shadows. After a few minutes there was a loud thump and a shriek from upstairs.

B Team shared a laugh. Katrina said something

about two big days coming up, said good night, and left the four sitting together in companionable silence listening to the serenade of frogs, crickets, and cicadas. All may have been sharing the same thought. That it could be the last time.

Suddenly, a cool breeze pierced the warm night air ruffling hair and clothes and shifting the mood. The wind chimes and the leaves of the cottonwood trees sang in response to the harbinger night wind. It blew through almost instantly, but left behind a distinct aroma, the promise of a rainstorm. When they saw lightning in the distance, they took it as a cue and mutually agreed to adjourn for the night.

"Can I take a pure human through a pass?" Litha asked Deliverance.

"I won't lie to you and say, 'No', but it would not be in your best interest for me to show you how. There are far more who do not survive it than those who do."

She sighed. "Okay. How can I be sure I'm taking the pass closest to where Storm is?"

"I want to show you something. But first I have two gifts." Smiling, he handed her a pendulum. "It's made of black diamond from Ovelgoth Alla and it's programmed for my life signature. You'll always be able to find me. Anytime. And it comes with one more thing."

He tilted her chin up with his forefinger so that she was looking at him full in the face. "Your demon name. I wasn't there to name you, as I should have been, as I wish I'd been. But, life is for learning and I'm claiming a do over - giving you your Abraxas name now. It's Liberty."

Litha fell in love with it as soon as the sound had left his lips and knew he had chosen well. She had to run it over her vocal chords.

"Liberty." She said it almost reverently while she clutched the black diamond pendulum in her hand. It also felt like it belonged there. Her expression said she accepted his treasures in the spirit intended and he was satisfied.

"I don't have anything for you."

The demon laughed. "Litha, you've already given me what I want most - time spent with you."

Those words pierced through the remainder of reserve she had erected around her heart. While she was trying to decide what to say, he turned away suddenly and picked up her luggage, two vintage, Gucci soft sides filled with the wardrobe she'd acquired piece by piece during times when he was "busy" with incubus business.

Daddy had spoiled his little girl rotten. She'd enjoyed every minute of it and had the loot as a bonus. She hoped it was going to be a trousseau.

Litha followed him into the null space and tracked him through the ride he chose. When they stepped out, they stood in a parking lot with him smiling like he had feathers on his chin. He set the luggage down.

"What?" she asked looking around to see what could be so amusing.

"It's yours," he said.

There was nothing there except an outrageously divine automobile sitting alone under a parking lot spotlight. It was a red Aston Martin

DBS convertible, perhaps the shiniest car she had ever seen.

"You don't mean this?" She pointed to the car. She stared for a minute and then treated him to her throaty laugh that was music to his ears.

"All yours. Pink slip has your name on it. It's in the glove compartment."

"Let me see." The passenger door was unlocked. She slid in and opened the glove compartment, half expecting some practical joke to jump out at her. What she found was a new passport and driver's license with a good photo of her and a pink slip that, true to his word, had her name on it. Litha Liberty Brandywine. She opened her mouth to ask how he had managed that, but before she got the question out, she saw the sales price listed on the receipt, and almost choked. "Three hundred thousand dollars?"

She got out of the car, closed the door, and stepped back like she'd done something wrong by sitting in it. "That's..." she stopped for just a second to calculate, "...four times what I make in a year. And it's completely overwhelming."

He beamed at her.

"I'm not sure I should take it. I'm not sure I *can* take it. I don't think I can even afford the insurance on my salary."

"Come now. Did I not miss everything? Birthdays, graduations, soccer games? Let me be a proud Dad. As far as insurance, upkeep, all that stuff, it's taken care of."

"It is?"

"Trust me."

"I have a standing policy of running the other direction whenever someone says, 'Trust me.'"

He smiled broadly. "That's my girl."

"I didn't play soccer."

"Then that's one less thing I missed."

She realized that she was hesitating to say goodbye. How odd. "If I get Storm to marry me, I don't think his friends will appreciate you showing up for a father daughter dance. Not after you abducted Kay's fiancée and caused so much trouble."

"Father daughter dance," he mused. "Well, just as long as you know I would want to."

"The phrase, demon's daughter, has kind of a dark poetic ring. I could get used to it."

"That's my girl." Deliverance gave her a hug that said he hoped this wasn't the last time he'd see her. He put her bags in the trunk and pointed toward the road. "You take this road that way for thirteen miles. Just think about him and the seven-monks-pendulum will take you right to him."

Litha went up on her toes for one more hug. "Dad, I..."

Well, well. Life was full of surprises. The demon had cajoled and entertained and manipulated his way into her heart. Words caught in her throat when she realized she felt overly emotional about saying goodbye. She would probably always find it strange having a father who appeared to be thirty and it would only get stranger as she continued to age, but no one had any choice about the dads they get. Maybe they weren't all demons, but none of them were perfect either.

The road was the triple threat: narrow, hilly, and curvy. Oh. And it was also pitch black, not a street lamp in twenty miles. The fact that there was no one else out was a blessing because headlights coming at you in utter darkness could be disorienting. Litha had never been a car enthusiast, far from it, but she'd have to be in discarnate form not to appreciate the virtues of an ultimate driving machine like that: the smell, the feel of the leather, the luxurious numeral clock, and the way it drove. Talk about "handling" had never interested her before, but now her consciousness had been raised to the level of devotee. The car seemed to respond to her thoughts.

With every mile she got closer to Storm she felt like her heart was beating a little faster. She was glad the top was up on the car because she thought she saw lightning. She had worn a sleeveless white cotton dress because she expected the air to be warm and sultry. Seeing the lightning she wondered now if she shouldn't have picked something heavier. Or brought a sweater.

She was following the pendulum by the lights from the dashboard. It pointed straight ahead.

Everybody had gone to bed. Storm lay on his back on top of the cotton quilt cover on the screen porch cot wearing nothing but jeans. It was too hot for a shirt and too public for underwear. He had thought sleeping semi-outdoors would help settle his mind, but his thoughts were a jumble. They were there for a happy occasion, but he felt shrouded in sadness.

Ram and Elora were going to be parents, as mind boggling as that was. And, although nothing had been said, it only stood to reason that their days as active knights were coming to an end in the *very* near future. Kay and Katrina would be married the day after next and Kay wasn't coming back. He knew he should be feeling happy for his friends.

Swinging his legs around, he sat up on the side of the old iron army cot and lit a small, thin, black cigar. He sat smoking and listening for what he thought might be distant thunder. The glow of the cigar end seemed almost like company when he took a drag. And his thoughts went back to Litha. Again.

He was thinking that what had happened with Elora hadn't just left him shaken. It had left him handicapped with no confidence where women were concerned. He groaned out loud when he remembered the first time he saw Litha. The brash and beautiful witch had taken his breath away when she'd breezed in with her intoxicating scent and a field of electrical excitement that hovered in the air around her. He'd had the good fortune to attract the unlikely attention of a woman like that and how had he responded? *I'm not interested in a relationship.* What a douche!

That's when it hit him like a shot to the solar plexus. His epiphany.

The best thing that had ever happened to him was that Elora Laiken had turned him down. Here, he had spent months feeling sorry for himself only to find out that it was a blessing of the richest kind. Alone on a cot on a screen porch, he laughed out loud at his own stupidity and his own wretched timing.

What he had felt for Elora was a suggestion of love, a protective, almost brotherly instinct. Was it a connection? Yeah. Was it chemistry? That, too. But it was a far, far cry from the cock throbbing, gut wrenching, desperate stuff of night sweats that he felt for that witch. With Elora he had never been fighting with his own hands, constantly pulling them into fists to keep from reaching out and touching. Waking Woden! The merciless, relentless need that never stopped day or night. That was, he supposed, what Ram and Elora felt for each other. And he had tried to interfere with that? Thank the gods he hadn't gotten away with it.

Until now he hadn't even wondered why he'd never had an urgent desire to make love to Elora. Hell. He hadn't even tried to kiss her until they were on the way to meet his family and present themselves as an engaged couple. Why was he just now recognizing that there was something terribly wrong with that picture? The only thing stranger than that was that she had even considered going along with it. Eventually it would have sentenced three people to a life of unhappiness.

That feeling of bleak emptiness when Elora chose Ram? That wasn't heartbreak. Now that it was too late, he saw it for what it was. The death of a false dream.

He had wanted someone to share his vision of life in a romantic villa on the Sonoma Coast high above the sea. When Elora had materialized out of thin air and reached out for him, he had mistaken the event as providence and latched onto the idea that she was *the* one. In his ignorance about life, women, relationships, everything, he had drastically oversimplified mating.

There was an opening for a woman in his plan. So he'd tried to insert Elora into that slot. Whether she fit or not.

Now he understood that he'd had a chance for love. He should have grabbed for it with both hands when the real thing was standing right in front of him in the form of a wonderfully quirky witch with deep green eyes and red, red lips, saying, "Pick me". Instead he pushed her away.

Fate gave him an incomparable beauty who wanted exactly the same things from life that he did and, instead of thanking his lucky stars and embracing his good fortune with all the unfettered passion it deserved, he had been suspicious, reserved, mean, maybe even cruel. When it came to fucking himself over, it seemed he was about to be inducted to the hall of fame.

What had he thought he was waiting for? The "girl next door"? He pushed out a breath and almost groaned out loud at his own stupidity. Since the day Sol had showed up in his middle school Vice Principal's office, what in his life had ever been ordinary? It was only fitting that the women in his life be extraordinary.

He could hear the game show emcee in his head. "Bachelorette Number One hails from another dimension. She loves chocolate and can kick tail six ways from Sunday. Bachelorette Number Two is a breath stealing, half-demon witch who might disappear right into a wall just when a guy finally gets around to being serious about kissing."

Come to think of it, the fact that she was a *sex* demon's daughter could explain a lot about the palpitations and erotic dreams, not that there was anything wrong with being attracted to a woman who could get you hard with nothing more than a glance.

As he was dropping the little cigar butt into a soda can, he thought he might have caught a flash of lightning out of the corner of his eye. He turned his head that direction and looked up into the night sky through the practically invisible screen, then decided it was his mind playing tricks and lay back on the cot.

She said not even demons could keep her away. He was grateful she had included that vow in her message to him. It had given him something to hold onto. And he would hold onto that until the world looked level. He'd learned his lesson about doubting her.

More lightning flashed in his range of vision. This time thunder followed a couple of seconds later. No mistake. A storm was coming. The temperature dropped fifteen degrees in a matter of minutes, transforming the hot, still night into an event charged with excitement. Everywhere his skin was exposed it felt like static brushed over tiny body hairs lovingly, urging them to stand up at attention.

The harbinger was a pleasant little breeze, but before there was time to adjust to the cooler temperature, it began to gust, blowing trees and bushes into a frenzy, kicking the usually calm waters of the river into ripples that sloshed against the banks. The air filled with the potent and pungent aroma of rainstorm coming. *Litha.* He hoped to the gods she was safe. Wherever she was.

He remembered what she had said the first time she ever spoke to him. *There's something about the rumble of thunder that's so primal, so carnal It's the ultimate turn on. Add the smell of a rainstorm coming and it's a witch's dream.*

Litha didn't set the odometer. She didn't know how Deliverance had managed to have the car waiting in that parking lot under a spotlight with zero miles on it, but having seen some of his best tricks, it would take more than that to surprise her. He said thirteen miles. She didn't know exactly how far she'd gone, but she knew her pendulum was more reliable than any satellite direction-finder technology.

The thunder was getting closer and the lightning was starting to put on a fine show. When silver white streaks forked and fired across the sky, it made the surrounding darkness look like the dark purple of magick.

Her intuition told her it was time to slow down seconds before the pendulum took a sharp left at a white gravel driveway and almost jerked out of her hand. She turned in and eased slowly forward when the pendulum resumed pointing straight ahead. Between claps of thunder she could hear the crush of gravel and white shells under the tires as the car ground over them.

On either side of the drive tall oleanders bloomed profusely with white flowers. The wind was whipping them back and forth so that some of the blooms gave way. After a minute the oleanders opened up to an expanse of lawn and a white, two-story house. She immediately killed the car lights.

She had no idea what she was walking into. It could be a relative's house. It could even be a girlfriend's place. She tried to set it aside as pesky, self-sabotaging imagination. The house was completely dark, but that wasn't going to stop her. Nothing would. That very night she was letting him know that she was back in Loti Dimension and still hot for him. Only him. No matter what. He could run from Edinburgh to Siena to the Texas Hill Country. Until she had reason to believe that she would never stand a chance with him, she was all in.

Just as she turned the car off raindrops started to hit the windshield. She had taken her shoes off for the drive and decided to just run for it as she was. She was pelted by big drops as she bypassed the front door. For whatever reason, intuition probably, the back door *felt* like a better option. She ran across the St. Augustine grass barefoot, around the silent house, rain falling harder with every step. She grabbed her hair away from her eyes where it was being blown and tangled, so that she could see where she was going. The screen porch door was unlocked. It squeaked when she opened it and stepped onto the threshold.

Her eyes had adjusted to the dark and she could see well enough to make out the figure sprawled on top of the cot, but even if she couldn't see him, she would have known he was there. Her spirit was drawn to his essence like creation had calibrated them to be magnetic to each other.

Storm hadn't heard her approach because of the noise of the storm, but the squeaky hinge worked as well as an electronic alert. He turned his head to see who might be trying to enter, uninvited so far as he knew, in the middle of the night. There, framed in the doorway with a series of lightning flashes behind her, stood a wild and beautiful witch wearing a romantic, white dress just damp enough to cling to every curve. It was a vision no fantasy could ever hope to match. Storm held his breath, marveling at the complexity of the mind and the torturous nature of the tricks it can play. Even though his heart could barely stand looking at the vision, at the same time he was afraid to blink because it might vanish with the tiniest movement.

She took a step toward him, away from the door. "Do you want me here?" She asked her question and now stood motionless, heart beating fast, but not breathing - waiting for his answer.

The instant he heard her voice he knew it was no dream. Litha had no idea how fast a Black Swan knight in his prime can move. Before she had time to register that he was coming for her, Storm had her in his arms, smothering her mouth in a kiss that said: "I learned my lesson. Mountains may crumble. Seas may go dry. But I will *never* let you go again." She moaned against his mouth as her body went soft against him. He responded by tightening his arms and pulling her upward until she could wrap herself around him.

The feel of his bare skin under her hands was heaven, just as she'd known it would be. The heat of the witch's damp body, molded to his own, escalated his arousal to a frenzy of desire he hadn't known was possible as both of them were discovering that waking sex with each other was a hundred times more potent than nightwalking. He said her name against her lips like he was reassuring himself that she was real, then renewed the fervor of his silent pledge to kiss her mindless.

A near deafening crack of thunder shook the house. The wind whipped up, making trees bend and shake while wind chimes danced hysterically and almost flew off their hangers. The steady rain turned into a driving downpour that sounded like a tropical storm. The lovers paused when they heard noise coming from the house. It was hard to place because it sounded like a stampede.

Kay's sisters pounded down the wooden stairs, each trying to be first. They hit the screen door without stopping, as they had countless times as children. It didn't occur to any of them that it might be latched and it wasn't. It swung open in immediate surrender. They ran out into the night laughing, exhilarated by the cool rain and the exuberance of youth, without ever noticing Litha entangled in Storm's strong arms, wrapped firmly around her waist while her legs wrapped firmly around his.

In seconds the girls were drenched to the bone, still determined to get the lawn furniture cushions in out of the rain even though it was far too late to rescue them.

Reluctantly Storm let Litha slide down his body until her feet could touch the floor, but he did not relinquish the hold he had on her.

When the Norns had dashed out of the bunkroom to gather lawn cushions, Katrina had set out to close all the windows open to the north, the direction the rain was coming from. The four women had passed by Ram and Elora.

Thirty minutes earlier Ram had walked Elora to the door of the bunk room holding her hand, then set about giving her a goodnight kiss that would make her remember why sleeping without him was a dumb idea. Half an hour later they were still standing there necking like teenagers on dormitory steps with him alternately kissing and whispering in her ear what he would do to her if she came back to his room.

"Phone sex in person, Ram?" She put her lips to his ear and whispered back, "I like it. It could be a new trend."

"You know, should you change your mind, I'll be in that room there." He pointed across the hall. "And I would no' mind wakin' to find you crawlin' into my bed in the middle of the night."

The voices of the Norns carried up the stairs as they were shrieking and laughing about being wet through and through. Then, abruptly, everything went quiet. Katrina came out into the hall and looked at Ram and Elora. Something about the sudden silence was alarming. Kay must have thought so, too. He opened his door. "What's happened?"

The four of them hurried downstairs and out onto the now-crowded screen porch.

When Katrina saw Litha she let out a sob and rushed to throw her arms around the witch.

Elora turned to Kay's sisters. "Go change now before you cool off too much. I'll make you some nice chocolate tea." The sisters were torn between their curiosity and their shivering. Plus, they were used to giving the orders, not taking them. To the relief of all Order personnel present for the homecoming, the three sisters seemed to telepathically agree that they could ask questions later and silently withdrew to find towels and dry clothes.

When they were gone, Elora whispered: "We have five minutes to come up with a cover story." Then to Litha, Elora said: "We're all so glad to see you. And it just so happens we have an extra bed."

At Ram's suggestion, they agreed on an explanation and nominated Ram to tell it. He told Kay's sisters that Litha had helped Katrina get through her emotional trauma after she was returned and that Katrina had invited her to come to the wedding if she could. They were satisfied by that explanation. And, truthfully, he was so convincing Elora almost believed it herself.

She told him privately that it concerned her how easily he came up with an extemporaneous story that was a completely manufactured lie, not to mention the aplomb with which he told it. Ram just laughed and said: "I was no' born the day we met, you know."

Litha borrowed something to sleep in because

it was raining too hard to retrieve her Gucci luggage from the car.

After disgusting chocolate tea and a celebration cigar, Storm went back to the cot on the porch to sleep alone, or stay awake alone, his heart swollen almost to the size of the erection he was still packing.

As he thought about how quickly things can change those thoughts turned to the future and what might be on the next page after Kay's wedding.

He confronted the fact that his feelings of loss were only partially about Kay leaving The Order. The truth was that he was on a collision course with anachronism - a vampire slayer with no vampires to slay. He didn't know how long it would take Baka's task force to eradicate the virus, but it was coming. Soon. The sooner the better.

He had been there to help usher in a new age and that was really something. Something to tell grandchildren if his work was common knowledge by then. Fact remained, a wise person knew when it was time to turn the page.

He'd spent more than half his life saving to buy a vineyard while, at the same time, never *really* picturing himself as anything but a Black Swan knight. He thanked providence that sometimes fate had a way of arranging change even when you were too dumb to find the path on your own.

He didn't know what he'd done to deserve a gorgeous witch who wanted to make love to him, make wine with him, and make a life with him, but he found himself imagining sharing a bed in a Sonoma Coast villa with a green-eyed, demon's daughter. And that time he knew he'd got it right.

In the darkness, lying on his back on a screen porch cot, listening to the rain that had turned into a quiet, soothing drizzle, he smiled at the ceiling.

Life is good. Strange. But good.

Sweet delicious Litha.

CHAPTER 20

The women had stayed up too late talking in the darkness, giggling like kids away at camp. Things that might not be funny otherwise were funnier when you were supposed to be going to sleep.

Katrina had previously arranged the wedding party as three bridesmaids, not wanting to distinguish between any of her future sisters-in-law. She shocked everyone, Litha most of all, by insisting that she would be maid of honor, and Katrina made it clear she wouldn't take no for an answer.

When the fairer sex woke the next morning, the men were not in the house. They were found at the front of the house on the gravel drive standing around a fire engine red, convertible Aston Martin like it was an altar. The rain had not done a thing to sully the mirror finish paint.

On her approach Litha used the remote key to pop the trunk open. "Would somebody help me with my luggage?"

Storm settled an instantly heated gaze on her and walked toward her like she was the only person alive. This attention from him was such an abrupt about face from when she had slipped dimension that she hadn't even begun to adjust to seeing him with an expression of desire on his face. Desire for her. Barely suppressing a full on shiver, she leaned up and whispered in his ear, "It's a gift from my father."

Storm's eyes were lit like firecrackers when he looked down at her with just a hint of a smile. Life was going to be *so* interesting. "I take it you had a good time."

She laughed. "I confess."

"How 'bout a ride?"

She smiled. His eyes went straight to her mouth and stayed there while he watched her lips form the question: "Want to drive?"

He dragged his gaze up to her eyes and without looking away said loud enough for the others to hear: "We're going to go pick up stuff for breakfast. What do... *y'all* want?"

They got a list and directions to the H.E.B. in Kerrville. The sun was out and, after the big rain, every leaf was shiny. The world looked and smelled new, like it had been polished bright for a wedding. Litha handed Storm the keys. He stopped right before they pulled out onto the highway.

"Did I mention I missed you?"

Litha's heart turned over. "No," she said quietly, grasping at the anticipation of what she hoped was coming next.

"Well." He treated her to a suggestive smile that she'd had no idea he possessed. "I did. A lot."

After breakfast Litha went to the bunkroom to open her luggage and shake out some clothes to see what might look good enough to wear into town with the other women for the ritual preparing of nails, both finger and toe. That was when she discovered her father's bigger surprise.

One of the two Gucci suitcases was filled with clothes she had bought while Deliverance was "busy". Each item of clothing was a memory: this one bought in Buenos Aires, this one in Paris, and so on.

The other bag, the bigger and far heavier of the two, was filled with cash. She had no idea how much and zipped it closed as soon as she saw what was in it. She was sure there was enough money there to buy her vineyard, no matter what they asked. She just hoped this wasn't cash that the treasury department was looking for. She stowed the bag underneath the bunk bed and started trying to process what it felt like to be rich.

Storm spent most of the day making preparations for a special project. He borrowed a car to go into town promising to be back in plenty of time for the wedding rehearsal at five. Everyone who had come for the wedding was invited to the resort upstream for the rehearsal dinner and disco lessons after.

Storm didn't find out until the actual rehearsal was underway that Katrina had insisted that Litha be her maid of honor. Litha was a little embarrassed about it, but she was also a little pleased. She told Storm that she supposed Katrina was partial to women who agree to take her place in hostage situations.

All the participants walked through the mock ceremony, taking instructions from Katrina's mother, who wasn't especially thrilled about either the rushed wedding or the greatly pared-down concept, but since she assumed this meant a grandchild was on the way, she cooperated with as much grace as she could muster.

The configuration was typical. Kay and Katrina would leave the bridal bower first. Litha was then to take Storm's arm so that the two of them followed bride and groom down the aisle. When Litha hooked her arm through Storm's, he tightened his hold pulling her closer into his body which made her laugh, astounding him with the knowledge that he had the power to give someone such delight with such a small gesture.

When the wedding party arrived at the resort, a little crowd of guests had already assembled outside by the pool. They were having crawfish etouffee, stuffed jumbo shrimp, pasta jambalaya, blackened redfish, dirty rice and beans, green salad, and jalapeno corn bread with a choice of Bananas Foster, sweet potato bread pudding, or plain Blue Bell ice cream for dessert.

Ram took one look at the spread and turned to Elora with a grin. "I plan to eat 'til I can no' stand up."

"You know you worry me," she said. Then putting her mouth next to his ear she whispered. "If you refrain from outright gluttony, I will sneak out of the girls' dorm tonight."

He narrowed his eyes and looked suspicious. "Promise?"

"I do. But only if you have enough energy to make it worth my while."

She could see devilish wheels turning and was

glad she'd planted that thought. Clearly, a night on his own had made her mate eager.

He nuzzled her ear and whispered, "We will need to secure tape for your pretty mouth or every soul in this open window county will know you slipped away to your elf's bed."

She laughed, but wasn't entirely sure he was kidding. Ram stole looks at her throughout dinner that said he was enjoying the idea of illicit sex and that he fully planned to make up for the previous night's deprivation.

Between the parents of the bride and groom, aunts, uncles, cousins, boyfriends and various other "essential" friends, there were about fifty guests present.

Storm and Litha were seated at the wedding party table, but not together. He just wanted this over with. He had plans.

She had worn a red silk sundress that made the sexy color of her skin look even warmer and more touchable. It made her lips appear even redder than usual, a good trick considering, and made her eyes sparkle. Or maybe it was just the way she looked at him that made her eyes seem to sparkle.

His own eyes never left her for more than a minute at a time. Each time his gaze came back to her, he found himself appreciating every little thing as if it was the first time he'd seen her.

After dinner, Katrina's mother proudly introduced the disco instructor they had brought in from Houston and his lovely assistant, with fanfare. They called all would-be participants to the dance area and demonstrated a few moves. First, they gave a brief overview on the "spirit" of disco dancing. Then, when the guru of dance gave the signal, a sound tech cranked the big speakers and the night was filled with the thump, thump, thump of disco bass.

Some of the partygoers were old enough to have danced disco when it was in vogue. Others had picked it up for retro parties. Then, there was Katrina who was a fanatical devotee and Kay who was fanatically devoted to making Katrina happy - no matter the cost to his image.

Ram wanted to dance. He looked around for Elora, but she was involved in conversation so he hit the floor by himself. Ram seemed to make a habit of being extraordinary and his dancing was no exception to that rule. He was wearing loafer type shoes with leather soles that slid easily so that he could move effortlessly. Elora had often thought he possessed dancer-like grace whether he was sparring or hunting or just walking across the Hub. He managed to move with the joy and abandon of elves, without sacrificing the tiniest bit of masculine dignity. He didn't go in for exaggerated pelvic grinds or bumps; the kind of "dancing" that many men mistake for playfully sexy when its effect is similar to throwing cold water on femme spectators. No indeed. His rhythmic movement was an instant magnet to feminine attention.

Perhaps it wasn't fair that one person seemed to come packed with more than his share of gifts, but fate doesn't concern itself with balance. He was enjoying the music, enjoying the sensation of the dance and was completely oblivious to the fact that he was Pan in the flesh.

One of Katrina's cousins saw that he was dancing alone. Not knowing anything more about him than that he was scrumptious and a fabulous dancer, she thought to seize an opportunity. She appeared in front of Ram, far too close, and began dancing suggestively. Aggressively so. He took an abrupt step backward and gave her a look that would have sent most women slinking away. But, the pseudo-temptress was either oblivious to body language and facial expression or she was under the influence of far too many frozen margaritas, which, in fairness, did have a tendency to sneak up on partygoers.

Elora had just happened to glance toward the dance floor. When Ram looked over the top of the girl's head, what he saw was flame headed, wrath-of-goddess charging toward them with eyes blazing in fully incensed battle rage.

Just before she reached her target, Elora raised her right hand. Ram could read her intention. The girl was about to be 'snatched baldheaded'. He quickly stepped around the body in front of him, caught Elora's wrist in his right hand, and braced himself, allowing her to slam into his body instead. Though he was vibrating from the blow, he caught his wife around the waist with his other arm, pulled her into a tight, slow dance pose, and refused let go.

Where his grip held her wrist he could feel her pulse pounding. She was so angry she was breathing like she'd been sprinting. Under some circumstances that would be exciting, but he couldn't let that distract him from his purpose, which was to calm his bride and talk her down from wanting to murder a severely misguided little horndogess.

There was a part of him that was ecstatic about having a mate whose passionate excesses were a match for his own. She fought and fucked and argued as hard as he did. And, it seemed, she was every bit as possessive.

Elora started to jerk away, still seeing red and needing blood under her fingernails. He grabbed on tighter and swayed with her slowly, cheek to cheek, offering quiet murmurs of reassurance that he was hers alone. Of course she could have overpowered him if she'd wanted to, but that made having her submit to his demand all the sweeter. "It makes me so hot when you are territorial with me."

He felt her body soften and begin to relax a little. She pulled her head back far enough to look him in the face. "Then you must be burning up with fever all the time."

Ram tilted his head back so that his eyes were half lidded and lifted the corners of his mouth. "Aye. 'Tis definitely so."

"You saved that skank's hair, Hero, but she will not be getting a chance to thank you for it."

He chuckled softly. "Could have been more than just her hair at risk from the fire I saw in your eye. I saved *you* from causin' a scene at our teammate's weddin' rehearsal dinner; somethin' you never would have done when we first met."

"I know." She relaxed some more and her shoulders sagged. "What's wrong with me?"

His smile grew bigger as his tone turned to

teasing. "You seem to have developed a severe intolerance for others sniffin' 'round your mate. Could mean you love me."

"You think?"

"Remember that night when we were on break at Notte Fuoco? When you grabbed that woman's hair?"

She narrowed her eyes. "That *woman*? You mean the drunk slut with the ridiculous pony-do? Yes. I remember."

He thought she was unbearably adorable when she was jealous. "I'm thinkin' that you had already recognized me as your mate. At least in your heart. Your brain just had no' caught up yet."

Elora wasn't accustomed to feelings of extreme anger or impulsivity or even aggression for that matter. There was nothing desirable about those emotions. In fact, the sensations were altogether uncomfortable. She had felt so threatened she couldn't breathe when she saw another female moving in on her mate. Maybe it was a burden to be paired with somebody so beautiful and charismatic. She mulled that over for only two seconds before deciding that he was worth the price - whatever it was.

Her pulse and breathing had returned to normal. She responded to Ram's observation with a tiny little smile and the raspy, bedroom voice that never failed to bring his manhood to full attention. "Tell me what you have in mind for later."

He buried his face in her neck where he could drag in her wild jasmine scent and grinned against her skin. "Ravishin'."

Storm was on the sidelines giving the demonstration a look that could have passed for the "evil eye", but, when the dancing started, his interest ignited. It would have been impossible not to pick Litha out in her red, silk sundress. She wasn't dancing with anyone in particular because this was supposed to be a lesson. Storm's assessment was that she moved like he imagined a fertility goddess would dance if she visited Hunt, Texas on a warm night during the season of Beltane. He looked around to see if anyone else was looking at his witch because he could use something to do, and throttling perverts might be the perfect thing to take the edge off.

While he was looking around, she came up behind him and spoke. Thank the gods for years of training or he would have jumped

"Do you disco?" she asked, coming around to his side.

"Not even if a legion of demons was after me."

She laughed, but was thinking: "How about just one?"

"I do waltz though."

"You do not."

The responding glitter in his eyes said maybe he was telling the truth. He pulled her into a dance pose, but they quickly learned that there was no way to waltz to disco music.

"Okay, there's another option."

"I'm listening."

She became very aware of the warmth of his big hand covering hers. He lowered his other arm to wrap around her waist and gently pulled her closer until there was not a hair's width between them. She hissed in a breath of air softly, but not so softly that he didn't hear it.

"There's also very, very slow."

Litha was going to have to revise her opinion of herself as worldly woman because damn if that didn't actually make her knees feel mushy.

While the rest of the guests jumped and jived, Storm and Litha swayed gently in each other's arms. Storm didn't think he'd experienced many moments in his life that could be called magical. There were plenty he would call peculiar, weird, and even bizarre, but magical... not so much. He was thinking that Litha was opening up a whole new world of experiences he'd never had before. She was a miracle.

"Who's that with your friend, Storm?" Kay's mother asked him.

"Someone from work. Her name is Litha Brandywine."

"They certainly are a handsome couple."

Kay had to agree that they almost looked like they had been conceived as a matched pair.

Litha was trying to impress every sensation onto long-term memory, especially the promise implied by the erection pressing against her, captivating the attention of both her mind and body. She was wondering how long they were expected to stay at the party and was thinking about suggesting an escape when they were interrupted by Dandie.

"That's cheating y'all." She grabbed Litha by the wrist to drag her away, saying that they were about to form a circle and have a ladies only dance around the bride. Litha looked back at Storm apologetically as she allowed herself to be tugged away. Storm was thinking the whole concept of a ladies only dance was misguided because it was bad manners to upstage a bride and Litha couldn't help it.

The women danced around Katrina proving conclusively that when it comes to dancing chicks rule, with the exception of Rammel Hawking.

While the women demonstrated every possible form of joy and gyration, Kay made gentlemanly rounds pouring shots of Irish whiskey. When Storm held up his hand to pass on the offer, Kay raised an eyebrow. "You need to talk?"

Storm just smiled secretively. "Got plans later."

Kay was curious, but moved on to the next outstretched glass without another word.

Storm took one of the cars and drove back to the house before the party broke up. He changed into jeans and a tee shirt then set out with a flashlight. About forty yards up river he found just what he was looking for; a vacation home similar to the one Kay's family owned, lovingly attended with an expanse of short cropped, wide bladed grass sloping down to the widest part of the river. Best of all, it was evident that no one was in residence.

He returned to the screen porch to retrieve the supplies that he had stowed under his cot and had just let the screen door swing closed behind him when he heard the crunch of cars pulling onto the shell and gravel drive. He hurried away so he wouldn't be seen.

When Litha finished the bride's dance, she was disappointed that she couldn't find Storm and was even more disappointed that he wasn't at the house either. While she was wondering if she'd said something wrong, she pulled out her pretty, thin, white nightgown. It was cotton which meant it could breathe, just the right thing for a warm Hill Country night in a river house with the windows left open.

Storm unzipped the nylon sleeping bag and laid it down first to provide a barrier against the wet grass. On top of that he put two layers of new cotton blankets. When he had opened the packages earlier in the day, he thought they smelled funny, like chemicals, so he had personally run them through the washer and dryer. He didn't know how to use laundry appliances, but with the women gone into town, between himself, Kay, and Ram they figured it out by means of trial and error. He made the excuse to them that he needed more cover on the porch.

He smoothed the wrinkles out of the soft blankets and was proud that, when he put his face into the fabric, they smelled sweet like good clean soap.

He took out the bottle of wine. He'd been surprised and ecstatic to find a bottle of Cairdeas Deo brandy. It wasn't cheap. She had said it was a very good brandy. And it was fitting that a brandy she was named after be the very best. It seemed

Kerrville had some well-heeled wine patrons among the wealthy who vacationed and retired there.

The wine store had told him that his best bet for really good crystal would be one of the antique traders. Storm found two matching stems of art glass there and, again, they weren't cheap, but he was set on winning a woman whose father could give her an Aston Martin on a whim.

He rearranged everything three times, then stood there staring at it, talking to himself, and wondering if the anxiety he was feeling meant that he was losing his nerve. For crap's sake, he was a Black Swan knight from Bad Company no less. Not a fifteen-year-old boy. Even though that was exactly what he felt like.

He summoned his intent and set off for the house with single-minded determination. The only thing in heaven or hell that could stop him now was the witch herself.

The six women had decided that Katrina's last night as a single woman should include a lecture on sex - the one that most mommas don't deliver - and that each one of them would contribute some really juicy tidbit. The only rule was that Katrina was forbidden from participating because the Norns said they did not want an image of their brother engaged in coitus. Ew.

They sequestered themselves in the corner bunkroom with a stash of wine coolers. As the tidbits grew progressively juicier and wilder, the volume of the collective giggling, interspersed with squeals, grew in direct proportion.

With stealth befitting Black Swan knights, Ram and Kay picked up yard chairs and long necks and took up a post in the shadows of the back lawn directly underneath the open bunkroom window. As eavesdropping vantage points go, it couldn't have been better. They could hear everything said in the room above as if they were sitting on one of the bunks. Even the whispers.

Kay was grateful for the cover of relative darkness so that Ram couldn't see his face turn red every couple of minutes in response to some new and outrageously raunchy thing one of the girls said to each other. Who knew women could be so graphic? Especially his sisters! It was just wrong.

At one point Ram was laughing so hard he had one hand over his mouth and a forearm over his ribs trying to brace his stomach and contain himself so as not to give them away. He almost blew it when his wife referred to him as "cockzilla". A mental note was filed away to whisper that back to her when he had her at his mercy, as promised, sometime later than night.

They talked at length about what they liked in men, physically and otherwise. Ram was delighted and gratified right down to his well-formed toes that what Elora described was, basically, him. She ended by saying that what is said in the bunk room stays in the bunk room.   "Just as long as everybody understands that the beautiful blond is with me."

"I already told you I don't do chicks, Elora." Squoozie stroked her pale blond mane feigning indignant.

Words could never describe how much Ram and Kay were enjoying the absolute perfection of the simple pleasure of sitting in lawn chairs, each in the easy companionship of someone with whom they had stood beside and confronted mortality on many occasions. As they sat in silence, taking an occasional swig of beer, listening to the crickets, the frogs, an occasional plop of a fish in the water, and, best of all, the voices of women talking about matters of love, they were perfectly at peace.

Recognizing the moment for what it was, they were each recording a precious snapshot, knowing that change was coming, but that this would be a memory to forever keep in their hearts on the other side of the transition. There was a painful bitter-sweetness when life's journey took a turn. It made friends savor an appreciation of what might have been taken for granted.

At the same time both men became aware that someone was approaching the house. Decades of training kicked in and a sudden tension instantly robbed them of the relaxed state they had been enjoying. The alert, however, was quickly set aside because, even in the darkness, they recognized the shape and gait of the tall figure walking toward the house. They were glad they didn't have to give away their strategic position by yelling: "Halt! Who goes there?" like an ancient night watch.

Storm just nodded on his way past like there was nothing remarkable about his having disappeared earlier or about the fact that he had been out walking alone on the river at night. The screen door squeaked and then shut with the clatter everyone had come to associate as a paired sound. He stopped momentarily at the bottom of the stairs, then took them two at a time and didn't slow until he was standing outside the bunkroom door knocking.

From the lawn chairs below Ram and Kay could hear the knock and subsequent silence and each could easily imagine the women looking at each other, wondering who it might be. Elora was closest to the door so she got up and opened it.

Storm eyes lit on her and quickly slid past searching for... "I need that woman." He nodded toward the witch sitting cross-legged on one of the top bunks.

Elora regarded Storm affectionately. *Yes. You do.* Seeing that he wanted entry she stepped aside and opened the door wider.

As every head turned toward her, Litha unfolded her legs and started to climb down from the bunk. She was so stunned it almost felt like an out-of-the-body experience to hear her knight publicly deliver four simple words that, so far as she was concerned, formed the most exciting sentence ever spoken. *I need that woman.*

Before Litha got to the second step of the little ladder designed for children, Storm had gripped her by the waist, turned her around, and let gravity pull her forward so that she was bent over his shoulder. She gasped as he carried her away with one arm locked behind her knees and one hand alternately bracing and covering her finely upturned tush.

"Where are you taking...?" In that position she didn't have enough breath to get out the whole question.

"To finish what we started."

When Storm pushed through the screen door and carried Litha past Ram and Kay, they looked at each other and grinned as the door slammed behind him. He had toted her all the way to the river's edge before she got enough breath to get out a whole sentence.

"Hey, cave man. Put me down." It wasn't just that her lungs were being squeezed in that position. It was all the fondling taking place between Storm's free hand and her derriere that caused a near nonstop series of gasps.

He stopped abruptly, bent, and gently lowered her until her feet touched the ground. He was so strong that he wasn't showing any sign of exertion at all. "Are you going to come peaceably?"

There was enough moonlight for him to appreciate seeing her mouth slowly spread into a beguiling smile that was partly due to the fact that Litha's shapely ass was still tingling from the pleasure of being thoroughly explored by Storm's big, warm and highly curious hand. "Absolutely."

The bunkroom was quiet for a long time. Ram and Kay looked at each other wondering what was going on in there. They were agreeing silently, semi-telepathically, that it just wasn't in the nature of women to be perfectly quiet for such a long time. Certainly not *these* particular women.

Finally, Squoozie pulled a pillow in front of her

midsection and hugged it tight. "Ugh. Was that *not* just *the* most romantic thing you *ever* saw? Or even heard of? Seriously?"

All the pretty heads nodded at once and everyone murmured their agreement.

Elora glanced at her watch surreptitiously while thinking that she was more than ready for the others to go to sleep. She had a hot date waiting in the room across the hall.

Katrina was thinking that separating bride and groom the night before their wedding was a stupid custom that should by no means be tolerated by a modern woman. She glanced at her watch surreptitiously wondering how much longer before the others went to sleep.

Two of the Norns were wishing they had stayed with their boyfriends in one of the river cabins and surreptitiously looked at their phones under the covers thinking they might send a test text to see if a lover was still awake. The last was wondering if everybody in the house would hear the buzz of a vibrator.

Litha slipped her hand in Storm's. They were barefoot, but there was nothing but manicured lawn where they were walking and the wide bladed grass felt cool and soft beneath their feet. When they came to a stop in front of the pallet, Litha felt every cell stand up and look around. The intention was unmistakable. She looked over the world's best surprise before turning her face up to Storm. "You've been busy," she said softly.

He knelt down on the pallet and held up the

bottle of wine. "Guess what I found."

It was dark but she had her intuition to rely on. "Is that...?"

"...Cairdeas Deo brandy." To her the gesture was as moving as if the knight had laid the Golden Fleece at her feet and he looked just that proud to have procured it. She knelt down in front of him as he gestured with the bottle. "Want some?"

She shook her head and reached for him instead. "Just you, Storm," she said. "You're..." She never got the chance to finish that sentence. The words were drowned in a kiss that was at once demanding, compelling, and possessive. It was fierce. It was ruthless. It was relentless. She could see that, once Storm made up his mind about something, he committed to it and came for it head on, holding nothing back. She hoped to the gods she was going to be that thing he had made up his mind about.

Storm gave Litha exactly what she wanted. Not tepid touches. Not lukewarm timidity. What she wanted from him was the full commitment of unflinching passion, the kind that burned like demon fire. Not the kind that sought mere orgasm. The kind that aspired to a roaring triumph over lust that was so consuming it was excruciating. However impermanent it might have been.

His kisses engulfed her so completely that she knew nothing, cared about nothing, but the moment they were sharing. She was transported to a world every bit as unique as those she had visited with the incubus, a world where nothing existed other than the muscled body and battle hardened soul of the knight she clung to; the one who was urging her to lie back while not yielding her mouth for an instant.

He settled himself gingerly on top of the witch's luscious body as if he was taking great care to be gentle with her and, at the same time, savoring the raw experience of sex in real time with real touches and scents and sounds.

He slowly ran a hand up and down the skin of her bare arm. She was perfection to the touch and he couldn't get enough. The nightgown was so thin he could feel every rise and swell of her as if there was no fabric barrier, but he needed more. He wanted skin on skin and he wanted it right then. Enough time had been wasted while he played the fool. Everything he wanted was moving her sweet, warm body beneath him and, by gods, he was grabbing his chance for love with both hands.

Storm had the neckline of the pretty cotton gown clutched in both fists and was about to jerk his hands in opposite directions when he flashed on an image of little pearl buttons flying all around. He drew himself up short. If he ripped her clothes, she would have to return to the house wrapped in a blanket and a blush because he would be the ham-handed lover she'd once implied he was. He didn't want that for her. He didn't want her to be embarrassed because he was too eager and he didn't want to be inept at lovemaking.

He looked down at the red ribbon sash at the waist of her gown. Something about that streak of soft, satiny red against the palette of pure white was arresting in its subconscious promise of raw, unvarnished, uninhibited sex. He took hold of one end of the ribbon tie. "Can I help get you out of this?" He pulled on the ribbon, trying to free the knot with big, masculine fingers.

"Here. Let me do that." She said it softly, wondering if he would remember that she had once said that to him in a dream.

He surrendered the red ribbon to her expertise with every intention of undressing while she did. He took hold of the hem of his tee shirt and started to pull upward, but his eyes caught and locked on her fingers undoing little mother of pearl buttons, such an effortless thing for her that would have made him look and feel clumsy. Still as a statue, he watched as she undid buttons to her navel, enough buttons to free the gown so that it would fall past the swell of her hips in a maddeningly soft swish of fabric. The loosened front closure gaped open with temptation, causing Storm to silently beg to see and touch the secrets still hidden beneath the gown. He was holding his breath in anticipation. Another minute and he would have forgotten all about his honorable intentions of preserving the integrity of the garment.

Rising to her feet with the grace of a dancer, almost as if she was performing an ancient ritual of seduction, she pulled the gown open, exposing her breasts, and let it slide from her shoulders so that it drifted down and pooled at her feet in front of where Storm was frozen in place, on his knees.

He was looking up at Litha's gloriously naked body, his lips parted, his hands still clutching the hem of his shirt. With eyes riveted on her nipples, his tongue absently poked out to wet his bottom lip and he swallowed so that she could see his throat work even in the moonlight.

The celebrated knight who was known for decisiveness, envied by others for his ability to think quickly in dubitable situations, was mesmerized, lost in indecision. He didn't know where to start. There were too many things he wanted all at once. One of those was to tell Litha that she was, without question, the most magnificent woman ever created. That was what he wanted to say, but his brain wasn't cooperating well enough to allow his mouth to form words.

Seeing that Storm was paralyzed and essentially struck mute by the sight of her nakedness was the sexiest and most flattering tribute Litha could have been paid. She would have been charmed right down to her socks, had she been wearing any. His rapt attention made her feel like nothing less than a goddess. One would think that a guy living in modern times, when there's no shortage of nudity to view, would be indifferent, even bored. But looking at Litha in the moonlight, her secrets bared to his view, she might as well have been the first unclothed woman he'd ever seen.

The eroticism of being so graphically and intensely admired by the man she loved heightened the excitement of every nerve ending and cell fiber to the point of needing touch like breath. Not to mention that her clitoris had bloomed into a deliciously demanding swell.

Litha returned to the nest her would-be lover had made on the ground, took the hem of Storm's shirt from him, lifted it away and flung it aside. The

VICTORIA DANANN

sight of his bared upper body was as exciting to her as hers was to him. Knowing that she was going to be in his arms momentarily, skin on skin, made her breath come even faster. She urged him to his knees and reached for the waistband of his jeans.

When the backs of her fingers smoothed across his stomach, he jerked out of inaction, quickly getting himself out of his own pants. Unable to wait for another second, Litha threw her arms around Storm's neck and arched into him. The velvet smooth sensation of bodies meeting made Storm groan out loud. It was a sound that Litha cut short by a decidedly needy kiss and a throaty moan of her own, inviting and imploring at the same time.

Storm explored every inch of her that could be reached with his hands without relinquishing the kiss. As he eased her down he cupped one breast and took its nipple under advisement, first visually and then with his tongue, relishing the way it grew harder and more demanding under his agonizingly slow ministration. When he slid his hand down her body toward her core, Litha first tensed in anticipation then jerked her pelvis toward him pleading for touch. His fingers eased up her inner thigh until he made contact with the heat between her folds, so wet and ready for him. She started to cry out, but he quickly put a large hand over her mouth.

"Litha," he said quietly and breathlessly into her ear, causing a shiver to travel the length of her spine while her nipples drew up even tighter. "Sound travels on the river at night. We have to try to be quiet unless we want to put on a show."

She nodded.

"Are you ready for me?"

She shook her head.

"Do you want me to take my hand away from your mouth?"

She said something into his hand that he couldn't understand. He lifted his palm from her lips.

"You're welcome to smother my screams, but only if you're wearing a condom."

He grabbed his discarded jeans, reached into a front pocket and produced several.

"Right   here."

She chuckled and whispered: "That's a lot of condoms. Are you bragging?"

"Let's find out."

The way she fitted him for protection was as much a turn on as everything else she did. He nestled into the cradle of her thighs and settled there, feeling like a perfect fit, as if the moment had been preordained at the conception of creation. She pulled her knees up and caressed him by rubbing her smooth calf against his back, urging him on. When he entered her, she cried out a pleasure that was complete and completely unexpected since she had never been particularly vocal, but, thanks to Storm's warm and capable hand, only the two of them knew it. In a strange way the necessity of secrecy added a heightened excitement to their lovemaking and punctuated the intimacy that only they two shared.

Litha's glowing skin was evidence that she was hot as a pressure cooker, on the verge of coming right away which was a merciful blessing for Storm. He wanted it to be good for her, but couldn't have held out long. His arousal had been desperate even before the tip of her tongue had peeked out to touch the center of his palm where he held it against her mouth, but that tiny touch of moisture threatened to send him spiraling out of control.

He reached between them with his free hand and slid the tip of a finger between her folds to gently tease the swollen bud. Her response was instant and fervent. When her walls began to grip and milk his cock he tightened his hand just a little so that her screams didn't go farther than the little world of their pallet on the ground. When he realized he was going to lose his own battle with a need to shout, he shoved his forearm so far into his mouth that he left teeth marks.

After a few seconds he realized he had forgotten how big he was and let his full weight rest on the curvy body supporting him. Thinking he might be crushing her, he pulled up quickly saying, "Sorry. Carried away," in a husky voice.

"No, that would be me who was carried away." She gave him a languid smile as her hand drifted down his spine in slow, satisfied, affectionate strokes. "S'okay. Felt good."

He brushed a kiss over her cheek and found wetness. He pulled back so he could see her, "Are you crying? I did hurt you, didn't I?"

She shook her head back and forth adamantly. "No." She said no, but her eyes were glistening. "Happy tears."

He relaxed just a little and put his elbows on

either side of her so he could push tears away with the pads of both thumbs. "Seems oxymoronic to me."

She laughed quietly. "You're too smart for your own good, you know that?"

"That's what they used to say when... I was a kid."

Even in the darkness he could see that she was looking at him with something in her eyes that could be mistaken for adoration if he let his imagination run away with him; that look he'd seen at dinner in Siena. He ducked his head and brushed his cheek against hers.

Later, on her knees, sitting back on her heels and not the least inhibited about her nudity, Litha said, "Remember when you said you wanted someone entertaining?"

He laughed softly. "Unfortunately I do. What an idiotic thing to say."

"Look at me for a minute and don't look away."

"Why?"

"I don't think you believed me when I said I could be entertaining. I'm going to prove it."

It had been a long time since a woman had tried to tell Storm what to do. Undoubtedly this was the first time he had ever been both pleased and amused to obey. After a minute passed he smiled and reached for her.

"Well, it's not that looking at you without clothes on isn't entertaining. Because certainly it is, but strictly speaking, I meant something more along the lines of..."

She put her fingers to his lips to shush him and

VICTORIA DANANN

smiled.

"Okay. Turn around now."

He turned his head and his mouth dropped open of its own accord. Thousands upon thousands of fireflies hovered over the river and danced in the trees on the other side. They swooped, darted, and flitted. It was a spectacle that was magical beyond imagination. Storm laughed out loud, a sound so joyful and so rare it startled him, almost making him jump like a puppy with a grown dog's bark.

In that moment, he realized he'd never felt that before - that special happiness that transcends life on earth, taking you to a place in spirit called rapture.

When he turned to look at Litha, there were fireflies encircling her, lighting her face. *So that's what love looks like.* When he thought about the fact that he might have missed this, might have missed out on loving Litha...

He laughed again as he reached for her and pulled her into a thank you and thank-the-gods-for-you kiss. Her naked body went soft and invitingly pliant as she made a sound that could only be called a murmur of happiness. When he pulled back and looked around, the fireflies were gone as if they'd never been there.

He smiled down at her. "Without a doubt you are the most entertaining woman who has ever lived. If you had just said so in the first place, we could have saved ourselves a lot of aggravation," he teased.

As they drank wine and nibbled from the cheese sampler he'd bought, Storm relaxed into the simple pleasure of being with a woman. He'd spent so much of his life in the company of men, doing things that were unsuitable for their delightfully softer female counterparts.

Lying on his back with Litha snuggled into his side, her head on his chest, he told her that he'd been thinking it was time for something different; that maybe all the changes around him meant moving on would be the best thing. Litha listened quietly, encouraging him to feel comfortable enough with her to say whatever was on his mind. She only hoped that whatever change he was envisioning had a place for her in it.

"Do you ever want to tell me what happened when you disappeared through that wall?'

She tensed. "Yes. But not tonight."

She knew she should have told him about her demon blood, but she had to know what it was like to be with him, even if it was only once. If it was wrong for her to withhold that little bit of information about herself, then she'd rather live with a little guilt than a lifetime of wondering.

Litha tiptoed back into the bunkroom. She saw that Elora's bunk, directly underneath hers, was empty. Katrina was AWOL as well. She pulled the sheet up to her waist. She was glad she didn't have a bunk mate, because she smelled like sex; sex mixed with Storm's muskiness. It was powerful and raw and she wanted to permanently imprint the scent on her memory so that she could make it last forever. She closed her eyes and smiled in the darkness.

Elora woke with a start. It took a second to remember where she was. She'd slept in too many different beds in too many different rooms lately. She shook her mate and called to him in a forceful, breathy whisper.

"Ram! Ram!"

He opened his eyes, raised his head and glanced around to see what might have disturbed his wife, but found nothing threatening in the darkness or the silence.

She grabbed his hand and pulled it over to cover her flat tummy. "I felt the baby move."

He came fully awake then, turning toward her and pressing his hand gently, but more firmly. They lay still, waiting, looking at each other in the dim light, and sure enough, after a few seconds her stomach seemed to move of its own accord under his palm. Ram's face split into a grin so big it was contagious and Elora found herself grinning back at him with only the moonlight as their witness.

Without moving his hand away, he snuggled closer.

"What's his name?"

"Aelshelm Storm Laiken-Hawking. We'll call him Helm."

Ram mouthed it in the darkness like he was trying it on. Then he whispered, "Helm! Stop eatin' out of the dog bowl right now or we'll be in big trouble with your mum!"

Elora found out how hard it can be to laugh without making a sound. Ram began a series of possible scenarios that all began with Helm exclamation mark. At length Elora realized he could go on like this forever, probably recounting incidents from his own history. It could have been her imagination, but it seemed to her that every time Ram whispered, "Helm!" the baby jumped.

"Stop!" she laughed. "The baby knows his name and *doesn't* know you're teasing. He thinks you're scolding him and his objection is being registered by the lining of my womb."

Eventually she was forced to stop his litany midsentence with her own mouth. Which was okay with him.

THE WITCH'S DREAM

CHAPTER 21

Storm was glad to be wearing a long sleeve shirt. He turned it up at the cuff to just under the teeth marks he had left on his own skin. Throughout the day, whenever no one was looking, he pulled his sleeve up to admire the bite print and relive the memory of how it came to be there. Having marks on his body was hardly novel. Vampire hunters sustain a lot of bodily evidence of violence. But this was the first time he had ever delighted in a skin deep memento.

The wedding invitations, sent electronically because there was no time to do anything else, had stipulated Shoes Optional, Bare Toes Preferred. Kay and his groomsmen wore jeans and untucked, pinpoint oxford shirts with button down collars, sleeves rolled up. Kay's was white. Storm's was yellow. Ram's was blue.

The bride, her maids, and Elora wore solid color, summery dresses in various shades of the wearer's choosing. Katrina's, of course, was white. All the women carried bouquets made from delicate stems of yellow orchids plaited with end branches from the huge willow tree across the river.

The priest from the Congregation of the Children of Norway waited at the head of the bridal bower that had been procured from a rental place in San Antonio. He looked a little warm in his robes, but was smiling. Next to him, all four members of Bad Company stood together looking like they belonged that way.

The music started. It was a greatly slowed down version of "Bang My Bell" played live on a single electric mandolin. Squoozie was first to walk the carpet aisle that had been laid on top of the grass. She was followed by Dandie, who winked at her boyfriend on the way by, then by Urz, who smiled at her boyfriend on the way by.

Next came Litha who moved with such grace it almost seemed she wasn't touching ground. Her dress was a featherweight, boat necked, jersey knit, the same deep green as her eyes. It draped her curves beautifully and fell to mid shin where it fluttered around her legs in a handkerchief cut. When she'd bought it, she never expected to wear it barefooted, but somehow it worked. Her focus was trained on Storm standing at the end of the aisle next to Kay. She wore a serene, Mona-Lisa smile like a woman well-loved, and never took her eyes away from him.

Storm started to swallow, but felt his throat constrict with some hard-to-identify emotion that might be longing.

Last, of course, was Katrina who looked every bit the radiant bride. No one would guess that she had been abducted and held captive in a demon's lair less than a fortnight in the past. Kay could not have looked happier and his friends could not have been happier for him.

When the bride and groom took their places, the wedding party turned toward them as they had been instructed to do in rehearsal. That left Storm and Litha experiencing the wedding ceremony facing each other, three feet apart. Their eyes were locked on each other as they listened to the priest talk at length about the history and significance of marriage, about its implications personally, socially, and economically. The clergyman talked about the blessings of life partnerships that do not waver, but grow stronger and sweeter over time. He talked about the wonder of love, its healing properties and sustaining gifts, and what a miracle it is when the right two people find each other in such a complicated world.

Katrina had to nudge Litha to get her attention so that she could hand off the bouquet and join hands with Kay. The priest related the story of the couple's meeting on the first day of kindergarten, how she had cried when her mother had left and how Kay had rushed to console her and let her know that she had a friend and that she would never be alone.

He went on to tell the guests that the couple had chosen to compose their own pledges to each other. The bride went first and recited a variation on traditional vows. She stumbled a couple of times because she was emotional and everyone present was moved by the obvious depth of her feeling.

Then it was Kay's turn. He looked down at Katrina with absolute adoration shining in his eyes. "You could say my vows are lyrical because they're taken from one of your favorite songs. I knew I could never say what's in my heart any better than this.

"I, Chaos Erik Caelian, vow that I'm never gonna give you up, never gonna let you down..."

By the time Kay got to the third line of the chorus, Katrina had big tears running down her face as did Kay's only groomswoman, the knight who never failed to cry at the slightest suggestion of sentimentality. Storm and Litha had resumed their silent communion.

When he finished reciting his vows, the priest pronounced them married. After they kissed, Katrina retrieved her bouquet, then everybody including Katrina laughed when Kay surprised the bride by swooping her up in his arms to carry her down the aisle to the joyous recorded music of "Bang My Bell" played in real time. If anybody could pull that off and look good doing it, it was Kay.

Litha turned toward the guests with her bouquet in her right hand and waited for Storm to offer his arm, but he stood transfixed and immobile, still staring at Litha.

Storm was a good listener and he had listened to the proceedings with careful solemnity. Kay had loved Katrina since they were babies, while Storm had known Litha for only a matter of days if you counted the time she was in this dimension. And, yet, with every line Kay said to Katrina, Storm had been looking at Litha thinking: "That's exactly how I feel about her. That's the face I want to see morning, noon, and night for the rest of the strange life that seems to be playing out for me."

He was hit with a stroke of clarity as surely as if a lightning bolt had descended from the sky and touched him in the solar plexus. And he was decided.

Like the pair who had just married, he didn't want to waste any more time either. So, instead of offering his arm to walk Litha up the aisle behind the bride and groom, he turned away from the little congregation, putting the wedding guests at his back and held out his left hand to Litha.

She had no idea what he was doing, but, whatever it was, she was all in. From the moment she had gotten a look at the tall, dark knight who stepped into the headquarters foyer on a rainy day in Edinburgh her heart had informed her that she was never going to be the same and wouldn't want to be. The bouquet was transferred to her left hand so that she could put her right hand in his, which then left them facing the priest.

At the other end of the carpet, Katrina had been set on her feet and signaled for them to stop the music. The wedding guests grew quiet and waited, not knowing what to think.

Storm was wearing the sort of look of intensity that only he could generate. "Marry me." He squeezed her hand just a little. "Right now."

Litha's eyes went wide and her lips parted as she took in a gasp. Her confused emotions raised goose bumps all over her body at the same time her eyes filled with liquid. One of those tears spilled over onto her cheek.

Storm stepped in to her as he reached up to catch it with his free hand. "None of that. It's going to be good." She searched his face. He was so powerfully confident and so reassuring. "Our life is going to be a firefly picnic." That smile didn't give any indication that there was any doubt in his heart. Which was one of the reasons why it was going to be so hard and so painful to make all that hope and magic come crashing down on their heads like an avalanche.

She leaned into him and whispered. "I can't. There's something I have to tell you."

When he pulled back to look at her, she saw the disappointment that crossed his face. He turned to the crowd. "Okay, everybody. Just relax. Back in five."

He grabbed Litha's hand and pulled her toward the river, just far enough away so they could talk without being heard.

"Speak," he said.

She looked around, anywhere but directly at him, and rubbed her palms on the skirt of her dress. This was a development she couldn't have anticipated or prepared for in a hundred years.

"I really should have told you before."

"Litha. Come on. How bad can it be?"

She mustered the courage to look up into his face, pressed her lips together then blew out a breath. "Depends on how you look at it. No matter what, you can't tell anybody else."

His disappointment was turning into concern and he took on that all-business, serious expression that was vintage Storm. "Alright."

She told him the whole story. Start to finish even though she told it fast and abbreviated parts of it. She didn't think the fact that Storm was so still and quiet was a very good sign. She finished with,

"That's it"

"That's it? Katrina told us that as soon as she came back."

Litha was shocked. "You knew already?" He nodded. "So you're saying it's okay with you? That I'm... only part human?"

Storm hesitated for a beat and then laughed. "Litha, my three best friends in the world, the rest of B Team - not one of them is fully human. I'm the odd man out. Kay's a berserker. Ram's an elf. Elora - well, I guess she's elf plus. Why would it make any difference to me? Demon's just a word.

"You risked everything to rescue somebody you didn't even know. Goodness just doesn't come any shinier than that. If demon blood is part of what makes you who you are, then I'm glad for it."

Of all the possible reactions Litha had imagined, well, that wasn't one of them. She hadn't realized how tense she was and how much she'd been dreading this moment until relief settled over her. She threw her arms around his neck.

Then he added, with a touch of awe, "*And.* There's the car."

She pulled back so she could see his face and determine whether he was kidding or not. He just looked at her and blinked once.

"Well, regardless, that's not all."

"That's not all?" he parroted. "You just said 'that's it'."

She positioned herself so that his body blocked her from the view of the wedding assembly. Then she pulled a little ball of blue and orange flame into her hands.

"Okay. I heard about that, too, but seeing it is really something else. We're going to need some ground rules for arguing with each other."

"I didn't even know I could do this until that night in the Hung Goose pub. I was so crazy jealous seeing you dancing and touching those other..."

"So I guess Elora was right. I *did* owe the bill for the damage that night."

She looked confused. "The bill?"

"Yeah. Elora insisted that the fire was my fault and made me pay the bill for damage and lost business. We argued about it. It seemed irrational to me to conclude that it was my fault, but I agreed to pay for it because..." He sighed deeply, looked out at the river for an instant, and then back at her, "...because I felt guilty I guess. What I did that night was shameful. I *was* trying to provoke your jealousy. The damndest thing is that I couldn't even tell you why." The corners of his mouth twitched. "Of course, I didn't know I was *literally* playing with fire." That got a tentative smile from her. "But I can tell you I'm sorry I put you through that."

He put his arms around her and eased her closer. "If you did that to me, I'd want to do a lot more than just burn the place down. And I would probably hurt people who touched you more than I should. I won't share you with other boys."

She looked up at him like she wasn't ready to believe her own good fortune. "You still want me."

His arms tightened and he brushed his lips over her nose. "Litha Brandywine, my very own half-demon, fire-starting, incredibly sexy witch, you're looking at the guy who's never gonna give you up."

What she saw in his face and heard in his voice let her know that he had settled into a love for her that was burning as steady and even as the flame of a pilot light. But what completely undid her was that what she saw in those intense, black eyes just happened to be what she needed most in a mate. Fearlessness.

The priest had just finished dabbing his brow and chin with a white handkerchief. "I can't marry you. It wouldn't be legal and, no offense... " He glanced from one to the other. "...but I'm guessing you're *not* Children of Norway."

"No offense taken and you're right. We're not, but that's okay. We don't care about legalities and we're not religious." He looked at Litha. "We're not religious are we?" She shook her head emphatically and he turned back to the priest. "We're making promises to each other and that's enough for us. We're the kind of people who keep promises. Maybe you could just say the words. Pretend if that's what works for you."

The priest hesitated for a few seconds, considering, then seemed to relent.

"Very well. Do you..."

"Hold on a minute." Storm looked toward the rear of the little gathering and raised his voice. "Can somebody find the groom and send him back up here? One more time?"

Everybody laughed and in under a minute, Kay was standing next to Storm grinning.

The priest began again clearing his throat. "Do you have vows?"

Storm nodded then fixed his gaze on the prize

standing in front of him. He took her bouquet, turned and, reaching past Kay and Ram, handed it to Elora. When their eyes met he had a moment's hesitation seeing tears running down her cheeks, but almost immediately realized she was also smiling, positively glowing, which meant she was happy for him. *Women and their "happy tears".*

He had spent half his life studying vampire. Now he was going to spend some time learning about women. His handsome face broke into an open, carefree smile that was so much more expressive, so much more boyish than Elora had ever seen on him before. What that look said to her was: "See. There's happily ever after for me, too!" And she cried because she wanted that for him more than anything she could think of.

Storm faced Litha and held out both his hands palms up. When she placed her hands in his larger ones, a calm settled over her entire essence, causing her to feel perfectly at home and setting her spirit humming happily. She was thinking she might be crazy, but marrying this man was the single sanest thing she had ever done.

Eyes shining brightly, his full attention was focused on her alone. Storm was letting her know that he was giving a knight's promise. More potent than words. More binding than custom. He was taking an oath to finish what he was beginning and she could count on it till the end of time.

"I love you, Litha. I always will. I promise we'll work out the details to our mutual satisfaction."

Litha laughed softly, loving how that vow fit

Storm like a glove.

The priest turned to Litha. "And you?"

She said simply: "Everything. All the time."

Storm grinned in approval.

The priest looked at Storm and said: "Will you...?"

Storm provided his full name. "Engel Beowulf Storm."

"Will you Engel Beowulf Storm, pledge your troth as husband to this woman?"

"I have."

Turning to Litha the priest said, "Will you...?"

"Litha Liberty Brandywine."

"Will you Litha Liberty Brandywine, pledge your troth as wife to this man?"

"I..." Suddenly Litha was so overcome with emotion she couldn't get another word out. For the first time in her life she was literally rendered speechless. She wanted to say, "I do. I will. I have. I must." But her voice had frozen in her throat. She swallowed and tried again thinking, "Why now?" When nothing came out she started to look a little panic-stricken. But, there was no need to worry. She was no longer alone.

Storm pulled her into his arms and kissed her with a reserved sweetness that penetrated all the way to her soul. It was a new side of him she hadn't experienced before. All she wanted was to spend a few decades tasting all his moods. In her mind, as she watched their future unfold like a slide show in panoramic detail, every part of her relaxed into the euphoria of the moment. Her wedding day. So unexpected. So sweet. Life is strange. But good.

As soon as he released her, she opened her eyes and said in a perfectly clear voice, "I will." He gave her a heart-crushing smile that made Litha's stomach flutter.

The wedding guests applauded what had turned out to be a surprise double header, bonus celebration.

On the other side of the river, hidden behind a light green veil formed by the delicate, graceful branches of an old willow tree, Deliverance watched and listened. Feeling an invisible pull, Litha turned and looked across the river in the direction of the willow on the opposite bank. She absently palmed the black diamond pendulum she wore around her neck on a twenty-four carat gold, herringbone chain that looked marvelous against the unusual tint of her skin.

Sadness is quite out of character for incubus demons, but Deliverance found himself experiencing some odd sensations and assumed he must be coming down with something. He had a daughter and he felt pride in her. Equally unexpected on both counts. And he wished, more than anything at that moment, that he could simply cross the river and join the gathering, tap Engel Storm on the shoulder, perhaps shake his hand while terrorizing him with what the demon imagined might be appropriate fatherly threats of what he would do if Litha wasn't happy. Then he would hold Litha in his arms for a father daughter dance and say to everyone there: "This little girl is mine."

Storm and Litha lingered long enough to

collect well wishes and congratulations and have a couple of slow, slow dances. Even though it was late they decided they would pack up the car and find a little motel somewhere on the road. Storm said he didn't want to deliver the news to Sol that he wasn't coming back over the phone; that Sol deserved to be told in person, even if it meant driving all the way to New York.

By the time the wedding guests were gone, Storm and Litha had the car loaded. Kay and Katrina were leaving for their honeymoon in the Marquesas the next morning. After emotional goodbyes and promises to stay in close touch, the red sports car pulled out onto a dark road. Storm was thinking he could never remember being so excited. Or happy.

Litha was thinking that a couple of weeks before, she had thought everything she wanted could be found at the vineyard with the pink Italianate villa high above the Pacific Ocean. Now she was thinking that everything she needed was sitting beside her in the front seat of an outrageously extravagant auto gifted from a father she didn't know she had who was, by the way, a demon. And that life was strange. Strange and good.

A few miles down the road they pulled into a little motel with a VACANCY sign lit up in hot pink neon. The night clerk gave them a room that was ready for occupants in the sense that the window unit air conditioner had been turned on high and left that way after the sun went down. It was so cold their teeth were chattering when they finished bringing in luggage.

They decided to turn it off for a while, at least until it felt like the frost was gone. Litha pulled a blanket around her, but Storm had other ideas about how to get them warmed up quickly. They joked about having an old-fashioned honeymoon in the sense that their first time sleeping together and their first time in a bed together - while awake - was also the first night of their marriage.

EPILOGUE

Storm had done a lot of traveling for The Order. He knew his way around most of the world's big cities, but he hadn't enjoyed the simple pleasures of an old-fashioned car trip since he was a kid on family vacation. Truthfully, a road trip seeing the country from Texas to Napa by way of New York, in an Aston Martin alone with his bride - not terrible duty. And not a bad way to get to know each other either.

They talked about Litha's unique and irreplaceable abilities and decided she would continue to be available to The Order when necessary, but she would work from home when possible.

On the day the moon entered Gemini, Storm and Litha drove along a two lane county highway with the top down on the Aston Martin. The day was a vision. Yellow sunshine. Cerulean blue sky. Red convertible. Black top road. It was the kind of day topless cars had been invented for. When the villa came into sight, Storm slowed the car, eased over onto the shoulder, and came to a stop grinning at Litha like a man standing on the threshold of heaven, having just been welcomed in. If nothing else, he had learned how to savor special moments and let the sweetness melt in his mouth slowly.

Between the two of them, they had enough

VICTORIA DANANN

money to buy the place no matter how much the owners wanted. His was in the bank. Hers was in a suitcase in the trunk.

When they reached the gate, there was a sign that read For Sale. He pulled the car onto the drive, stopped in front of the sign, and looked over at his wife the witch.

"Did you?"

She just laughed.

"Never mind." Without looking away, he put the car into gear wearing that gorgeous smile she would never get tired of loving and put his suspicion away. "I don't care."

Maybe it turns out that the right thing is not *always* the harder thing to do. Letting himself fall in love with Litha was the easiest thing he had ever done, once he gave himself up to it. Was she made for him? And vice versa? He still didn't believe in coincidence, but somehow his perfect match had found him.

They had practically grown up next to each other without ever knowing the other existed. They both had the benefit of an unusual education that money cannot buy. They were both well-traveled. His travel experience was courtesy of The Order, hers was courtesy of a demon, but they arrived in the same place. They shared the same dream of a simple life making wine. They both worked for an organization committed to the philosophy that those with greater gifts bear greater responsibility.

There were three people whom Storm would

always call teammates. He would live out his life without ever qualifying that by calling them former teammates. To that odd trio of knights, he would always be available for any reason, at any hour, in this life and the next.

With all they had been through, each of them was well aware of how quickly things can change. The only thing in life they could count on absolutely was each other.

Of course, Sol had smoothly negotiated an agreement from him that he would report for duty if needed. It was the same acquiescence he had wrenched from the others. He had also flattered them by saying that "B" was being retired with them as it would be too much pressure for others to try to live up to Bad Company's reputation. Storm wished Lan could have known that.

POSTSCRIPT

Elora relaxed into the sublime perfection of a long weekend at her favorite place on Earth, the New Forest cottage where she had Ram and Blackie all to herself. It was her first time to experience the New Forest in spring with its spectrum of new leaf greens so intense it almost didn't look real. Nature had strewn colorful wildflowers throughout with a randomness that somehow always worked.

The dog was so joyful he grinned all the time in his doggy way with tongue hanging out and lips relaxed. He loved running through the forest with his owners on horseback and staying together in one room at night like a true pack.

After a simple dinner of roast chicken, apples, cheese, artisan bread and smuggled chocolate, she sat on the well-worn leather sofa and entertained Ram by retelling from memory, in as much detail as possible, the plot of a play that was well known in her dimension. As she spoke, she stroked the velvety insides of Blackie's ears and Ram listened patiently.

When she finished, he simply looked at her in a noncommittal way until she said, "Well?"

"Well what?"

"Well, Rammel, what did you think?"

He shrugged slightly. "It was a stupid story."

"Ram!" Elora could hardly believe her ears.

When he had accompanied her on her mission to entertain an injured knight at Jefferson Unit by telling him fairytales, Ram had always listened patiently and then, afterward, pronounced every one a 'stupid story'. So she shouldn't have been surprised. But she was. "The tale of what happened to the Capulets and Montagues is one of the most beloved and renowned literary works of my world."

"Then 'tis all the more shame that it is a stupid story. If you do no' want criticism, you should no' spread it about that the people of your world have such poor taste in tales."

"It's *not* stupid!"

"'Tis."

"Dickhead."

Ram looked stricken, as stunned as if he'd been slapped. "I can no' believe you just said that."

"Why not? *You* said, 'I do no' care if you call me dickhead so long as you share your bed with me' or something to that effect. Well, I decided this occasion called for taking you up on that."

From the look on his face she could see she'd really hurt his feelings. Ram didn't go sullen more than once in a blue moon. "I do no' suppose I was expectin' you to actually follow through."

"Well, it doesn't matter because you know I meant it affectionately."

"Does no' matter? And how is it you're thinkin' you can say dickhead affectionately?"

Her mouth turned up with a wicked guile that he, himself, had put there. "The next time I'm blowing you, I will remind you that you said that."

He laughed, unable to hold either his good

nature or his buoyant personality down for long.

"Okay," she said, "I told you a story and risked your unnecessarily harsh critique. So now you sing for me."

He treated her to her unique version of his killer smile, the one that was just for her, as he stood to retrieve his guitar. "As a matter of fact there is somethin' special I've been workin' on for just such an *occasion* as this."

Ram pulled the strap over his shoulder, sat on the ottoman in front of Elora, tuned quickly and began to play the acoustic guitar he kept at the cottage. She didn't recognize the song, but he might have rearranged it. The instrumental intro didn't give up a clue. She didn't recognize it until he began to sing the lyrics of "Never Gonna Give You Up", unplugged. She decided to add musical genius to his already long list of remarkable attributes. His voice that somehow managed to be sexy and angelic at the same time, along with the gift of the song, created an intimate moment she would never forget. It made her heart swell and feel too big to be confined by her chest. And each time she thought she could not love him more, her capacity expanded.

Helm responded to his father's voice by wiggling happily as if he was dancing a jig. It made Elora laugh out loud.

And there it is. Given the world they lived in, Elora knew the importance of savoring quiet, precious moments. And, at that very minute, The Lady Laiken, knight of The Order of the Black Swan, was certain she was the happiest elf alive in that dimension or any other. She begged for two encores, which secretly delighted the musician.

When Rammel finished for the third time, he carefully set his guitar aside. The light in her eyes and her pleas for more were all the thanks he needed. Nevertheless, only a fool passes up a bird nest on the ground. So he turned to her with a gleam in his eye.

"Now about that blowin' you spoke of..."

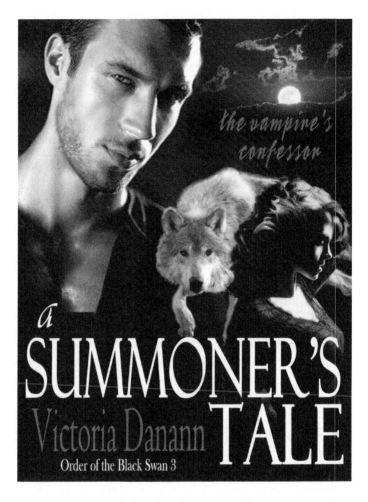

A Summoner's Tale by Victoria Danann (Chapter 1 excerpt)

BLACK SWAN FIELD TRAINING MANUAL

Section I: Chapter 1, #1
The plural of vampire is vampire.

When the rush of activity subsided, he found himself alone with his own thoughts; a condition that was more than familiar since he had spent hundreds of years that way. Without the distraction of his friends' banter, since his proposed staff had left Edinburgh, he had begun to see his task not just as a job, but as a mission, one immersed in the duality of joy and gravity.

He had never considered himself to be impatient. Quite the contrary, everything he had ever pursued in earnest, from painting to music to writing, had depended upon patience. But, his cognizance of the enormity of the burden he had accepted was growing in direct proportion to the time that was passing. Every day that nothing was accomplished was a day when more people had their humanity taken from them, another day when vampire remained imprisoned in bodies infected with the foulest disease imaginable, and, also, another day when people died.

Everyone who had been assigned to work with Baka on his project was gone. Everyone except Heaven who had turned out to be anything but. The large work space, intended for several people, seemed deserted with him alone most of the time. He worked from early in the morning until late into the night. When Heaven was there her moods ran the range of a shallow bell curve from disagreeable to surly to sullen. He admitted that he had provoked her on their first meeting for reasons that were a mystery to him. Something about her instantly put him on edge and made him feel anxious.

Even though that feeling persisted, he had attempted to make amends so that they could work together amicably. To no avail. She was prickly to the core, spurning every effort on his part to develop a rudimentary standard of civility. She behaved as if simple courtesy was more than she could manage which meant that "nice" was a goal way too distant.

He not only had to work with a person who detested his very presence, but, adding insult to injury, it seemed he couldn't shake an inexplicably strong attraction to her. He found himself staring at the curve of her cheek when her head was bowed over work. Or the shine of her chestnut hair when she walked through a ray of light. Or the way her lips pursed whenever he gave her something to do. It was damned aggravating.

To make matters worse, he seemed to have lost interest in pursuing other women.

At exactly fifteen after five she checked her wristwatch, closed an open folder of proposed budgets, rose as she rolled her chair back, pulled on her sweater jacket, draped her purse strap over her shoulder and, like every other day at the same time, walked out of the office without glancing his way or saying goodnight.

He sat back and heaved a big sigh. *Alone again. Naturally.*

Baka had been a person with a well-developed sense of morality, and a well-functioning conscience before he became a vampire. During the last hundred years of life as a vampire, having survived long enough to blessedly recover his understanding of right and wrong, he had turned himself in to The Order, voluntarily serving as their consultant and consuming only artificial sustenance.

No. He had never been short on conscience. And that conscience was rubbing a hole in his brain telling him that it would be wrong to simply sit at a desk and plan a strategy on paper while, at the same time, *doing* nothing. So, keeping his own counsel, for better or worse, he determined that he would continue to work as a bureaucrat during the day, but would spend his nights - at least part of them - looking for others he might help back to the light.

He had worked with Monq at Jefferson Unit labs to develop a delivery solution. Taking a page from the methodology of the late Gautier Nibelung, they had decided that the safest and most effective approach would be dart gun. Each dart was outfitted with a tiny canister that would puncture on impact releasing a formula that was part stun and part cure. The proper dose of stun solution had been determined by tests on Baka himself. So he knew it worked. First hand. Obviously vampire must be incapacitated while the viral antidote works. As medicinal remedies go, it is fast working, but not instant. There is a delay of two to four hours between introduction to the system and complete reversal of the disease, depending upon the age and constitution of the individual.

His plan wasn't perfect. It depended on encountering one vampire at a time and extracting him, while paralyzed, without engaging other vampire. Tricky, but the alternative was waiting for a task force to be vetted, assembled, and trained.

And waiting was the one thing he couldn't manage. Maybe it wasn't the smartest thing he'd ever done, but, hell, he'd had a long life.

To his advantage, he still had certain attributes that were extra human. Not like comic book heroes. More like human plus. No one knew if these benefits would fade away over time, but, for now, he was a little stronger, a little faster, and could see in the dark a little better than most people. All traits very useful for vampire hunting.

It just so happened that he found his assigned base of operations in prime territory that qualified as a vampire magnet on all counts. In Edinburgh's Old Town there was a large pedestrian population that came out at night *and* it was built on top of an underground system that was not utilized to any extent that would interfere with the needs of vampire. All this was literally in sight of his office - five minutes' walk away.

In a darkly poetic way, it was fitting that vampire would thrive in Edinburgh's underground city which consisted of a system of tunnels, caverns, and cells cut into the much softer sandstone under the rock that the above-ground Old Town is built upon. It's a place with grisly history where thousands of hapless poor lived in darkness, packed together without sanitation and with the vilest of criminals. Plague victims were not removed and buried or burned, but just sealed in their cells.

Modern day Ghost Tours offer a shallow excursion - shallow because individuals don't want to stay in the underground very long. Words like "creepy" are frequently used even by hard-core insensitives. That leaves miles of maze for a vampire haven.

Baka had been a vampire long enough to know all about how they think. He knew that the days of the Beltane festival would be a gorge fest for vampire. The Royal Mile, just over the heads of vampire living in the Underground, would be packed with crowds of visitors to the city, visitors intent on celebration and revelry, danger being the last thing on their minds. It would be a blessing to vampire in the original sense of the word which was bloodletting; when, as a rite of passage, young pagans would stand in a pit under a grate where a bull was sacrificed and bathe in the gift of the blood that showered down upon them.

These are things that weighed heavy on his heart and occupied his mind when he was left alone with his own thoughts.

So Baka finished his day, went to dinner alone, and slowly savored every bite of actual food. Afterward, driven by a heartfelt desire to do some good in the world, he pulled on a pair of cargo pants and equipped the dozen pockets with two dart guns and as many canisters as he could carry without being slowed down. He descended the stairs to the main foyer wondering if, even partial redemption for a long life of misdeeds, is possible. The fact that he was not accountable for that infamous history should have given him some peace of absolution. But didn't. He said good evening to the doorman and headed out into the night.

Printed in Great Britain
by Amazon